Waiting Since Forever

Kiltie Jackson

ISBN-13: 978-1-9998666-4-8

DEDICATION

For Craig and Ross

The best nephews in the world.
xxx

ONE

'Oh, for crying out loud! Seriously?'

Clarissa Walton listened to her father huff and puff as he read the morning newspaper. Despite the new digital age, George Walton still preferred a good, old-fashioned newspaper and she could tell from the way he was snapping the pages over that he was not happy with the articles contained within. Although, her father seemed to be perpetually dissatisfied with life so why should today be any different. She picked up another slice of toast and had just begun to butter it when her father's voice broke out from behind his miniaturised broadsheet.

'Do you really think you should be having that, Clarissa? You need to learn to temper your appetite in your youth to ensure you don't run to fat in your middle age. Your husband won't thank you for letting yourself go, you know.'

For the briefest of seconds, Clarissa felt a surge of annoyance at her father's tone but it was gone before she fully realised it had been there.

'I'll do an extra fifteen minutes on the treadmill when I

go to the gym this evening.'

'Be sure that you do. Teach your body discipline now, it'll thank you in years to come.'

'Yes, Father.' Clarissa had been listening to this mantra from her father nearly all her life. It had been teeth and sweets when she was a child, now it was food and fat as an adult. Her mother had been receiving this particular nugget of wisdom for as long as she could remember and she'd gained inclusion to it when she'd turned thirteen. Now, aged twenty-three, it was as common an expression as saying good morning or goodnight and although she barely paid any heed to the words, the hidden threat of her father's displeasure was never missed.

'I'm sure Tristan Faulkner would be considerably less interested in you if you started putting on poundage.'

'George, that's enough! Clarissa is only just into a size ten, she has nothing to worry about with her weight.'

George lowered the paper and looked over the top at his wife.

'Estelle, Tristan Faulkner is a gifted young solicitor who has all the promise of an exceptional career in front of him. Clarissa is lucky to have someone so remarkable showing an interest in her.'

Clarissa saw her mother open her mouth to reply but not wanting to endure another argument over breakfast, she dropped the offending slice of toast onto her plate, placed her napkin on the table beside it and, as she stood, said, 'Father, are you almost ready to go to work? I just need to brush my teeth and I'll be ready to leave.'

George looked at his watch. 'I'll be waiting at the door for you in five minutes. If you're late, I'm going without you.'

'See you in five, Father!'

'Five MINUTES, Clarissa, five MINUTES. I've told you before – you will speak properly in this house.'

'Yes, Father. I'm sorry. I'll see you in five minutes.'

The growl in her stomach – the result of foregoing that extra slice of toast – had Clarissa looking at her watch; it was almost lunchtime. She decided to finish checking the file she was working on before stopping to eat.

She'd almost completed her task but when she tried to turn the last two pages, she found them stuck together. After carefully prising them open, she was annoyed to see a signature had been missed.

'Damn it!'

It's a good thing I'm thorough, she thought, because this error could have thrown out the whole deal. She decided to pop up to her father's office, get his signature on the all-important dotted line, and then have lunch.

As it was quicker than waiting for the lift, Clarissa took the stairs up the two floors to the senior partners' offices. When she arrived on the corridor of power, as it was known by the rest of the staff in the firm, all was quiet. The deep-piled, expensive maroon and grey carpet swallowed up her footsteps. The PAs on this floor were "ladies who lunched" every Friday, so there was no one around to announce her presence. She was sure, on this one occasion, her father could eschew his usual protocol given the urgency of the situation.

She was just approaching the boardroom when she heard voices floating out. Angry voices at that. The blinds were closed but Clarissa immediately recognised the harsh tones of the company's construction partner, Paddy Archer. The other voice was her father's.

As she stood in the corridor, debating what to do next, she couldn't help but overhear the heated conversation. At first it didn't really register what she was hearing but when the words began to sink in, she clamped her hand to her mouth in shock. Some seconds passed before she turned on her heel and rapidly exited the way she'd come, the file in her hand completely forgotten.

A few minutes later, sitting in the staff kitchen, picking at the salad in front of her, Clarissa was sighing over her loss of appetite. She stared at the pages of her book but was unable to concentrate – mostly due to what she'd just overheard but also because Elspeth Reid and her cronies were talking loudly over in the corner. As usual, she was sitting on her own. This was the downside of being the boss's daughter – no one trusted you to keep any office gossip to yourself and so didn't share their secrets. She'd never done anything to earn this distrust, it simply came with the territory. It was believed she would tattle-tale back to her father so her work colleagues maintained a wide berth. Clarissa let out a little sigh. She hadn't really wanted to do her article clerkship at her father's legal firm but he'd been quite insistent and she hadn't been able to come up with a good enough reason for refusing. George Walton had opened the Oxford branch of his London firm ten years ago and it had proved to be a highly successful venture. It was a well-respected establishment in the centre of Oxford and for anyone else, being articled there would have been quite a coup.

Suddenly, Elspeth let out a loud groan.

'I don't believe it! Ashley has only gone and cancelled for tonight! She's got a stinking cold and has gone home to her bed.'

Clarissa looked up to see Elspeth waving her mobile phone around the table, letting the other three girls see the evidence of Ashley's cancellation.

'Surely you'll be able to find someone else for the ticket?'

Elspeth pulled a face. 'I don't know if I can – it's a bit short notice and not everyone is into hypnotic shows, even if it is the world-famous Michael Duval. That's thirty-five quid down the drain because she was supposed to pay me for it tonight. Bugger!'

Out of nowhere, Clarissa heard herself saying, 'If you're really stuck, I could take her place.'

Elspeth spun round in surprise but it was nothing compared to the shock Clarissa herself was feeling. What the hell? Where on earth had that come from? She'd never had any interest in going to a hypnotic show, although she'd seen Michael Duval on the television and apart from being drop-dead-gorgeous, he was immensely talented.

'Are you sure Daddy won't mind? I didn't think it would be the sort of thing he'd approve of – his little diddy darling going to the theatre to see something as uncouth as a hypnotist. It's not exactly "Swan Lake" or "The Marriage of Figaro" you know!'

'I don't think it'll be a problem. I won't tell if you won't!'

Darla Sutton leant over to Elspeth. 'Look, given the short notice, it's unlikely you'll get anyone else. You might as well accept the offer… unless you want to be thirty-five quid out of pocket?'

Elspeth nodded. 'Yeah, I suppose you're right.'

She turned back to Clarissa. 'Okay, the ticket's yours! The show begins at seven thirty and we're planning to go for a bite to eat beforehand. If you want to join us, we're meeting in the pub next door at five o'clock.'

Clarissa smiled. 'Thank you, Elspeth. I'll see you there.'

She picked up her things and left the kitchen, leaving Elspeth and her friends to talk about this new turn of events. While walking up the corridor, Clarissa realised she was relieved not to be going home. After the conversation she'd overheard, she didn't think she could face seeing her father just yet. By the time she got back to her desk, a little bubble of excitement had started to grow inside her and she began to look forward to this unexpected night out.

TWO

'Oh yes, nice one! Here, guys, listen to this.'

Gerald Wainwright lifted his head. What did big-mouth Barry have to say for himself now? This new open-plan office the company had insisted on implementing had a lot to answer for. In the old days, he could close the door to his office and shut out the constant drone that was Barry Bennett's voice but now he had to endure it day after day with no let up. How was it possible for one man to talk so much about absolutely sod all?

'What you got, Baz?' Jason Temple, Barry's sidekick, called over from where he was standing at the photocopier.

'I've had an email come in from that last-minute ticket website. They're offering half-price tickets for tonight's Michael Duval show, just up the road. Anyone fancy it?'

Jason and a few of the other lads in the office called out to say they were in.

'Oh, hang on a minute... damn, we only get the discount on parties of six or above. How many are interested? Put yer hands up.'

Four hands shot up in the air. Gerald looked on in

amusement. They might be a top five-hundred accountancy firm but you didn't need a degree to see they were short on the numbers. He dropped his head back down and returned to analysing the paperwork in front of him.

A few minutes later he jumped as a hand slammed down on his desk. He looked up to see Barry Bennett standing in front of him.

'Yo, Gerry, why don't you come along to this gig tonight? I'm sure you'd enjoy it, do you good to let your hair down a bit. Or should I say, let the Brylcreem have a night off!' He laughed at his own joke while looking around to ensure he'd been overheard.

Gerald cringed inwardly for two reasons. One, he HATED being called Gerry, and two, Barry's mockney-cockney, Eastenders tone grated hard against his eardrums.

'I really don't think it's my kind of thing, Barry, but thank you for asking.'

Gerald cringed again but this time at his own lack of courage. What he really wanted to say was, 'Fuck off, Barry, you fat git! I wouldn't hang out with you if you were the last fat bastard on the planet!' Time and again, however, his nerve always failed him and he ended up being the epitome of politeness. There again, as Barry's boss, it probably wouldn't go down too well with the HR department if he did give in to his desire. He may have gotten away with it forty years ago but not now in this uber-PC world they lived in.

'Aw, go on, Gerry. Pleeeeeease! We only need one more to get the cheap tickets. I'm sure Marjory'll let you off the leash for one night!'

Gerald was all set to refuse a second time until Barry mentioned Marjory. In a toss-up between who was the biggest thorn in his side, there wasn't much between Barry and Marjory, his wife! Both were as annoying and as irritating as the other and, between the two of them, they made Gerald's life pretty miserable be it at work or at home. However, in a head-to-head such as this, Barry was the lesser of the two evils! At least there would be others in the group which might help in diluting the Barry-concentration a little.

'Oh, all right, I'll be your sixth man!'

'Excellent!' Gerald cringed for a third time as Barry did the air guitar riff from the movie, "Bill and Ted's Excellent Adventure". Honestly, Gerald surmised, it's no wonder he kept getting headaches – all this cringing couldn't be doing him any good at all.

As Barry walked away, Gerald wondered what kind of show it would be because, if this Michael Duval bloke offered any kind of relaxation therapy, Gerald was going to be the first one to put his hand up as a volunteer, for if the tension in his shoulders got any worse, they'd be hanging off his ears like a pair of earrings.

He let out a sigh as he took off his glasses to give them a rub clean before returning to the paperwork on his desk. Soon, he was oblivious to the office chatter going on around him.

An hour later, a diary reminder popped up on Gerald's computer. He felt his stomach tumble when he read it – he'd been dreading this part of the day but it was something which had to be done. He opened his desk drawer, took out the envelope Karen in HR had given him, and made his way to one of the meeting rooms out by reception. Using the phone in the room, he made an internal call and then sat down to wait.

A few minutes later, the door opened and one of the office secretaries, Sarah, waddled in. Gerald jumped up to pull out a seat for her.

'Hi, Sarah, thank you for coming down. May I offer you something to drink? Tea? Coffee?'

'Oh, no thank you, Gerald. This one seems to have his foot permanently stuck in my bladder so every drink I have means a loo trip five minutes later.'

She rubbed the large bump in front of her. Sarah was a petite girl and Gerald had often wondered, as he'd seen her grow over the months, if she'd still be able to walk by her due date.

'Well, let me know if you change your mind.'

He sat down on the chair next to her. 'Sarah, I believe this is your last day in the office.'

'Yes, and I have to say, I'm looking forward to the next three weeks – just putting my feet up and relaxing. The journey to and from work has been tough this last month or so.'

'Well, before you go, I need to give you this.' He handed over the envelope.

'What is it?' Sarah looked at him, her face suddenly turning pale.

'Just open it…'

Gerald turned to look out of the window as she ripped the envelope open and took out the paperwork inside.

'Oh, my goodness… you cannot be serious? Honestly?'

He turned back to see tears in Sarah's eyes. Oh, bugger! He hadn't expected that!

'Yes, honestly.'

'But, Gerald…. why? Why have you done this?'

'Sarah, I know how tough things have been for you the last few years – the babies you didn't get to hold and then John being made redundant just weeks after you found out you were expecting again, but no matter what was going on in your life, you've always had a kind word and a smile for everyone around you. Every week, when you know I've been to visit my dad, you ask how he is and each Friday, when you know I'll be seeing him over the weekend, you ask me to send on your kind wishes. You're a lovely person who's had to deal with some pretty rough times so when I was standing at the photocopier a couple of weeks ago and overheard you saying you couldn't afford to buy the cot-bed you really liked, I decided that I would get it for you. As a thank-you gift from my dad and I.'

By this time, the tears were pouring down Sarah's face. Gerald grabbed the box of tissues from the nearby cupboard and handed them over.

'Oh, Gerald… it's too much, I can't accept this…' Sarah hiccupped as she blew her nose.

'Yes, you can, Sarah, please. I've done it all correctly – I asked Karen in HR to sort it out to ensure there was no data protection breach and she's arranged for the cot to be delivered to your home next week. The details should all be in there.' He nodded at the letter in her hand. 'I don't know your address so you don't need to worry about me being some kind of creepy stalker or anything like that.'

Sarah leant to the side and took a hold of his hand. 'Gerald, of all the things I might imagine of you, that could never be one of them. You are a lovely, sweet man and if I wasn't so "puffed up" right now,' she looked down at her big tummy, 'then I would happily deck Barry Bennett for the way he speaks to you.'

'Oh, don't you worry about him. As my mother would say, he's all talk and no trousers!'

Sarah giggled as she pushed herself up from the chair. She leant over and as best as she could manage, gave him a hug.

'Thank you so much, Gerald. It's a wonderful gift and I am deeply grateful.'

With more than a little bit of awkwardness, Gerald patted Sarah's back. 'No need to be grateful, Sarah, I just wanted to do something nice for someone nice who deserves a bit of a break. Now, off you go and if you don't mind, I'd really appreciate it if you kept it to yourself. I don't want the whole office to know.'

'Mum's the word – literally!' Sarah giggled again and made a zipping motion with her fingers across her lips as she left the room.

When the door had closed quietly behind her, Gerald let out a sigh of relief. He was glad that was over with. He'd tried to get Karen in HR to inform Sarah of his gift but she'd refused saying he should be the one to pass on the news. It had been lovely to see the joy on Sarah's face and to know she'd been happy, but one thing was for sure, he wouldn't be doing this again for a while – he didn't need the stress.

THREE

Clarissa sipped her glass of wine and felt herself begin to relax. Now that they were away from the office, Elspeth and the other girls weren't as scary as she'd pegged them to be. They were including her in their conversations and making sure she felt a part of the group. After a couple of drinks at the pub, they'd moved on to an Italian restaurant and Clarissa had really enjoyed the pizza she'd ordered although, with her father's voice rumbling in her head, she'd gone for the low-calorie half-pizza / half-salad option. Under her breath, she'd cursed her father but she simply could not bring herself to order a full-sized pizza even though she desperately wanted to. But that aside, it had been a good meal peppered with fun conversation.

They had arrived at the theatre and were grabbing a last-minute drink at the bar when Elspeth began teasing her about the attention she'd been getting from Tristan Faulkner.

'So, how many dates have you had?' she asked.

'I'm not sure, maybe six or seven…' Clarissa knew exactly how many dates there had been – fourteen – but she didn't want to share that with anyone. It was bad enough her father considered them to be an item without others thinking the same. She was still unsure about Tristan and was not about to commit herself to anything just yet so the less folks knew, the better it would be in the long run.

Elspeth opened her mouth but before she could speak, the bell rang and a tannoy announcement came over asking everyone to make their way to their seats as the show would be starting in five minutes.

The girls quickly necked the wine left in their glasses before trouping single file into the auditorium. Clarissa made sure she was at the end of the line, thus keeping a distance from Elspeth and making it impossible for her to ask any more questions.

They found their seats and Clarissa was surprised at the close proximity to the stage. She'd be able to give her mother a good report on how Michael Duval looked close up. Her mum had expressed her envy at Clarissa's luck in getting a ticket and wished her a great night. She hadn't told her father she was going out for the night – there was no need to prod the dog with the stick for Elspeth had been right on the money when she'd said he wouldn't approve. Furthermore, he'd have openly forbidden her to attend which would've resulted in a row and taken the shine off the evening. It was better to deal with the fallout tomorrow, after the event.

The house lights went down and the room fell quiet as the show began.

Dry ice began to seep from underneath the curtain and loud booming music began pounding from the speakers. A deep dramatic voice announced the hypnotist and the curtains swung open to reveal the man himself, standing in the centre of the stage wearing… a shirt and jeans?

Seriously?

Clarissa blinked at the under-stated appearance of

Michael Duval. He always wore suits on the television so she would have expected one of those at least.

The dry ice faded away, the music ceased and the stage lights came up to reveal Duval standing in a plain, empty space.

'Ladies and gentlemen, thank you for being here tonight. I welcome you to my show and I hope you all have a fun and entertaining evening. Now, some of you might be wondering why there is no fancy stage-set and no fancy suit – the truth is, what I do doesn't require any of those things. My type of hypnosis is simple, straightforward and requires no fancy gimmicks. Are we all happy with that?'

A muted response came back from the audience.

'I said, are we all happy with that?'

This time the audience replied with more enthusiasm.

'Excellent.'

Michael Duval placed the microphone in the stand and asked for the house lights to be turned up.

'Right, everyone, please could you all stand up and copy my actions.'

There was a buzz of noise as the theatregoers placed handbags on the floor, laid jackets on their seats and stood up.

'Okay, ladies and gentlemen, I want you to begin by shaking your hands in front of you to release any tension. Just like this…'

Clarissa copied Michael's movements and looked along the row to see Elspeth and the other girls doing the same.

'Perfect…' She looked back towards the stage. 'Now, I want you all to clasp your hands in front of you, like this, and hold them like that until I tell you to unclasp them.'

She clasped her hands as instructed, smiling along as everyone else did the same.

'Thank you. Now, please unclasp your hands.'

Clarissa tried to unclasp her hands but couldn't. She

pulled harder, but nope, they were totally stuck together.

'Could those of you who were able to unclasp their hands please sit down.'

A moment later, approximately half of the room remained standing.

The hypnotist gave a little smile and Clarissa quickly looked around her. She was relieved to see both Elspeth and Darla were still standing.

'Now, ladies and gentleman, please put your hands, still clasped, straight out in front of you, like this, and hold them there for a moment.'

She hesitated briefly before doing as Michael Duval requested. A few seconds passed before the audience members still standing were asked to unclasp their hands and put them down by their sides.

For the second time, Clarissa found she could neither undo her hands nor move them from their current position, stuck out horizontally in front of her. She tugged and pulled but to no avail.

'Could all those whose hands have now unclasped and are by their sides, please sit down. Thank you.'

She sneaked a quick peep to the side. Phew! Thank goodness Elspeth was still on her feet! The two of them shared a quick grin at their joint dilemma.

'Thank you. And finally, for the last bit before we move on with the show, could all those still standing, please put your hands above your heads, hands still clasped, like this.'

Knowing that resistance was now futile, Clarissa put her clasped hands up in the air and hoped that this time, she'd be able to sit down. There weren't that many people still standing and she felt rather exposed. She didn't like being the centre of attention and she knew people were now looking at her.

'Okay, ladies and gentlemen, for the last time, please unclasp your hands and put them down by your side.'

Last time? What the hell does he mean by “last time”? Clarissa was weaving from side to side as she tried to unclasp the hands that were stubbornly refusing to do her bidding. It was with no small amount of horror that she watched Elspeth shake her hands out and sit back down in her seat. Her face fell as Elspeth gave a little shrug and an apologetic smile.

She turned back to the stage when Duval spoke once more.

‘Thank you everyone for your participation. May I ask those still standing to make their way to the stage.’

Eh? What? ‘No, no, no, no, noooooooooo,’ she mumbled. This could not be happening to her. She tried again to undo her hands and almost fell over in the attempt. Most of the other audience members had already approached the stage and she could feel the eyes of those still in their seats watching her and her struggles.

The realisation quickly dawned that she had no choice here, she had to go through with whatever was coming next. Clarissa stepped out into the aisle, making a mental note as she did so that, the next time the girls in the office had a spare ticket for anything, she was going to keep her mouth well and truly shut!

FOUR

Gerald was sitting between Jason and Barry, wondering how on earth he'd managed to be seated thus. He'd made sure a few of the other lads were between them when they'd walked in from the bar. Up till now, the evening hadn't been too unpleasant – they'd had a meal at the pub a few doors along from the theatre and it had been relatively painless. His co-workers had mostly talked about football and he knew he'd surprised them when he'd offered some knowledgeable insights during the conversation. For his sins, he'd been a lifelong Aston Villa supporter and he still liked to spend afternoons watching the games with his dad. It didn't happen so often now that his dad had moved out to the retirement village near Lower Ditchley, but he still managed to get them to a few games through the season. When the weather was particularly bad, and played havoc with his dad's arthritis, they would watch whatever games were being shown on the television.

A sharp elbow in the ribs from Barry brought him back into the present.

'Hey Gerry, ain't this the ticket? I 'ope he does that

thing when he gets folks up from the audience on the stage. I'd love to be knocked out – I bet it's amazing!'

Gerald really hoped Barry didn't have the ability to read minds because right now, the only kind of "knocked out" he was wishing upon Barry would have to be administered by a good right hook. Thankfully, before the temptation to apply said "right hook" was too much to resist, the lights went down and the show began.

A few minutes later, having made the sensible decision to remain seated when the hypnotist had asked everyone to stand, he felt Barry's meaty fist grab the back of his collar and haul him up to his feet. 'Hey, Gez, you not joinin' in? Up you get, we're all in this togevver!'

His second attempt at refraining from participating was met with another sharp elbow in the ribs, this time from Jason. At this rate he was going to be black and blue by the time he got home.

Within ten minutes, he was wishing he'd opted to stick with the bruised torso as he looked up at the hands clasped firmly above his head. You have *got* to be kidding me, he thought. How in hell's name had this happened? Everyone knew these guys put "plants" in the audience, none of the participants were ever genuine… were they? Well, it seemed this one was for no matter how hard he tried, Gerald couldn't bring his arms down or pull his hands apart.

When he was instructed to make his way to the stage, he let out a groan. He did not need this! Why had he let Barry talk him into coming along? Now he was shafted either way! If he refused to join in the shenanigans on the stage, Barry and Jason – along with the rest of the office – would hound him over it for goodness only knew how long. If he did choose to participate, they'd forever be taking the piss, not allowing him to forget it for as long as they worked together. He was damned if he did and damned if he didn't! Talk about the devil and the deep blue sea?

'Well, are ya goin' up or wot? Not chicken, are ya?'

Barry's hot, beery, breath on the side of his face was enough to prompt him into action. He sidled out past Jason and began the walk of doom towards the stage. Spotlights were weaving around the room, picking up the poor unfortunates as they made their way forwards. One of them landed on him and blinded him through his glasses. This caused him to stumble and he felt his face grow scarlet. He didn't know how long this humiliation was going to last in the short-term but he knew the aftermath would last a lifetime.

Clarissa allowed herself to be helped up the stairs by the two staff members standing there. She was glad of their assistance for walking up stage steps with your hands stuck high up above your head was no easy task. Michael Duval came across and guided her to a spot on the stage. Once everyone was in place, she discretely looked around and counted eight poor unfortunates standing with their hands above their heads. One poor man, four places along, appeared utterly mortified. Mind you, she thought, he didn't really look the type of person you'd expect to find at a show like this. He had dark, slicked-down hair, cut in an old eighties style mullet, sported heavy, black-rimmed glasses and when paired with his brilliant white shirt, sleeveless woollen tank-top (she didn't know those things still existed) and his suit trousers with the ultra-sharp creases in them, he looked as much like a fish out of water as it was possible to be. Just at that moment, he glanced sideways and caught her eye. She gave him the smallest of smiles and turned back to face the front, realising she'd missed what Michael Duval had been saying.

Just then, the hypnotist snapped his fingers and her hands flew apart and fell down to her sides. She gave them a shake, just as she'd done when this farce had all begun, and felt the blood flow back into her numb digits. She felt the air move behind her and looked around to see the back curtain rising up and a number of chairs lined up. Michael Duval asked them all to take a seat.

There was a bit of a scuffle but soon everyone was sitting. Duval came over and moved one or two people around but he was quickly satisfied he had them all sitting in the correct order. He turned to the audience, spoke a few words and then snapped his fingers. Immediately, Clarissa felt herself slump in her chair with her eyes closed. She tried to open them but they were so heavy and it was too difficult. She could hear everything that was going on around her but her body felt both heavy and light and she was quite unable to move.

Michael Duval began to explain to the audience that he would shortly be telling them a story and in this story, there would be a number of key words. Each participant on the stage would be assigned one of these words and when their key word was mentioned, that person would then perform an action which he would put into their head. She listened as he walked along the line telling the first person they would whinny like a horse, another would be a mime artist stuck in a box, someone else would be starving hungry, and so on. When he came to stand in front of her, she was fully aware of his presence. Still, she could neither move nor open her eyes. She felt his hand upon her shoulder.

'When I say the word "feet" you will smell a horrible stench coming from the person next to you. It will be the most disgusting smell you have ever come across in your life.'

The pressure on her shoulder eased as Duval walked

away. She'd been moved to the end of the row of chairs in Duval's reshuffle and he shortly returned to place an empty chair beside her. Clarissa was surprised at her level of awareness of what was going on around her. She'd always believed that being hypnotised meant being totally out of it – almost like being asleep – but it would seem not. She still couldn't open her eyes though or move any part of her body.

The hypnotist was now calling for a volunteer from the audience and there was a round of applause. She felt the vibration of footsteps as they walked across the wooden stage, coming to a stop at her side. Someone then sat down in the empty chair.

Duval launched into his story and Clarissa could hear the other people lined up beside her performing their acts as he spoke. He was just describing the problems he has buying shoes because he has such large feet when she began to smell the most hideous aroma. Her eyes flew open and she looked at the man sitting on her right-hand side. She, as discretely as possible, put her hand under her nose and moved her chair a little to the left. Duval walked over to her.

'Is everything okay, miss?'

'Err… yes, yes, it's fine.'

'Are you sure?'

'Yes, I'm sure.' She glared at the man on her right.

Duval placed his hand on her shoulder. 'Sleep,' he said.

Clarissa felt herself slump back down in her chair. What on earth? She knew what had happened but couldn't *believe* it had happened. She had genuinely smelt the most disgusting stink. How could that be? She was aware of her surroundings; she knew what was going on about her but she was still susceptible to Duval's commands. Her head was so busy thinking through the situation that she failed to listen to the hypnotist's words. The next thing she knew, the foul aroma was making its way up her nostrils once again. She could feel herself gagging from how awful it was. This time, she didn't care about offending anyone, she moved her chair as far as it was possible to do so from the man sitting beside her.

Duval came over to her again. 'Miss, are you sure everything's okay? You don't look very happy?'

Unable to control her thoughts, her mouth or her actions, Clarissa jumped up from her seat, ran behind the hypnotist, pointed to the man and yelled at the top of her voice, 'He's stinking! He needs a bath, so he does! He clearly hasn't seen soap or water for weeks!'

The audience roared with laughter as Duval led her back to her seat and put her back into "sleep" mode.

As he finished off, she sat listening, utterly mortified at what she'd said to that poor man. There was no smell now and she knew the man wasn't in the least bit smelly. She hoped there'd be an opportunity to apologise to him. However, when the audience began clapping and the chair was removed from her side, she knew that saying sorry was not likely to happen. She felt relief that this ordeal must be nearly over but it was short-lived as Duval began to explain to the audience how his job entailed a great deal of travelling around the world and how he particularly liked to see each country's national dance.

Once again, she was aware of him moving down the line, giving out his instructions – one person had to perform a ballet whenever he mentioned Paris, another had to do Cossack dancing when he said the word Russia. She was lumbered with doing the flamenco when Spain came up. Oh, great!

Sure enough, Duval launched into his second story and she felt the stage tremble under her feet as various dances were performed across the boards. She gave her best attempt at a flamenco, twice, and felt she hadn't done too badly. As she was finishing off her second stint, and was being led back to her chair, she caught a quick glimpse of the gentleman she'd spotted earlier. His sharp-creased trousers were now hidden beneath a long, tulle, tutu. As she sat down and was put back into "snooze" mode, she realised he'd been given the ballet to dance. She was quite sure that he was, or would be, absolutely appalled by that. She felt rather cross with Duval for he'd clearly picked on the man by giving him that dance to do. She listened as the hypnotist wrapped up his story and announced to the audience at large that he was about to bring the performers out of their slumber and, when he did so, he would like everyone to give them a massive round of applause as a thank you for their participation, for without them, the night would have been considerably boring.

'However, ladies and gentlemen, before I send these wonderful people back to you,' Clarissa sensed Duval coming to stand nearby, 'I always like to finish by saying… When you all awaken, you will be as you were. However, know this – you are strong, you are kind. You are courageous, you are not stupid. Live your life to the fullest, find your dreams and follow them. Be the person you have always wanted to be because if you can get up on a stage and perform in front of hundreds of people, you can do anything you set your mind to! You are amazing. Don't ever forget it. One… two… three…'

Duval clicked his fingers and Clarissa felt the heaviness seep from her. She sat up in her chair, blinking her eyes. She heard the applause and cheers coming from the audience but she didn't take much notice, she was too busy enjoying the sensation of calm relaxation flowing through her. Even though she'd been aware of what was going on around her throughout the whole performance, she felt like she'd just awoken from the deepest of sleeps and her body was completely rested. She'd never felt like this before and she took her time walking back to her work colleagues, trying to relish the sensation for a few seconds more.

'Wow! Clarissa! You dark horse. Who knew you could dance like that? Have you had lessons in flamenco?'

The questions came at her thick and fast and she tried to laugh them off, saying she'd seen a few films and hoped she'd done alright. Elspeth finally came to her rescue.

'Okay, girls, give Clarissa a break. She's been a great sport tonight. Shall we pop to the pub for a quick one before we go home?'

The answer was a unanimous yes. Elspeth turned to Clarissa. 'Will you be joining us?'

Clarissa thought for a moment before replying, 'Yes, I will.'

Elspeth couldn't hide her surprise at this. 'What about Daddy? Won't he be annoyed his little girl is late home?'

Clarissa's answer shocked them both.

'Fuck him! After that, I need a drink!' Whereupon, she put her arm through Elspeth's and let herself be led to the nearest bar.

FIVE

Gerald tried to find the girl he'd caught looking at him on the stage before the performance had begun. Something about her had been familiar but he didn't know what. He was hoping a second glance might help him to remember. He twisted round but people were moving and getting up from their seats and he could no longer see anyone who'd been up on the stage with him.

He felt rather strange inside. It was the first time he'd been hypnotised and it hadn't been at all what he'd expected. Sometimes, he'd been fully aware of what was going on around him throughout the evening's events and then at other times, he would suddenly come to – just like wakening up from a deep sleep when, for those first few seconds, your brain has kicked in but your eyelids and body are still heavy with slumber.

He knew he'd been prancing around the stage pretending to be a horse but it was the ballet attempt which had him feeling truly humiliated. Barry Bennett was going to make his life hell now. Of all the things the hypnotist could have made him do, that was by far the worst.

'Hey, Gerry-boy, what a show, eh? You certainly keep your talents well hidden.'

Gerald almost choked as Barry slapped him with great force on the back. 'When did you begin your secret life as a ballerina? You kept that one quiet!' Barry guffawed loudly while Gerald quietly picked up his jacket.

'Maybe we should be calling him "Geraldine",' piped up Jason.

Barry thought this was hilarious and said as much while they walked outside.

'So, Geraldine, are you joining us for a drink before you go home? You can give us another dance…' Barry raised his hands above his head and began twirling around on the pavement.

'No, I won't join you, thank you for asking. I need to be getting home.'

Gerald inwardly cursed the politeness of his reply. He so wanted to cut Barry Bennett down to size but he'd never been able to stand up to the bullies in his life and that wasn't going to suddenly change now.

He raised his hand in a farewell wave and walked away, Barry's mocking tones ringing in his ears long after he'd left them behind and driven home.

Gerald pulled onto the driveway and was dismayed to see the flicker of the television behind the lounge curtains. He'd hoped Marjory would be in bed by now – he couldn't face her tonight.

'Is that you home then?' came the strident tones from the lounge doorway as he removed his shoes and put on his slippers.

'Yes, Marjory, I'm home.'

'I hope you had a good night out while leaving me here to fend for myself.'

'I'm sure you managed – you usually do,' he muttered beneath his breath.

Gerald stepped through the door and took in the sight of the empty takeaway boxes still littering the coffee table. A couple of Pringles tubes were laid on their side, devoid of any contents, and some chocolate wrappers were scrunched up amongst the debris. Debris that Gerald knew he'd been cleaning up in the morning.

'I'm off to bed,' he said to the back of his wife's head as she continued to watch some low-level reality show on the television.

'I'll be up shortly.'

'No need to rush.' He walked up the stairs with heavy feet and hoped he'd be asleep before Marjory joined him. Only ten months before, he'd thought he was the luckiest man in the world as he'd watched her walk down the aisle towards him. Now, he had to face the fact his father had been right about her – she was a lazy, slovenly mare who'd just wanted to find someone to keep her and run around after her. 'She's a selfish one, lad,' his father had said, 'you don't want to tie yourself to someone like her, she'll only make you miserable.'

The week after they'd come back from their honeymoon, she'd quit her job saying it was too stressful for her but she hadn't bothered to find another one. She didn't lift a finger to help around the house and expected Gerald to cook and clean when he got home from the office. He'd mentioned the fact that, as she was at home all day, maybe she could take on the household responsibilities but the ensuing row had been almost apocalyptic. He'd tried not doing any housework and only cooking for himself, but she'd simply ordered takeaways and left the mess lying around afterwards. It was three days before he cracked and cleaned everything up, unable to live in the stench and mess any longer. He'd caught her smirking as he'd vacuumed around her and realised then that he'd been played. Since then, she'd grown fatter and smellier, only having a shower and washing her hair on the days she visited her mother.

Gerald put his toothbrush back in the holder and looked at his reflection in the mirror. He was barely forty-six yet he could easily have passed as being a decade older. He'd been bullied at school, bullied at work and now bullied at home, and it showed. The only time he hadn't been bullied were the three glorious years he'd been at university. That happiness, however, had been short-lived and now his eyes were lifeless and he couldn't remember the last time he'd smiled. He caught sight of a tub of tablets sitting on the shelf, left over from when his dad had moved out. He picked it up and looked inside – it was almost full. He stared at it for a few moments before, with a heavy sigh, he put the lid back on and returned it to the shelf. He didn't even have the courage to end it all. He walked into the bedroom, changed into his pyjamas and got into bed.

Marjory had come upstairs and begun snoring like a rhino long before he was able to eventually still his mind and go to sleep.

SIX

Clarissa woke up with a small groan. Where was she? There was a tap at the door and she realised that this is what had woken her.

'Come in,' she called hoarsely. She was clearing her throat as the door opened and the scent of coffee floated in, quickly followed by a hand carrying a steaming mug through the gap.

'Are you up for one of these?'

'Am I ever! Get it over here now!'

Elspeth walked in, looking as fresh as a daisy, and handed the mug to Clarissa who'd managed to pull her aching limbs and torso up into a sitting position.

'How are you feeling?'

'Achy, although,' Clarissa took a big sip of the coffee, 'this will really hit the spot, thank you.'

'You're welcome. I'll bet you're glad I forced that pint of water and the vitamin C tablets down your neck now!'

Clarissa had a vague memory of Elspeth demanding she take her "No Hangover" cure last night and she had to agree, it certainly seemed to have worked. She was absolutely knackered from dancing into the wee small hours but her head, although groggy, was pain-free.

'Thank you for looking out for me last night and for allowing me to crash in your spare room, Elspeth, I really appreciate it.'

'Hey, not a problem. It was nice to see you let your hair down – you always come across as being so strait-laced and uptight. You're a young girl but you behave like you're in your early forties. It's not right, love, you should be out there, enjoying the fun of being young.'

'I know, but my father… well… he's rather strict…' Clarissa's voice tailed off. In the last twenty-four hours she'd come to realise just how strict her father was and how unreasonable he could be. She'd had so much fun last night but now it was time for her to go home and face the music. She knew her father was going to be absolutely livid.

'Grab a shower before you leave. It'll make you feel better. I've put a towel in the bathroom for you.' Elspeth stood up and Clarissa thought she was going to speak again but after a few seconds, she simply gave a small smile and left the room.

'What do you mean, you "went out with the girls from work"? Haven't I forbidden you from associating with the other members of staff?'

'You don't seem to mind me "associating" with Tristan Faulkner though, do you? What makes him so special, huh?'

Clarissa and her father were screaming at each other in the kitchen. She'd been starving when she'd arrived home and had headed straight to the kitchen to make some toast before going up to her bedroom. Unfortunately, this had been one of the very few Saturdays when her father *hadn't* gone into the office and he'd come in from the garden just as she'd put the bread in the toaster.

'Don't you back-chat me, young lady!' George roared, his face turning puce with anger.

'I'm not back-chatting, I'm asking a perfectly reasonable question. Why am I allowed to speak and see Tristan but not the other staff members? Would it be something to do with the fact that his father is a "Sir" and you're aiming to marry me off to him? After all, that would be right up your social-climbing alley, wouldn't it?'

Clarissa turned her back and began buttering the toast which had just popped up. She couldn't believe she was speaking to her father like this – where was it coming from? Normally, she wouldn't say boo to a goose but right now, she was all full of fire and fight and was enjoying standing up for herself. Elspeth was right – she had been behaving like a middle-aged woman and dressing like one too. She caught sight of the tweed skirt she was wearing and was vowing to burn it as her father spoke again.

'That does it, Clarissa, you are grounded! I will NOT have you associating with those girls, they're clearly a very bad example on you and I was right to insist you keep away from them.'

Before she could answer, her mother walked into the room.

'What on earth is all this noise? George, the windows are open, do you want the neighbours to hear you screaming like a common fish-wife?'

George had been about to continue his tirade but his wife's comment saw him snapping his mouth closed again.

'Father is expressing his disgust that I chose to spend the evening with the girls from the office and didn't arrive home until this morning.'

'Where did you stay, dear?' Clarissa watched her mother place the bouquet of flowers she was holding calmly in the sink and run in a little water.

'I… err… stayed at Elspeth's, one of the paralegals from the office.'

'Oh, good, you're making some friends. And did you have a fun time?'

'Estelle! This is not the time for small-talk, I have just informed Clarissa that she is grounded. From now on,' he said to Clarissa, 'you will be coming home with me every evening after work until I deem you are suitably repentant of your actions.'

'Grounded? Repentant of my actions? Father, I am twenty-three years old, a bit old for you to be grounding me, and this is the twenty-first century, I have the freedom to do what I want.'

'Not while you live under my roof you don't!'

'Fine! I'll move out and find my own roof to live under.'

'ENOUGH! YOU WILL NOT SPEAK TO ME LIKE THAT! YOU WILL SPEAK TO ME WITH RESPECT!'

Clarissa looked her father up and down before replying in a stony tone, 'If you want my respect, Father, then I suggest you try earning it!'

She threw her toast onto a plate, stormed out of the kitchen and up the stairs to her bedroom, slamming the door hard behind her.

She walked over to the dressing table and put the plate down, her appetite now gone. She took in the appearance of the face staring back at her – the flushed cheeks and the slightly open mouth through which she was panting, but it was her eyes which had her attention. They were sparkling! She'd never seen them shine like this before.

Clarissa suddenly realised she looked alive!

For the second time that morning, Clarissa was woken up by gentle tapping on the bedroom door.

'Come in,' she sighed, knowing her mother had arrived to give her a lecture on her earlier behaviour. Her dad had had his say, now it was her mother's turn.

'Hi, sweetie, I've brought you a hot chocolate,' Estelle Walton slipped in through the door and placed the large mug, overflowing with cream and marshmallows, on the bedside table before sitting down on the end of the bed.

'Hi, Mother. Thank you for the drink.' Clarissa was surprised to receive this treat but managed to hide it as she took a sip. When she'd misbehaved in the past, her mother did not come bearing gifts.

'How are you feeling now you've had a sleep?'

'Better, thank you, but I meant what I said – it's time for me to move out. I hope you're not here to try and talk me out of it.'

'Not at all, my dear, I'm here to make sure you don't change your mind.'

'I'm sorry… what?' Clarissa placed the mug back down heavily on the table.

'You heard me, Clarissa, you're long overdue finding your wings and flying the nest. I'm just glad you've managed it before your father had you married off to that obnoxious Tristan.'

'You don't… you don't like Tristan?'

'Can't stand him, dear. Horrible, slimy little weasel that he is! He spends more time with his head up your father's arse than he does talking to either of us when he's here.'

'Mother!' By this time, Clarissa's chin was almost on her duvet.

'What?'

'You… talking like that… it's… it's—'

'It's not me? Is that what you mean?'

'Umm, yes!'

'Clarissa, darling, these are the words that are in my head most of the time, I simply never say them out loud.'

'Why not?'

'Because I have to maintain the standards your father has imposed upon us.'

'So, why are you saying them now?'

'Because you've finally woken up to the farce of a life we live here. You have no idea the joy it gave me to hear you shouting back at your dad today.'

'The joy?'

If Clarissa was in any way surprised by the change in her own behaviour this morning, it was now completely surpassed by this change in her mother. Where was the quiet, insipid, woman who always agreed with her husband and lived to serve his every need?

'Mother, I don't understand…'

'Oh please, call me "Mum" – Mother is so affected!'

'But Father hates "mum and dad"!'

'Fuck your father!'

'MOTHER!'

Estelle shrugged. 'What? As of this moment, I no longer care what he thinks or feels about my behaviour.'

'Okay, Moth—, I mean Mum, enough now! What is this all about?'

Her mother took her hand and began to talk.

'I was nineteen and studying accountancy at university in London, when I first met your father. He was older than me, kind, attentive and quite different to boys my own age. Maturity can be quite a head-turner. When I took him home to meet my parents, well… they totally fell for him and his charms. My father was bowled over by this young man who had every intention of making the law his career, for he'd been a labourer all his life and he always felt a bit inferior when in the company of *"thems that has learning"* – his expression, not mine. When George announced his intention to marry me, I never got to say "yes", for my parents were too quick to say it for me. I expressed my doubts about being too young and wanting to finish my accountancy course but I was ignored and my father told me I should be grateful that a nice young man like George wanted anything to do with an ugly duckling like me.'

Clarissa gasped aloud. 'He didn't say that? Surely not?'

'Oh, he surely did. Your grandfather was, I can say with hindsight, rather a tyrant and that's why he liked your father so much – they were two of a kind.'

'You could have refused and continued studying.'

'This was an era, Clarissa, when too many people still expected women to stop working after they were married. A few years later, I'd have been able to fight it but your grandfather had old-fashioned principles and he was simply glad I was getting wed.'

'I see.'

'It wasn't too bad at the start but when George got a job at a top London law firm, his lifestyle expectations changed. He set his heart on becoming a partner in the firm and that meant meeting certain standards. Suddenly, I had to learn to bake like a French patisserie chef, cook cordon bleu, and keep house like Martha Stewart. He wanted to entertain all these high-flyers in the legal world and I was expected to always be better than the time before. I hated it – that kind of life was not for me. I began to hate the man he'd become. I tried to talk to him but he wasn't prepared to listen.'

'So why didn't you leave him?'

'I'd started to think about it but then something happened – I fell pregnant.'

'You could still have left him.'

Her mother smiled at her.

'I could have but for two things – I didn't have any means of supporting us both; my parents would have disowned me for disgracing them and – far more importantly – your father wouldn't have let you go. He'd been desperate for me to become pregnant; it was another thing for him to compete with his peers and brag about. He *might* have let me go but he'd have fought tooth and nail to keep you and there was *no way* I was giving up my child. So, I did the only thing I could do – suck it up, as the saying goes, and ensure you had the best upbringing it was possible to give you.'

'You've stayed with him all these years for me?'

'Yes, I did. That was the choice I made and don't you dare feel responsible in any way. I had to ensure he didn't overpower you although he hasn't made it easy for me – I feel I've been fighting a daily battle for the last twenty-odd years.'

'But… I don't understand – you've always supported him and backed him up.'

'Not always, darling. Do you recall those Girl Guide camps you hated going to each year? I didn't insist you went just for the hell of it. I hoped you would find your spirit of independence and that one year you'd come home and turn into a rebellious teenager. But you never did. You simply told me how much you hated them and that you were glad to be home. And then, when you were applying to universities, I encouraged you to look at some more far-flung options such a Cambridge or Birmingham or Southampton – anywhere that would get you away from George and his controlling influence – but you chose Oxford because your father pretty much bullied you into it. I didn't even want you to do law.'

'So, why didn't you try harder?'

Estelle looked down at her lap and when she looked back up, Clarissa saw the tears in her eyes.

'Clarissa, I tried so damned hard. That was why I forced you to do the secretarial course at school – I convinced your father that being able to speed type would be beneficial in this new computer age but the truth was, I wanted you to have a skill you could use anywhere in the world. There is always a need for secretaries and so no matter what happens in your life, if the worst ever comes to the worst, you'd still be able to work and keep yourself. In this new, virtual age, you can even work from home.'

There was silence as Clarissa digested all her mother had told her.

'What will you do if I move out?'

'I don't know,' she sighed. 'I'll wait until you are settled and then decide. If I'm being honest, it's a bit scary to think about it.'

'I think you should leave him! Get out and find your own life.'

'That sounds delightful, dear, but…'

'But what? I've heard the way he talks to you. I've seen the way he undermines you – if I'm not here, then you have no reason to stay.'

Her mother took her hand.

'I know, darling, but when you've spent your whole life being told you're not good enough, it becomes really difficult to think that you are. I suppose it's like being institutionalised – you want to get out but are terrified of what being out will bring.'

'If you could do anything, Moth— Mum, what would it be? What would YOU most like to do?'

'I'd love to take myself off travelling – you know, buy one of those little camper van things or a motorhome and travel around the UK, learning more about the country I live in. George was always too busy trying to impress with his city breaks to Paris and Barcelona and thought staying close to home was something only the working classes did.'

'Then you should do it! Go for it! Live your life!'

'Let's get your life sorted out first, Clarissa. Then I can begin to sort mine.'

‘It’s not that easy for me either, Mum. I can move out but I need to stay at the firm until I’m fully qualified. I’m kind of stuck too.’

‘I understand but… well… as it happens, I have this for you. It’ll give you some breathing space while you make whatever changes you need to make.’ Estelle pulled a piece of paper from her skirt pocket and handed it over to Clarissa.

‘What’s this?’

‘It’s a bank account in your name. I opened it when you were born and whenever I had some money to spare, I’d put it in there. As the years went on, and your father became successful, I was able to deposit larger amounts. I’d like to think there’s enough in there to free you up to make your own choices.’

Clarissa looked at her mum, once again astonished at the secrets now being revealed to her, before looking down and slowly unfolding the paper in her hand. She looked at the numbers written down, looked at her mum and then looked at the numbers again.

‘Seriously? But that’s… that’s a fortune, Mother!’

‘It’s not a fortune, Clarissa, but it’s certainly enough to allow you to do whatever you want – within reason of course.’

Tearing her eyes away from the numbers swimming in front of her, Clarissa looked at the woman who had given up so much for her. Sure, her mum may have had a comfortable life when it came to material things but she hadn’t had any real happiness and, in that moment, Clarissa realised she didn’t know her mum at all. She’d gotten a small insight into her life this afternoon but Clarissa wanted to know more. Clarissa wanted to get to know her mother.

‘Actually, Mum, I’ve just had an idea and I think you might like it… why don’t we BOTH go travelling? Let’s buy a motorhome and tear up the motorways of Great Britain together – what do you say, shall we do it? Does that sound like a plan?'

'What? Seriously?'

'Yes, seriously.'

She watched the joy spread over her mother's face. 'Oh, Clarissa, I would absolutely love that. Are you sure?'

'As sure as I've been about anything. Let's do it! Let's do it as soon as possible.'

'How about Monday, when your father goes to work? Shall we go looking at motorhomes then?'

Clarissa looked into the eyes that were so like hers and made the same observation now that she'd made about herself earlier – her mother's eyes were shining and sparkling.

She had come alive.

They had *both* come alive.

SEVEN

Gerald took a deep breath as he stepped out of the lift onto the floor for his office. It was Monday morning and he was dreading this. He'd spent all weekend worrying about today and wishing he could find a way of avoiding it. Unfortunately, an airplane hadn't fallen from the sky and landed on his head nor had an earthquake occurred right under his house and swallowed him up, which meant he had to face the music that was Barry Bennett. His only hope was that Barry would grow bored of mocking him sooner rather than later.

He pushed open the double doors, wishing as he did so, that his desk wasn't situated in the far corner. He'd barely made it past half of the desks when the strains of "Swan Lake" filled the air and Barry and Jason appeared, up on their tiptoes and flapping their arms.

'Good morning, Geraldine, come to show us your moves have yer?' Barry called over to him in a high-pitched, falsetto, voice.

'Ha, ha, Barry, very funny.' Gerald forced himself to keep walking although he could feel his legs turning to jelly. He made it without stumbling, tripping or falling and sat down gratefully in his chair. His secretary placed a cup of coffee on his desk and, giving her a smile of thanks, he grabbed it up and sipped it gratefully. He took his time sorting himself out, all the while gritting his teeth at the shenanigans happening a few feet away. Barry had begun telling anyone and everyone who would listen what had happened on Friday night at the theatre. Just as he'd reach the end, someone else would come in and he'd start all over again.

Barry was on his seventh telling of the story in less than two hours and was, yet again, playing "Swan Lake" on his PC while calling on "Geraldine" to come and show everyone how it should really be done when something inside Gerald snapped.

'ENOUGH!' he yelled at the top of his voice. 'THAT IS ENOUGH!'

'Err, I'll say when it's enough, Geraldine, and I'm not quite done yet. Maybe in anuvver ten or twenty years or so, me old mucker, but not just yet.'

Had Barry not called him Geraldine again, in front of the whole office, Gerald might have let the matter go, but that was the final straw. He threw his stapler across the room, marched over to where Barry was sitting, grabbed him by the tie and twisted it in his fist until it was putting pressure on Barry's windpipe.

'NO, BARRY, I WILL SAY WHEN IT IS ENOUGH, YOU FAT, IGNORANT, STUPID, BASTARD!' He lowered his voice. 'You think you're so funny and clever when the truth is you're just thick and pathetic. If you were so clever, you'd be able to come up with witticisms that are not at the expense of your colleagues, but you can't. All you can do is pick on those around you and your little group of acolytes join in – NOT because they like you, you stupid arsehole, but they hope that by doing so, you won't pick on them. It's time for some home truths, Barry – I hope you're man enough to cope although I have my doubts. No one likes you, Barry, everyone detests you. You're a rude, bad-mannered, foul-mouthed, racist, sexist, fat bully. You always have been and you always will be. Well, I've had enough of your abuse and so has everyone else around here.' From the corner of his eye, Gerald had noticed the smiles growing on the faces around him and this only served to bolster his confidence.

'From now on, you will treat everyone here with the respect they deserve. You think you're so admired but I suggest you take a look at how everyone is laughing at you now. No one has come to your defence, which I'm sure tells you what you need to know. We think you're scum, Barry.'

Gerald leant forward, twisted the tie a little more and said menacingly into Barry's face, 'And my name is GERALD! Not Gerry, not Gez and *not* Geraldine. It's GERALD! Have you got that? *I said, have you got that*?'

Barry just about managed to nod his head, so tight was Gerald's grip.

'Good! Oh, and one more thing – drop the fake cockney accent. Everyone knows you were born in Cowley. It just makes you sound like a thick twat, but then, I suppose that's exactly what you are!'

Gerald loosened his grip on Barry's tie, shoved him back in his chair and returned to his desk, where he switched off his computer, picked up his jacket and briefcase and walked towards the office doors. Before he walked through, he turned to face his staff again. The room was so quiet he was sure they could have heard a pin drop. He looked at the faces staring in his direction, a mix of shock, surprise and joy spread across them.

'Right,' he said loudly, 'I'm going to be out for the rest of the day, but when I return tomorrow, everything changes around here. There WILL be respect shown to every staff member BY every staff member and God help anyone who thinks they're above this new regime. Have I made myself clear?'

He took the murmurs and nods as assent, turned and walked out of the office.

When the lift arrived and the doors closed behind him, he slumped against the wall and tried to still his trembling body. He was shaking from head to toe and he could feel the adrenaline flying through his veins. Where the *hell* had that come from? Never, in his entire life, had he ever raised so much as a finger against anyone who was making his life miserable. He usually just waited it out and hoped the perpetrator would grow bored and find a new target. He all but staggered out of the building and into the small café next door where he ordered a double espresso and sat down at the breakfast bar along the window.

He was sipping the last few dregs in the cup when he stopped staring unseeingly out of the window and took note of the shop across the road. It was a hardware shop. Suddenly, an idea came into his head and before he had the chance to change his mind, he picked up his briefcase and hurried out.

As he stood waiting for the traffic to clear, he began to smile. It seemed that if today was to be a day of change, he might as well go the whole hog. What was that saying again? Oh yes, "in for a penny, in for a pound" and with that thought in mind, he crossed the road with a definite spring in his step.

EIGHT

The new-found joy in Gerald's downtrodden little soul nearly did a runner when he stepped through the front door of his home. The stale smell of a fry-up was hanging heavy in the air and he walked into the kitchen to find a pile of dirty, greasy pans in the sink. A half-hearted effort to soak them had been made but the water was now cold and the fat lay thick upon the top.

The worktops were equally as messy with an empty baked beans tin lying on its side, the remains of the sauce dribbling out and making a little congealed pool. The loaf of bread sat opened up, the slices falling out like dominoes and the crumbs from the toast were spread all around it. The butter hadn't been returned to the fridge and he could see orange stains from the marmalade around its edges.

Gerald dropped his carrier bag on the table with a sigh. The kitchen had been pristine when he'd left this morning. He hadn't ever been over-the-top house proud, but he liked things to be clean and tidy. Since Marjory had moved in, however, that had become a distant memory. He pulled his phone from his pocket, took a photograph of the mess and then set about his task for the afternoon.

First of all, he went up into the loft and brought down two suitcases, which he took into the master bedroom and placed on the bed. He then, with great care, removed all of Marjory's clothing from the wardrobe and dresser and folded everything neatly into them. He picked up some other knick-knacks and put them in too. He looked carefully around the room and satisfied he had packed everything that belonged to his wife, took the cases down the stairs and put them by the front door.

Gerald then walked into the lounge, turned a blind eye to the mess and looked about him to see if there was anything here which belonged solely to Marjory. Apart from a few DVDs, and a couple of cheap, tacky, china figurines, there was nothing. He squashed these few extra pieces inside a suitcase and locked it. Both suitcases were then put out in the porch after which, he went to the garage, grabbed his tool kit and proceeded to change the locks on both the front and back door. He also added an extra bolt to the inside of the French windows.

Satisfied that everything was now in order, he picked up the cases, walked to the end of the driveway and placed them carefully on the small patch of grass beside the wall. He looked at his watch and saw that Marjory would be home from visiting her mother soon. He unbolted both of the large, iron gates and, for the first time in a long time, he closed them to, battling for a moment with the ground bolts to get them in place. He saw headlights turn into the lane at the far end as he was feeding the thick sturdy chain through the ironwork – the padlock had just snapped into place as Marjory pulled up.

The angle of the car meant he couldn't see her face behind the windscreen as the glare of the headlights hit his eyes, but he soon heard her voice when she rolled down the window and yelled through it.

'Oi, you daft arsehole, what're you playing at with closing the gates? Open them up, I want to get in and have my dinner, I'm starving.'

'Sorry, Marjory, but no can do. You no longer live here and your suitcases are just over there if you would like to retrieve them.'

'YOU WHAT?' Her screech was loud enough to scare some pigeons out of a nearby tree.

'I think you heard me but, just in case you didn't, you are no longer a resident at this abode.'

'Are you kicking me out?'

'Yup, that's exactly what I'm doing. Marrying you was one of the biggest mistakes of my life but today, I am putting it all to rights.'

The car door opened and Marjory heaved herself out and waddled over to the gate. For the first time, he really saw just how much weight she'd gained in the time they'd been married, although he wasn't surprised because all she ever did was eat and watch television. From the day she'd stopped working, she'd just lazed about and he was now looking at the end product of her slothfulness. It was considerably unappealing.

A fat finger was prodded through the gate. '*Marrying me* was the best thing you ever did, leaving me is your biggest mistake. You were a lonely, single, middle-aged man when I met you and that's exactly what you'll go back to being.'

'You're right, Marjory, I was lonely when I met you. I'd spent many years caring for my father and when he moved over into the retirement village, I found being here on my own difficult, but I have since come to realise that I would much rather be lonely and on my own than spend another second under the same roof as you.'

'You'll regret this, Gerald Wainwright! I'll take you for every penny you have. You won't be so sure of yourself when I'm moving into the house and YOU'RE moving out because I'm going to get a good solicitor who'll ensure I get everything.'

'I think that is very unlikely, Marjory, for two reasons.' Gerald smiled calmly and raised his hand. 'Reason one,' he raised his index finger, 'You haven't worked for the best part of a year so I doubt you have the means to pay for a sub-standard solicitor never mind a good one, and reason two,' he lifted his middle finger, 'the house is not mine and you can't have what is not mine to give!' He let his two fingers float in the air a moment longer before returning his hand nonchalantly to his trouser pocket.

'What do you mean, the house is not yours? Of course, it's yours! You live in it and pay the bills!'

'Sorry, dear, but the house is still in my father's name. You can't touch it!'

'But you've got his power of attorney – the house was supposed to be signed over to you when that paperwork was completed…'

'Ah yes, that… I'm afraid my father didn't, or doesn't, like you Marjory. He's considerably more astute than I am and he saw you for what you are the first time he met you. When he realised I couldn't be convinced to end our relationship, he refused to sign the paperwork. So, the house is still in his name and I have no power over anything. Bummer, huh!'

In the fast-fading light, Gerald could see Marjory's face moving from shock to anger and back to shock again. He couldn't help the little frisson of satisfaction that ran up his spine. He wasn't a cruel man by any means but Marjory had mistreated him for too long and now her hens were coming home to roost.

'But… what will I do? Where will I go? I have nowhere to stay!'

'Oh, come now, Marjory, I'm sure the eternal delight

that is your mother will be thrilled to have you back living under her roof. I now know why you kept us apart until the wedding day – you were scared I'd look at her and see what you'd become. Well, you got that right because you're becoming just like her and there's no way I'm sticking around to see the finished article. Now,' he glanced at his watch, 'I have to get back indoors and clean up the mess you left behind. You'll be hearing from my solicitor in due course.'

Gerald turned and walked back towards the house.

'Oi, you get back here! I'm not finished talking to you… Gerald! GERALD!'

'But I'm done talking to you,' he whispered, as he closed the porch door behind him and locked it. He walked in the front door without a backwards glance, closed it and locked it with the new key. He then leant against it and slumped down to the floor, shaking from his courageous act. Never in a million years would he have thought himself capable of standing up for himself the way he had done today. A variety of emotions were coursing through him, crashing against each other as they vied for a position in the rankings – was he happy? Scared? Exalted? Uncertain? He really didn't know but eventually, after sitting on the floor for goodness knew how long, it came to him. There was no question on how he felt.

He was relieved!

NINE

'Oh, Mum, I didn't realise motorhomes were this expensive. Maybe we should have a rethink on our plans.'

Essie Walton looked at her daughter's concerned face. Yesterday, Clarissa had refused to go to work and, after George had left for the office, the two of them had sat at the dining table making plans and drawing up lists of all the places in the UK they wanted to visit. They'd yet to work out a route but there was plenty of time for that. The first task in hand was sorting out the motorhome. Last night, Clarissa had informed her father she wouldn't be in the office for a few weeks as she needed some time out. He'd tried to bully her into submission but Clarissa had changed and she was having none of it. She'd stood up to George and had informed him that, just like every other member of staff, she was entitled to holidays and she intended to take them. This had shut him up and he'd gone off to London this morning in a state of high dudgeon. Essie had been so proud of her daughter and had told her as much as soon as her husband's car swept off the driveway.

'It's knowing I have your support that's making me so brave, Mum' Clarissa had whispered in her ear as they'd clung tightly together in a hug. 'I wouldn't have been anywhere near as courageous without you rooting for me.'

'Yes, you would have, darling. You have more strength inside you than you realise. Now, come, let's go and do some car shopping!' She'd given Clarissa a grin full of so much mischief that Clarissa had melted into a fit of the giggles and it had taken the whole of the journey from the house to the caravan and motorhome establishment before she was able to stop.

Essie looked around the motorhome they were both standing in. It was brand new, the latest model and she loved it! She loved it even more because she knew George would hate it. This would be his worst nightmare for a holiday but she couldn't think of anything she would enjoy more. She sat down on one of the front seats and swivelled gently from side to side. Clarissa was sitting opposite on one of the beige leather bench seats.

'Clarissa, trust me when I say we can afford this.'

'But, Mum, it's almost half of the money in the account. It's too much. We can just as easily get a second-hand one, that would be just as good. Or we could rent one, that would be even better.'

Essie leant forward and looked earnestly into her daughter's troubled face.

'Clarissa, firstly, that money is ALL yours. None of it is going towards this venture. That's for you for when you finally decide what you want to do with your life – something I hope this trip will help with. Secondly, one of the few positive things I have learnt from being with your father, is that we never settle for second best. Or in this case, second hand. Also, a rental would be no good because we don't know how long we'll be away for. Thirdly, when we're finished with our travels, and know where or what we're doing next, we can sell it and make some money back. We can easily afford to buy it new because, what you are not aware of is, your father decided to make some financial changes – for tax purposes – a few years ago and they included putting a number of bank accounts into my name.'

'You mean…'

'Do I have access to all his savings? Yup, that would be correct!' The mischievous grin returned to Essie's face and Clarissa's giggles raised their head once more.

'Oh, don't you start those again, my girl, or you'll set me off and that won't hold much sway when I try to barter the price with young Paul over there.'

'You're going to barter?'

Essie smiled at the surprise in Clarissa's voice.

'Of course, I am, dear. Your father may have forced me to join the local WI because he thought it created the correct family image but I've learnt many things in my time there and bartering was one of the first. Never accept anything on face value, always see if you can get a better price.'

The young salesman caught her eye and wandered back over to them, trying desperately not to appear too anxious or overly enthusiastic. Essie smiled at his thinly veiled attempt and mentally rubbed her hands with glee. She was going to have this one on toast!

An hour later, once a price had been agreed and a few extras thrown in, Essie signed the paperwork and the date was set for them to collect their new means of transport, in a week's time.

When they got back in the car to leave, Essie turned to Clarissa.

'You know what? I think this calls for a celebration. Since your father's away, why don't we have afternoon tea in Oxford and then buy some guide books and roadmaps to begin plotting our route?'

'I think that sounds perfect. Let's go.'

The two women set off into town, chattering and laughing as they discussed their plans. They arrived in Oxford and Essie set about trying to find a parking space. She didn't like using the multi-storey car parks after her car was badly dented in one a couple of years before. This meant trying to find something on the street, which was always more of a headache.

She was so busy looking further down the road she didn't see the man stepping out from between the parked cars until Clarissa let out an almighty scream but by then, it was too late. She was unable to stop in time and hit the man who thudded onto the car bonnet before rolling off to land on the tarmac in front of them.

TEN

Gerald had woken up late that morning. It had been a late one the night before as he'd scrubbed the house from top to bottom, trying to eradicate the presence of his, soon-to-be, ex-wife from it. While he'd been scrubbing and scouring, he noticed how shabby the house had become. It hadn't been decorated since his mother had moved out, leaving his father to look after him and his older sister, Flora. Flora had occasionally nagged them to drag the interior of their home into the twenty-first century, and vague promises had been made that they would do so, but after her death, there had been no more nagging, no more promises and no interior improvements. A long list of items now lay on the kitchen table and Gerald studied it while sipping his coffee and eating his toast.

Once he'd cleared up after himself, he took a deep breath and switched his mobile phone back on. When he'd had to decline the seventh phone call from Marjory last night, he'd turned it off and put it away in his briefcase to avoid the temptation to read the texts that were also pinging away every few minutes. Knowing Marjory's foul mouth when she was in a temper as he did, Gerald had a fair idea what to expect and, a short time later, he wasn't disappointed. She'd called him all the names under the sun, plus a few more besides, and had made threats of what she would do to his person if she ever laid her hands on him again.

It was reading these that made his left eye begin to twitch. His new-found courage was something he was still growing into and the memories of Marjory's temper tantrums made his stomach churn. The tender skin on the inside of his left arm began pulling and he leant over to retrieve the tube of cream to ease it. Marjory had always claimed that putting the boiling hot pan, which had just come straight off the hob, onto his arm had been an accident. It wasn't long after they were married and, at the time, Gerald had believed her. It hadn't taken long, however, to adjust his thinking and he now knew she'd done it on purpose. There had been too many other incidents, such as a foot "accidentally" tripping him when he was carrying fresh cups of tea, or a "stumble" on the upper landing that had seen him fall halfway down the stairs, or the cold tap being turned on all too frequently in the kitchen when he was up in the shower. He didn't know how many times he'd been scalded over the months, but it was rather a lot.

In more recent months, there had been less "accidents" as they had turned into outright physical abuse. She would goad him into a corner and rain slaps and punches around his head while screaming into his face. He'd moved his chair into the corner after the time she'd hit him from behind with the iron. One night he'd come home to find all his suits in tatters because he'd been in a meeting at work and hadn't taken her phone call.

Last night, Gerald had finally admitted to himself that he was a victim of abuse. Most people think of women as being the abused partner in a relationship; it often takes another couple of mental steps to attribute the same to a man. His first instinct had been one of shame, but as he'd scrubbed vigorously at the bathroom floor, he'd let the anger and shame flow out. By the time the bathroom floor had been wiped down and was shining brightly, the anger had gone and he'd been left with a deep sense of emptiness, unable to really comprehend what he'd been dealing with in his short marriage.

Now, in the peaceful silence of his home, he took a deep, calming breath, put down his phone and went to have his first "safe" shower in ages. He stayed in it a little longer than usual, relishing the constant temperature of the warm water before getting out and dressing.

After closing the door on Marjory's screeching last night, he'd made two telephone calls – one to the office to advise he was taking a week's holiday and the second to the family solicitors which had resulted in a rather important appointment this morning that he didn't want to miss. He picked up his briefcase and was about to place the required paperwork inside when he stopped mid-action. No! It was time to lighten up a bit. He took a rucksack from the hall cupboard and placed the items in there instead.

Before leaving the bedroom, Gerald peeped carefully through the net curtains to see if Marjory was around. He'd have been more than a little surprised to see her, for while it was late in the morning for him, it was most certainly the crack of dawn by her standards. He looked up and down the quiet country lane and satisfied that she wasn't hanging about, he quickly ran down the stairs and out to his car. With haste, he opened the gates, drove through, and then made sure they were firmly closed and locked again before driving off in the direction of Oxford.

A lovely warm glow had lit up inside him when Gerald left the solicitors office a few hours later. It had been agreed that he could divorce Marjory on the grounds of unreasonable behaviour and his childhood habit of keeping a diary – suggested by a teacher to help him cope with the school bullies after his mother had moved away – had stood him in good stead. He'd recorded many examples of his wife's behaviour and these had gone into the petition. Photographic evidence had also been added for good measure. He knew Marjory would try to refuse the divorce so he'd had to ensure his evidence was tight enough to prevent any wriggle room on her part. He was prepared to offer a settlement of five-thousand pounds to her, going up to seven thousand if she pushed hard enough but, as the house wasn't his and there were no children to consider, his solicitor felt this was more than generous considering the marriage wasn't even a year old. All being well, he'd be free of her in a few months.

So engrossed was he in his thoughts, Gerald wasn't paying any attention to the traffic as he stepped out to cross the road and knew nothing of the approaching car until it swept him off his feet, spun him across its bonnet and then dropped him with some force in the middle of the road.

He lay there for a moment, inwardly bemused that he was actually seeing stars. His favourite childhood cartoons of Bugs Bunny and Daffy Duck had all been true. Go figure!

He closed his eyes as a sensation of nausea came over him and when he opened them again, the sky above had been blocked out by two beautiful, but rather concerned, faces. Faces that were both extremely familiar to him.

His eyes flitted from side to side, taking in what he was seeing before he managed to whisper, 'Essie? Essie Parker, is that you?'

No one got the chance to reply as a larger-than-life

figure suddenly bore down upon them. 'I saw it all, I will be your witness, ladies. This man just stepped out onto the road, he didn't look or check for traffic. I saw it happen. Here's my card, call me if you need me. I'll be happy to speak to the police.'

Gerald was raising himself up into a sitting position when he heard the word "Police" being bandied about.

'No, no police, I'm fine, honest. Just a little bashed about. I admit full responsibility and will pay for any damages.'

He looked up at the flamboyant voice who appeared to be wearing equally flamboyant clothing but everything was blurry, as not only had his glasses fallen off in the tumble and he was squinting in an attempt to see properly but his hair had fallen forward over his face.

'Here you are, sir, they fell when you rolled off the bonnet. They don't appear to be damaged although the left arm is a touch wonky,' said a gentle voice softly in his ear as his glasses appeared in front of him.

Gerald put them on, pushed his hair back off his face and looked round to see the younger of the two hovering faces kneeling beside him.

'Hi, I'm Clarissa.' She put out her hand towards him and Gerald gave it a shake. This all felt rather surreal – did people really go around introducing themselves so politely after a road traffic accident? 'Do you think you can stand, sir? We need to move so we can clear the road, there's a couple of cars backed up now.'

The older woman came over just as Clarissa was helping him to his feet and picked up his rucksack.

'Mrs…' she looked at the business card that had been shoved into her hand, '…Ward has said we may park on her driveway as she is on her way out and won't be home until later this evening.' She pointed to the house where a large SUV was reversing out and turning onto the road. A brightly coloured arm came out of the window and gave them all a wave as it drove off.

'Clarissa, do you want to stay with the gentleman while I park the car?'

Gerald walked with Clarissa and sat on the low garden wall of the house where her mother was parking their car. Gerald knew they were mother and daughter – the resemblance was too strong for them not to be. They shared the same pale-caramel blonde hair, milk-chocolate brown eyes, oval face and large, but beautiful, mouth.

Clarissa was asking him how he was feeling but he wasn't listening as his eyes were too busy drinking in the vision of beauty in front of him. A vision he hadn't seen for over twenty-five years.

ELEVEN

Essie looked at the man sitting on the wall in front of her. He was looking at her with a strange expression on his face. It was almost dreamy-like and she was becoming concerned that he did in fact need medical assistance. He was giving no indication of being hurt but there might be something going on internally.

'Look, I'm going to call for an ambulance. I don't want to risk moving you until you've been properly checked over.'

'No, Essie, please, I don't need an ambulance, I'm fine. Just a little bumped and bruised but nothing drastic.'

'Are you sure? I really do think— Wait a minute… how do you know my name?'

Essie realised then that he'd whispered her name just before Mrs Ward had interrupted them.

'Don't you recognise me, Essie? I know it's been a while and you've certainly aged better than I have but I didn't think I'd changed *that* much.'

Essie leant in for a closer look. Now that he mentioned it, there was something familiar—

'Gerald? No, it can't be… is it? Gerald Wainwright?'

The smile that spread across the invalid's face was all the answer she needed.

'Oh, my goodness, how are you? Okay, stupid question but… Oh, my goodness, I can't believe it's you!'

'Let's just say I'm a lot better for seeing you, Essie.'

'Do you two know each other?'

Essie straightened up. 'Darling, this is an old friend from my uni days. We were on the same course and roamed around together.'

She turned back to Gerald. 'Gerald, I'd like you to meet my daughter, Clarissa.'

'Err, Mum, we've kind of already done that bit.'

Clarissa smiled before also turning towards Gerald. 'Gerald, I need to ask – were you at the theatre on Friday night? At the Michael Duval show?'

'Yes, I was. When I saw you on the stage, my first thought was that you looked familiar but I didn't get the opportunity to dwell on it before I was unceremoniously dumped into some kind of stupor.'

'You were the poor soul he made do the ballet, weren't you?'

'Yes!'

No one missed the grimace on his face.

Essie stepped back into the conversation. 'May I suggest we take this reminiscence party somewhere more comfortable and preferably where there is coffee and cake. Warmth would also be good, Gerald, as you may not have noticed it but you're shivering. Come on, let's go and find somewhere.'

'What about the car, Mum? Are you just going to leave it here?'

'Sure! Mrs Ward made it quite clear she won't be home till later this evening so it'll be okay to sit there for a couple of hours.'

Satisfied that Gerald could walk and move okay, Essie led the way back to a small coffee shop she'd noticed earlier when she'd turned into the road. The smell of the freshly ground coffee beans embraced them when they walked in the door and Essie drew in a deep, deep breath – this, along with fresh cut grass, was a scent she could never get enough of. Her mouth began to water as a waitress walked by with a large mug of something delicious looking, topped with fresh cream and cinnamon.

They sat down on the two large, leather sofas by the window – Gerald and Clarissa on one, Essie sitting opposite. A small coffee table sat between them. The waitress soon came to take their order and then they all sat back, silent for a moment as they reflected on how they'd come to be there together.

'Gerald, I know I keep asking but are you sure everything's okay? I can't help feeling you should be getting checked out at the hospital.'

'Essie, honestly, I'm fine. I'll let you know immediately if I begin to feel otherwise.'

'So, Gerald,' Clarissa leant forward with a cheeky little gleam in her eye, 'I have to ask – what was my mum like in her younger days? Was she as bossy then as she is now?'

'Cheeky child! How did I manage to fail so badly as a parent?'

The joint laughter took a moment to pass and then Gerald replied, 'Clarissa, I'm afraid I have nothing untoward to say about your mother. She was the sensible one who always looked after everyone else and tried her best to keep us out of mischief. Although, she did once dance on the table in the pub while stone cold sober!'

'Noooooo! She did not! Seriously?'

Essie chuckled at the look on her daughter's face. 'Gerald Wainwright – you tell the whole story here!'

Seeing her old friend had no intention of expanding on

his comment, she turned to her daughter.

'What you have not been told is that "someone" – not mentioning ANY names,' she glared mockingly at Gerald, 'had commandeered my handbag and wouldn't return it until I had, and I quote, "lived a little and let my hair down". I jumped up on the table and danced up there to prove I wasn't the straight-up and down little madam he regularly accused me of being.'

'In fairness, Essie, you were always a little on the prim side. It was our job to loosen you up. A role, I believe, Bobbie and Ritchie were only too happy to take on as their own.'

Essie smiled as she remembered her old friends. 'Bobbie was the worst – she was always an advocate for women's rights and I'm sure she spent more time trying to buck the patriarchal system than she did actually studying.'

'Well, she must have done something right because she qualified top of the class and now holds the top position for a worldwide firm, in their Manchester office.'

'Wow! Good on her.'

Essie couldn't help the small stab of envy on hearing of her old friend's success. They'd promised to conquer the world together until George had come along; now it seemed Bobbie was managing just fine without her.

'Well, Essie Parker, you had the chance to be there beside her – you were both brilliant, you know.'

'Oh, I'm not so sure about that, and it's Essie Walton these days.'

'Oh, so you married George then?'

'Yes, and you'd have known that if you'd come to the wedding!'

Essie tried to keep the bitterness out of her voice. It had hurt her no end when her closest friends hadn't bothered to attend her wedding.

'Well, maybe if you'd sent an invite, we'd have been

there. Bobbie was gutted when she didn't get one. I know she declined being your bridesmaid because it's a concept she didn't agree with but there was no need to exclude her completely – that was cruel.'

'I didn't exclude her. I didn't exclude any of you. You were all invited. You were my closest friends, why would I not want you at my wedding?'

'None of us received an invite, Essie.'

'But… I wrote them out myself. I even put in little letters for you, telling you how much I was looking forward to seeing you all. George posted them the next day—'

Essie suddenly stopped talking and looked at Clarissa. Her mind was whirling as it digested this new piece of information.

'No! He wouldn't… would he?'

'Mum, I wouldn't put it past him! He's such a control freak!'

Clarissa turned to Gerald. 'I'm going to take a guess here that my father didn't approve of you, or Mum's other friends.'

'Well, I don't like to speak out of turn but we rarely saw your mother once George came on the scene. On the few occasions we did meet up, it was uncomfortable and he made no effort to hide the fact he'd rather be somewhere else.' Gerald glanced at Essie. 'I'm sorry, Essie, but it's true.'

She sighed. 'I know it is, Gerald, I can't disagree with you. I'm simply trying to get my head around him doing that. After all, one invite going astray in the post I could accept but not all three. What's actually worse is that, when I got upset about it before the reception, when I realised none of you were there, he had the bare-faced audacity to say that my friends were clearly not friends at all.'

'But, Mum, surely you knew they hadn't accepted the

invites before the wedding day? You could have chased them up beforehand.'

'Your father took charge of everything. Remember, my parents were not well off and George was standing the cost for most of the event. He felt this gave him the right to take the reins – the only job I had was to buy a nice dress and arrive on time.'

'Seriously? You let him get away with that?'

'Clarissa, I'd only just turned twenty, your father is seven years older than me and seemed so sophisticated. I was naïve and knew very little about the circles he moved in. It seemed the easiest thing to do. Don't forget, my parents were thrilled to see someone like George show an interest in me – they would have gone to the wedding walking on their hands if George had asked them. They cared far more about what he wanted from the day than what I wanted at all.'

'I'm sorry, Essie, none of us realised. We just thought we'd been shunned in favour of the new toffs you were mixing with.'

'Hey, Gerald, it's not your fault, you've got nothing to be sorry for. It's one of those things but I'm glad I now know the truth.'

She gave him a small smile, to reassure him, but inside, she was seething. The realisation that George had been so manipulating even before they were married, made her feel sick. How many lies had he told her over the years to ensure she remained the dutiful little wife?

Just then, from the corner of her eye, she caught Gerald trying to stifle a yawn.

'I saw that, Gerald. I think it's time to get you home although I really would prefer to be taking you to hospital to get checked out. Concussion can kill, you know!'

'Essie, I feel okay.'

He stood up but she noticed a slight wobble when he

did.

'Fine! If you won't go to hospital, then we're driving you home. You're not getting behind the wheel of a car today. Clarissa, you take our car and follow. Gerald, I'll drive yours.'

'Really, Essie, there's no need—'

'Gerald, it's not up for discussion.'

Clarissa leant over and, putting her hand up by the side of her mouth, mock-whispered, 'Gerald, Mum's in bossy WI mode now – I'd just give in if I were you because you ain't gonna win!'

Essie laughed at her daughter's cheeky comment.

'Exactly! So come on, hand over the keys and you can direct me on where to go.'

TWELVE

They were just turning into the lane which led to Gerald's house when he suddenly whispered, 'Shit! Quick, stop the car!'

Essie slammed on the brakes, glad that Clarissa wasn't too close behind.

'What's the matter, have I taken a wrong turn?'

'No, that's my house just up there but look…' He pointed through the windscreen. 'Marjory's car. She must have been sitting there waiting for me all day.'

'Marjory?'

'My wife. Well, soon to be ex-wife. I was just coming back from seeing my solicitor when we, erm… bumped into each other.'

'I see. And how long have you been separated?'

Gerald looked at his watch. 'About twenty-one hours!'

'WHAT?' Essie's head nearly came off her neck as she turned to look at him. 'Less than a day?'

Gerald nodded, a sheepish expression on his face. 'It's a long story, which I'm happy to share but getting past her,' he nodded at the car blocking the gates of his house, 'is going to be a problem.'

Just then, Essie's mobile rang. It was Clarissa sitting behind her, wanting to know why they'd stopped. Essie looked at Gerald and was surprised to see what looked like fear on his face. She quickly came to a decision.

'Clarissa, change of plan – we're going back to ours. Are you able to reverse and go back out to the main road? Yes? Excellent. Do that and we'll do the same. We'll meet you back at the house.'

She looked at Gerald as she placed the phone back in the car well.

'Right, you're coming to stay at ours tonight. DON'T argue,' she put her hand up to stop him speaking, 'I wasn't happy about you being here on your own tonight anyway, not after your accident, so it makes sense that you should stop at ours for the night.'

'Won't George mind?'

'He probably would but as he's in London, it doesn't matter.'

'Do I get any say in this?'

Essie watched in the rear-view mirror as Clarissa reversed and turned. She looked at Gerald as she put the car back into gear.

'No, Gerald, I'm afraid you don't.'

An hour later, Gerald and Essie were sitting nursing mugs of coffee at her kitchen table. They'd picked up a Chinese takeaway on the route home and, once eaten, Clarissa had gone to her room, giving them some privacy to catch up on the years since they'd last seen each other.

Gerald looked up from his coffee mug.

'Why did you assume I'd be on my own this evening?'

'I don't know.' Essie gave a small shrug. 'You didn't

seem "married", if you know what I mean. No ring, although I know lots of men don't wear them, but there was just… something. I really can't say what. How long were you married for?'

'Ten months.'

'Oh!'

Gerald could understand the shock on Essie's face. No one expects a marriage to fail that quickly. He wondered what to tell her – could he be honest? Or would that make him look a total pansy? He didn't want to look weak but his solicitor had reiterated his own thoughts – men are victims too and they need to learn to talk about it.

'Look, Gerald, I'm not going to pry, but if you want to talk – now or any other time – I'm here for you. We were close friends once; I'd like to think we could be again.'

The kindness of Essie's words helped him to make up his mind and he blurted out, 'It was an abusive marriage and I was the victim.'

'Oh no, Gerald! I'm so sorry.'

'It's just one of those things. I was a mug. I married her before I really knew her properly and found out very quickly afterwards that she'd played me for a fool.'

'That's not your fault, Gerald, you did nothing wrong. You placed your trust in someone and they abused it – that puts them in the wrong, not you. How bad was it? Was it mental abuse? Physical?'

'Both.' He looked down at the table and blinked, trying to clear the tears from his eyes.

'Hey…' Essie got up and moved chairs to sit beside him. She put her hand on his arm and rubbed it gently.

'I'm sorry, Essie, I just feel such an idiot. My dad tried to warn me but I was so infatuated, I refused to listen to him. I'd been lonely for so long and she was the first woman who'd shown any kind of interest in me since I can't remember.'

'But… I don't understand, the girls at uni were always giving you the eye – what changed?'

'I'd just qualified when Dad developed rheumatism and it was quite severe. We now know it as rheumatoid arthritis but back then, rheumatism covered everything. He went from being an active, mobile person to being a semi-invalid within a few months. It was horrible to see. My sister Flora was married and with a small toddler, so it fell on me to take care of him. I didn't mind – he'd looked after us when my mum left so it was my turn to return the love. As time went on, however, I had less time for myself and it became a merry-go-round of going to work and then straight home to look after Dad. I didn't get the chance to meet girls or even speak to them and even if I had, what was I going to do? I didn't have the wherewithal to develop a relationship with them. I suppose I just ended up being out of practise.'

'So, what changed? Did your dad…' Essie's voice trailed off.

'Die? Oh, gosh, no! With the wonders of modern science, a new medication was developed which helped to combat a number of his symptoms. He's still ill, don't get me wrong, but he got back some of his mobility and with it came the desire for his independence. The house, with its narrow doors and upstairs bedrooms and bathrooms was no good for him but a ground floor flat, with nice wide doors and everything on the level was perfect, so he moved into the retirement village just up the road from here and reckons it's the best thing he could have done. He's made new friends who look out for him, he gets to go on days out and he's absolutely loving it! He still has days where his illness is beating him but at least he now also has days where he beats it.'

'But, let me guess, this suddenly left you at a loose end? You went from being a carer with every hour and every minute accounted for to… well… nothing! You had all this time to spare and no idea what to do with it.'

Gerald started in surprise. 'Yes, that was it exactly. How do you know that?'

'I'm in the local WI and we've had a few women join us over the years who've been in exactly the same place – cared for their elderly parents for many years and when the care is no longer required, for whatever reason, they suddenly find they have to build a new life but with no idea how to go about it.'

'Yes, that's exactly it. It also leaves us totally unprepared for those who have a mind to take advantage. I must have some kind of radar because it was the very first time I'd been out on a works do for years. By the end of the night, Marjory had latched onto me and barely six months had passed before we were married.'

'Wow! That was fast!'

Gerald nodded. 'I reckon she knew she couldn't keep up the act for long so she put all her efforts into getting me down the aisle as soon as possible. I didn't see that, of course, and was just utterly flattered that someone wanted me that much. I knew I wasn't a great catch in the looks or personality department but she didn't seem to mind. Of course, I now know she didn't give a shit about me, all she was looking at was the cushty life she was going to live once the ring was on her finger.'

'How long was it before she changed?'

'Pffft! Weeks! If that! We were barely back from our honeymoon when she quit her job, saying it was too stressful, but no effort was ever made to find another one. From then on in, it was all downhill.'

Gerald pulled back the sleeve of his shirt and showed Essie the burn from the saucepan, explaining what had happened along with all the other incidents which were supposed to have been accidents but were not.

When she suddenly stood up and began filling the kettle to make a fresh round of drinks, Gerald realised he'd been talking about himself for over an hour and half.

'Oh, Essie, I'm sorry, I've been banging on about my troubles all this time, you should have told me to shut up.'

He sat back in surprise when Essie spun round and he saw the look of fury on her face.

'Don't you apologise, Gerald, for being brave enough to share what that bitch has put you through! What an evil cow! If she was here right now, I swear I'd swing for her. I'd knock her teeth right down her throat, I really would! When I knew you all those years ago, you were a lovely, kind boy and I don't believe that's changed now you're a man, so how *dare* that nasty cow take your trust and kindness and abuse it like that. It makes me furious.'

'But, Essie, what about you and George? Let's be honest here, your marriage doesn't sound so good from where I'm sitting.'

Essie finished making the fresh drinks and sat back down beside him.

'You're right,' she sighed, 'I'm in no position to talk.'

'Has he ever hit you?'

'What? Hell, no! That's the one thing he's never done. I'd have left him in a heartbeat if he'd ever raised a finger towards me or Clarissa. But,' she looked into his eyes and Gerald felt his heart give a little squeeze as he beheld the sadness on her face, 'I'm beginning to realise he has mentally abused me for years. The way he speaks to me and treats me is close to how my father spoke to my mother and I. I didn't know it was wrong. I grew up in an environment where the man laid down the law and the women in the house were expected to follow it. Bobbie was just beginning to teach me it shouldn't be like that when George came into my life and her lessons were forgotten.'

'And you never realised what he was doing?'

'Not until it was too late. He'd been controlling from the beginning of our relationship but with my dad being that way… Then, when I was close to plucking up the courage to do something about it, I found out I was pregnant. I had no choice but to stay with him for my baby's sake. I thought my friends had abandoned me, my parents adored George so there would've been no help from them and, as you know, I never did finish my accountancy course so I had no qualifications to help me through. Something in me broke then and George must have sensed it because after that, he grew more personal with his comments and insults such as telling me I was fat, my hair wasn't right, my clothes were all wrong, I was holding him back in his career because I wasn't good enough, I'd served the wrong food to an important client he'd brought to dinner… I could go on but I'm sure you get the picture.'

'When did you become aware that this was wrong?'

'It was when all those sexual abuse cases began to be mentioned on the news. Suddenly, there was an onslaught of programmes on the television and articles in newspapers about how men treat women and one day, I was reading an article about how women are being conditioned from a very early age to believe they're not as good as men. I read all the examples being given and I nodded my head to every one of them. That's when I became aware of the possibility that both my father and my husband had been mentally abusing me all of my life.'

'But, still you're here. You haven't left him. Why not? Clarissa isn't a child anymore…'

'It's strange, Gerald, but things have changed in the last five days. Up till now, I was waiting for Clarissa to find her independence, always hoping she'd come home one day and say she was moving out. I wanted her away from George's influence. While I'm here, I'm a buffer between them and I'm able to dilute his behaviour towards her. Well, she went out on Friday night with some girls from work to see the Michael Duval show, ended up staying out all night, which she never does and arrived home on Saturday morning all fired up and telling her dad where to shove his controlling ways. Honestly, I was so proud of her.'

'You say Clarissa has changed since Friday night?'

'Yes, that's right.'

'Did you know she ended up on the stage as part of the act?'

'No, I didn't! She never mentioned that. Is that what she meant earlier when she referred to you both as being his stooges?'

'Yes. We were both hypnotised by him and, at the end, he gave a funny little speech where he told us to go forth and be brave, be courageous and live the life we've always wanted to live – or words to that effect. You say Clarissa was different when she got home on Saturday, well yesterday, I did things I never *ever* thought I would have the courage to do, one of them being to boot Marjory's fat ass out the door.'

'Are you thinking this Duval chap has put some kind of, what… spell… on you both?'

'I don't know about a spell but the timing is far too much of a coincidence in my book.'

Essie sat back in her chair with a look of wonderment on her face. She looked at him and Gerald waited for her to speak.

'I don't really know what to say.' She gave him a look of confusion. 'I've never really held much sway with hypnotism – I've watched the TV shows and I enjoy them as pure entertainment but I always thought the "participants" were plants. I never for a moment believed they were genuine.'

Just then, Clarissa walked into the kitchen, dressed in her pyjamas and dressing gown.

'Are you guys still up talking? Haven't you seen the time?'

Gerald looked up at the clock and was shocked to see it was after midnight.

'Gerald has been telling me about Friday night – you didn't mention, darling, that you'd been up on the stage.'

'Didn't I?' Clarissa paused for a moment. 'No, I didn't. The argument with father, and our subsequent conversation, pushed it from my mind.'

'I was telling your mum about the little speech Mr Duval gave just before he woke us up and I was wondering if he somehow put a sort of hypnotic spell thingy on us as I'm definitely not feeling the same now as I did on Friday. Something has certainly changed in me. Your mum was saying that you appear to be more assertive than you've previously been.'

Clarissa gave a small laugh. 'No, Gerald, I don't for a moment believe I'm "enchanted" in any way. When I came off that stage, I desperately needed a glass of wine to help me get over the fact I'd been up there. It was later that night, while I was dancing in the nightclub with my friends – something I never got to do because my father disapproved – and I realised what Duval had said was right; if I can go up on a stage and do what I did in front of hundreds of people, then I CAN do anything. That was when I decided I was no longer going to be the meek, mild-mannered, girl my father had forced me to be. From that moment on, I was going to be the person I wanted to be and he could like it or lump it. This is my life to be lived how I want to live it.'

Gerald was silent while he thought over Clarissa's words. Eventually, he replied, 'I still think he might have enchanted me, as you put it, because I've never stood up to people the way I've stood up to Barry and Marjory. I've always wanted to but never had the courage.'

'Perhaps,' Essie put her hand gently over his, 'the situation on Monday was simply the straw that broke the camel's back. We all have our tipping point and maybe you'd just been pushed too far for too long. Once the dam was broken, you couldn't stop the outpouring of the injustice you've endured all these years and you've faced up to the bullies in your life. The thing you'll find is that now you've finally had a taste of how it feels to be strong and assertive, you'll do it more often. And that's not a bad thing.'

'Hmmm... maybe...'

'Anyway,' Essie stood up and began clearing the empty mugs from the table, 'it's late and time for bed. I'll show you to the guest bedroom.'

A short time later, Gerald lay on his side in the guest bed, staring at the pale blue curtains which were backlit by the brilliant moonlight outside. He was mulling over what Clarissa and Essie had said. Was it merely a coincidence that the worm inside him had turned at the same time he'd been hypnotised? Had he finally been pushed over the edge and he'd snapped? Was it even conceivable that he *had* made these changes off his own back? As he lay there, he began to feel a small glow of pride growing in his belly. To hell with the hypnotist idea – why should Duval get the plaudits for something he'd done himself. Gerald smiled as he turned his back on the window and snuggled down into the quilt. He was responsible for this change in his demeanour and... what was that expression? Oh yes, he was going to "own it"!

With that thought on his mind, he was soon fast asleep.

THIRTEEN

Essie walked into the kitchen the following morning to find Gerald sitting at the table, looking through the motorhome brochures she'd left there the night before.

'This is a nice one. Well laid out and attractive inside.'

She looked at the one he was pointing to.

'Yes, I thought so too. It's the one we've bought.'

'I have to say, Essie, I'd never have put George down as being the motorhome type. He always struck me as being the posh hotels in Paris or secluded villas in Tuscany type.'

'You supposed correctly, Gerald, that's him exactly. No, the motorhome is for Clarissa and myself. We had a long talk on Saturday and I shared with her what I told you last night and now we're making plans to go travelling together. While we're away, I'll have space and time to get my head in order and figure out what to do next. We've decided to start with a road trip around the UK together. George doesn't yet know about it.'

'You haven't told him?'

She smiled at the surprise in Gerald's voice. She turned

from the sink where she'd been refilling the kettle and grinned at him.

'Nope! We haven't told him. We might tell him when we're all ready to go. There's less chance of him trying to interfere and ruin things that way.'

'You don't think he'll notice the vehicle sitting on the driveway? They're not easy to hide, you know.'

'I'm going to have a word with my friend, Sukie. She and her husband own Ditchley Manor and she has quite a bit of land. I'm sure she'll be fine with me parking it somewhere out of the way.'

'If you need to, you're more than welcome to park it at my house. There's plenty of space and it could keep Vanda company.'

'Vanda?'

Gerald's face went slightly pink under her questioning look.

'My old Volkswagen camper van.'

'Oh, you have one of those cute, little campers? I love them! If there weren't two of us going on this trip, I'd have been quite tempted to have bought one of those. How long have you had it?'

Essie placed the fresh coffee pot on the table and sat down.

'I've had *her* for several years. She was a complete wreck when I got her – to be honest, I think it was the rust that was holding her together. She became my little restoration project. When my dad was still at home, it was something I could do while he was asleep or watching television. I could tinker away in the garage but I was nearby if he needed me.'

'What colour is she? Does she have all the mod cons?'

'She was built in 1966, she's powder blue and white, has the split front screen, the double side doors – complete with the louvre windows – and the pop-up top to allow better headroom. She's a left-hand drive, which took a bit of getting used to, and has power sod-all!' Gerald grinned at her as he said this. 'I think I'd develop a fine pair of biceps if I was to take her on a long journey.'

'You haven't been away anywhere with her?'

'No, I've not really had the chance. I've driven her about locally, on road tests and stuff, to check she ran okay and to keep the engine and battery ticking over, but the opportunity to go away on a holiday simply hasn't arisen. I couldn't have left Dad and then when he moved out, I met Marjory and she would far rather lie by the poolside in Ibiza than travel around the country in a camper van.'

'I'm afraid your wife is slipping further and further down in my estimation, Gerald, if you don't mind me saying so.'

'Essie, she's at rock-bottom in mine so no offence taken.'

'And would I be correct in thinking Vanda is from camper VAN?'

'You would. I'm afraid I'm not the most original soul to have walked the earth.'

'It sounds good to me.' Essie smiled at him. 'Now then, can I interest you in some breakfast before we get you home? I have to go to the supermarket later so I thought I would follow you home to ensure you get there in one piece and then I can carry on to do my shopping.'

'Oh, I don't want to put you to any more trouble, Essie, you've already gone out of your way to help me.'

'It's no trouble at all, Gerald, I'm almost passing your front door. Now, how does sausage, bacon and eggs sound?'

She smiled when Gerald concurred that her breakfast suggestion sounded very tasty indeed.

Essie followed Gerald down the main road and indicated when he turned into the lane that led to his house. She didn't know this area very well and was having a good look around when Gerald's car came to a stop in front of her. A few seconds later he got out and walked towards her. She rolled down the window and was perturbed to see him looking quite anxious.

'Are you okay, Gerald? Was the drive too much for you?'

He let out a sigh. 'Marjory is here again. Or still here – I don't know which. I can't see her having stayed here all night but equally, she's never usually up at this time of the day either.'

'You need to face her, Gerald. You can't avoid her a second time.'

'I know.' Gerald straightened up and looked down at her. 'Stay in the car, Essie, she can be a vicious bitch and I don't want you getting caught up in this.'

He walked away and she heard a door slam. A loud, screeching voice soon filled the air but Essie couldn't quite make out what was being said. A strong breeze was blowing and taking the words in the other direction. Nor could she see anything. Gerald's car was raised higher than hers so any possible view through the windows was blocked.

Suddenly, there was a scream and she was scrambling out of the car door when she stopped to grab her phone. Within a few seconds, she had the video option running and she was making her way towards Gerald's front gate.

Essie stepped around the front of Gerald's car and saw a woman, with the girth of an elephant, twisting Gerald's arm up his back and slamming his head off the roof of her car. Gerald, although of reasonable height, was slight of frame and she was using her considerable bulk to hold him in place.

'STOP THAT RIGHT NOW!' Essie held up her phone, making sure she was recording the scene.

Marjory stopped banging Gerald's head up and down but she didn't release him. 'Fuck off! This is none of your business, ya nosy bitch.'

'Release him right now or I'm calling the police.'

'You put that phone away, this is nothing to do with you. Beat it or you'll get what he's getting.'

'That's where you're wrong, Marjory. This is everything to do with me. I work for the company representing Mr Wainwright and you are currently providing us with excellent evidence. Your actions are being streamed live back to my office and I only have to say the words for my secretary to be making a phone call to the local constabulary.'

'He's had the cheek to say he wants a divorce and blames ME for the breakdown of the marriage. He says I've physically abused him – what a fucking nerve. Those things were all accidents.'

'And is twisting Mr Wainwright's arm up his back and banging his head off the roof of your car *also* an "accident"?'

Marjory immediately let go of Gerald and stepped away from him. 'I got the paperwork yesterday, special courier delivery they were, like he couldn't wait to get rid of me. I was upset, that's why I reacted like I did.'

Essie watched in astonishment as Marjory managed to squeeze out a few crocodile tears to go with her tall story.

'Well, Mrs Wainwright, I strongly suggest you get back inside your vehicle and leave ASAP. I will be making a recommendation that a restraining order is put in place immediately, as you're clearly unable to control your emotions at this time and the last thing we wish to see is anyone being hurt.'

'But—'

'INSIDE your vehicle now, please, Mrs Wainwright.'

Marjory's mouth opened and closed a few times but nothing more was said. She finally got into her car and with a screech of tyres, sped off down the lane. Essie motioned to Gerald to stay quiet as she kept the video running a bit longer. Once she was satisfied that Marjory wasn't returning, she switched it off and let out a sigh of relief. Gerald was leaning against the side of his car and she went to stand beside him.

'Thank you, Essie, you were wonderful. For a woman of her size, she can move fast and she had me trapped before I realised what she was doing.'

'You didn't hit her back? You could probably have managed an elbow in her face.'

'I could never hit a woman, Essie, no matter how much I was provoked.'

Essie felt her admiration for him go up several notches. He was hanging his head and kicking a stone around with his foot.

'Gerald, not using violence is something to be proud of. Don't be ashamed because you're essentially a good, decent, bloke. I admire you for your restraint if I'm being honest. I wanted to punch her lights out when I saw her bashing you about.'

'Seriously?'

She gave Gerald a small side glance. 'Oh yes! My hand was itching to smack her one in the teeth but I knew it would be detrimental for you in the long term so I held back. However, do not underestimate how tempted I was!'

Gerald grinned at her. 'In truth, I would have loved to have seen that, but I get where you're coming from. I have to say though, Essie, saying you worked for my solicitors was a genius idea. I don't think she'd have backed down so quickly if she'd known you were just a friend.'

'It was the first thing that came to mind. I'll email the

video to you and I recommend you forward it to your solicitors immediately and get a restraining order sorted because she strikes me as the type who'll return for another round.'

'I'll get it done this afternoon. Now, I need a coffee after all that excitement, will you join me?'

'Absolutely! I could do with a few minutes to get myself together before driving into town.'

Gerald took the chain off the gates and they both drove in. Essie looked around the tidy, herringbone bricked, driveway and saw that Gerald was right when he'd said there was more than enough space for her motorhome. She looked at the house in front of her as he relocked the gates. It was a detached house, built from the local Cotswold stone with double fronted bay windows and a recessed front door. She imagined it had once sported wooden storm doors but these had been replaced by double glazed porch doors.

'Nice house,' she said over her shoulder.

'Thank you. My great-grandfather had it built. He was an engineer or something similar and was involved in the construction of the railways in the late 1800s.'

'I can see why Marjory's so keen to get her hands on it.'

'Well, she's got no chance. It's still in my dad's name!'

'Good! Somehow, I don't think she'd appreciate it.'

They stepped inside the front door and Essie immediately exclaimed over the beautiful, tiled flooring of the hallway. Everything about it spoke to her. She adored old buildings. Her own home had been one of the last to be built in Ditchley before the previous lord of the manor had put the covenant in place that no future building was permitted. It was a nice enough house, and very spacious, but it lacked the character of older builds.

Gerald led her into the kitchen, apologising for its

tattiness as he did so. 'The whole house is desperately in need of updating and it's now my next project. Vanda is complete so I need something new to occupy my time. It really should have been done years ago.'

'In some ways, Gerald, it might be a blessing that it wasn't. You may have been tempted to remove some of the old features – as was the way of things fifteen or twenty years back – which would have been a terrible shame. Now you know to keep those lovely cornices and tiled fireplaces and find ways of working with them.'

'My brother-in-law, Matt, is a builder. He renovates old buildings and he'd have had something to say if we tried any of that!'

'Well, I'm sure you'll do a great job here.'

The kettle boiled and Gerald soon placed a mug of coffee in front of her. 'Would you like to see Vanda?' he asked.

'Oh, yes please!'

Gerald led the way through the side door to the garage, explaining it had been a later add on to the house. He pulled the light switch and the pride shining out of his face as he pointed towards the gleaming vehicle in front of them, was so bright it could have lit up the garage itself.

Essie had to admit that Gerald had done a wonderful job on her. Her blue and white paintwork was perfect, her chrome bits were shining and not a single speck of dust sat on her windows. Gerald took a key from his pocket and unlocked her side doors. There was just enough space to allow them to open right out. As Essie stepped inside, he informed her that he had also had the large tent which attached to the side of the camper to provide more space when she was set up and in use.

It was, as Essie had expected, smaller than the motorhome but that didn't detract from the overall quaint cosiness. She admired the black and white tiled floor, the pale wood fittings and the petite fridge fitted under the sink.

'I'm guessing, Gerald, that you chose not to stay true to the original fittings inside as I'm sure Vanda wouldn't have had a fridge when she rolled off the production line.'

'Too right! She's all original on the outside but I've souped her up on the inside. If I ever do get to go somewhere in her, there's a limit to how much of my creature comforts I'm prepared to give up.' Gerald's grin stretched right across his face and it reminded her of the boy she'd once known, all those years ago.

'Well, I hope you get to achieve that dream sooner rather than later. Now, I must get on. After all the drama of this morning, I need to do something really mundane and buying groceries is about as mundane as it gets!'

Gerald led her back into the kitchen and locked the door behind him. He reached up and placed the key in a tin on top of the kitchen wall units.

'Secret hiding place?' she asked.

'Yes. I refused to allow Marjory unsupervised access. I didn't trust her not to do something out of spite so I made sure the door was always locked and I changed the hiding place of the key every time, just in case she was spying on me.'

'Probably a wise move.' She picked her coffee mug up off the table and took a sip. 'And, talking of wise moves, do you want to give me your contact details – phone and email – so I can send that video to you.'

'Absolutely. I'll do that now.'

Twenty minutes later, Gerald led the way back out to the driveway and opened the gates for Essie to drive through. She opened her window and stopped as she pulled up level with him.

'Gerald, it's been lovely seeing you again. Please keep in touch and don't be a stranger now that we've found each other again.'

'Don't worry, Essie, I'll make sure we stay in contact.'

She gave him a smile and a wave as she drove off. She looked in her rear-view mirror and watched his stance change – instead of standing straight and tall, his shoulders dropped and an air of dejection wrapped itself around him as he pushed the gates back together.

This image played on Essie's mind all the way to the supermarket and the whole time she was filling her trolley. She absentmindedly placed her carrier bags in the boot of the car and continued to mull over the change in Gerald as she'd left.

By the time she got home, she'd made up her mind. She quickly put the groceries away, poured a glass of wine, picked up her phone and reading the number he'd written out, tapped on the screen.

When the call was answered, she got straight to the point. 'Hi, Gerald, it's Essie. What are you doing on Tuesday? Do you fancy meeting for lunch?'

The grin on Gerald's face when he ended the call from Essie would have given the Cheshire cat a run for its money. He knew he'd never have had the nerve to get back in touch with her and he'd honestly thought he wouldn't see her again. This deserved a little treat and there was a nice malt whisky in the cupboard waiting to be opened. His heart gave a little skip at the thought of seeing Essie again. It would seem, he mused, as he cracked the seal on the bottle, that while he may have locked away his feelings for Essie a long time ago, his heart had never forgotten her.

FOURTEEN

Gerald walked into the office with a spring in his step. His week away had been productive and he was almost sorry to come back to work. For so many years, the office had been his escape from his home life but that was no longer the case. His niece, Flora, had popped round for a visit and when he'd mentioned his decision to decorate the house from top to bottom, she'd offered to lend a hand. She'd completed her art and design course at college and would love to put some of what she'd learnt into practise. He'd emphasised to her the need to maintain the traditional elements of the house but with a fresh new look. Flora had offered to pick up some design magazines for him to look through and mark out what he liked. Now that he'd made up his mind to do this, he really wanted to get on with it – having to do his day job was a little bit of a nuisance.

'Morning, Gerald, nice to see you back.'

'Morning, Barry.' Gerald swallowed down his surprise at Barry's subdued greeting and made his way to his desk, less surprised to see the piles of paperwork on it awaiting his attention. He placed his briefcase on the floor, grabbed a coffee from the kitchen and sat down to deal with it all. He was so immersed in the files that the shrill ringtone of his office phone made him jump in his seat. Seeing it was the big boss, David Rowson, he quickly answered it.

'Good morning, David, how are you today?'

'Good morning, Gerald, not so bad, thank you. Could you come along to my office at your earliest convenience, please?'

'I can come now, if that suits.'

'Perfect.'

The call was abruptly ended and Gerald looked at the buzzing handset in shock. While David Rowson was a man of few words when it came to telephone calls, he never hung up without ending the call in the correct manner. Gerald quickly made a note on the file he'd been working on, placed it to one side and, running a hand over his head to ensure his hair was tidy, he set off down the corridor to the managing director's office. The same thought entered his head as it always did when he walked along the directors' corridor – they'd been quick to emphasise the benefits of an open-plan set up for the general staff and management but much less keen to give up their own little castles. He often wondered if they were aware of how much the general staff resented them for this.

When he reached the MD's rather plush corner office, he tapped on the open door and stepped in.

'Ah, Gerald, do come in and close the door behind you.'

David pointed to the seat in front of his desk for Gerald to sit down and they exchanged a few minutes of small talk before David finally got to the reason for summoning him.

'Gerald, we've been crunching the numbers and sorting out the forecasts for the coming financial year and in doing so, it would seem that we're not going to hit the targets we originally set. We're doing a reforecast but it looks like we're going to have to make a few redundancies.'

‘Excuse me? Redundancies?’ This had been the last thing he’d expected to hear.

‘I’m afraid so. We’re looking at roughly three or four across all departments. I need you to decide whose jobs can be most easily split up and absorbed into the day-to-day tasks of the remaining employees. Ideally, if you can lose four, that would be best.’

Gerald’s head was reeling. Four staff members? How the hell was he going to manage that? Everyone was busy and they already had more work than they could cope with.

‘I’m sorry, David, but I don’t understand – we’ve got more clients now than we’ve ever had. How can we possibly be making redundancies?’

‘The board have set the numbers and we have to ensure we meet them.’

Gerald looked at David for a moment and then the penny dropped.

‘Oh, I get it! The board have set a higher target than usual because they want a bigger cut of the dividends. They’re after a bigger pay out and don’t care what it takes to achieve it.’

The MD looked at him but said nothing. The fact he didn’t refute the comment told Gerald he’d got it in one.

‘I’m guessing this is not negotiable?’

‘I’m afraid not.’

‘Can I make the proposal for voluntary redundancies first? It might be less painful if folks thought they were being given a choice.’

‘If you think it’ll help. We will, of course, be offering a generous package for those who accept.’

David passed some paperwork over the desk and at a glance, what was being offered was not unreasonable.

Gerald stood up. ‘Leave it with me. How soon do you need to know and for those who accept, would it be an immediate departure?’

'The sooner the better, Gerald, and yes, for whoever accepts, it would be immediate.'

Gerald nodded his understanding and made a quick exit from the room. His stomach was churning as he marched back along the corridor and he couldn't decide if it was due to the shock of having to make the redundancies or anger at the reason why. By the time he reached his desk, he'd decided it was the latter. His position meant he got to see the board reports and the profit margins and he knew the company made nice healthy turnovers every year. The workload of his own department screamed to him that this year was no exception. All of this was down to a bunch of fat cats, who already had more money than they could spend in one lifetime, being greedy and wanting more. They didn't give a toss about the lives they wrecked in the process.

Gerald got up and walked to the kitchen area, discreetly looking around the room as he did so. Elaine, who'd just bought her first home with her fiancé and was now planning their wedding, smiled at him as he walked past. Steve, whose wife was expecting their first child, had his head down and his earphones in because the classical music he played helped him to concentrate better. Even Bolshy Barry, the bane of his life but an excellent father who adored his wife and two children, was concentrating so hard on the spreadsheet open on his computer screen he didn't see Gerald pass by. He couldn't see any of them volunteering to leave so how on earth could he possibly choose who to let go?

When he returned to his desk with his coffee, Gerald sat down and stared at the blank screen of his PC for several minutes. He'd never been one to shy away from difficult business decisions but this was something else. As he sat, a small idea popped into his head and it only took a matter of moments for it to grow into a very big idea.

He pulled the paperwork David Rowson had given him nearer and read it more closely, after which, he grabbed his calculator and worked out a few figures. He booted up his computer, sent a few emails, sorted out some files, sent a few more emails and then closed everything down.

Two hours after leaving David Rowson's office, Gerald was back in it, advising him he was taking the voluntary redundancy offered to his department. This time, he got to enjoy the shock on the MD's face.

'But… Gerald, you don't need to do that! Why would you choose to go?'

'Several reasons, David. Firstly, my salary is pretty much equal to four staff members, so it's easier all around. Two, I don't have the same commitments as most of my team so it won't have the same impact on me and, thirdly, I've been here since I graduated, it's time I moved on and found something else.'

'But… all the knowledge you have—'

'Other people in the department also have the same knowledge. We only ever employ the best. I would recommend you give Steve a promotion – create a new position that is lower than the one I hold, that way you don't have to give him a huge raise.'

'Well, I did not see this coming!'

'To be honest, David, neither did I but now that I've made the decision, it feels absolutely right. I've been stagnant in my life for too long – it's time to make some changes.'

'Well, if you're absolutely sure…'

'I am!'

'Fine. I'll speak with HR to get everything arranged.' David stood up, came around from his desk and stuck out his hand. 'It's been a pleasure working with you, Gerald, I wish you the very best for the future.'

Gerald gave the proffered hand a swift shake, turned

and walked out of the room. Once again, as he marched down the corridor, his stomach was churning but this time it was with sheer excitement. He already knew what the next few months had in store and he couldn't wait.

'Vanda,' he whispered under his breath, 'gird up your loins, girl, we're hitting the road!'

FIFTEEN

Essie picked up her coffee mug and listened to her friend, Sukie, ranting at her. She'd just spilled all the beans on the state of her marriage to George and Sukie was expressing her disappointment at Essie for not having confided in her sooner.

'Essie, I can't believe some of the things he's said to you… they beggar belief! I tell you, if Pete ever spoke to me like that… well, let's just say he'd be enjoying hospital food for a very long time!'

'I grew up in an abusive household and was conditioned to it, Sukie. I didn't notice that George was behaving the same way as my father. I mentioned the state of things to my mother but she wasn't sympathetic – why would she be, her own marriage was no better than mine and she'd put up with it all those years, so why couldn't I?'

'But, Clarissa… she's always been so shy and quiet – George must have had some kind of influence there?'

'He did but whenever possible, I would try to be a buffer between them. It wasn't easy because… well… George is George! You've had dealings with him, you know what he's like.'

'Yeah, a blustering little ball-bag, too full of his own importance and too fond of his own, overly-loud voice. I'm sorry, Essie, I know he's your husband and I mean no offence but my hands clench every time I hear him!'

Essie couldn't help but laugh at Sukie's more-than-accurate description of her husband. 'Sukie, no offence taken because you're only speaking the truth.'

'So, what do you intend to do now? Are you going to leave him and get a divorce? Clarissa's old enough now, surely, that you can finally get away from him?'

'Well, I have a lot more to tell you but before I start, you might want to make another coffee.'

When the fresh mugs were on the table, and Sukie had sat back down, Essie filled her in on the last ten days of her life.

'Oh my! Essie! That is a wonderful plan! Well done you!'

'You don't think I'm mad or off my trolley, do you?'

'Absolutely not! Travelling around the country, bonding with your daughter and having fun – what's mad about that? How are you going about it? Hotels? B&B's? Camping?'

Essie laughed along with Sukie on the last option. 'Seriously, Sukie, do I look like the kind of person to mess around with tents?'

'No, but you've surprised me so much this morning, I now believe anything is possible.'

'Well, you're not too far off the mark…' She pulled the motorhome brochures from her bag and pushed them across the table.

'No way!' Sukie picked them up and flicked through them. 'You're planning to buy one of these?'

'Already bought it!'

'What?'

'Yup! We should've picked it up today but there was a delay so we're now getting it in a few days.'

'Brand new?'

'Oh yes! I wanted something quite special for us both.'

'What did George say about it?'

'He doesn't know yet.' Essie almost choked on her coffee as she laughed at the incredulous look on Sukie's face.

'How have you managed to get away with that?'

'When the new Oxford office was opened, George decided it was time to get "savvy" with his finances. Over the years he's built up a portfolio of rental properties in London and Oxford, which meant, from a tax point of view, he was being hit quite hard. He transferred most of them into my name, including the house we currently live in, and also the bank account the rents are paid into. In other words, he pretty much transferred the "business" to me. To say the bank balance is a healthy one would be an understatement. Although, there's been a teeny-weeny little dent put in it since last week!'

'Oh, my goodness! I'm guessing it never occurred to him that this might go against him in the future…'

'Sukie, the man is so arrogant, it would never cross his mind that I'd ever consider deceiving him.'

'So, will you divorce him?'

'I don't know how I feel right now. Seeing Clarissa come out of her shell this last week and start to become the woman I always hoped she'd be, has been quite a thrill. I still need to come to terms, however, with the knowledge that I can walk away from him if I want to. I will use this trip to work out how I feel and what I want. I need time away from him and from this life he has created for me to decide what I want to do next.'

'And what about this Gerald chap? Where does he fit in?'

Oh, he doesn't fit in anywhere. We're just old uni chums and it was great to catch up with him again.'

'Essie Walton, you're blushing! So, c'mon girl, fess up the juice. I'm not daft, you know!'

Essie felt the warmth of the glow on her cheeks as she thought about the Gerald she'd known when she was younger.

'Okay, okay! I admit, I did have feelings for him when we were students. Back then, he was terribly shy, but once you got to know him better, he was funny, witty, full of life and great company to be in.'

'And now?'

'He's… different. Life hasn't been kind to him and it's changed him.'

'In what way?'

Essie thought for a moment. 'You know when you watch programmes on TV and there's a dowdy, middle-aged man with the Brylcreem hair, thick black glasses and dodgy, knitted tank-top? Well, that's Gerald! To a "T"! He's your stereotypical middle-aged man. It's like the joy that used to be in him has drained away and he's now just a shell going through the motions.'

'How sad.'

'It is. He deserved better.'

'Well, maybe now he's kicked his bitch of a wife into touch, he'll change back to how he once was.'

'I hope so. After all that he's been through, it would be good for him to have something nice in his life.'

'And you might be his "something nice"?'

'Oh, stop it, Sukie. Behave!'

Sukie grinned at her. 'Do you plan to keep in touch?'

Essie felt the colour rise in her cheeks again as she answered, 'Well… we're kind of meeting up for lunch tomorrow…'

She waited for her friend to stop laughing although

Sukie had such a hearty, full-bodied laugh that she couldn't help but join in.

'So, it's "watch this space" is it?' Sukie finally managed to splutter.

'No, it is not! It's only lunch, nothing more. Besides, I'm about to go off racking up the miles around the UK in a few weeks, there'll be no opportunity for anything else.'

'Hmmm, we'll see!' Sukie grinned at her again.

'Anyway, getting back onto the topic of my imminent travels, may I ask a small favour, please? When we pick up the motorhome, would you mind if I parked it somewhere on the manor until such times as we're ready to leave? I just know George will not take the news well and I don't want to risk him sabotaging the vehicle or causing any other problems. If it's hidden away, we can get it prepared and then just go when the time is right.'

'Of course, you can, that's no problem at all. The garage next to the Big Gatehouse should be big enough and it's not being used – you can put it in there.'

'That would be perfect, thank you.'

'Happy to help. All I ask in return is that you send lots of postcards when you're out on the road. The twins would love them and I'll be able to teach them a bit about this gorgeous country we live in.'

'I think I can do that!'

'Super! Now, we have just enough time for one more cuppa before I have to go and pick up my darling little heathens from playgroup, so you can fill me in on all the places you plan to visit.'

Essie retrieved a notepad from her handbag. 'It's a short list so far, Sukie, but I'm sure you'll be able to help me with some more suggestions.'

'Oh, I'm quite sure I can!' Sukie grinned as she stood up.

Essie sighed quietly to herself. Telling Sukie everything

hadn't been as difficult as she'd thought it would be and now that she'd told one person, it wouldn't be so hard to tell others when the time came to do so.

SIXTEEN

'And it was with the greatest of joy that I walked away from the desk which I have laid ownership to for almost twenty years!'

'Wow! How does it feel? How do *you* feel?'

Gerald and Essie were sitting at the back of the Inn on the Green pub in Lower Ditchley and he'd just filled her in on the latest change in his life.

'Very refreshing, since you ask.'

'But aren't you concerned about getting another job? I mean, isn't it harder for older people like us to find work? I'm sure that's what I've read.'

'The redundancy package was a good one and my living expenses over the years have been minimal, which means I've got plenty of savings to tide me over. I'm considering starting up my own small business, looking after just a handful of clients. Enough to keep me occupied but not so many that it becomes a full-time job.'

'And will you be able to find enough clients?'

'Well, I did "accidentally" send the company client details to my private email address before I left. I know there are a handful of smaller accounts who would probably be interested in a more bespoke service.'

'Erm, are you supposed to do that? Is that not called "industrial espionage" or something similar?'

Gerald let out a small laugh. 'Industrial espionage is probably a bit strong. My contract states I can't contact any of my previous clients within six months of leaving the company. After that, they're fair game.'

'So, what do you intend to do for those six months?'

Gerald leant forward, the smile on his face stretching from ear to ear. 'I'm following your example – I'm hitting the road! Vanda and I are visiting my mother in Scotland but we'll be going the scenic route and taking our time about it. There are so many places I've always wanted to see and now I'm going to do it!'

'Gerald, that's fantastic news. Well done you for having the nerve to go for it. You must be so excited.'

'I really can't wait, Essie.'

'What about the house, though? Do you want it to be empty while you're away? Don't forget, I've met your wife – I wouldn't trust her an inch.'

'I'm going to have a word with my niece. She wanted to help with the decorating so I'm going to make her an offer which I hope she won't refuse – she can live in the house while I'm gone, do all the decorating and I'll pay her for her services.'

'Nice one! Do you think she'll go for it?'

'I hope she will. She's twenty-two and I think living at home with her dad is feeling a little claustrophobic now. I'm sure she'll relish the chance of some freedom.'

'And you trust her not to have too many wild parties?'

'She's quite responsible. Losing her mother when she was young meant Matt had to bring her up on his own. He did a great job and she's a fabulous girl. I trust her not to do anything too crazy.'

'Great! That'll be a load off your mind if she does accept. Did you sort out a restraining order against your wife?'

'I would need to press charges to get one of those but my solicitor is sorting out an injunction against her. With your video, and the details I provided to him previously, he can't see there being a problem in getting one. By the time it expires, the divorce should have gone through and, all being well, that's the last I'll see of her.'

'Fingers crossed for you.'

'So, have you told George yet that you're going off on this trip with Clarissa?'

'Not yet. I need to prepare myself for the argument that'll follow and psych myself up to deal with the verbal abuse that will fly my way.'

'He's that bad?'

Essie began sharing in more detail what her life with George was like and Gerald listened with growing anger at the way this beautiful woman had been treated. George had taken a girl with so much to offer and bullied her into being someone quite different. Gerald looked at Essie sitting opposite him and saw the well-dressed wife, in her twin-set and pearls, of a successful London lawyer. She looked exactly like the "ladies who lunch" crowd with her perfectly coiffed hair and expertly applied makeup. The girl he'd known in college hadn't cared much for clothes and had often come out wearing colours which clashed and outfits that suggested she'd gotten dressed in the dark. Makeup had been a swipe of lip gloss and a "hairdo" was scraping her lovely, thick blonde curls up into a ponytail. The sleek, highlighted bob, manicured and polished nails and colour-coordinated outfit were as far removed from "his" Essie as it was possible to be.

'Why didn't you put your foot down, Essie, when he began all his shenanigans? You never had a problem standing up for yourself when we were young and at uni.'

'I know. It's just… well… I was in love, or thought I was, and in the beginning, I was trying to please him. Trying to be the perfect wife for a man with ambitions. I just did as he asked, worked on "becoming better" and put a great deal of effort into being his perfect little hausfrau!'

'How do you feel now?'

'Liberated! I feel free to move on. The change in Clarissa has removed the weight from my shoulders and it's great.'

'I saw a lot of your younger self in her, when we were chatting. She has the fire you once had.'

'Well, that fire in Clarissa was a slow burner but it's a fully-established flame now. She's found her voice and believe me when I say she's no longer scared to use it. George came home from London on Friday and started with his usual antics as soon as he walked in the door. Without going into too much detail, let's just say Clarissa didn't hold back on sharing her views on his behaviour with him!'

'Well done that girl! What did George say?'

'He spent most of the weekend in his study. Clarissa and I, on the other hand, had our first ever proper girlie night together. We got a couple of bottles of wine, some pizza, ice-cream and chocolates, took up residence on the sofa and watched a couple of chick-flicks. Something which George would never have permitted in the past! We had a great time.'

Gerald looked into Essie's big brown eyes. They were shining with joy and her face was glowing with her smile. Despite her well-put-together exterior, the girl he'd loved was still in there. It cheered him no end to know that George Walton hadn't killed her off, despite his best efforts, and that with a little bit of time, she would rise again. He reached into his jacket pocket and pulled out a small package.

'This arrived this morning, just as I was leaving, so I brought it with me.' He unwrapped the packing to show Essie the UK Travel Guide book he'd bought. 'I thought it might give me some more ideas of places to visit – do you fancy going through it with me?'

'Oh yes, what a marvellous idea. Let me just get my notepad out.'

The two of them spent the next hour, heads together, poring over the book and making notes, neither of them aware they were being watched.

SEVENTEEN

Clarissa was spending the morning helping her friend Saffy revise for her mock exams. They were in the café of The Cabookeria, the village bookshop and café, and despite the six-year age difference, the two girls got on well. Saffy was mature for her age and she was also the only true friend Clarissa had. Her father's overbearing ways had managed to lose most of her friends in the past but Saffy let his obnoxious comments roll off her like water off a duck's back. She would simply make polite noises until Clarissa came to the rescue and dragged her up the stairs to her bedroom where they would close the door and giggle like kindergarten children. Clarissa knew that Saffy's reluctance to be intimidated by her father drove him nuts and she loved it. Lately, she'd had even less sympathy in that area and she'd filled Saffy in on all the details when they'd taken a short break from studying.

'You did WHAT? Seriously? Oh, man! I wish I'd been there to see that.'

'I'm glad you weren't, it was bad enough with half of the girls from the office witnessing my humiliation without you being there too!'

Saffy roared with laughter as Clarissa described her night of being Michael Duval's stage puppet but when Clarissa went on to describe the events that had followed – including using the "F" word regarding her father's feelings about her staying out late that night – Saffy almost choked on her mocha coffee.

'Blimey, Clarissa, I didn't think you even knew that word. You never swear!'

'Well, sometimes you just have to. Trust me, the expression "Take a load off" was never more appropriate than it was that night. As soon as I said it, it was as if a great weight had been lifted from my shoulders. All my life, my father has hung around my neck like the proverbial albatross – pushing and pushing for me to be perfect in every way. I had to have perfect manners from the minute I could walk, the perfect vocabulary from the minute I could talk. I've always had to dress "just so", listen to the music he considered to be acceptable, only read books which were educational… Have you heard of "The Stepford Wives", Saffy?'

'I saw the film with Nicole Kidman.'

'Well, I was a Stepford Daughter! Brainwashed into being what *he* thought I should be and not allowed to be my own person.'

'But, what about your mum – surely she's at fault too for letting him get away with it?'

Clarissa repeated what her mother had said to her that day in her bedroom. 'To be fair, she did try to help me to get away from him a few times, I just didn't see it like that. With hindsight, I can appreciate that she often took the flak on my behalf.'

'And now you're off travelling – you lucky thing. That'll be so much fun.'

'It'll be nice to spend time alone with Mum and get to

know her properly without the spectre of my father hanging over us.'

'Does he know of your plans?'

'Not yet. The intention is to get the motorhome, park it at Sukie's place and load it up over the next few days or so. Once we're all ready to set off, then we'll tell him.'

'Have you left your job then?'

Clarissa smiled while recounting the conversation she'd had with the HR department. There had been much astonishment when she'd advised them that, for the foreseeable future, she would be out of the office and if there was a problem with this, they could take it up with her father. Something she knew they wouldn't do as his boorish manner was not restricted to his home and family life.

'Be sure to text me regularly with your whereabouts and take lots of photographs. I'll try not to be too jealous as I wilt under the pressure of maths, English and science exams.'

'You'll be absolutely fine and I know you're going to do well. Believe in yourself, Saffy, you can do it!'

'I'm sure I will, but if you'd mind just going through this passage with me again, that would be great.'

Clarissa smiled and began to explain again how the root of X squared equalled Y multiplied by Z. Algebra had been a favourite subject.

It was a couple of hours later, when Clarissa was stepping out of the bookshop, that she spotted her mum walking into the Inn on the Green. She called for her to wait but the pouring rain must have muffled her voice for Essie didn't appear to hear and the door swung closed behind her.

Clarissa put up her brolly and, trying to avoid the puddles, made her way across the village green to the quaint little pub. She'd only ever been in here once before – unsurprisingly, her father hadn't approved of women being in pubs but she'd sneaked in on her eighteenth birthday for a glass of wine. She arrived at the door and gave her brolly a good shake before going inside where the noise hit her like a train. It was lunchtime and the place was packed. Clarissa quickly realised it was a Tuesday and one of the days when the coach trips came in. She pushed her way through the crowd and saw the back of her mother's head by a window in the room at the back of the pub. She was about to call over when she noticed her mum wasn't alone – she was with Gerald.

Clarissa took a moment to observe them. They looked completely at ease in each other's company and were laughing as they perused the menus on the table. Clarissa didn't for a moment think there was anything untoward in them meeting – Gerald was, after all, just her old friend from uni – but she was fascinated with the way they were interacting. Her mother was quite animated and glowed as she smiled. Gerald appeared to have shrugged off the diffident gloom which seemed to accompany him and looked like an altogether different man.

Seeing Gerald get up and walk towards the bar, she stepped behind a pillar and waited until he'd placed his order and returned to his seat before stepping over to the bar herself and ordering a bowl of soup. She managed to secure one of the high bar stools nestled under one of the wooden drink shelves which were wrapped around various pillars in the pub. From here, she could see her mum and Gerald but with very little chance of being seen herself. She wasn't spying per se – it was more that she couldn't recall ever seeing her mum looking so… vivacious! Even from this distance, she could see that Essie's eyes were shining and her smile was so bright, she looked a good ten years younger. It was interesting to see and made Clarissa despise her father a little more, knowing how he'd suppressed her mother's natural self all these years.

As she ate her soup, Clarissa watched Essie and Gerald poring over a book and her mother making notes. While she dunked her bread, she saw them laugh and share good natured banter while discussing what lay on the pages in front of them. Finally, they stood up and made their way out of the pub, seemingly oblivious to everyone else around them.

Clarissa returned her empty soup bowl to Percy the landlady, who was run off her feet behind the bar, and asked for a glass of chardonnay when she had a moment. She didn't want to run out the pub right behind her mum, she needed some time to think over what she'd seen and consider what to do next.

Her opportunity came that evening over dinner when Clarissa let her mum know she'd spotted her in the pub. Once again, her father was in London and staying overnight so they were taking the opportunity to have pizza and garlic bread while sitting at the kitchen table – three more things her father abhorred so three more things Clarissa and Essie were deriving great enjoyment from.

'Mum, I saw you and Gerald having lunch in the pub today.'

'Did you, darling? You should have joined us.'

'I didn't want to interrupt – you both appeared to be enjoying yourselves.'

'Well, I've known Gerald for many years, even though we lost touch but despite that, it felt as if all the time in between had slipped away and we were students once again. He could always make me laugh and hasn't lost that knack.'

'I noticed. I don't think I've ever seen you laugh or

smile as much. You looked very… relaxed. You never look like that with Dad.'

'Being in your father's company is not exactly relaxing, dear. One is always too busy minding one's P's and Q's – you know what he's like.'

'I do. I guess that's why it was nice to see you in a different light. To see you looking happy.'

Essie didn't answer right away and Clarissa began to think the conversation had come to an end when she replied, 'You're right, Clarissa, that's exactly how I felt. I hadn't given it any thought but now you've brought it up, yes, I was happy. At one point I felt quite giddy and blamed it on drinking wine at lunchtime, however, I now don't think it was that at all. I think it was my senses going into overdrive due to being in the company of someone with whom I can be myself and I don't need to put on an act.'

'Funny, that's the exact thought that crossed my mind. I was actually quite angry with Father for stifling your natural joyfulness all these years.'

'I allowed him to do it though, sweetheart, I have to take some of the blame.'

'But you did it for my sake.'

'I did, but it's all water under the bridge now. We can't go back and change it; we can only change what's ahead of us. And what's ahead of us right now, is a very exciting road trip. Gerald was showing me a UK tourist guide book he'd bought and I've made a few notes of places which might be of interest to visit.'

'Why did Gerald have a guide book?'

Essie explained to her about Gerald's redundancy, how he'd been inspired by their own road trip to venture off on one of his own and that he'd bought the book to get some ideas as he took the slow road up to visit his mother in Scotland.

'His mother lives in Scotland? Is she Scottish then?'

'He never actually said, come to think about it, but her name's Flora – which is quite Scottish, I think – so maybe she is.'

'Is visiting Scotland going to be on our agenda?'

'I would like to think so, it's a long time since I've been up there for a visit.'

'I don't remember us ever visiting Scotland…' Clarissa's face scrunched up as she dug through her memories.

'You haven't been there, darling, it wasn't good enough for your father. Well, not to go on a family holiday that is! He didn't mind going up when it was a shooting weekend with all his twatty, upper-class, cronies but he preferred family holidays to be places he could brag about. That's why you've seen Barcelona, Paris and Madrid but not Glasgow, Edinburgh or Stirling!'

'Soooo… if Gerald is doing a road trip on his way to Scotland, and we're doing a road trip which includes a visit to Scotland, why don't the three of us join forces and go together? Obviously, Gerald would be in Vanda and we'd be in our motorhome – which we now need to find a name for – but we could drive up in tandem.'

The look of surprise on her mother's face was quite the picture and Clarissa wished she'd had her mobile on hand to capture it.

'You're suggesting Gerald joins us? Wouldn't you feel put out – like he was intruding on our girl-time together?'

'Mum, we'll still have plenty of bonding time when we're driving on the road but I think having Gerald with us would be nice. From what he was saying last week, and from what you've told me tonight, I think he deserves some fun too. A road trip with friends surely has to be better than doing it alone.'

'I suppose…'

'Mum, it's only a suggestion. If you'd rather it be just

the two of us, then I'm fine with that. I'm just throwing the option out there.'

'And you're absolutely sure you wouldn't mind if he tagged along?'

'Oh, don't put it like that, Mum, you make Gerald sound like a spare peg. I would be quite happy for the whole experience to be shared among the three of us. I like Gerald and would be delighted for him to "join our gang". If we're all heading in the same direction, it would be daft not to – don't you think?'

'Do you know what I think, Clarissa? I think you're a wonderfully generous and kind-hearted girl. I'll give Gerald a call and ask him to meet up tomorrow. We can put it to him then.'

'Cool! I'll leave it with you. Right,' Clarissa stood and moved her dirty plate into the dishwasher, 'I'm off upstairs to try and whittle down the clothes I want to take but can't, clothes I really need to take but can't and the clothes I don't want to take but they'll be the most practical so I must!'

She bent down to give her mum a kiss on the cheek before leaving the room. She paused on the stairs when she heard her mum speaking.

'Gerald? Hi, it's Essie... What are you doing tomorrow? Are you free to meet up, because Clarissa and I have a proposition for you?'

Clarissa giggled quietly as she continued on up to her room. Her mum calling another man to proposition him? She never thought she'd see the day.

EIGHTEEN

'Are you absolutely *sure* you ladies don't mind me tagging along? I know this is supposed to be your special bonding time.' Gerald glanced in the rear-view mirror and caught Clarissa's eye as he asked the question. Clarissa leant forward and placed her elbows and forearms on the back of the two front seats.

'Gerald, I can absolutely assure you that I have no problem with you joining us on our trip.'

'I just feel as though I'll be intruding on your plans.'

'Gerald Wainwright!' Essie gave him a look of exasperation. 'You will not be intruding – we've invited you to come along with us. We want to visit the same locations so it seems crazy not to travel along together. You in Vanda and us with our new monster.'

Gerald flicked on the indicator and turned into the car park belonging to the motorhome showroom.

'Look, Gerald, if you don't want to "ride shotgun" with us, just say so. We don't want to force you along if you'd rather travel on your own.'

Bringing the car to a halt and switching off the engine,

he turned around to look at Clarissa and Essie. 'Ladies, I would love to be your "wingman" and if you're quite sure I won't be intruding, I accept your very kind invitation. Although,' he looked at Clarissa, 'using your expression in its original form, I'm pretty lousy with a gun so we'd better hope the bandits are occupied elsewhere.'

The two large smiles which greeted his answer caused a warm sensation to spread across his chest. It had been a long time since he'd felt this happy and he couldn't decide if it was a result of being included in something or if it was down to knowing he'd be spending some serious quality time with Essie. Whichever it was, it felt good.

The three of them got out of the car and made their way to the showroom door. Today was the day Essie and Clarissa were picking up their new motorhome and Gerald had offered to drive them there so they could return together in their new vehicle.

It didn't take long for the paperwork to be completed and signed off and once done, Paul walked the three of them through to a large, open area behind the showroom.

'Ladies, sir, I'm going to pass you over to Val who'll now go through all the small details of your vehicle. After that, she'll get you behind the wheel to practise driving it before you go out onto the open road. It's been a pleasure.' He made the introductions, held out his hand to give theirs a firm shake and trundled back inside.

'Hi, lovely to meet you. Please, come with me and I'll give you the lowdown.'

Gerald took in the lady in front of them. Her ash-blonde hair was pulled back in a no-nonsense ponytail, her face was devoid of makeup and her blue eyes sparkled as she smiled at them. She oozed trustworthiness and Gerald immediately felt they'd be safe under her tutelage.

She led them over to the solitary motorhome and Gerald couldn't help but admire it. It was so clean, shiny, and

BIG! Vanda was going to be dwarfed by this beauty.

'Wow! It's lovely. But it's also huge! I don't think I'd fancy driving that!'

Val turned to look at him with a smile. 'This is one of the smaller models. I've driven several that are bigger than this.'

'Really?'

'It's easier than you realise, trust me. By the time we're finished here this morning, you'll all be driving this like you've been doing it for years.'

Gerald noticed the bright smile on Essie's face as she looked at the new acquisition. He wished he could take a photograph but didn't think it would go down well. Val was showing them how to go about disposing of the waste, how to refill and what to use to plug in for battery charging purposes, so he felt it would be more productive to watch and listen to her than swooning like a love-sick teenager over Essie. There'd be plenty of time for that in the weeks to come.

They moved inside the van and Gerald couldn't help but be impressed. The furnishings were luxurious and not a single inch had been wasted. The motorhome was well laid out and had everything they'd need. Val opened a door and showed them the bathroom / toilet area, unclipping and swivelling to reveal how to change it from a loo with a small hand basin into a full-blown wet room complete with shower. That was something Vanda definitely lacked.

Val moved to the back of the motorhome which was currently set out as two single beds. She explained about the blackout blinds and the fly screens, how the cupboards were all automatic locking to ensure nothing opened and fell out whilst on the road and then, with a Paul Daniels flick of the wrist and a Debbie McGee smile, she transformed the two beds into one double bed. A moment later, after another push, twist and shove, they had a nice cosy seating area. Essie and Clarissa took it in turns to perform the same transformations under Val's watchful eye. Gerald declined when she looked at him, saying that it was unlikely he'd be required to do it as he'd be travelling in his own van.

'Oh, what do you have?' Val asked with interest.

'A 1966 VW camper van.'

'Nice one!' She gave him a nod of approval.

Satisfied she'd shown them all the inner workings of the motorhome, right down to the safety net that went across the double bed artfully hidden away above the driving cab, she sat them down and began to explain a few "driving" things like "always get someone to guide you into your plot when reversing in as it's easy to forget the bike holder on the back". After that, she got Essie behind the wheel.

'Essie, I want you to drive the van around the yard, following the arrows and then reverse it back into this space, please.'

Val sat next to her in the passenger seat while Gerald and Clarissa buckled themselves in on the bench seats behind. From here, they had a good view of what Essie was doing and could hear Val passing on her instructions. Gerald saw Essie lightly stroke her throat with her forefinger before turning on the ignition. The small action had him spinning through his memories to the night before their first exam, in their first year at uni. They'd all been revising together – Essie, Bobbie, Ritchie and himself – but Essie's nerves were getting the better of her and she'd been sitting stroking her neck, her movement becoming more agitated as the evening wore on. Eventually, the motion became too distracting for Bobbie and she'd tied Essie's hands behind her back with her long, Tom Baker style scarf. No amount of wriggling could undo Bobbie's firmly tied knots and it had fallen to Gerald to turn the pages of Essie's text book for the next few hours. Every time he did so, she graced him with a sweet smile of thanks and that was the night he began to fall for her—

'Gerald, are you listening?'

'Huh? What?'

Clarissa gave him a gentle poke in the ribs with her elbow. 'Your turn behind the wheel, move it!'

'Oh, right! Sorry!' He quickly changed places with Essie and listened carefully to what Val was saying. He'd completely missed Essie's attempt and the words of wisdom Val had imparted to her. Fortunately, though, and with no small thanks to his occasional rides out in Vanda, he got around the small course with ease and was able to handle the motorhome without any difficulty. He then swapped with Clarissa and sat down next to Essie.

'That was so much easier than I expected it to be,' she whispered.

'Good! Do you feel more confident with going out on the open road?'

'Yes, I do.'

'Even better because if I'm not mistaken, we're heading towards that gate over there and there's real, live traffic on the other side of it.'

'Yikes!' She grabbed the sleeve of his jacket, her clenched fingers pushing against his arm. Their warmth seeped through the thin material and the skin underneath felt as though it was being scorched. Gerald managed to swallow down the sigh which almost escaped from his lips. After all these years, Essie still had an effect on him, and despite all those years, he knew he'd never have the nerve to tell her.

NINETEEN

It was Tuesday morning and Sukie looked on while Essie gave Marvin, as the motorhome had now been christened, the onceover. She was checking his water inlets were all firmly locked, the awnings were tightly closed and the cupboards inside – now full of clothes, toiletries, crockery, food and any other things they thought they might require – were also securely fastened. Their bikes were leaning against the garage door, waiting for Gerald to arrive with his so they could be secured together on the bike-rack at the back.

Clarissa walked around behind her mum, double-checking, as they'd agreed, to ensure nothing was missed.

They'd taken Marvin out for a fuel stop yesterday – Essie driving him to the garage, Clarissa driving him back and both were now fairly confident they'd be okay behind his wheel.

Clarissa was inside Marvin checking all was good when Sukie moved to stand beside Essie and asked, 'What did George say when you told him?'

She let out a sigh. 'He still doesn't know.'

'What?'

Sukie's jaw dropped open as Essie hesitated in answering, thinking back to the previous morning…

Essie watched George finish knotting his tie and checking it was properly positioned in the mirror on the wardrobe. 'George, what time do you think you'll be home tonight, I need to talk to you about something?'

She'd been trying to sum up the courage to speak with him all weekend but had kept putting it off and now, here they were, Monday morning and departure day was tomorrow. The discussion had to be tonight – she'd run out of time.

'I'm back down in London again today and I expect to be there all week so I won't be back until Friday.'

'Excuse me! And you're only just telling me this now?'

'I didn't see that it was all that important to tell you. I don't need you for anything – we have no events coming up.'

'George,' she let out an exasperated sigh, 'I'm your wife, you're supposed to keep me in the loop with these things.'

'Exactly! You're my wife, not my keeper, and I don't need to give you my daily itinerary.'

'No, I don't need your daily movement sheet, George, but some form of communication would be nice. For goodness' sake, your secretary knows more about your life these days than I do! And this is the third week in a row you've been down in London – maybe we should look at moving back there if this carries on.'

'Estelle!' He spoke her name in the same tone of voice her father had used when he was talking down to either her or her mother. 'The firm is working on a big case and I'm currently needed in London.' He turned his back on her, pulled his suit carrier from the wardrobe and placed three of his suits inside. A further three were thrown on the bed, accompanied by the words, 'Those need to go to the dry cleaners, see to it.'

His commanding tone and dismissive attitude were the final straw for Essie. Sod you, she thought, I'm telling you fuck all!

She walked into the en suite and was in the shower as George drove out the gates, still oblivious to the imminent departure of his wife and daughter.

'So, he doesn't know yet?' Sukie looked at her in bemusement.

'Nope! He'll find my note when he returns on Friday.'

'Would it be too rude to ask what you wrote?'

Essie turned to her friend and smiled. 'I kept it simple. *"Gone travelling!"* with a smiley face.'

'That's all?'

'It's more than he deserves!'

'And his suits?'

'Still lying on the bed where he threw them! He can sort out his own dirty washing, I'm not his slave! Now,' Essie briskly changed the subject, 'you have my new phone number, because the old one is now switched off?'

'I do, it's already in my phone.'

'I've put the re-direction on my mail, and also Clarissa's – thank you so much again for agreeing to let me divert it to you, there's less chance of George finding out where we are if he can't access my bills.'

'Would he open your post?'

'Too right he would! In a heartbeat!'

'Wow! Pete would never do that. In fact, he won't even open anything that has both our names on it unless I'm there with him.'

'The thing is, Sukie, Pete respects you. To George, I'm just another thing he possesses. There's a big difference.'

Just then, there was a shout and a holler, and Essie turned to see Jenny Rowland and her daughter, Saffy, coming down the drive towards them.

'I'd hoped to catch you before you set off,' Saffy said, as she ran the last few yards and threw a large hug around Clarissa who'd stepped out onto the driveway.

'You told Saffy? We said no one was to know.' Essie looked at Clarissa in dismay. It had been agreed that no one, bar Sukie, would be told of their plans to ensure George was kept fully in the dark.

'Don't worry, Essie, your secret's safe. Your husband will *never* hear anything from us, I can assure you of that.'

Essie felt herself relax. Sukie had passed on a few stories about George's behaviour on the rare occasions when he'd graced Jenny's bookshop and tearoom establishment with his presence. He'd been rude to the staff, snapping his fingers, demanding preferential treatment such as ordering items not on the menu and insisting they make them otherwise he'd put bad reviews on the internet. He hadn't endeared himself in any way to Jenny, and Essie knew she'd most likely relish the opportunity to get one over on him.

'Thank you, Jenny.'

'Essie, it'll be my pleasure.' She gave a cheeky little grin. 'I'll let Sukie know if he does happen to come asking.'

'What about Saffy?'

'Oh, don't you worry about that sassy little madam. She'll soon send him packing with a flea in his ear. I'm afraid "respect for her elders" stops short when it comes to George.'

'I can understand that!'

'We've brought you a going-away-travelling gift.'

Saffy handed over a bag to Clarissa who unwrapped the prettily wrapped item inside.

'Oh, nice one, Saffy! What a clever idea.' She held up the box and showed Essie the games compendium they'd been given. 'These will be perfect for the days and nights when we're taking it easy. After all, we won't be out and about all the time. Thank you.' She gave Saffy another hug.

A horn tooting had them all turning around to see Gerald driving Vanda up the drive towards them. He pulled alongside Marvin and got out.

'All set?' he asked.

Essie smiled at him. 'We sure are.'

'So, where are you off to first, or is that also a secret?'

'First stop is Wales. We're staying in Snowdonia National Park for a few days so we can explore some of the nearby beauty spots and then we'll be making our way towards Chester. After that, who knows? We're not planning too far ahead – we want to play it by ear and just go where the notion takes us.'

'And, talking of going,' Gerald looked at his watch, 'we need to get moving to make sure we arrive on time. I don't fancy trying to set up in the dark if we're late – especially with this being our first time and not yet fully up to speed on how it all works.'

His comment set off a rush to load up the bikes, followed by a quick flurry of hugs, kisses and well-wishing and then Essie was behind the wheel, switching on the ignition and following Gerald out the manor gates. She glanced in the mirror and saw Sukie, Jenny and Saffy waving them off. She did a couple of toots on the horn, stuck her arm out of the open window and gave one last wave in return before turning onto the open road and out of their sight.

She looked at Clarissa. 'You okay?'

Her daughter turned towards her with the biggest smile

she'd ever seen on her beautiful face.

'Oh yes, Mum, I am more than okay. I can't believe we're finally on our way. This is going to be so much fun.'

Essie looked back towards the road with Clarissa's smile duplicated on her own face.

'It sure will be, my darling, it sure will be!'

TWENTY

They'd been driving for about an hour, when the walkie-talkie on the dashboard crackled and Gerald's voice came over the waves. 'Hey, how's it all going back there? Everybody happy?'

Clarissa picked it up. 'Hi, Gerald, yes, we're all good here, how about yourself?'

'Absolutely fine and dandy, Clarissa. We should reach Stourport in half an hour or so. If we get split up at any traffic lights, I'll pull over to wait for you.'

'Okay, see you soon.'

Clarissa popped the handset back on the dashboard and looked out of the window at the passing countryside. One of the first things they'd agreed on, when the three of them had sat down to discuss the planning of their journeys, was to avoid motorways whenever possible.

'There's so much lovely countryside and little villages to see which we'll miss if we go on the motorways.'

Clarissa had agreed with her mother. The whole point of the trip was to chill out, relax and take it easy. Gerald had come up with the suggestion of the walkie-talkies.

He'd explained that some of the areas they'd be heading towards might not have good mobile signals and the "Wee-tees" – as they now called them – might be a better option. They were also better than phones as they could legally be used when driving while mobile phones could not, therefore, making it easier to keep in touch when on the move.

She looked over at her mum. They'd been lucky with the weather; it was a perfect, sunny, spring day and the sunlight streamed into the cab, making her mother's blonde hair shine. She'd been due to have it cut two weeks ago but had cancelled the appointment stating that longer hair could be more easily maintained when they were on the road. The extra bit of length suited her and Clarissa thought it made her look younger. It had been interesting watching her mother morph from the well-made-up, perfectly maintained woman she'd been into this more relaxed, easy-going person. Her makeup today had consisted of a light sweep of tinted moisturiser, a quick flick of a mascara wand and a lick of lip gloss. The full-on eye makeup, foundation and blusher brushes had all been relegated to the "only for special occasions" league. If one was being fanciful, Clarissa thought, you could almost say that freeing herself from the confines of her makeup bag had allowed Essie to break the other chains which had been wrapped around her. Gone were the tailored slacks, twin-sets and two-inch heels – her mother now sat beside her wearing jeans, a polo shirt and trainers with a sweatshirt slung over the back of the seat. She was humming along to the music on the radio and looked as though she no longer had a care in the world.

'What do you think Father will do when he sees the note?'

'Hmmm, let me think. First of all, he'll pump out his chest in total effrontery that we've dared to do this. He'll then make several huffing and puffing sounds as he scrunches the note in his hand and drops it back on the kitchen table. He won't believe we've actually gone until he looks around the kitchen and realises there's no dinner being cooked, at which point, he'll stomp around the rest of the house, slowly becoming aware there are no other signs of life and the only lamps on are those on the timers. He'll let out a "Grrr" of anger, march back to his briefcase, yank his mobile out of the side pocket and try to call me. When it goes directly to voicemail, he'll call you. Upon getting no reply from either of us, there is a seventy percent probability that the phone will be thrown across the room.'

'Only seventy percent?'

Her mother smiled at her. 'He's not long replaced the last one which was smashed in a fit of temper. He won't want to spend seven-hundred pounds on another new phone. Keeping Apple's share price up won't sit easy with him.'

Clarissa chuckled at her mother's very apt account of her father and his behaviour.

'With that description, I can't possibly think why you would *ever* consider leaving him! The man sounds a total delight!'

Her dry comment resulted in her mum letting out a bark of laughter which Clarissa joined in with. It was still quite new to hear her mother sounding like this and it thrilled her all the way through to know she had been the cause of her mum's merriment. She mentally crossed her fingers, hoping this trip would see them enjoy many more such moments.

They drove into the little town of Stourport-upon-Severn and Essie made sure she kept Gerald in her sights. Once or twice a car pulled out in front of her but she was always able to see Vanda. They'd driven almost through the whole town before, finally, the indictor flickered on the camper van and it drove into a large car park belonging to a pretty pub called, "The Old Beams". They got out and Essie rolled her head around to relieve the tension in her shoulders. Marvin was easy enough to drive but she'd been tensed up on the journey due to this being the first time she'd driven him properly. She was sure it would wear off as she became more used to being behind his wheel.

'Give me a moment, I just need to pop inside.' Gerald strode off towards the main door while Essie continued to rub out the knots at the top of her back. It wouldn't be so bad after lunch as Clarissa was taking over the driving for the next stretch.

Gerald arrived back beside them. 'I was just letting the manager know we have a table booked for lunch but we're taking a look around first. I didn't want him to think we'd just parked up in his car park and buggered off. We might have ended up clamped or towed away.'

'Were they alright with that?'

'Absolutely, and even said we are more than welcome to use their facilities before we go.'

'Cracking idea!' Clarissa was already halfway to the door before Essie had even picked up her handbag and locked Marvin up.

'I think I'll join her!'

'See you both out here in a few minutes.'

'How do you know about this place?' Essie asked Gerald as they waited for the lights to change on the little stone bridge over the River Severn.

Gerald's voice was wistful as he replied, 'We used to come here for family holidays when I was a kid. We had an old caravan then and we would be here for two weeks every year up till I was about eight or nine.'

'Fun times?'

'Oh, the absolute best. Flora and I would paddle in the river, spend our pocket money – which we'd saved up for weeks – in the fairground or on candy floss and enjoy the freedom of being able to run wild. It was bliss.'

'Why did you stop coming? Did you become teenagers and suddenly places like this were no longer "cool"?' Essie nudged him gently in the ribs.

'Not quite, although I'm sure that would have happened eventually. As it was, my granny died, my mum went up to Scotland to sort out the funeral and didn't come back.'

'Oh, Gerald, I'm sorry.'

'We never returned after that. Dad sold the caravan and began doing longer hours at the office. I don't think we ever had another family holiday together after that.'

'Do you know why your mum never returned?'

'No, I don't, Dad would never tell me. In all these years, I've never heard him say a bad word against her. Even now, I think he still loves her.'

'Does she still love him?

'I don't know but I plan to ask when I see her.'

'Oy, you two, get a move on! The waltzers are open and I want to indulge my inner child by having a turn.' Clarissa, who'd been walking ahead and not party to the conversation, turned to wave and chivvy them along.

'Come on, Gerald, let's go and be kids again. No more melancholy for today, eh!'

Essie smiled, took his hand and dragged him across the road to the little fairground opposite, purposely turning a deaf ear to his protestations that he didn't get on well with this particular fairground attraction.

TWENTY-ONE

Gerald looked at the menu in front of him. He was still feeling a bit rough after their stint in the fairground. He'd have been fine on any of the other rides but he and the waltzers had never been the best of friends. It had been made worse by the young attendant, who'd clearly taken a shine to Clarissa, making a point of spinning their car twice as fast and twice as much as was necessary. While Essie and Clarissa had squealed their delight, he'd been doing everything in his power not to projectile-vomit all over the place. He'd walked behind the ladies after that, as they sauntered around the town admiring the little gift shops they passed, so as to avoid them noticing his queasiness. He'd surreptitiously taken some tablets and hoped they'd kick in soon.

Essie went to the bar to place the order and commented on the age of the building when she sat back down.

'It's been here since the 1500s,' Gerald informed her. 'My dad's a bit of a history buff and he liked to remind us of that every time we visited.'

'So, you've been here a lot then?' Clarissa asked.

‘I’d say quite a few times. We came here the first night we arrived and the last night before we left. It was always considered to be *the* special holiday treat.’

‘Has it changed much since then?’ Essie asked the question as she gazed admiringly around her.

‘Oh yes! It was darker and smokier back then. Those were the days when smoking was still allowed in pubs and restaurants so everything was always a bit dingier.’ He followed Essie’s example and took in the fresh cream-coloured walls and pristine white ceilings, the beautifully exposed beams which lent the pub its name, and the décor of knick-knacks dotted around. Here and there, old, stained-glass windows set in oak, created little nooks and crannies for the clientele to sit in. A roaring fire filled the room with warmth and finished off the welcoming ambiance of the place. ‘It’s considerably classier now, I can tell you.’

‘Do you know that this is only the second time I’ve been in a pub since I left uni?’

‘No way!’ Gerald sat back in surprise. ‘I’m not insinuating you’re any kind of a lush, Essie, but you were a regular member of our group when we had our little forays into The Castle Bar.’

‘George didn’t like seeing women in pubs – he thought it was common.’

‘So, where did you go on nights out? The park to feed the ducks?’

Essie gave a small laugh. ‘Not quite. Wine bars were acceptable, and restaurants, obviously. But never, ever a pub.’

‘Correct me if I’m wrong here but didn’t he meet you in a pub? Isn’t that just a little bit hypocritical – he can frequent pubs but you can’t?’

‘You’re not wrong, Gerald, and yes, it is hypocritical, but that’s George for you – hypocritically sexist all the way through to the bone!'

'When was the first time?'

'The day we met for lunch a couple of weeks ago.'

'Blimey, Mum, you weren't kidding that day when you said you no longer cared what Father thought as you were in the pub barely a week later.'

'Blame Gerald, he's a bad influence on me!' She winked at him as she lifted her glass of sparkling water to her lips.

'Err… good try, girlfriend, but I seem to recall *you* changed the venue from the café in town to the pub in the village.'

Essie shrugged. 'When you said you weren't going to be in town, it didn't make sense for us both to waste time heading that way when there was a place close by with a reputation for great food.'

'And talking of great food…' Clarissa inclined her head towards the waitress walking towards them, 'I think this might be ours.'

A few oohs and ahhs met the arrival of their lunch as it was placed in front of them and apart from some giggles when Clarissa's stomach let out an almighty growl, there was silence as they worked through the vast plate-loads in front of them.

They hadn't long set off on the second part of the journey when Clarissa suddenly announced, 'I like Gerald!'

Essie looked across at her. 'Well, I'm kind of glad to hear that as I would hate to break the news to him that his company was no longer wanted.'

'He makes me laugh and he's good for you.'

Essie started a little at this last bit. 'I'm not quite sure what you mean, darling…'

Clarissa gave her a quick, sideways glance. 'Whenever we've been out as a family, with Father, you were always uptight. I know now that that was down to his expectations and the ramifications afterwards if you ever – in his eyes – let him down. With Gerald, however, that strain is absent. You laugh frequently, you talk more often and you're really relaxed. You totally change – you're a different, and if I may say "better", person around him.'

Essie pondered on Clarissa's words before she replied. 'I suppose I am. Maybe it's because I knew Gerald all those years ago, before I was forced to don airs, graces and twin-sets. He's one of the few people who knows the real me – the girl I was before your father came along. He treats me now exactly as he did then – pulling my leg over silly things and making funny comments that make me smile. By *not* treating me differently, he helps me to be different.'

'Is that all it is?' Clarissa sneaked another sidelong look at her. 'Nothing more?'

'More? What are you talking about?'

'I was just wondering if you secretly fancied him?'

'CLARISSA WALTON! I'm a married woman—'

'Err, yeah… married to a dickhead! You're allowed to look, you know!'

'Clarissa, I married your father for better or for worse, and forsaking all others, so even though he may have behaved abominably, I'm not about to go out, eyeing up other blokes.'

'Well, there's nothing stopping you while you sort out your divorce, then you can hit the road running when you sign the decree absolute!'

'Clarissa, I don't even know if I want to divorce your father. I don't know what I want right now except to have some fun, some freedom and to spend quality time creating beautiful memories with you.'

'Okay, Mum. I'll just say this and then I'll park it –

Gerald is good for you and you could do a lot worse than to hook up with him. I know he'd treat you right!'

She leant over to turn up the volume of the radio and began singing along to the music, leaving Essie to ponder over what had been said.

TWENTY-TWO

They made good time and pulled into the caravan park in Blaenau Ffestiniog, in the middle of the Snowdonia National Park, just before five p.m. Essie jumped out to guide Clarissa as she reversed into their space and Gerald pulled into the next one, parking Vanda up facing forward, rather than reversed, for they planned to put up, and put out, their awnings to create a little corridor between the two vehicles. When they'd been planning the finer details of their trip, they'd spent some considerable time discussing what to take until Clarissa suggested they pool their resources as it made more sense than taking duplicate items in both vans. Gerald would sleep in Vanda at night, and had his own small toilet should he need it, but he'd shower, eat and hang-out with Clarissa and Essie in Marvin at all other times. When they went off on day excursions, they'd go in Vanda because she was smaller and more "user-friendly" when it came to parking. Gerald had put them both on the insurance as named drivers and Essie had done the same with Marvin's insurance. This allowed for them to work out driving rests if they were on a longer journey.

A kitty had also been set up where they all put in the same agreed value each week and this would cover all feeding expenses be it meals out or food bought in. Essie was adamant that Gerald would not be paying more than his fair share. She couldn't forget his evil, money-grabbing, bitch of a wife in a hurry and she wanted to ensure he felt an equal member of their little gang.

They quickly got themselves settled. There was a small incline on Gerald's lot, so Essie had to help him with his levelling ramps to prevent him rolling down towards the driving cab while he was asleep. Essie's lot was pretty flat, though, so she was spared that hassle for today.

'Shall we take a stroll around and see what's what?'

'Sure, Gerald. You coming, Mum?'

'Yup, two seconds – I'll just take the butter out of the fridge so it can soften up for when we come back.'

'What's for dinner tonight?'

Essie looked at Gerald as they walked past the communal showers and made their way to the little gift shop and convenience store. 'I've kept it simple as I didn't think we'd want anything overly substantial as we'd stopped for lunch, so it's a sort of ploughman's lunch. Crusty bread, cold meats, cheese, pickles, potato salad and some delicious macarons from Sam's bakery in the village. Is that okay?'

'It sounds perfect, Essie. Thank you. I've got a macaroni cheese and bacon bake in the fridge and I picked up a ciabatta loaf from the bakery as I passed by this morning, so I hope that'll do for tomorrow night.'

'Gerald, that'll more than do, I'm already looking forward to that.'

'I'll sort something out when it's my turn – I didn't see the point in preparing something for three days from now as we don't yet know what we're doing. I don't want you to think I'm not doing my bit.'

‘Clarissa, we certainly wouldn’t think that so don’t you be worrying. Now, how about a small race up the hill to that tree – that should get some fresh Welsh air into our lungs and help us all sleep tonight.’ Gerald pointed towards a small hill just off the path they were walking along.

‘You’re on!’ Clarissa had already sprinted off with Gerald hot on her heels. Essie let out a small groan – she hated running! She never went on the treadmill when she hit the gym, she always made a beeline to the elliptical machines. She watched Gerald and Clarissa put some distance between her and them and with a sigh, she kicked up her heels and went haring after them. She wasn’t going to be the butt of their jokes for the rest of the night for not joining in. Just like The Three Musketeers, they were going to be all for one and one for all. She simply wished the “one for all” bit had been a bit less energetic!

The following day, they drove south and visited Portmeirion where the cult sixties sci-fi programme, “The Prisoner”, had been filmed. Essie and Clarissa instantly fell in love with the pretty little town which had been perfectly preserved and still looked exactly as it did in the TV shows. Gerald had watched the shows repeatedly when he’d been a boy and spent the next few hours filling Essie and Clarissa in on the various landmarks, houses and shops and explaining where they’d all slotted into the series. He repaid their patience of allowing him to waffle on uninterrupted with some lovely ice cream from the little gelateria. Many photographs were taken and a couple of postcards were purchased before they returned to Vanda and made their way to Harlech with its stunning ruin of a castle which loomed tall over the town. Essie had made up a small picnic with the leftovers from last night’s supper, which she took from Vanda’s little fridge and put inside a rucksack. They set off towards the castle, laughing and joking about who'd pass out first from climbing all the steps inside and admiring the new bridge which they'd read about online.

'Oh boy, I enjoyed that, but I'm shattered now! Pass those sarnies over, Mum.'

Essie and Gerald had just laid out the waterproof travel rug and Clarissa was quick to grab a corner. 'I do like a good 'splory castle and that was *definitely* a good one!'

'Splory?' Gerald looked at Essie.

'Our word for "exploring". It came about when Clarissa was little and it's kind of stuck.'

'Fair enough.' Gerald sat down on the opposite corner to Clarissa and leant back against the ancient wall behind him, looking out towards the sea. Essie sat and assumed a similar position. All three ate in silence – the fresh sea air along with the energy used to explore the old ruin having given them all a fierce appetite.

Finally, replete, they tidied away the tubs and spent a few more minutes admiring the view.

'Do you think it's changed much since it was first built?' asked Clarissa.

'I expect it's pretty much as it was back then although I suspect the caravans may have come along at a later date. Mind you, that one over there,' Gerald pointed to a static caravan in the middle of the park behind the castle, 'looks pretty dilapidated, so there's a good chance it's been here as long as the castle!'

'Oh, Gerald!' Clarissa and Essie both laughed at his silliness.

Gerald stood up, chuckling as he did so. 'Come on, you

two, time to move if we want to get down to Barmouth. Now, it's a proper little seaside town – I think you'll like it.'

He held out his hand and helped Essie to her feet. The rug was rolled up and put back in the rucksack.

'Right, last one to the van is a squishy-faced nincompoop!'

The three of them power-walked back to Vanda as fast as they were able – pushing and shoving each other aside in a bid to ensure they weren't last. The laughter and jesting which accompanied them only served to impede progress and they all arrived at the same time. In no time at all, Vanda was back on the road, laughter and singing slipping through her open windows as the light-hearted mood continued for the rest of the day and right up until bedtime.

Gerald's last thought, as he pulled the quilt around him, was that he couldn't remember the last time he felt this free.

TWENTY-THREE

'C'mon Mum, chop-chop! We've got a busy day today, no time for tardiness. Gerald, are you up and about?'

Clarissa was up, dressed and raring to go. She'd arranged a little surprise but it was something with a timed slot so they needed to get going very soon to ensure they didn't miss it.

'What's the rush, Clarissa? It's barely half-past seven.'

'I'm just excited to be going up to Colwyn Bay, Mum. I've heard The Pogues and Kirsty McColl singing about it every Christmas for as long as I can remember and now, I'm finally going to see it.'

'Sweetheart, I don't think it's all that special – it's just a stretch of sand.'

'But I also want to see the town and don't forget we're planning a few more castle visits too.'

Gerald's voice finally came crackling into the camper. 'Yes, Clarissa, I'm up and will be with you both shortly. Essie, can you take Clarissa's batteries out, please, she's far too energetic for this time of the morning.'

By 8.15, they were piling into Vanda, Essie grumbling

that she hadn't even had time for a coffee.

'Don't worry, Mum, we can have a nice brunch when we get to Penrhyn Castle.' Clarissa turned to Gerald who was about to get into the driver's seat. 'Gerald, I'll drive today. You need to have a break.'

'There's no need for that, Clarissa, I'm happy to drive.'

'No, Gerald, I'm driving. You haven't had time out yet, it's your turn to rest. Now sit down over there,' she pointed to the bench seats where she'd sat the day before, 'and chill out.'

'Blimey, Clarissa, I think you forgot to take your bossy tablet this morning – are you sure you don't want to go back and get it?'

'Very funny, Gerald, now sit!'

She glanced at her watch as she adjusted the seat and mirror. This was the first time she'd driven a left-hand drive on the roads and she was hoping she adapted to it quickly. They had over an hour – as long as they didn't come across any tractors, sheep, or sheep on tractors, they should get there just in time.

'Erm, Clarissa, where are we going?' Essie was looking around as Clarissa pulled off the A5 onto a side road with a dead-end sign.

'It's okay, Mum, I read there's a great viewing point up here so I thought we could spare a few minutes to see it.'

'Oh, okay.'

Clarissa smiled inwardly – so far, so good, although she knew her luck would shortly run out. She didn't know exactly how her mother, or Gerald for that matter, was going to react to her surprise but she suspected it might not be joyfully received… at least, not in the first instance.

She drove through the gate and it was impossible to miss the large sign which announced their destination,

"Zip World Velocity 2. The fastest zip line in the world."

She pulled into a parking space and was already out of the van before her mother could say anything.

'CLARISSA!'

'Yes, Mum?' She peered around the back of Vanda with a look of assumed innocence upon her face.

'Why are we here?'

'Like I said, Mum, it has some wonderful views. There's a café just up there where you can see right across the valley.'

She looked at her watch. She had fifteen minutes to persuade her mum and Gerald. It was going to be cutting it fine but then again, it also meant there was less chance of her mum backing out once she realised she was booked in to go hurtling through the quarry at over one hundred miles an hour.

Clarissa led the way up to the viewing platform and they arrived just in time to see two people taking off. They were all suited up and looked like little red pea-pods as they hung horizontally on the zip-lines.

She watched her mother's face as she took in their descent. 'What do you think of that, Mum? Fancy it?'

'Most definitely not, never in a million years!'

'Well, that's a pity, because I've booked the three of us in for a ride.'

'You've done *what*?'

'You heard me, Mum, we're going up there!' She pointed to the platform high above their heads.

'You have got to be joking…' Gerald looked up and she actually heard him gulp.

Essie was considerably less restrained. 'No fucking way are you getting me on one of those!'

'Aw, Mum, come on. It'll be a blast. This whole trip is about trying new experiences and having adventures.'

'I would prefer adventures where the risk of serious

injury was considerably reduced. No, I won't do it.'

Clarissa was about to make a second plea when Gerald said quietly, 'If you're not planning to do it, Essie, then you can hold the coats.'

'Excuse me? Are you saying, Gerald, that you're going to go up there, on THAT thing?'

'Yup, that's exactly what I'm saying, Essie.'

'But—'

'But what? Clarissa has gone to the trouble of arranging this and while I concur it would never have made it onto my list of the top ten things to do when in Wales, now that we're here, I'm going to give it a go. Like Clarissa said, it's time for some new adventures. Now, I would never force anyone to do something they really didn't want to, but the Essie I knew all those years ago – the one I believe you're trying to rediscover – would never have walked away from such an opportunity.'

Clarissa looked on in amazement. She most certainly hadn't expected Gerald to be her knight in shining armour when it came to talking her mum round but she recognised the signs of her mum crumbling under his gentle persuasion.

'Oh, all right then. But only because I don't want to be the odd one out. Right now, Clarissa, I really don't like you.' Essie turned and stomped away towards the main office.

'Gerald, I could hug you! Thank you SO much for that.'

'Clarissa, I didn't want to see you disappointed, but if I'm being honest, at this moment, I don't like you very much either.' He peeled away and quickened his step to catch up with Essie.

Clarissa felt a little stung at Gerald's comment and hoped that once they'd all zipped through the air and reached the other side in one piece, her surprise would be better accepted.

Essie climbed onto the table as instructed and lay quietly on her stomach as she was tightly locked up and strapped in. She listened carefully to the woman beside her as she repeated where to put her hands and told her in no uncertain terms that she must keep them in this position until she reached the other side. They should only be released if she saw the instructors flapping their arms at her; this meant she was coming in too fast and needed to slow down. She pulled down her goggles and waited as the assistant checked everything was secure. Nodding that all was good, the front part of her harness was clipped above her onto the carriage on the zip-line, followed swiftly by her legs.

'Right, Essie, I'm going to remove the table.'

The table underneath her was lowered to floor level and the zip-line gave a small groan as it took her weight. She was now hanging in the air like a piece of best rump beef behind the butcher's counter. She turned her head to see Gerald dangling in the same position. A quick look the other way saw Clarissa also suspended, her head sticking out over the edge of the platform.

'Clarissa, I just want you to know that as of this moment, you are disinherited.'

'Okay, Mum. No problem!' came the cheeky reply.

Essie looked straight ahead and felt her chest tighten as she looked out into the blue sky in front of her. She closed her eyes and took in gentle puffs of air, just as she had done when she was in labour. How ironic was it that the cause of her learning to breathe in this manner was also the cause of her having to do it again? She glanced down at the lumps of rock directly below her as her stomach twisted over in knots.

'Hi, Essie, I'm just double-checking you're all strapped

in securely.'

The deep, male voice letting her know he was satisfied her harness had passed muster did little to make her feel any better. She really couldn't believe she was doing this.

She didn't ever do things like this and she was beginning to feel dizzy.

No, she couldn't do it! She wasn't cut out to be *this* adventurous, no matter what Gerald said. She was about to turn to her assistant and ask to be taken down when the countdown began and before she could object, she was zooming off through the air.

With her eyes squeezed tightly closed, she felt the wind slap against her face and, as she picked up speed, her lips and cheeks begin to quiver and wobble. Her whole face felt as though all the muscles had suddenly turned to jelly.

She opened her eyes just as the ground fell away below her and she was gliding over the beautiful blue lake, the fluffy clouds in the sky reflected in it and the sunlight glinting on the surface. She raised her head and looked forward into the distance. It was a gorgeous, spring day and she was flying through the air like a bird. From nowhere, a fountain of joy burst through her and she all at once felt released. Released from George, released from the life he'd forced upon her, released from the responsibility of being a mother, released from everything. For those few brief seconds, she felt like a balloon which had escaped and she was floating off into the sky, never to be seen again.

'Oh, shit!' She saw the ground instructor madly flapping his arms, letting her know she had to try to slow down. She shoved her arms out to her side and flapped for all she was worth until he gave the signal that all was good. She pushed down her right hand and grabbed the shepherd's crook, which helped to bring her to a standstill. In no time at all, her feet had been released and she was back on terra firma once more. Her knees buckled slightly, but fortunately her instructor caught her and helped her up until the jelly sensation passed.

'So sorry,' she said, feeling embarrassed.

'No problem at all, ma'am. It happens a lot. Did you enjoy it?'

'Yes, I did! I wasn't expecting to but it was quite something.'

The instructor simply smiled and nodded. No doubt he'd heard that a thousand times, Essie thought as he walked off and Clarissa and Gerald came towards her.

'Well, Mum, am I still disinherited?'

'You damn well deserve to be, putting me through something like that! Are you trying to kill me off early?'

'I'm sorry, I thought it might be something you'd enjoy. You know, kick start the old adrenaline and all that...'

Essie was too high on excitement to let her daughter suffer any longer.

'Clarissa, I bloody loved it! Not to begin with, but about halfway down, I experienced this wonderful feeling of total freedom and felt a rush of pure joy explode through me. It really was quite amazing. Thank you for arranging it.'

She gave Clarissa a tight hug and the two of them, laughing and joking, walked off arm in arm.

Gerald walked a few yards behind the ladies, feeling quite sick and once again using every ounce of his self-control not to throw up. His legs were wobbling and his head was pounding. That had to be up there as one of the worst experiences of his life, which was saying something considering he'd been married to Marjory, but it was the truth. He'd hated every second of the ride. He hadn't wanted to come over as a wimp, and it had been horrible seeing Clarissa so disappointed that her carefully planned surprise hadn't been as well received as she'd anticipated, but he couldn't help regretting that he hadn't mentioned his dislike of heights sooner. Fingers crossed this would be the only incident as he didn't think he could go through anything like it a second time.

TWENTY-FOUR

The following day, they upped wheels and made their way to the outskirts of Chester, stopping along the way for a mooch around Llangollen and a meander around Wrexham. Upon looking at their maps, and their list of places to visit, the general consensus had been to book pitches for a few nights and make the campsite the centre point for visits to Chester – which Clarissa declared herself a new fan of after their brisk walk around the city walls where she came across the centuries-old, quaint little wonky houses with their tiny wooden doors and instantly declared herself awash with house envy – Chester Zoo, and Cheshire Oaks where, much to Gerald's amusement, both ladies had been keen to inform him they were not interested in all the "designer clobber" and were just intending to pass through to say they'd visited. Their "passing through" took almost a whole day what with Essie taking a whole hour to decide she *would* buy the Radley handbag she'd fallen in lust with while Clarissa had to give herself a self-imposed spending limit to prevent the need for a second motorhome just to carry her purchases. Both ladies managed to talk him into buying a pair of Sketchers trainers which he happily concurred were exceptionally comfortable.

It was, however, unanimously agreed that the highlight of this stage of the road trip was their day in Liverpool. They set off early in Vanda, parked up at the Seacombe ferry terminal and took a ferry across the Mersey to Liverpool. Essie and Gerald insisted on singing the famous Gerry and the Pacemaker's song while Clarissa made her way to the other side of the boat, pretending she didn't know them. When they disembarked, all three were thrilled to find the statue of the city's most famous export, The Beatles, a short walk away from the main door of the ferry terminal and many photographs were taken with it. Essie had them creased up in laughter as she badgered Clarissa into taking a photograph of her kissing Paul McCartney. The angle of the statue's head made it look as though he was returning the favour. She also had a picture taken on her phone which she sent to Sukie with the caption that Sukie wasn't the only one to have snogged a rock god!

Clarissa lingered for a moment as her mum and Gerald walked off together along the quayside. She watched Essie throw her head back in laughter at some comment Gerald made and a second later, he was laughing too. The light-hearted sound of their merriment floated towards her on the wind and it hit her that she'd seen her mother laugh more in the last few days, since they'd embarked on their trip, than she could recall seeing in all the years before. Time seemed to be falling away from her mum's shoulders and Clarissa was beginning to see the girl she'd once been before George Walton had come into her life and sucked all the joy from it.

As she strolled along behind the older couple, Clarissa wondered if there had ever been anything more than friendship between them as they were a perfect fit – both physically and emotionally. Gerald was taller than her mum but only by about half a foot or so and his normally perfectly placed, dark brown hair was blowing about in the breeze coming off the river. It made him look less "middle-aged" even though he was still dressed in cord trousers, a flannel shirt and a tank-top. The thick, black-framed glasses didn't help either and Clarissa made a silent vow to herself that she'd be giving him a makeover before this trip was over. He was also so attentive to her mother and ensured she always went first or had first choice. Essie also reciprocated in a similar manner which could sometimes be frustrating when all Clarissa wanted was a decision to be made. She'd also noticed they were now doing the old "finishing each other's sentences" thing although she was sure neither of them had realised. It felt a bit strange seeing her mum in the company of another man, even if he was bringing out the best in her. The only man she'd ever seen with her mother was her father and he was a selfish, manipulative pig. She was realising that, the more she saw her mum open up and begin to shine, the more intense her dislike for her father was becoming. She was just wondering at which point her dislike would turn to loathing and the loathing would fester into hate when her mum stopped, looked around and called on her to catch up.

Clarissa pushed away the dark thoughts in her head and, with a radiant smile, quickened her pace and linked arms with them both, saying as she did so, 'Honestly, you two! You're like a pair of schoolkids, giggling away to yourselves. I can see I'm going to have to be the adult around here and keep you both in check!'

'Oh, Clarissa, don't be such a fuddy-duddy. I'll have you know that I am old enough to know better but young enough not to give a shit!'

'Mother!' Clarissa knew her feigned shock was fooling no one and this was confirmed when Gerald replied, 'I'm wot she said too!'

Amidst more howls of laughter, the three of them made their way to the meeting point for their Magical Mystery Tour.

'Well, this is disappointing.'

'Mum, we've walked up and down now for almost an hour, trust me, it's not going to happen.'

'But I saw it on the television – people go back in time on this street!'

After the tour had dropped them off at the famous Cavern Club, Essie had expressed a wish to visit Bold Street, not too far from where they stood. It was known as the "timeslip street" and many reports had been made over the years by people claiming they had, for a brief moment or two, slipped back in time. Clarissa was initially interested but her mum had been walking up and down the street now for ages with no success and the novelty was quickly wearing off.

'We can come back some other time, Mum, and try again, but I think for today, it ain't gonna happen. Please, can we now move on?'

'Well… I have a little surprise for you both, if you would like to follow me.' Gerald treated Clarissa and Essie to one of his little, shy smiles – the kind, Clarissa had begun to realise, he made when he was unsure about something or uncertain how a suggestion might be received.

'Oh yes, and what that might be, Mr Wainwright?' She gave him a not-so-gentle nudge in the ribs.

'It's a surprise. You treated us to something different the other day, now it's my turn.'

'Please tell me we're not about to abseil off the Liver Building…'

'No, Essie, nothing quite as daring as that, I can assure you. Although I think I know a certain dare-devil around here who'd be game!' He returned Clarissa's dig in the ribs with the same level of vigour she'd put into his.

'Funny you should say that, Gerald, for it is on my "To-Do" list.'

'You have a "To-Do" list? Since when?'

'Since I woke up to what an asshole my father is, Mum, and realised I was missing out on all the fun stuff in life because of him. The more daring something is, the more I intend to do it!'

'I see! Well, just be careful and don't come running to me when you break both your legs bungee jumping off Tower Bridge or wherever they do these things.'

'Such a funny mummy, aren't you! Anyway, I was planning to save that for when I go off to Australia – might as well try it where it all began.'

'Australia?' Essie's voice was faint.

Clarissa put her arm around her mum's waist. 'Don't worry, mother of mine, that won't be for a couple of years yet.'

'Thank goodness for that!'

'It makes more sense to travel around Europe first and I'll probably do the States after that.' Seeing Essie's face drop further, Clarissa quickly decided to change the subject – clearly her mum wasn't yet ready to hear the next step in her plans.

'Gerald,' she turned to him with a beaming smile on her face, 'what's this surprise you have for us then?'

'It's about a fifteen-minute walk from here but I hope you enjoy it – it's not something well-known but it's certainly different.'

It took them just over ten minutes to arrive at Gerald's secret destination.

'The Williamson Tunnels Heritage Centre – what's that

when it's at home?'

Gerald gave them his shy smile again. 'Erm, tunnels built under the city of Liverpool by a bloke called Williamson. It's only a little exhibit – we'll be here an hour at the most.'

Clarissa looked at her mum and could see she wasn't too sure about this one, but then, she hadn't been at all sure about the zip-line and look how much she'd enjoyed that – eventually! 'Come on now, Mum! Remember we promised we'd try new things and have adventures – Gerald is merely joining in.' Clarissa beamed at Gerald. 'You first, lead us forth into another adventure.'

'Wow! That was so interesting, thank you for such a lovely surprise, Gerald.' Essie blinked as they came out of the Tunnel Heritage Centre into the bright sunlight of the day. She fumbled around in her handbag for her sunglasses. 'I can't believe no one knows the real reason for them being built.'

'I think the guide may have the right suggestion though, that he did it to keep his workers in employment when they may otherwise have been unemployed. I did like the story that he had them moving bricks from one place to another for no reason other than to keep them busy. I'm glad you enjoyed it.'

'I certainly did and it's made me realise I need to be more open minded to new experiences. It's all very well talking about wanting to try new things, I must work on actually doing them without reservation. Both you and Clarissa are teaching me that. Thank you, Gerald.'

'I think you were allowed to be reserved about scooting down a zip wire, Essie, that's not your run-of-the-mill new experience, is it?'

‘Perhaps not, but the fact I enjoyed it so much is proof that I need to be more gung-ho and less uptight. Mind you, twenty-odd years of living with George Walton will do that to you.’

Gerald was about to reply when Clarissa, who’d been quiet since they’d left the tunnels, suddenly said, ‘Do you think we could be walking over the top of one of those tunnels right now?’

Essie stopped in her tracks and Gerald did the same. ‘D’you know, Clarissa, I never gave it any thought but the guide did say they don’t know exactly how long the tunnels are or how many because they’re still being excavated.’ She looked down at her feet. ‘Maybe we are…’

For the rest of the walk back to the dock to catch the ferry, they all took turns in exclaiming, ‘Could this be a tunnel?’ in silly voices and pulling daft faces which created much laughter along the way.

TWENTY-FIVE

'Blackpool!'

'Bakewell!'

'Blackpool!'

'Bakewell!'

Gerald heard the raised voices as he walked towards Marvin whose windows were open, allowing the sounds inside to escape. He'd been out to collect the Chinese takeaway they'd ordered while Essie and Clarissa were supposed to be getting the table ready for them to eat.

He went to knock on the door but stopped himself just in time. Essie had told him a number of times that he didn't have to knock, he could just step inside. When he'd voiced his concern on doing that and perhaps finding either her or Clarissa in a state of undress, it had been agreed he should only knock in the mornings and at any other time, the privacy screen would be pulled across in order to spare his blushes.

He opened the door and stepped in to find Clarissa and Essie staring at each other over the small pull-down table which had been set in preparation for his arrival with the takeaway.

'Okay you two, time out. What's the face-off for?'

'We were discussing where we should head towards next. Mum wants to be all boring and go to see stately homes and stuff in the Peak District but I want to go to Blackpool and have some fun at the Pleasure Beach.'

Clarissa shuffled round to make space for him to sit down while Essie got up to pour the wine he'd also brought back.

'Clarissa, I'm more than happy to go to Blackpool but I'd like to see some of the stuff in the middle of the country first. Once we hit Blackpool, we'll almost be in the Lake District and then it'll make no sense to double-back on ourselves. This way, if we head there next, we're just going across the country.'

'Hmph!' Clarissa slumped down in the seat with a sulky face and Gerald was reminded that although she was quite grown-up and mature most of the time, she was only in her early twenties and the odd relapse into a teenage tantrum was allowed.

'I may be able to resolve this issue quite amicably,' he said, as he took the foil containers from the plastic bags and placed them on the table. The aroma was making his mouth water as he spoke. 'I agree with Essie on this because—'

'Oh, I might have known you'd take Mum's side!'

'Actually, Clarissa,' he gave her a sharp look, 'if you would permit me to finish, you'll hear why.'

'Sorry.' The apology was quiet and reluctant.

'Traditionally, the Pleasure Beach – I'm assuming you're referring to the amusements and theme park – doesn't open full-time until Easter, except when it's a late Easter in which case, it opens a few weeks before, and it gets very busy around the holiday period. My suggestion would be that we tour around the Midlands for the next couple of weeks and *then* make our way to Blackpool. By that time, the Easter holidays – which start next week in case you didn't know – will be over and the kids will have returned to school. This means two things – one,' he stuck out his thumb, 'we'll be able to get booked into a decent campsite as all the good ones will be full by now and two,' the index finger popped up, 'the queues for the rides will be shorter if we go mid-week and we won't spend most of the day standing around waiting. That's only my suggestion but I think you'll agree it makes sense.'

Essie placed the wine glasses in front of them on the table and sat down. 'How come you're so au-fait with the timings of the Pleasure Beach? Are you one of these mad roller-coaster fans who likes to travel the world going on all the big dippers etc?'

'Blimey! No, not at all!' Gerald felt the pit of his stomach drop away at the thought. He downed a quick gulp of wine and took a moment to spoon some of the egg-fried rice onto his plate. 'One of the lads I used to work with, Barry, would take his family there every Easter without fail. The whole office would be treated to the full spiel from the moment he began looking for somewhere to stay – they never went to the same hotel or B&B twice, draw your own conclusions from that – to the drama of his missus getting her holiday gear together, the kids fighting over who was sharing a room, and getting the dog into the kennels and the cat into the cattery. He'd always finish at lunchtime on the Thursday before Good Friday and I swear the office would collectively breathe a sigh of relief once he'd gone. After a few years of that, one soon learns how it all works!'

'Another good reason for giving it a miss at Easter is that you might bump into the delightful-sounding Barry and his brood and I get the feeling you'd rather avoid that.' Clarissa waved her crab claw around as she spoke.

'You'd be absolutely correct! I'm really hoping I'll never see him again and it would be sod's law that we'd meet if we were in Blackpool at the same time.'

'Fair enough, we'll go with your suggestion. It makes far more sense when you put it like that and I most certainly don't want to waste my days waiting in lines for the rides. Good call, Gerald.' She picked up her wine glass and chinked it against his.

Gerald, conscious that Essie hadn't said much, looked at her over his own glass. 'Are you okay with that suggestion, Ess?'

She gave him a glimmer of a smile. 'It sounds like a good plan to me. We can look at locations and campsites after dinner and get those sorted out.'

'Are you okay, Essie?'

Gerald was helping to clear up after dinner. He'd noticed Essie had been quiet throughout the meal and he wanted to know why. Clarissa had gone to a nearby bar with some youngsters she'd met on the campsite. This was the first time he and Essie had been properly alone together since they'd set off on their travels.

'Yeah, I'm fine.'

The tone of her voice belied her words and Gerald wasn't going to be fobbed off.

'Essie, you're not fine – don't try telling me you are – so please, what's wrong?'

'Honestly, Gerald, I'm okay. Just a bit tired after our long day out.'

Gerald hung the tea-towel on the hook to dry, gently put his hand on the small of Essie's back and guided her to the table.

'Have a seat and I'll pour us some more wine.'

When the replenished glasses were in front of them, he

sat down, took a sip and then looked Essie directly in the eye.

'Essie, I know something isn't right and I'd really like you to share it with me. Please.'

She gave him a sad look and, in that instant, a thought slammed into his head. It nearly took his breath away and it was with some trepidation that he allowed the words to come from his mouth.

'Am I the problem? Is that why you can't say? Do you want me to leave you and Clarissa alone? I can go if that's what you'd like – I don't want to encroach upon the time you're spending with your daughter.' The words tumbled from his lips at the same speed as his super-fast beating heart and he could feel a cold sweat of fear beginning to break out. The last few weeks had been idyllic and he wasn't ready to part ways with Essie once again.

'What? Oh, Gerald, no! Absolutely not! You couldn't be further from the truth.'

A hand came over the table and laid itself softly over the top of his. 'I'm not good at sharing how I feel because no one has ever asked me how I am or noticed when I'm out of sorts.'

'George—'

'—Never gave a monkeys! I don't think he's ever asked me how I feel in all the years we've been married. My role in the domestic set-up was to ensure *he* had an easy life and my purpose was solely to look, and run around, after him – making him look good and easing his way up the career ladder.'

'Surely Clarissa…'

'She's young. The young rarely think like that. They notice their friends when they're down but parents don't get the same treatment. We're not expected to have bad days – we're only ever allowed to be sunny and bright.'

'Well, I'm here now and I'm asking – what has made

you feel down this evening?'

He watched as Essie battled with her inner emotions. Several times she opened her mouth to speak and then closed it again having said nothing. It was clear she was struggling to break the seal around the part of herself that had been so tightly contained for over twenty years. Well, Gerald was in no rush and he waited patiently for her to be ready to share. He'd almost finished his wine when she finally spoke.

'I was having a wonderful day until we arrived back this evening. When you set off for the takeaway, Clarissa and I began discussing where to go next. When I didn't immediately fall in with her desire to go to Blackpool, she became really stroppy. It was almost like she'd gone from being twenty-three to thirteen. She didn't want to listen to reason and kept talking over me whenever I tried to explain. It really threw me because I thought we'd become closer of late.'

'Was she a terrible teenager?'

'No, anything but. George would never have permitted such behaviour. She was the meek, well-mannered, young lady he expected her to be. She excelled at school, never broke curfew and was the perfect child.'

'Then, if you don't mind me saying, I think she's earned the right to throw a teenage tantrum once in a while if she's never done so before. If I'm speaking out of turn – and please say if I am – but I can't help feeling that George has cowed you both all these years and Clarissa is now learning how to exert herself. You told me yourself how she's been changing since that night out. She's beginning to think for herself and we all make mistakes when we're learning something new – it's how we find out there's a right way and a wrong way.'

'I don't see it like that – it feels like my daughter has suddenly pulled away from me and there's a large, cold, void between us. Even when she went out this evening, there was still a chill between us.'

'I'm not a parent and the only experience I've had of young girls or children is second-hand through my brother-in-law, Matt, as he tried to bring up my niece on his own after my sister died. Flora was, and still can be, quite headstrong and she almost drove her poor father into the grave next to his wife on more than one occasion as she grew up. You have been spared those traumas… until now!'

'Dare I ask what diabolical things your niece got up to?'

'Probably best that you don't!'

Essie laughed at his dry reply and he felt his own mood lift at the sound. He never wanted to see her down or upset and from the sound of things, she'd had more than enough of that during her life with George.

'So, any advice on what to do about Clarissa?'

'I'd say do nothing. Let it pass and don't blow it up into a big deal. With luck, she'll realise her behaviour was out of order. If not…' he gave a small shrug, 'so be it. Move on and let it go.'

'You're a rather wise man, Gerald Wainwright, and that is a perfectly sensible suggestion.' Essie stood up, quickly bent over to kiss him on the cheek then got the remains of the wine from the fridge.

'Shall we finish off this bottle over a film and some chunky crisps?'

'Depends what film you had in mind…'

'The Life of Brian?'

A massive grin sprinted across his face as memories of their little college gang watching that film on an almost weekly basis, sprung to mind. They used to have competitions to see who could quote the most lines.

'That sounds absolutely perfect! I'm in!'

TWENTY-SIX

Clarissa stomped across the field of the campsite. She'd met some girls yesterday when she'd been getting supplies at the camp shop and they'd invited her to join them in the nearby pub this evening. She'd jumped at the opportunity because as much as she loved her mum, and was growing ever fonder of Gerald, she needed some time in the company of people her own age. She also felt really bad at being such a bitch to her mother. She didn't know where the display of temper had come from but it was a side of herself that she didn't wish to see too often. It had left her feeling quite out of sorts so she was glad to have some breathing space away from the confines of the motorhome to get her head straight.

As she passed by the campsite shop, she made a quick detour and went in. It had dawned on her that there'd been garlic in her takeaway and it might be prudent to purchase some mints.

She was standing in the queue, which was not moving at any speed thanks to the gentleman at the front changing his mind on all of his purchases, when a voice suddenly whispered in her ear, 'Och, lassie, ah widnae recommend they mints, they've got holes in them!'

She spun round to find herself face-to-face with a broad chest encased in a blue Scotland rugby shirt, the collar open and a light dusting of reddish-gold hair peeping around the buttons. She lifted her gaze and met a pair of dark-blue eyes smiling down at her. Above them sat a pair of thick, but defined, eyebrows in the same reddish-gold hue as the chest hair she'd first spotted and an unruly mop flowed around a face that while not overly handsome, was most certainly interesting. The nose looked like it may have fallen foul of a tackle or two on the rugby pitch, the cheeks were a little too rounded and the lips were just a touch too full. But the smile which sat upon those lips… Oh boy! It was the most beautiful smile Clarissa thought she'd ever seen on a man. It was open and friendly but at the same time, hot, sexy and lustful. The small gap in his front teeth made her think of a little boy full of cheeky mischief. She'd bet her last pair of knickers that that smile had gotten this man into bother more than once. She gulped down a mouthful of air, realising that she felt quite breathless, and replied, 'Hmm, is that so? Maybe I should ask for a discount then, seeing as they're damaged goods.'

'Ye could try, but ah dinnae fancy yer chances. Yer man there looks a right tight sort.'

The soft Scottish accent was light and musical and not the deep, throaty roar you'd expect from someone who looked to be about six foot six across the chest and eight foot high!

'You could be right there. I think I'll do my good deed for the day and take them off his hands without comment. It would be wrong to leave them behind – even damaged goods are worthy of love and attention.'

'You're a right wee good Samaritan. That's a very generous thing to do. There's a place reserved in heaven for good people like you.'

'Thank you for your praise, kind sir. I hope my mints agree with you.'

'Well, they do have holes in them and we don't know how they got there. Maybe they have a dark, sordid past and used to run in a gang. They may have gotten the holes from a drive-by shooting. You get Allsorts on the sweetie counter you know.'

'That's a bit of a heavy assertion to be making. I'd like to think they were a lot more Smarties than that.'

'Next!'

Clarissa turned away to be served and, glancing over her shoulder as she walked out the door, gave the witty, handsome stranger a farewell smile.

She was walking slowly along the path, putting her purse back in her handbag, when she heard a shout behind her.

'Excuse me…'

She turned to see the man from the shop walking towards her. With those big, long legs, it only took a few steps to bring him to her side.

'Look, please feel free to tell me to sod off but I was wondering if you'd like to go for a drink? There's a very nice pub just across the way.'

'That's actually where I'm headed. I was just taking my mints there for a consolatory drink. I think they deserve one after being so maligned by your good self.'

'Then perhaps I should buy your mints a drink instead…'

'Clarissa Walton.' She held out her hand.

'Ross MacKenzie.' Her hand disappeared inside his but the finger-cruncher she'd been expecting did not come. Instead, her hand received a nice firm shake and it tingled lightly when Ross let it go.

By this time, they'd reached the pub and Ross opened

the door, stepping to one side to let her enter first.

'I'm afraid I'm actually meeting some people here,' she told him wistfully. This was one of those occasions where she deeply loathed the good manners she'd been brought up with. What she really wanted to do was find the darkest corner of the pub and kiss this man until the Statue of Liberty sat on her ass!

'As am I, but I can still buy you a drink if only to say sorry for hitting you with my inane banter back there in the shop.'

Just then, she spotted the girls from the campsite on the other side of the bar. She waved at them and they waved back. The two men they were standing with also waved. Their friendliness made her feel even worse for wanting to ditch them for this stranger by her side.

'Thank you for the offer but I enjoyed the banter so there's no need to apologise.' She nodded her head in the direction of the other girls. 'My friends are waiting.'

With a smile, she turned and pushed her way through to the back of the bar. When she reached Fliss and Becky, she was surprised to find Ross still behind her. Before she could say anything, the bloke standing beside Fliss called out, 'Hey, Ross, me old cobber. You made it! I was beginning to think you'd gone off walkabout!'

Clarissa looked from Fliss, to the man by her side, then to Ross and back to Fliss again.

'You all know each other?'

'Well, kinda.' Fliss grinned. 'We picked this reprobate up just outside London. He was hitchhiking and it seemed a nice thing to do. He was wearing his kilt, how could we not?'

'Oh!' She didn't know what else she could say to that.

Ross stepped in to explain. 'One of my best mates owns a motorcycle shop in Blackpool. He came off his own bike a couple of weeks ago and broke his leg. His cousin is currently helping him in the shop but he has to return to his own job next week. I said I'd help out until he's back on his feet. Quite literally!'

'I see. Is there any reason why you didn't just get a bus or a train there? Or even drive up?'

'Let me get some drinks in and I'll explain.' Ross took the orders and Fliss introduced her to her and Becky's boyfriends while he was away.

When he returned and everyone had taken their glasses, Ross carried on talking as though there had been no interruption.

'To answer your question, I couldn't drive as I part-own the car with my brother and he needs it for work.'

'What does he do?'

'He's a GP and needs it for callouts and emergencies.'

'Fair enough, but hitchhiking? Isn't that dangerous?'

Ross looked at her, pointed his finger to his chest, and said, 'Seriously? Do you think anyone's gonna mess with this?'

Clarissa realised how daft her comment was and laughed. 'When you put it like that, I suppose not. But why hitchhiking?'

'I enjoy it. I've been doing it since I was a student and I've met some amazing people over the years. Yeah, there's been a few assholes too – some lorry drivers can be right twats – but most folks are kind and genuine. I like the fact that, for a few hours, I get to share the lives of people I would never otherwise meet. It's actually how I met Karl. He gave me a lift on the back of his bike – he had a spare helmet which just about fitted me – and we ended up hanging out for the best part of a month. We've been best buds ever since.'

'I see. I have to be honest, it's not really something I think I'll ever try.'

'What? Hitchhiking or riding a motorbike?'

'Well, I haven't done either so far but I think I'll definitely give the hitchhiking a miss. A ride on a motorbike? I think I'd be prepared to give that a go.'

'I'd say that was a good choice. It's quite thrilling – as long as you're with someone who's experienced and treats the bike with respect.'

'I'll keep that in mind should the opportunity ever come up. So, how long do you think you'll be in Blackpool for?'

'Probably a couple of months, I expect. Karl reckons he'll be in plaster for roughly eight weeks and it'll be another few weeks after it comes off before he can move around freely again. Thankfully, it wasn't a complicated break so it should be pretty straightforward.'

'And what will you do after that? Go back to work?' Clarissa was curious as to what he did and how he'd been able to get so much time off to help his friend.

'Not for a few months. I'm a structural engineer and I've recently finished a contract. My next job is overseas but doesn't begin until October so I was planning to head home and help out on the farm over the summer, get in the harvest and then go off after that. I haven't been home properly for a few years so I know my mum will be a happy bunny to have me there. I'm the youngest so I always get spoiled rotten when I go back.'

'How many siblings do you have?'

'Two brothers. Fraser's the eldest and he works the farm with my dad. Kenneth – he hates being called Ken or Kenny, which is great fun when we want to wind him up – is the doctor and we share a flat just outside London. What about you? Any brothers or sisters?'

'No, I'm an only child. It would have been nice to have had a sister but given the circumstances, that was never going to happen.'

'Oh! Bad childhood?'

Clarissa hesitated before replying. 'Let's just say

“different” and leave it there.’

‘Sure thing. So, now you know just about all there is to know about me, tell me something about you. What’s a nice girl like you doing in a gin-joint like this?’

‘Hanging out with people I’d never usually otherwise meet?’

Ross grinned at her words and she felt that tug in her stomach again. Dear goodness, that bloody smile…

‘Nice reply!’

‘Cheers! The simplest answer is that I’ve taken time out to do some travelling with my mum and her friend.’

‘Time out from what?’

‘Being a trainee solicitor. I’m currently an articled clerk at a law firm in Oxford.’

‘I see. Don’t articled clerks get worked into the ground and have to submit holiday requests in blood upon parchments made from their own skin?’

‘Usually but when your father owns the company and you have a HUGE falling out with him and need some time away…’

‘Gotcha! So, where have you been so far and where are you going next?’

‘Let me get my round in, and we should maybe talk to the others for a bit as we’ve done a good job of ignoring them since we arrived. We can talk more again later.’

‘Okay, pretty Clarissa, I’ll hold you to that.’

She took the drinks order and made her way to the bar. While she waited to be served, she used the time to clear her head. As she’d been talking to Ross, she’d felt herself becoming light-headed, almost as though she was falling under his spell, and she needed to put some space between them for a few moments. She’d never met anyone as mesmerising as he was and it felt nice but strange. The more they talked, the more she wanted to know about him. She hadn’t really had any boyfriends as a teenager –

another symptom of her father's controlling nature – and Tristan was the only man she had been in a serious relationship with. Her experience was limited but she was quite sure that what she was feeling now was rare. When the barman eventually took her order, she changed her own drink from a vodka and lemonade to just lemonade – all things considered, it might be best to give alcohol a miss for the rest of the night.

TWENTY-SEVEN

Essie was in bed, reading her book, when she heard a giggle and whispering outside the van. She'd taken Gerald's wise words on board and wasn't going to make any mention to Clarissa of her earlier behaviour but that didn't prevent her stomach from knotting up as she wondered how her daughter would be when she returned. She didn't have long to wait – the door opened a few minutes later and she heard Clarissa closing it carefully behind her so as not to make a noise. The dividing screen was pulled across at the end of the bunk so she couldn't see Clarissa to gauge her current mood.

Just then, a soft whisper carried up to her. 'Mum, are you awake?'

'Yes, darling, I am.'

The screen was moved aside and Clarissa came to perch beside her. 'Mum, I'm so sorry for being a bitch earlier. I don't know what brought it on or why I got the hump over something so petty.'

Essie breathed an inner sigh of relief. Everything was okay again. She reached down and patted Clarissa's hand.

'Hey, don't worry about it. We all have off days. You were probably just tired after our long day out.'

'Maybe…'

'Anyway, did you have a nice evening?'

'Oh, yes! It was wonderful.'

'Really? Want to tell me more?' The immediate brightening of Clarissa's face had not gone unnoticed and Essie was curious to know what could have turned an ordinary evening down the pub into something much greater.

She didn't have to wait too long to find out the something "much greater" was called Ross, he was Scottish and had a great sense of humour. The girls Clarissa had set out to meet got a brief mention but it appeared that "Ross" had received the bulk of her attention. The whole story of how they met was shared and also all the information Clarissa had gathered after that.

'Inside leg measurements?'

'Sorry?'

'I was asking what his inside leg measurements are. I think it's the only thing about him that you haven't told me.'

Essie grinned as Clarissa's face went bright scarlet.

'Oh, Mum!'

'I'm teasing you, darling. It's great that you've met someone nice although at the risk of sounding like an old fuddy-duddy, the timing could have been better. Travelling around the country is not the best beginning for a new relationship.'

'Who said anything about a relationship?'

'Your face did. This Ross is not someone you "just met in the pub" – there's more to it than that, I can tell.'

Clarissa let out a sigh. 'You're right, Mum, there is more. I've never met anyone who made me feel the way he did tonight. I can't quite put a finger on it but it was like an instant attraction. I don't know if he felt the same way about me though.'

'He told you he's heading to Blackpool and we'll be there ourselves in a few weeks. Does he know that?'

'Yes, he does. He gave me his phone number and made me promise to call him as soon as we arrive.'

'Well, I'd say that sounds very positive. I'll bet you're wishing even more that we were going there tomorrow.'

Clarissa didn't reply straight away but when she did, Essie was both surprised and relieved at her answer.

'Actually, Mum, I think I'm glad that we're not. My feelings were so intense tonight that I'd like some time to sort of… well, come to terms with them, I suppose. The purpose of this trip is for us to bond together – despite my teenage tantrums – but also for us both to work out what we want from our lives going forward. That's my priority right now and a relationship isn't really on the agenda. We'll see what happens when we get to Blackpool. Now, I'm going to bid you goodnight and get myself to bed – we're shipping out early tomorrow.'

'Okay, darling. Goodnight, sleep well.'

'And you, Mum.'

'Oh, Clarissa, one last thing, maybe a wee apology to Gerald when you next see him, for tonight…?'

'Of course. Absolutely. Love you.'

'Love you too, gorgeous girl. See you in the morning.'

Clarissa closed the screen behind her and, as she switched off her little overhead bed-light, Essie grinned in the darkness. Everything was going to be just fine, as Gerald had said it would be. Thinking of Gerald made her smile even more. The feelings she'd once held for him, all those years ago, were beginning to resurface and while they may not be appropriate, it made her feel good to know she was still capable of loving.

The next three weeks passed in a whirl of day trips all over the middle of England. They found a campsite near Alfreton in Derbyshire and its location was a great central point which gave easy access to almost everywhere they wanted to visit. They began with Lichfield, taking in the beautiful three spires of its cathedral and enthusing over the items held within from the Staffordshire Hoard – the amazing find of Anglo-Saxon gold and silverware, currently believed to be the largest ever discovered. They stopped off at the National Arboretum on the way back and paid their respects to all those who'd fought in the wars while defending their country with Gerald sharing a few of the memories his grandfather had passed on about his time in the military. There were photographs taken with Robin Hood when they visited Nottingham and curses when the walk back *up* Steep Hill in Lincoln was considerably more painful than the walk down – 'Clarissa, if we ever do this again, YOU can bloody walk, but I'll be taking the bus!'

Essie, however, had fallen quite in love with Lincoln, the upwards climb of Steep Hill aside, and had relished poking about in the myriad antique shops which filled the streets around the castle. She also fell deeply "in like" with Chatsworth House and sent Sukie a photograph with the caption, **"Someone has a bigger pile than you, dearie..."** to which there was a quick reply – **"Think of all the hoovering..."**

They cycled along the Manifold Trail, just outside Leek, and soothed their aching coccyx by drinking wine from the vineyard near Bakewell. The same visit also saw them try a proper, traditional Bakewell pudding, which was declared to be much tastier than the smaller iced tart they were more used to.

By the time they were making their way towards

Blackpool, Essie was looking forward to having a few easy days in one place. She needed some chilling out time and Gerald agreed. Once they parked up, there'd be no more driving that week. They could get buses into the centre of Blackpool and there were some lovely nature walks not far from the campsite.

When they arrived at the campsite, they were, however, disappointed not to have two pitches next to each other. Gerald wasn't too far away, only one row behind and a few pitches along, but they'd become used to sharing their spaces and putting items in whichever van was closest at the time.

'It's not a great hardship,' Gerald commented. 'I usually come to you, it just means I'll need to walk a little further.'

'Are you sure you're okay with that? I can always ask if we can be moved.'

'Essie, look around you – the place is rammed. We were lucky to get the pitches we have. Just leave it, we'll manage.'

'Okay, if you're sure…'

'I'm sure. Now let's get set up, then we can make our way into the town. I'm gasping for a beer and some nice, fresh, fish and chips.'

'In that order?'

Gerald smiled.

'Preferably together!'

TWENTY-EIGHT

Clarissa was happy to have finally reached Blackpool and to be seeing Ross again. They'd kept in touch via text and FaceTime and she was now desperate to be in his company. She hadn't shared with her mum that they'd kissed when he'd walked her back to the van after the pub – some things you just don't tell your parents! – and she hadn't known until that night that it really was possible to melt when someone placed their lips upon yours. She'd always put that expression down to being romantic baloney, but not anymore. When Ross had placed his soft, gentle kiss on her lips, every nerve ending had gone zinging off in a different direction and her knees had barely managed not to buckle beneath her.

She looked at the map on her phone. Ross had told her to meet him at the entrance to Central Pier on the shore front as he reckoned it was probably one of the easiest places to find and hardest to miss. She looked up and seeing it in the distance, agreed with him on that point. She'd caught the bus into town with her mum and Gerald but had declined to dine with them; she suspected Ross would most likely want to go for a meal since he was meeting her straight from work. Or, from helping out his friend, if she was being precise.

From the calls they'd had, it sounded like he was really enjoying himself. He'd never worked in retail before and he was finding it most enjoyable, especially interacting with the customers. He'd told her that he only ever met the clients he was building structures for or the workmen actually doing the building. He rarely, if ever, met the staff who'd be working inside the buildings, the residents in the apartment blocks or the customers who stayed in the hotels.

The front of the pier was busy when she reached it and the smell of hot doughnuts wafting on the air made her stomach rumble. She was starving. She looked around for Ross but couldn't see him and when she checked her phone, she saw she was a few minutes early. She strolled over to stand by the balustrade and look out over the sea. The wind blew through her hair and she was glad she'd decided to leave it loose otherwise it would have been a windswept mess by now. This way, she only needed to run a brush through it to tidy it up. Her stomach growled again, this time more loudly, and she began to wonder if there was time to sneak in one little doughnut before Ross arrived. Not wanting to be embarrassed by her body making obscene noises, she made her way to the stall and joined the small queue. She watched the machinery making the doughnuts and found it quite soothing. She was so engrossed in the simple process that she almost jumped out of her skin when a soft, Scottish burr murmured in her ear, 'You don't want to buy those, they've got holes in them!'

She burst out laughing, whirled around and surprised herself by throwing her arms around Ross and giving him the biggest of hugs. Ross was quick to return the favour by lifting her up in his arms and spinning her around.

‘Hey, gorgeous lady, what’s a nice girl like you doing hanging around in a place like this?’

‘Are those the only two lines you have to offer?’ she chortled, as he placed her back on the ground, although he didn’t release his hold.

‘I confess, my repertoire is limited but it has worked up till now.’

‘Oh, tried it on a number of ladies, have you?’ Clarissa forced her voice to be light and carefree but inside, a sharp pang of jealousy had just head-butted her in the solar plexus. What was it about this man, she thought, that kept bringing about all these new emotions that she’d never had to deal with before? Whenever she’d been out with Tristan, and other women had made a play for him, she hadn’t been at all bothered and had even once told a rather drunken spectacle that she was welcome to him. Clearly, he’d annoyed her that night. Okay, he’d annoyed her more than usual for she’d come to realise that Tristan had annoyed her most of the time. This realisation had come about after another FaceTime with Ross had ended and she was missing him. She’d never missed Tristan and on the few occasions where they’d FaceTimed, she’d been glad to hang up and get back to whatever he’d interrupted.

‘Absolutely not. I kept my best lines for you. I wasn’t wasting them on just anybody, you know.’

‘They’re your *best* lines? I am *so* glad I wasn’t around to hear the worst ones…’

‘The cheek of it! And there was me about to treat you to a hot, albeit damaged and holey, doughnut…’

‘Okay, I’m sorry. Please, let me have a damaged doughnut.’

‘I’m really not sure—’

Just then, Clarissa’s stomach let out the loudest of rumbles. Ross looked down and looked back up at her reddening face.

'Was that you?'

'Yes, I'm starving and the smell of the hot dough and sugar is sending me bonkers.'

Ross turned to the girl on the stall, who'd been waiting patiently for them to sort themselves out, and asked for three doughnuts.

'Three?'

'Yes, one won't be enough and two each is too many. We'll split one between us and that'll be just right until we go for dinner.'

'I don't want to be pedantic here but you haven't actually *asked* me if I'd like to join you for dinner.'

Ross was putting his wallet away in his pocket as she said this. He looked up in surprise.

'Yes, I have. Haven't I? I must have done…'

She took the warm doughnut he was holding out to her and took a bite. Ohhhhhhh… that tasted so good. Her mouth full, she shook her head in reply to his question.

'Nope,' she muffled through her teeth.

'I am so sorry. How rude of me, Clarissa, I would never normally make such an assumption.'

She swallowed and resisted the urge to take another bite before answering. Ross hadn't even begun to eat his yet and she didn't want to look like the doughnut equivalent of the Cookie Monster.

'It's okay.'

'No, it's not. It was rude. Please, would you like to join me for dinner tonight?'

Her stomach growled again – one bite of doughnut was not enough to quieten its voice.

Amidst their joint laughter, she accepted the invitation.

'Great. I've found a fabulous, little Italian restaurant not far from here but it doesn't open until seven, so do you fancy a wee stroll along the pier to kill some time?'

'I fancy that very much.' And you, her inner voice

screamed, but she was careful not to let that one slip out.

'Oh, my goodness, my trousers feel fit to burst!'

Essie sat back and placed the dessert spoon on the side of her plate.

'I did warn you that a large cod and chips might be too much, especially given how you were drooling over the desserts menu.'

'But I was starving! I couldn't help myself.'

'Then maybe you should've passed on the dessert?' Gerald was teasing her – he'd learnt she still had the sweet tooth from her younger days although he could tell from her slender frame that she rarely indulged it.

'What? Pass up on apple crumble with custard? Not a chance, my son! Not! A! Chance!'

She gave a small laugh and he watched as her finger ran around the edge of the bowl, scooping up a couple of small droplets of the bright yellow sauce.

'Well, tell you what – why don't we take a walk along the front and burn off some of the million calories we've just consumed?'

'That sounds good to me.'

Gerald paid the bill and helped Essie put her coat on. They might now be in April but the sea air was still fresh and nippy, so they'd both wrapped up warmly when they came out.

They crossed over the road to the promenade and stopped to watch a tram coming towards them.

'They're quite wonderful. I know trams are coming back in some of our bigger cities but they don't quite match the ones you get here in Blackpool. These are so old and romantic.' Essie gave the old vehicle a wistful look.

'We can get one back down, if you like, on our return

trip.'

'That sounds lovely.'

He hadn't brought any gloves so Gerald stuck his hands in his jacket pocket. A moment later, he felt Essie's hand slip into the crook of his arm. He didn't say anything, just gave her a smile and squeezed it against his side. She smiled back at his action and for a time, they walked in companionable silence along the seafront, enjoying the view, the fresh air and the quieter hustle of the thinned-out crowds. Blackpool after seven p.m. and outside of school holidays was a nice place to be.

They'd not long passed the pier where Clarissa had met Ross earlier, when Essie spoke.

'Did you sort things out with your solicitor?'

'Yes, it's all good. They're going to courier the paperwork over from their Preston office tomorrow.'

That morning, just before they'd left Derbyshire, Gerald had received a call from his solicitors advising him that the decree nisi for his divorce had come through and needed signing. When he'd advised them of his whereabouts, they'd suggested sending the papers by courier if the campsite were happy to sign for the package. He'd called back ten minutes later to say there would be no problem with that and to send them up.

'How do you feel, now that's it's almost over?'

Gerald thought for a moment before replying.

'A little bit sad but mostly I'm relieved. I think I'm sad at being a divorcee rather than from breaking up with Marjory. Being detached from her is a big relief.'

'I'm surprised you ended up with someone like her, Gerald, you could have had the pick of the girls back in uni.'

'Life happened and I lost what little confidence I had back then. When Marjory showed an interest, I was flattered and fell for it.'

'Little confidence? Gerald, you were oozing confidence from every pore when we were at uni.'

'It was false bravado. Inside, I was always terrified.'

'Then you hid it well. That's why all the girls found you so attractive and fell at your feet.'

'Not *all* of them.'

'What do you mean?'

'There was one girl who didn't throw herself at my feet. I fancied her way above all the others but she never showed any interest. Well, not in that way.'

'You're kidding me? How come we didn't know? You never told us about her.'

'I didn't want you all teasing me. You guys had decided I was some kind of lothario and it was easier to let you carry on thinking that. That way, I could continue to love from afar with no risk of being forced into showing my hand and having my heart broken.'

'Aw, Gerald, you were in love – that's far deeper than "fancying" someone…'

'I know.'

'Did you ever do anything to let her know she was important to you?'

He didn't answer straight away. This was it – make or break time. He could tell Essie the few words that might make her realise she'd been the girl of his dreams or he could tell a little white lie and let it pass by. Before he could decide, however, Essie spoke again.

'You did, didn't you? I can tell from your face. Did I know her? Who was she? What did you do?'

He chose to ignore the first two questions and answered the last one instead.

'I sent her a Valentine's card.'

'And?'

'She went off with someone else.'

Essie stopped walking, withdrew her hand and turned

to look at him.

'She never did! Oh, Gerald, how cruel.'

'It wasn't. I suspect she didn't know the card was from me. There was never anything in her behaviour to suggest that she did.'

'Then you must have been close for you to notice that.'

'Close enough…'

Essie peered at him and he tried to keep his expression as neutral as possible.

'What was the card like? Was it a feeble little number that she was possibly less than impressed with and so made no effort to find out who it was from? You should have said, I would have helped you to choose one.'

Here goes nothing, thought Gerald. 'No, it was a good card. One of those padded ones you used to get in a box. It had a black kitten on the front, with a big floppy yellow bow—'

'—holding out a red rose?' Essie's mouth dropped open.

'Yes, that's the one. You remember?'

'Too right I remember the card, it's the same one George sent to me.'

'Did he?'

'Did he what?'

'Send you that card?'

'Of course, he did. He put his initials inside – G.W. for George Walton.'

'Or Gerald Wainwright…' he said quietly.

Essie's mouth opened and closed a few times before she was able to speak.

'YOU sent it? But… when I thanked George…'

'He happily took the credit because he'd been trying to get your attention for ages.'

'That was the night we began going out together.'

Essie walked over to a nearby stone bench and sat

down. Gerald gently lowered himself down beside her.

'Are you okay?'

'No, not really. I've just found out that my controlling, manipulative bastard of a husband is a lying shite-bag and has subjected me to the best part of twenty-five years of misery over a fucking lie!'

'I'm sorry, I shouldn't have said anything—'

'Yes, you should have! Twenty-five years ago! Why did you let me think it was him? Why didn't you tell me the truth?'

'You seemed to be happy and I didn't want it to appear like sour grapes by telling you the truth. Anyway, do you think you would have listened? The fact that you thought the card came from George and not me is telling in its own way. You didn't think of me like that and so it was best not to rock the boat.'

'Oh, Gerald, you bloody fool! I cared about you and desperately wanted to be your girlfriend but you never gave any hint that my feelings were reciprocated. All these gorgeous, beautiful girls were hanging around you like bees round a honey pot and I didn't believe I could compete with them. When I got that card, my first thought *was* of you but I immediately dismissed the idea as being fanciful. George, in my mind, was the most obvious sender. He never denied it so I had no reason to think otherwise.'

'The opportunity he wanted fell in his lap and he ran away with it.'

'And broke two hearts into the bargain.'

Gerald stared out at the sea for a time. Essie sat quietly beside him, most likely trying to take on board what she'd learnt, just as he was trying to come to terms with the fact that she'd felt the same way about him back then. The next question was how did they feel about each other now?

'There's a pub over there, Gerald, fancy getting a

drink? I could do with one right now.'

'Me too.'

They stood up and, as they waited for the traffic to clear so they could cross the road, Gerald decided the answer to the next question would have to wait for now.

TWENTY-NINE

'Gerald, are you okay? You're as white as a sheet.'

'Yeah, Gerald, you look like you're about to throw up.'

'I'm fine, honest.'

Gerald hoped he sounded convincing because the truth was, he was absolutely shitting himself. The four of them – Ross had met up with them today as the shop closed on Wednesday and Thursday – had finally arrived at the Pleasure Beach theme park. Clarissa was in her dare-devil element and had been trying out every ride. Essie, taking courage from the zip-wire event, wasn't too far behind. They'd been Steeplechasing, Tobogganing, Grand Nationaling and Big Dippering. They'd caught their breath in The Tunnel of Love (a bit embarrassing when he and Essie had been in the same little boat together) and had laughed at the exceptionally un-scary Ghost Train.

Despite his intense dislike of heights, Gerald had been able to cope with just about every ride he'd been dragged onto. Even the Revolution had been conquered. This, however, was the final hurdle and he felt more like hurling than hurdling. They were waiting in the queue for The Big

One. Standing at a height of 235 feet and reaching speeds of up to 85 miles per hour – yes, he'd made the mistake of looking it up – this was the tallest rollercoaster in the UK and he was about to get on it. Did he feel sick? You bet he did!

The train rolled into the boarding bay and the next batch of victims got on. The queue moved along again and he looked at the smiling, expectant, faces all securely tucked into their little carriages. What was wrong with these people? How on earth could something like this be enjoyable to them? It was a modern form of torture!

'Gerald, are you sure you're okay? It's just… you're looking a little green around the gills, as the saying goes.'

He turned to Essie who was looking at him with concern. Ross and Clarissa were behind her, worried expressions on both their faces. He hated that he was worrying them like this so decided to come clean.

'I dislike heights. They make me feel quite ill.'

'WHAT?' Three voices came back at him in unison.

'But, Gerald, you've been on all the tall rides today,' said Essie.

'You did the zip-wire in Wales,' Clarissa responded incredulously.

'Man, why have you no said anything?' Ross's accent broadened with his disbelief.

'I didn't want to spoil anyone's fun by being a boring old man. The rest have been bearable but this…' He pointed upwards, flinching as the screams from the ride came floating back towards where they were standing. 'This is something else and it's taking every ounce of willpower I have not to walk out.'

'But, Gerald, if you really don't want to do it, it's not a problem. Please don't feel forced into it.' Essie looked at him with gentle eyes and spoke softly, no hint of recrimination in her voice.

'I *have* to do it!'

'No, Gerald, you don't.' This time it was Clarissa reassuring him.

'Yes, I do. My old man's done it twice and I'll never hear the end of it if I bottle it!'

'Your dad has been on The Big One?'

'Yes, Essie,' he sighed, 'my arthritic father has done this twice. Some friends of his, Sadie and Bernice, organised a trip to Blackpool for the old folks in the retirement village where they live. Apparently, he dosed himself up on painkillers and tried every-bloody-thing going. Said he'd had the best day out for as long as he could remember. He went on about this particular ride for months afterwards. He's determined to come back and do it again before he curls up his toes. I'll never hear the end of it if I don't give it a go.'

'I don't recall you having a problem with heights when we were at uni.'

'I didn't then, it's grown over the years. Maybe it's an age-awareness thing, I dunno.' He gave a small shrug.

The track below them began to crackle and vibrate. The train was coming back in for the next load of thrill-seekers and this time, he was going to be sitting amongst them.

'You'll be fine, Gerald. Hold my hand as we go round. I'm going to be right beside you. You can do this – I know you can.'

Essie gave his hand a quick squeeze before letting go to get into the little carriage. Ross and Clarissa got in the one in front. He was tightening the slip cord on his glasses when Clarissa turned around.

'Gerald, the good news is that, if you throw up, it'll go on the people behind you!'

'Oh, Clarissa!'

Essie took his hand again while Ross and Clarissa bumped shoulders as they laughed at her comment.

The attendant came along and checked the bar was down firmly across the front of them. Gerald could feel the sweat beginning to break out on his forehead and his hands became clammy. He tried to pull his hand out of Essie's but she held firm. The train moved off, rolled out of the boarding area, round the bend and then began its slow, steady crawl up to the peak, where it would then fall almost to the ground at breakneck speed.

'Gerald, here's a little tip for you, to make the drop less traumatic. Tighten your middle as though you were pulling your stomach right in while being desperate for a pee. It prevents that lurching, sickening sensation as we drop down. It might help.'

'Thanks, Essie.'

He did as she suggested and got it all together just as they went over the summit. The ground came flying towards him and they twisted away and up again before he knew what was happening. The ride flowed and twisted, turned and fell and ran around half of the park but none of it was as bad as those initial few seconds. In fact, he was just beginning to enjoy it when it pulled back into the station and he had to get off. Ross helped him out as his legs felt like jelly and his hands were shaking. No one said a word until they'd gone through the exit barrier and sat themselves down on a couple of nearby benches.

'How are you feeling?'

Gerald looked at Essie's hand sitting lightly on his arm as she asked the question. He took a moment to reply.

'Surprisingly well, as it happens. In fact, pretty damn good.' He began to laugh. It was a soft chuckle at first but rapidly grew into a full-on belly laugh.

'That'll be the relief coming out.' Ross gave him a smile and a pat on the shoulder.

'D'you know, Ross, I think it's actually the realisation of what an idiot I've been. As Essie said, I didn't used to have a problem with heights when I was young so why now? I've become a scared, boring, dull, unadventurous middle-aged man who doesn't know how to have fun.'

'Oh, Gerald, that's a bit harsh!'

'No, Essie, it's not. It's the truth. I thought I was being adventurous by going on this trip but I've not really changed inside at all – I'm still boring. Well, that ends right here, right now! It's time I really began to live again.'

He stood up, pulled his knitted tank-top down with a sharp tug, smoothed his hair to the side and straightened his glasses.

'Right! I'm going back on that thing and, this time, I'm sitting at the front! Who's coming with me?'

Not giving the others a chance to reply, Gerald hot-footed it over to the barrier and made his way back into the queue. His dad had done this ride twice? Well, sod you, Dad, he thought, he was about to do it three times!

At least!

THIRTY

Essie looked at Gerald sitting across the table from her. Ross had recommended a nice, secluded Chinese restaurant away from the usual tourist haunts and, therefore, usually only frequented by the local population. This meant their meal would not be disturbed by raucous hen or stag parties.

As she sipped her wine, Essie tried to put a description on Gerald's current demeanour. Was it possible for men to glow? Women glowed – apparently – but could the same be said of men? She wasn't sure but it would be a perfectly apt description at this time. His face was shining and happiness seemed to be spilling out of his every pore. She would swear that, as he'd walked through the door in front of her earlier, he'd actually been bouncing! Just then, Ross made a silly joke and instead of his usual quiet chortle, Gerald let out a loud, infectious cough of mirth. It was a sound Essie hadn't heard for an incredibly long time. Not since she'd been at uni and not since she'd met George and left Gerald, unknowingly heartbroken, behind.

She thought back to the revelations of two nights ago.

When they'd sunk a few brandies, while trying to come to terms with the words that had been spoken, they'd caught a taxi back to the campsite, sitting in silence for the whole fifteen-minute journey. Gerald had walked her to Marvin's door and before she could speak, he said, 'If it's alright with you, I'm going to have a time-out day tomorrow. Vanda needs a good clean and I could do with giving her a check-up to ensure all her working bits are in order.'

She'd managed to keep the sigh of relief to herself – she also needed some space to get her thinking straight. 'Actually, that suits me perfectly. I could do with giving Marvin a good going-over too. Shall we meet here for breakfast on Wednesday morning?'

Gerald agreed and waited until she was inside the camper before bidding her goodnight. There had been something unreadable in his eyes and she didn't know what he was thinking when he walked away. She'd watched his retreating back from the window and felt the tears finally begin to slip from her eyes, just a few to begin with but it didn't take long before they were pouring furiously over her cheeks. She wasn't quite sure what she was crying over – was it anger from knowing George had cheated her with his lies or was it heartbreak for the life she may have otherwise had – a life of happiness with the boy she'd loved then and the man she suspected she might still love now. Of course, there was no guarantee that, had she and Gerald got together, they'd have lived a life of blissful marital joy, but it was a choice she'd been robbed of making because George always got what George wanted – even if it meant lying to get it. And he'd wanted her!

She was in bed by the time Clarissa arrived home and when the whisper came, asking if she was asleep, Essie had pretended that she was. She was in no doubt that if Clarissa had come in to talk to her that night, she'd have told her the whole story because she hadn't yet had time to put her "game face" on. She would tell Clarissa everything eventually but she needed some time to come to terms with it herself. She was beginning to wonder how much more about George there was to find out and more to the point, just how much more damage had he inflicted.

'Mum, are you ready to order yet? You've been staring at the menu for ages.'

'Whoops, sorry!' Clarissa's voice brought her back to the here and now. 'I think I'll have the special house fried rice please with a side order of sweet and sour sauce, thank you.'

The waiter wrote down the details, retrieved the menus and left with a smile.

'So, Ross, where in Scotland do you come from?' Essie smiled as she made the effort to get to know more about the pleasant young man Clarissa had introduced them to earlier in the day. She'd ascertained he had good manners while they'd been physically throwing themselves all over the theme park, and he'd been most attentive with Clarissa without being in any way patronising. Given how George had behaved towards her, Essie was keeping an eagle eye out for history repeating itself but so far, everything was looking good. Mind you, it was early days yet and who knew what might come next.

'I'm from near Inverness. My parents own a dairy farm up that way.'

'Oh, does that mean you Dairy Milk then?' Clarissa giggled.

'I've been known to give it a wee Twirl,' Ross replied.

'Do you Wispa in the cows' ears to keep them calm?'

'Don't be so daft, that would be a very Flakey thing to do!'

'Ah, only the Fruit and Nuts do that, do they?'

By this time, both Ross and Clarissa were in fits of laughter – Clarissa being especially un-ladylike as she snorted like a pig while trying to restrain herself.

Essie looked at Gerald and couldn't hold back her own smile as he gazed upon the youngsters in complete surprise.

'Is this a private joke or can anyone join in?' he said in a dry tone. 'Just tell me the Topic and I'll Snicker with laughter right alongside you!'

His comment set Ross and Clarissa off again and it dawned on Essie what the gist of the joke was.

'You lot are Whole Nuts, you really are, and if I didn't have a serious dose of the Munchies, I'd be back at the van, Lion Bar down.'

'Mum, you are classic!'

'Thank you, Clarissa, although I do believe that is a biscuit! Now I think it's time we all calmed down or we'll be kicked out for making too much noise.'

'Sorry, Mrs Walton. It's my fault, I started this.'

'Not tonight, you didn't, Ross, and please, call me Essie.'

'I do need to take some blame, though.'

'I'll let it go but I do have one question… when the cows are all lined up waiting to be done, is it known as the Milky Bar?'

The laughter that ensued caused the waiters to look sharply in their direction but Essie didn't care. Silly, happy laughter was exactly what her poor, misshapen little soul needed right now and, looking at Gerald, she suspected he did too as he joined Ross and Clarissa in wiping away the tears from their eyes.

Once they'd had their fill of rice, crackers and noodles, Gerald returned to Ross's earlier comment on where his family lived.

‘Ross, when you say you live near Inverness, how near is “near”?’

‘About fifteen miles south, although it depends on the weather and which road you take.’

‘Do you know a place called Forres? It’s east of Inverness by roughly twenty miles?’

‘Aye, I know it.’

‘My family, on my mother’s, side are originally from there although she doesn’t live there now.’

‘Is she still in Scotland?’

‘Yes, she has a smallholding south-east of Forres, somewhere between Dunphail and Craigroy, on the side of Loch Ewing.’

Ross sat back and gave him a strange, surprised look. ‘I’m going to take a wee stab in the dark here, Gerald, but… your mother wouldn’t happen to be Flora MacDonald, would she?’

Now it was Gerald’s turn to be surprised. ‘Er, yes! How on earth would you know that?’

‘Ah, she’s very famous around our parts.’

‘She is?’

‘Oh, yes! No one has a way with the animals like Flora Mac and when a potion is needed to sort out any ailments, The Flora, as she’s known, is the first port of call for many of the locals. Quite often, they’ll go to her before they go to their doctor. Her knowledge of herbs, flora and fauna is unequalled. My family still have their farm, thanks to her.’

‘They do?’ Gerald felt almost faint at hearing all this praise for his mother. He’d barely seen her since she’d left them and their communication was sparse. That was one of the reasons why he was going to Scotland – to try and reconnect with her before it was too late.

‘Yes. When they had the foot and mouth outbreak, nearly all the dairy herds were being slaughtered. If that had happened to us, the farm would have folded and our livelihood would have been gone. Flora gave us something to mix in with the cattle feed and it kept them healthy. Three times the herd was tested and three times they came back with the all-clear.'

'That could have been just pure luck.'

'It could have been but two neighbouring farms didn't share that luck… My father is convinced Flora helped us and to this day, he is eternally grateful.'

'Gosh! I didn't know that. Unfortunately, we've been estranged for most of my life so I know hardly anything about her. She clearly has a gift.'

'She has that.'

Gerald fell silent and let the others talk around him – Essie and Clarissa were exclaiming on what a small world it was and Clarissa was roping Ross into being their tour guide when they got to that part of the country, a role Ross seemed more than keen to take on. It brought back to Gerald even more how little he knew of the woman who had birthed him. Although he had vague memories of her from his childhood, and they were nice memories of being loved and cared for, the pain of being without her always hit him hardest whenever she came to mind, so he'd spent the greater part of his life keeping the memories locked firmly away. It had been easier to believe she was a horrible, evil person and that he was better off without her. His father had never said a bad word against her, however, and when Gerald had, on occasion, said mean things, his father had always reprimanded him and told him not to speak badly of people he knew little of. It was, therefore, quite a shock to find out she seemed to be a bit of a local celebrity in the area where she lived. Meeting her was going to be more than a little interesting, that was for sure.

'Mum, Gerald, we're going to head off now for a bit, if that's okay.' Clarissa was preparing to leave with Ross.

'Of course, it's okay, darling. Off you two go and enjoy

yourselves, we'll settle up here.'

'Please, Essie, let me give you some money—'

'Absolutely not, Ross, this one is on us. Now go and have some fun. Are you heading anywhere in particular?'

'There's a nightclub I think Clarissa would enjoy…'

'Just make sure she gets home safely.'

'I will. And thank you for dinner.'

Clarissa leaned over and kissed both Essie and himself on the cheek. 'See you later.' She gave a small wave as they headed out of the door.

He looked at Essie. 'Are you okay with her going off like that?' He'd found himself becoming quite protective towards Clarissa, almost as though she were his own daughter, and he was surprised at his feelings of concern over her departure.

'I have to be, Gerald. I can't keep her tied to me for ever, no matter how much I would like to. You have to allow them to be free, it's the only way they'll stay by your side.'

He thought over her words for a moment. 'Yes, I can see that.'

'Besides, he seems a nice boy, so I don't think I've got much to worry about there.'

Gerald just nodded. Now that they were alone, he wasn't altogether sure how to proceed. Should he mention the other night and the secrets that had been revealed or should he stay quiet and follow Essie's lead?

He didn't get a chance to decide because at that moment, Essie broke the silence which had been growing between them.

'Gerald, about the other night and the things we said…'

'Er, yes…' He swallowed nervously, wondering what was coming next.

'I'm not ready to talk about it yet, I'm still trying to get it all straight in my head, so let's "park it" – which is what,

I believe, the young ones say today – and revisit it another time. Maybe when it's a little less raw. What do you say?'

He put his hand on top of hers and gave it a little squeeze. 'That sounds like the perfect plan to me. Consider it parked!'

Essie grinned at him and, as she returned the pressure on his fingers, said, 'I may be too old to go clubbing but I'm not too old to get shit-faced. How do you fancy a pub crawl? Last man standing pays for the taxi back!'

Gerald felt the heaviness inside him disappear with her words. They were back on stable ground again and memories of similar nights at uni came back to him.

'As I recall, young Estelle was a bit of a lightweight in her younger days, has she improved with age?'

Essie laughed and gave him a cheeky wink. 'That, dear chap, is for me to know and you to find out!'

THIRTY-ONE

'Shhhhhhhhhhhhhhhhhhhhhhhhhhhh!' Essie giggled as she placed her finger on her lips. 'We don't wantsh to wakesh up the other campersh,' she whispered, although not as quietly as she thought she had.

'You're the one making all the noise.' Gerald's voice came from behind her in the dark.

They were stumbling along the path, trying to find their vans. Gerald had forgotten to bring his little torch and Clarissa had gone off with the other one in her bag.

'Gerald, I thinksh I might be a little bit pished…'

'Only a little bit? I think we can safely say you're still a lightweight, Essie!'

'How come you're shtill shober?'

'I'm definitely not sober, just not as drunk as you.'

A sudden "oaffing" sound made Essie stop and turn around. She peered into the darkness, hardly able to see a thing.

'Gerald, are you okay?'

'Not really!' His voice floated up from the ground at her feet. 'I've tripped over a cable or something and I can't find my glasses.'

Essie bent down and groped around in the direction of Gerald's voice. She could hear rustling as he moved around.

'Gerald, what are you doing?'

'Trying to find my glasses. If you fancy helping, I'd be very grateful.'

Essie knelt down and as she did so, there was a crunching sound under her right knee. Gerald's rustling suddenly stopped.

'Essie, have you just found my glasses?'

'Erm… I think I might have…' She began giggling again as she tried to pick up the pieces she could feel under her hand.

'Oh, Essie…'

'I'm… shorry…' She could barely talk for laughing, even though she knew it wasn't funny, but somehow, it was. She felt Gerald move to her side and the shaking of his body told her he was laughing too. She grappled around, found his hand, and placed the broken pieces of his spectacles in it.

'You're good at jigsaws,' she squeaked, 'you'll be able to fix these!'

'I think it'll take more than that to fix them.'

She felt him stand up beside her.

'Come on, give me your hand, I'll help you up.' She felt his hand on her shoulder and she grabbed it, letting him pull her to her feet.

She stumbled against him and nearly had them both back on the ground.

'Oops! Shorry 'bout that.'

'Here, let me help.' His arm came around her waist and he held her against him.

'Ohhhh, Gerald, are you trying it on with me?'

She was vaguely aware of him stiffening next to her but

was too sozzled to realise why.

'No, Essie, your virtue is quite safe. Now come on, let's get you home.'

She felt him moving and a moment later, there was light.

'Ooh, I thought you didn't have your torch?'

'I've just remembered I have a torch on my phone. Now get moving before the battery dies, I don't think it has much juice left.'

Essie let Gerald lead her along the path. She was beginning to feel really sleepy. She was also beginning to feel something else.

'Oh Gerald…'

'Yes, Essie?'

'Ish it much further becaushhe… I really, really need to pee…'

She heard Gerald mutter something under his breath.

'What did you shay?'

'I said, "That's all I need!" Look, there's Marvin over there, have you got your key?'

'I can manage,' was her haughty reply. It wasn't her fault she had to go to the loo. Well, actually… maybe it was. That last snakebite had possibly been one too many.

Gerald placed her in front of Marvin's door and took his hand away. She hadn't been expecting that and lost her balance, banging against the side of the motorhome.

'Uh, oh!'

'Now what?'

'I've… um… dropped the keys.'

'Oh, for goodness' sake! Essie!'

'I didn't do it on purposhe.'

'The next time you suggest getting drunk, remind me to make other plans!'

'Have you not had a good time?'

'Yes, I have. It's been fun remembering what it was like

when we were students although I suspect the hangover will take much longer to recover from.'

'Gerald, what are you doing down at my feet?'

'Trying to find the bloody keys!'

'Gerald…'

'What?'

'I really have to do a pee right now. I think I'm going to wet myself.'

'Just hang on a second… ah, got them!'

Essie sensed Gerald standing up as she leaned against Marvin for support. The phone battery must have died for they were in darkness once again. Gerald put his hands on her shoulders and moved her to one side.

'Now what are you doing?'

'You're leaning against the door. I can't open it if you're leaning on it!'

She heard the clinking of the keys as Gerald found the right one and after a few attempts, he got the key in the lock and opened the door.

'Shee, you're not sho… shober yourself,' she hiccupped.

'I never said I was sober, just more sober than you.' He flicked a switch and the light came on, brightening up the area around them.

'Leave the light on for five minutes to help me find Vanda, okay.'

'Okay.'

She leant forward, grabbed Gerald's collar, pulled him towards her and kissed him soundly on the lips.

'Thank you for looking after me, Gerald, you're a shentleman. Goodnight!'

She stepped inside, pulled the door closed and dived straight into the toilet. She was so busy enjoying the relief of not having wet herself, the fact she'd just kissed Gerald didn't even register.

Gerald stood looking at the closed door in front of him as his lips tingled from the unexpected kiss. Feeling more than a bit dazed, he turned in the direction of his own little van, his fingers lightly touching his lips as he walked. So *that's* what a kiss from Essie felt like? A smile crossed his face and he gave a tiny skip. What a fabulous ending to a wonderful day. He'd just reached Vanda when Marvin's light went out.

'Sleep sweet, my beautiful Essie,' he whispered, and hoped the light breeze would carry his words to her.

THIRTY-TWO

'Here, this'll make you feel better.'

Clarissa handed two tablets and a glass of water to her groaning mother. She also pushed a cup of strong black coffee across the table.

'I am never drinking again,' came the muffled reply as Essie bent over and laid her head back down on her arms.

'Some role model you are, Mum. I didn't know you had it in you.'

Clarissa had never seen her mother even the slightest bit inebriated, so to find her this morning with a full-blown hangover had been quite a shock.

'I'm not sure if I should let you out with that Gerald one again, if this is the state he's going to bring you home in.'

Essie mumbled a reply.

'I'm sorry, Mum, I didn't get that?'

Essie raised her head a couple of millimetres and repeated, 'It wasn't Gerald's fault, this was my idea.'

'Your idea?'

'Shhhhhhhhhh! Too loud!'

Clarissa began to laugh. She couldn't help herself – it

was too hilarious seeing her mum like this. She clicked a picture on her phone and sent it to Ross with a quick explanation. A minute later, she got his reply.

"I know the perfect cure for a hangover. Tell your mum to be ready for me in an hour and to wear sturdy jeans along with a warm jumper."

There was a knock on the door and when she opened it, Gerald was standing there with a loaded plate in his hand.

'Bacon butties? All fresh and piping hot.'

'Oh, yes please! I'm starving!'

She stepped back to let him in and he placed the plate on the table in front of Essie.

'Urgh! Take them away!'

Gerald laughed. 'Not feeling so good, huh?'

'If you want to know what death warmed up looks like, Gerald, look at my mother!'

They both laughed again as Essie raised the middle finger of one hand in a gesture that would never be taught in any self-respecting ladies' finishing school.

Clarissa placed one of the butties on a plate and gave it to her mum.

'Come on, you, get eating. It'll help.'

'Don't want it!'

'Look, Ross is coming to take you out in an hour so you need to eat something.'

That had Essie's head coming up faster than it had moved all morning.

'Ross is wha—?'

'He said he knows the perfect cure for a hangover and he'll be here in an hour. As that was ten minutes ago, he'll be here in fifty minutes, so I suggest you eat that and get a move on.'

'But what does he have in mind?'

'He said you've to wear jeans and a warm jumper so I suspect he's planning a brisk walk along the seafront, letting all that good sea air clear your head.'

'I don't feel like I could walk the length of myself right now, never mind a jaunt along the seafront. Call him and cancel.'

'No, I won't. This will be a good opportunity for you to get to know him. Don't think I didn't clock you watching him closely yesterday, seeing how he behaved and stuff.'

'Do you like him?'

'Yes, I do. A lot.'

'Could it be serious?'

'I don't know, we've only had a few dates but I think it has the potential to be.'

'Okay, just for you, I will do my best.'

Clarissa noticed the grimace on her mum's face as she bit into the bacon butty in front of her, but she ate it all and had two cups of coffee before heading into the shower.

'So, Gerald, do you have any plans for the day now that it looks like my mum will be otherwise occupied?'

'I need to go into town. I broke my glasses last night so need to visit the opticians to sort out new ones.'

'How did you break your glasses?'

Clarissa found herself roaring with laughter once again as Gerald brought her up to speed on the antics of getting home the night before.

'Oh my, I wish I had been here to see that.'

'I think your mum's probably glad that you weren't. Having you witness the hangover from hell is probably painful enough for her.'

'Actually, Gerald, between the two of us, it's quite refreshing to see her like this. It's good to be reminded that our parents are human and capable of making the odd cock-up here and there. It's too easy to put them on pedestals and expect them to be perfect all the time.'

'I suppose you're right; it is.'

'I've got some shopping to do in town myself, so would

you mind if I joined you?'

'I'd be delighted.'

'Sorted. Shall we head off after Ross arrives for Mum?'

'That's perfect. I'll just go grab my jacket and lock up Vanda. Are you okay with getting the bus in? I don't feel up to driving this morning and I suspect I might not be legal yet either.'

At that moment, Essie came back through to the front of the van.

'Yeah, Gerald… how come you look so fresh and sprightly this morning when you had nearly as much as I did to drink?'

'That'll be the vitamin C tablets and pint of water I took before I went to bed. Guaranteed hangover cure which has never let me down yet!'

'Oh, that's what Elspeth gave me. It worked a treat!'

'Clarissa, I forbid you from drinking alcohol for the rest of your life.'

'Mum, I don't think you're in a position to be dictating that to me.'

'My darling daughter, I am in the perfect position. I would not wish this hangover upon anyone!'

Before Clarissa could reply, they heard the roar of a motorbike and when she looked out of the window, she saw Ross had arrived.

'Well, Mum, time to look sharp. Your date is here.'

'No! Not in a million years! Never ever!'

'Mrs Walton, I mean, Essie, please trust me. Once you've been on this for twenty minutes, you'll soon forget any hangover. I promise you.'

'I'm quite sure I will, Ross, for I expect my insides will become my outsides and be spread all over some road somewhere.'

‘Mum, Ross is a very good bike rider. He’ll look after you. You’ll be fine.’

‘Clarissa, I have never been on a motorbike in my life and I’m not about to start now.’

‘Actually, Essie, yes you have.’

Essie looked at Gerald in surprise. ‘No, I haven’t.’

‘Yes, you have. That lad at uni – Pedro, I think it was – turned up one day on his brother’s bike and was giving everyone a turn on it. You were one of the first to have a go and when you arrived back, you were saying what fun it had been. You loved it.’

‘I did? I don’t remember that at all.’

‘Trust me, you did. So why not take this opportunity to enjoy that thrill again. You’d be daft not to. Don’t let a little bit of fear hinder you – look at how liberated I felt yesterday when I let go of mine.’

‘Oh… alright then! Leather me up, Ross, it looks like I’m getting no choice here.’

Clarissa and Gerald watched as Ross helped Essie into the leather jacket and thick gloves he’d brought with him. When he’d slipped the helmet on, Clarissa quickly took another photograph. So many firsts today and it was barely ten in the morning!

She and Gerald waved them off and Clarissa hoped Ross could breathe okay because her mum was clinging onto him like a limpet.

‘Did she really go on a motorbike at uni?’

‘Nah! She wanted to but Pedro ran out of petrol before it was her turn. She was disappointed as she’d wanted to try it.’

‘So, you’ve just lied to her.’

‘I prefer to think of it as a slight altering of the facts. She *would* have loved it, if she’d had the chance of the ride.’

‘Well, I won’t tell her if you won’t.’ She gave Gerald a

grin, picked up her handbag and jacket and locked up Marvin.

'Come on then, Gerald, let's go and hit those shops!' She slipped her arm through his and they chatted easily all the way to the bus stop.

An hour later, Clarissa was standing in Sightsavers trying to keep an utterly shocked expression off her face. For the first time since they'd met, she'd seen Gerald properly without his glasses on and he looked completely different. He was verging on being quite gorgeous. Not Ryan Reynolds or Chris Hemsworth gorgeous, but more than alright for a normal bloke on the street. He was talking to Andrea – the assistant – about some replacement specs and had taken off his current goggles as he explained they were an old pair. While Andrea went away to talk to someone, Clarissa couldn't help herself and blurted out, 'Gerald, why do you wear such big, thick, black framed things? They do nothing for you.'

'Err… I don't know. I've always worn that style since I first began to need glasses in my twenties.'

'Were they in fashion back then?'

'Possibly. I've just gotten used to them and always stuck with what I knew.'

'Or, more likely, too scared to try something different.'

'Perhaps.'

'What about contact lenses? Have you ever tried those?'

'Urg, no! Putting my finger in my eyes doesn't do it for me!'

'So, you were happy to send my mother off on a big, Harley motorbike this morning but you can't face popping a contact lens in your eye?'

Gerald had the good grace to look sheepish at that

comment.

'When the assistant comes back, you're going to ask about lenses, okay?'

'Do I have to?'

'Gerald, don't take this the wrong way, but you're hiding behind those glasses you wear. You've got lovely eyes, such an unusual colour, but I've never noticed them before because they've always been overpowered by the dominant frames of your glasses.'

The assistant came back just then and with the help of a sharp kick to the ankle, Gerald asked about being tested to see if he would be suitable for contact lenses. After consulting the diary, Andrea informed him there was a free appointment in an hour. Clarissa made her write Gerald's name in it before he had the chance to answer.

'We'll see you in an hour.' Clarissa smiled at the assistant and marched Gerald sharply out of the shop.

'Right, Gerald. We've got an hour to kill and I know exactly where we're going.' She walked swiftly back along the pavement and into a hair-dressing salon they'd passed on the way to the optician. The sign in the window said "No Appointment Required" and Clarissa was about to take them up on that.

'Good afternoon, may I help you?'

'Hi, Mandy,' Clarissa looked at the name badge on the young girl's uniform, 'Do you have the time to cut this gentleman's hair for me?'

'Would it be just a trim?'

'Nope! I want a full restyle!'

'Eh?' Gerald butted in. 'Wait just a minute—'

'No, Gerald, you wait a minute! Don't you think you've dressed like an eighty-year-old for long enough? The last time I saw a haircut like yours was in a black and white movie released just after the war! Yesterday, you finally began to live again – your words, not mine! – so, let's continue the good work today. Allow me to give you a makeover. Please?'

She waited as he hesitated a bit longer.

'We can fit in a restyle if sir would like?' Mandy offered.

Clarissa threw Mandy a grateful smile and the girl nodded back at her, behind Gerald's back.

'Oh, go on then! It'll grow out soon enough if I don't like it.'

Clarissa rolled her eyes. 'Now that's what you call gratitude! Take him away, Mandy, and bring him back with something like this, if you think it'll suit.'

She showed Mandy a picture on her phone which she'd pulled off the internet as they'd been making their way to the shop.

'Oh, yes, I think that'll suit very well.'

'Do I get to see?'

'No!' came the reply in unison.

Forty minutes later, Mandy brought Gerald back to her. Clarissa looked up and a huge smile crossed her face.

'*Now* we're cooking with gas!'

THIRTY-THREE

Gerald found himself whisked back to the opticians with moments to spare before his appointment. Andrea did a double-take when he re-presented himself in front of her.

'Wow! Err… fabulous haircut, Mr Wainwright, it takes years off you, if you don't mind me saying.'

'Urm, no, not at all. Thank you.'

Gerald couldn't remember the last time anyone had given him such a spontaneous compliment. It gave him a little flicker of warmth inside.

He didn't need to look at Clarissa to know she had a smug look of righteousness about her – he could feel it emanating from her. She'd already informed him that once they left the opticians, she was taking him clothes shopping because "The Victoria and Albert Museum want their Boring Old Farts display back!" Cheeky madam!

Although… he had to be honest with himself, he was actually looking forward to it. His old dress style didn't suit his new, smarter, hairdo and if he was able to have contact lenses, then it seemed only right to go the whole hog and sort out some swanky outfits to match.

'Gerald Wainwright?'

He looked up to see the ophthalmologist standing in front of him. 'Yes.'

'Please, come with me.'

He stood up and looked at Clarissa who gave him a big grin of encouragement.

'Go get 'em, tiger!'

The test didn't take long and he wasn't altogether sure if he was happy or not to be told there should be no problem with him wearing lenses. The ophthalmologist passed his prescription to Andrea and she took him to a small area with tables and mirrors. She sat him down and told him she'd be back in a moment. When she returned, she had two packets in her hand.

'Mr Wainwright, these are samples of your lens prescription. You need to try these out for a few days, gradually increasing the length of time you wear them then come back for a check-up to see how you've got on and, if all is good, we'll sort you out with one of our payment and pre-order schemes. Now, I'll explain what to do and you just follow what I say.'

Ten minutes later, Gerald was blinking like a good 'un and swivelling his head, looking at everything around him.

'Oh, my goodness! It's like someone's switched the lights on!'

He couldn't believe how brighter and sharper everything was. There were no thick frames hindering his view and the whole world looked totally different. He walked over to where Clarissa was patiently waiting, scrolling through her phone to pass the time.

'Hey, you!' he said with a grin.

'Well? Are you good for them?'

'Got them in already!'

'Yay!' She gave him a massive hug. 'Well done, you did it! How do they feel?'

‘I can’t feel them at all. I have high-water content ones, or something like that, which means they’re hardly noticeable. I can, however, see for milessssssssssss,’ he dragged the word out with a laugh, ‘and that is awesome! Thank you for making me do this. I just wish I’d had the nerve to do it sooner.’

‘Hey, better late than never. Now, before we go, I’ve had a look at some different frames for your glasses, so let’s get those sorted out too.’

It didn’t take long for Clarissa to decide which frames didn’t make him look like a grandfather.

When the assistant was handing his credit card back, along with his receipt, someone jostled him from behind and the card fell to the floor. Quick as a flash, Clarissa bent down to pick it up. As she gave it back, she asked, ‘What does the “C” stand for?’

‘I’m sorry?’

‘The “C” – your middle name – what is it?’

‘Oh, it’s Craig.’

‘Nice! I like it.’

‘I do too.’

They were walking out of the shop when she spoke again.

‘Do you like it better than Gerald?’

‘What, Craig?’

‘Yes.’

‘If I’m being honest, I do. I’ve never liked my first name.’

‘Then why not call yourself by your middle name. Instead of being Gerald. C. Wainwright, you could be G. Craig Wainwright.’

‘I’ve never thought about it. Are you allowed to do that? Legally, I mean.’

‘Yes, you can, since you’re not actually changing your name, you’re simply using a different part of it. If you go to the bank, they'll change your cards to read G. Craig Wainwright if you decided you preferred that.'

'That's interesting to know. Although being called Craig might take some getting used to.'

'The thing is, you no longer look like a "Gerald" anymore. Well, you do a little bit because of the dodgy gear you're still wearing but once we get you out of that, you'll definitely be more of a "Craig". I dunno if that helps or not…'

'It's certainly worth thinking about. So, where are we going now?'

'First we're going to Next and then onto River Island.'

'I think I might be a bit old for trendy places like that.'

'Well, you'll have to suck it up because Blackpool doesn't have a "Grandpas R Us" shop!'

'I'm beginning to get just a little paranoid about my current attire, Clarissa. I haven't heard you say a single nice thing about anything I'm wearing. Is it really that bad?'

'Gerald… Craig… Let's just say that, if we were in the month of November, even the guy on the bonfire would be embarrassed.'

'Okay, point taken. Lead on and finish sorting me out.'

'It'll be my pleasure.'

Once again, Clarissa's arm looped through his and Gerald found himself being swiftly marched along the road. One thing was for sure, when Clarissa was on a mission, she didn't let up until she was done.

Essie stood on the edge of the cliff and felt the sharp salty sea breeze pull her hair away from her face. The sun was shining and she lifted her face upwards to feel its warmth. Right now, with the adrenaline coursing through her body, she felt as high as a kite and her earlier hangover had long disappeared.

Ross had taken her for a ride, following the coastline where possible until they'd arrived just outside Arnside. They'd parked up in a small layby and much to her surprise, Ross had produced an unexpected picnic. It wasn't anything fancy – some egg sandwiches, a couple of pork pies, a tube of ready-salted Pringles and a couple of bottles of water – but she was famished and would have eaten anything.

She walked over to where he'd laid out the picnic rug and sat down.

'How are you feeling now?'

'Considerably more alive than I did a few hours ago. Thank you for this.'

'It's my pleasure. I'd already planned this trip out today; bringing a passenger was not a problem.'

'You hadn't planned on seeing Clarissa today then?'

'No. She said she had to go into town so we arranged to meet later. It's good to have some space from each other – you need to know if you miss someone when you're figuring out how you feel about them. I don't like being all or nothing at the start of a relationship, I prefer the slow build. You put down better foundations that way.'

'That's a good way of looking at it, although some relationships can be perfect from the very first meeting.'

'I know. My mum and dad were childhood sweethearts. They met in nursery, became best friends that first day and have been together ever since. My brother, Kenneth, on the other hand, met a girl, fell in love and was married within eighteen months. Nine months after they said "I Do" they were filing for divorce. So, I've seen it from both sides and have decided this way of doing things is the best.'

'I think you're probably right. I don't want to see Clarissa rushing into anything – I want her to take the time to find out what kind of person she wants to be. She's not really had the opportunity to do that until now.'

'She did hint at something along those lines but I didn't want to pry.'

Essie took a drink from her water bottle, giving her some time to work out how much detail she wanted to go into.

'Let's just say "controlling husband and domineering father" and leave it at that.'

'Fair enough, I hear you. So, what do you think of these pork pies? They're hand-made on the premises and I reckon they're among the best I've ever tasted.'

Essie smiled at the young man in front of her. Kind and diplomatic… he'll go far, she thought as she agreed the pork pies were, indeed, rather tasty.

THIRTY-FOUR

'Hi, Mum, I'm home.'

Essie heard Clarissa call out and walked around to the other side of the van. Ross had been helping her with some of the less enjoyable tasks of touring the country in a motorhome. She'd initially declined his offer of assistance, when she'd told him what needed to be done, but had accepted after he'd replied, 'Och, when you've grown up mucking out a large herd of coos, very little ever fazes you after that.'

'Hi, sweetie, did you have a good day?' She kissed Clarissa on the cheek and looked behind her for Gerald. 'No Gerald? You haven't left him behind, have you?'

'No,' her daughter laughed, 'he's just gone to his van to put away his shopping. He'll be over shortly. Hey, Ross…' She caught sight of Ross and ran over to see him. Essie witnessed their embrace and knew, from their respective body language, that this was going to be more than a holiday fling. Now that she'd spent some time with Ross, she was happy for him to be Clarissa's "ever after" if it came to it, although she hoped he'd continue to give her space and be patient with her while she found the path she wanted to travel along.

She was pottering about inside Marvin when Clarissa popped her head around the door. 'Mum, that's us away now. I'll be home later.'

'Okay, be careful on the bike.'

Clarissa's head came back through the door. 'Oh, I forgot to ask – how was your bike ride? Was it fun?'

'I had a great time, thank you, and Ross is very capable so I enjoyed it a lot. I'm not about to rush out and buy a Harley though, if that's what you're hoping for.'

'Bummer!' She grinned. 'So, Gerald was right then – you do like motorbikes.'

'Actually, young lady, Gerald was very wrong! I remembered exactly what happened with Pedro and I'll be having words with him when he arrives here.'

'Oops! Then I'm outta here. Laters!' She waved and was gone, the roar of the bike masking Essie's own farewell. She pulled the door to – the breeze was blowing the wrong way and coming right through the doorway. It was only a few days until they were in May but the weather hadn't warmed up yet and it could still be nippy.

She poured herself a glass of white wine and relaxed in one of the rather comfortable cab seats. She picked up her book to read while she waited for Gerald to come over.

She was completely immersed in her thriller when there was a knock on the door.

'Come in, Gerald, it's open.'

A moment passed but he didn't enter.

'Gerald, the door is open, just come in!'

Still, no one entered and the knock at the door came a second time.

'Oh, for goodness' sake!'

With an exasperated huff of annoyance, Essie pushed herself up out of the seat, grabbed her wine glass – she might as well refill it while she was up – and walked over to the door, pushing it open with her foot.

'Gerald, I said just co—'

She looked up and her words died on her lips while the wine glass slipped from her hand and smashed against the edge of the step.

'Hi, Essie, I've brought over dinner. Does cold meat, cheese, salad and fresh crusty bread sound good to you?'

Essie couldn't speak. She looked at Gerald and the last twenty-five years just slipped away. His hair had been cut into a style not too dissimilar from the one he'd had at uni, the thick, black frames of his glasses – which had done a great job of hiding most of his face – were gone and she was looking at the Gerald she'd known and loved back then. She only knew she hadn't slipped back in time because there were faint lines around his eyes and a little bit of grey on his temples.

'Essie, are you okay? You've gone so pale…'

She gripped onto the doorframe and used it to balance while the lightheaded sensation passed.

'I'm…. err… I'm fine. Just got a shock…'

'Clarissa didn't say anything to you?'

'Not a word! I'm guessing this is all her doing?'

'Pretty much. Now, can I come in or shall we eat dinner here?'

Essie moved aside so Gerald could enter and then bent down to pick up the broken glass. She also checked there was none in the grass underneath as campsites were rather strict about such things.

She stood up and turned to see Gerald had dug out another wine glass which he handed to her. She sat on the bench by the table and took a large gulp, her eyes on Gerald the whole time.

'Good surprise or bad surprise?'

'Huh? Sorry?'

'How I look now – good or bad?'

'Do you like it?'

'That's not what I'm asking, Essie!'

'It's good, definitely good. I wasn't expecting it – it was quite a shock.'

'Yeah, I think I got that. If it makes you feel better, every time I've caught my reflection today, I've done a double-take.'

'It's so different and yet… so much the same. If I'd been asked to describe you, before we met up again, I'd have said pretty much thus!' She pointed her finger at him and waved it up and down.

'I'm going to take that as a compliment. Now, you sit there and I'll sort out dinner.'

Essie watched him as he moved about in the small space, trying to adjust to this change in his appearance. The dodgy old, mullet-style hairdo, with the crisp side parting and comb-over, was gone and had been replaced with a sharp short-back-and-sides but with some length on the top, which had been softly spiked up. Combined with high cheekbones that were no longer hidden behind obnoxious black glasses, it changed his whole look. The hazel eyes, with their little flecks of gold, could once again be seen and the memories came flowing back of them being sad, happy, laughing, cheeky, mischievous and scowling – all the various emotions Gerald had gone through in their uni days and which she'd observed from a distance, too shy to say anything that might make him realise her feelings for him were more than just platonic.

'There we go.'

Plates were placed on the table and Gerald took the seat across from her.

'Tuck in,' he said.

She picked up some of the French stick and buttered it slowly while her brain caught up with all the other changes

Gerald had undergone.

'No tank-top?' She admired the sparkling white T-shirt underneath the pale lilac casual shirt he was wearing.

'No! Clarissa was rather cutting in her opinion of those. She kept asking if I shopped at "Grandads R Us" which I thought clarified the point that I was dressing in old clothes.'

'I'm sorry she was so rude but she did have a point – tank-tops are rather seventies. How did you ever come to wear such things?'

'I can tell you exactly how. I was working on Vanda one day and it was a bit chilly, so I pulled on a sweatshirt but the sleeves kept slipping down and getting in the way. I was looking around for something else when my eye fell upon one of Dad's old tank-tops hanging up on a nail. I put it on and it was perfect. I was warm but didn't have any bothersome sleeves. From then on, I began wearing them more often and didn't give any thought to how I might actually look in them. They were just so practical.'

'I notice the thick corduroy trousers are also not in attendance this evening…'

She'd more than noticed their absence – the jeans he had on were clinging in all the right places and she hadn't been able to avoid seeing his nice, tight ass since it had been eye-level while he'd been moving about.

'Another Clarissa casualty, I'm afraid. She was rather scathing about those too, so they're gone and I now have a selection of jeans and trousers – chinos I think they're called – hanging up in the van.'

'Well, they suit you and I'm in agreement with Clarissa, I can't abide cords either.'

'Jeans have changed a lot since the last time I wore them – there's a greater selection of styles and they're better fitting too. I'm finding them considerably more comfortable than when I last wore them, and *that* was more years ago than I care to think about.'

'You look just how you did at uni.' She said the words quietly.

'Is that a bad thing?' His tone matched hers.

'No, it's just…' She raised her hand and dropped it again. 'With everything that was said the other night, and now seeing you looking like the Gerald I knew back then, it's… it's just a bit… oh, I can't explain it but I already felt mixed up inside and this not-so-new look hasn't helped.'

'I'm sorry.'

'Don't be! It's not your fault.'

'Some of it is though, Essie. If I hadn't been such a wimp back then and had spoken up sooner… if I hadn't been too shy to say anything…'

'But all those other girls you had dates with, you weren't shy with them. If you cared so much about me, why did you go out with them?' As she spoke, Essie realised that this was what had been bugging her since Gerald had broken his silence.

'They were just distractions, nothing more. I didn't think I was good enough for you, I never for a moment dared to think you might feel the same way about me. The only way I could deal with it was to date other girls and hope that, one day, someone might come along who could help me forget you. Except… she never did. The truth is, there was, and only ever has been, one girl that I have loved. And, after all this time, I don't believe it's ever going to change.'

Essie felt her heart fill with joy before immediately sinking again with sadness.

'Gerald, I can't make that same declaration to you. I'm married – regardless of what state that marriage might be in – and it would be wrong of me to give you any kind of hope or promises. I don't know what I'm going to do when we return home and I'm not yet ready to make a decision.

I'm just enjoying having this freedom right now and building a relationship with my daughter.'

'Essie, I fully understand. I'm not asking you for anything nor am I expecting anything either. I know you still have commitments elsewhere and that's fine. Being here with you, as your friend, is good enough for now.'

'But what if it stops being enough, Gerald, what then?'

'Then we'll cross that bridge when we come to it. Let's keep it simple and not place any expectations on each other. Things always have a way of working themselves out in their own sweet time. I say, for now, we just go with the flow and let whatever will be will be.'

'Blimey! Full on with the clichés this evening, are we not?'

'And here's another one – it's time for a fresh start! Well, for me anyway.'

'Really?'

'Yup! I sent the divorce papers back to my solicitor today. I'm almost officially divorced. It seems fitting that today was the day Clarissa decided on my makeover – I reckon that's why I was happy to go along with it – it seemed the right thing to do.'

'Is it appropriate to say congratulations?'

'In this instance? Absolutely! Clarissa also came up with another suggestion…'

'Gosh, she was full of them today.'

Essie listened as Gerald explained about changing his name. Or rather, using his middle name instead.

'If you prefer "Craig" to "Gerald" then do it. If I'm being honest, Gerald suited you yesterday but now, further to this transformation, I think Craig is more fitting.'

'Very well then, from this moment forward, I'm going to try Craig on for size. It'll take a bit of getting used to so I apologise in advance if I don't answer you right away.'

'Not a problem, CRAIG,' she emphasised his name

when she said it, 'it'll take a bit of getting used to for all of us but we'll get there. And, if you find you're not comfortable with it, we can easily revert back.'

'Thank you, Essie. Now, let's get this lovely grub eaten and then I can stick the kettle on. I fancy a nice strong cup of tea and a game of cards. Are you in?'

'I sure am. Let's see if I still have what it takes to kick your ass at snap!'

When Essie went to bed later that night, her hand aching from beating Gerald, or rather Craig, several times over, she realised some of the turmoil inside her had eased. Knowing the reason why Gerald… *Craig*… had been out with so many girls at uni had helped considerably. He hadn't been playing the field, he'd been trying to forget her. She turned over and let out a sigh. He was free now to move on but she wasn't. She was nowhere closer to deciding what to do with her own marriage than she had been when they'd set out on this journey.

THIRTY-FIVE

It was their last night in Blackpool and they were back in the little Chinese restaurant they'd visited previously. Essie had asked Clarissa if she wouldn't prefer to spend the evening with Ross on her own but she'd said it would be nicer for them all to dine together and they'd go off after that.

'How much longer do you think you'll be in Blackpool for, Ross?'

Craig passed round the bowl of prawn crackers as he asked the question.

'I think probably till the end of June. Karl's plaster cast is due off by early June and he'll most likely need a bit of physio on his leg before it's back in working order. I need to be home for July, to help with getting the harvest in.'

'But… I thought you said it was a dairy farm?'

Ross looked at Essie. 'It was but in the aftermath of the foot-and-mouth disease outbreak, it brought home to my family how vulnerable we were by relying on just one product for a living. My eldest brother, Fraser, took himself off to agricultural college to expand his knowledge and advised my dad to look at organic farming. He saw the merits of it so they made the decision to go down that route. The herd was reduced and a portion of the land was set aside for organic production. It was a bit tough through the conversion years but we stuck it out and it's now turning a profit. Only a small profit, but a profit all the same. My mum then decided that, with us kids being older and able to look after ourselves, she could muck in too. She commandeered some old workers' cottages, did them up and now rents them out as holiday homes. She also set up a farm shop and sells locally grown produce and homemade cakes and bread. The last I heard is that she's also toying with the idea of a tea-room although I don't know if it's come to anything yet.'

'I see. It sounds quite a big concern. Does your dad not mind that only one son has gone into the family business?'

'No, not that I'm aware of. Fraser was always going to follow my dad into farming, that was clear from a young age. He has a real passion for it and plenty of vision to keep it going from strength to strength. Neither Kenneth nor I felt the same way and we were encouraged to take whatever paths our hearts put us on. My father has always said the most successful farmers are the ones who love the job. That's our Fraser.'

'Can we come for a visit?'

'Clarissa! Don't be rude. Wait to be invited.'

'No, Essie, it's fine. I'm really hoping we'll all meet up again, especially when you'll be so nearby – I'm assuming you plan to stay with Flora, Gerald's… er… sorry, Craig's mum when you get there.'

'That's the plan, assuming she's happy to see us.'

'She doesn't know you're coming?'

'Um, no, not at this time. I don't want to give her the opportunity to say no. If we just land on her doorstep, it makes it more difficult to turn us away.'

'I see. Well, if there is a problem, you're more than welcome to come and stay with us. The cottages will probably be full – those American tourists love our close proximity to Culloden Moor and Loch Ness – but we'll be able to find you a place to park up.'

'Thank you, Ross, that's most kind of you.'

The waiter arrived with their food and the rest of the meal was spent talking about the locations they were planning to visit over the next few months.

When they'd finished eating, Ross and Clarissa went off for a bike ride leaving Essie and Craig to go for one last stroll along the promenade.

'I can't believe how much has changed in the time we've been here, Craig. Clarissa is falling in love – although I don't think she's realised it yet – you've become a whole new person and I've found out that my entire marriage has been based on a lie. I'm not coming back here again – I don't think I could cope with any more life changes.' Essie let out a large sigh.

'It's certainly been a revelation, but d'you know what, I'm glad because I think we're all in a better place because of it.'

'Speak for yourself!'

'Essie, the truths that have come out puts you in a position of power when it comes to your future choices. By knowing all the facts, you'll be able to make better and informed decisions, regardless of what those decisions are. Anyway, less of this maudlin talk. Let's head down to the Pleasure Beach and have another couple of turns on the Big One before we ship out. And, if you scream *really* loudly, I might even treat you to a candy floss afterwards.'

'You, Craig Wainwright, are turning into one smooth talker. Candy floss? You really know how to turn a girl's head!'

Their laughter floated away on the wind as they did an

about turn and made their way towards the amusement park, preparing to behave like teenagers once again.

THIRTY-SIX

Gradually, spring moved into summer and the three amigos made their way slowly northwards, taking in the beautiful sights the west side of the country had to offer. They meandered through the Lake District, admiring the brilliantly sparkling lakes nestled safely at the feet of the high, protective mountains around them. Windermere thrilled them and Coniston enchanted them but it was Grasmere where they felt the most soothed and at peace. Well, that was until Craig found out more about George and how much of a bastard he'd been to Essie.

They were standing respectfully at Wordsworth's burial place when Essie quietly recited a small verse:

Here I lie, in my place of rest,
Sleeping my final sleep,
I lived my life how I knew best,
And gave no cause for others to weep.
I quietly lived as an honest soul,
Never once did I tell a lie.
In every job I gave my all

I did not let life pass me by.
I always believed in the eternal quest
The good Lord by my side I did keep,
So, here I lie in my place of rest,
Sleeping my final sleep.

'Wow, Essie, that was beautiful, did Wordsworth write that?'

She mumbled something under her breath which Craig couldn't hear.

'I'm sorry, I didn't hear, say it again.'

She turned away, but he managed to catch her words this time.

'No, I did.'

He put his hand gently on her shoulder and turned her round to face him.

'Did you just say you wrote that?'

She nodded while staring down at her shoes. She looked exactly like a small child anticipating a telling-off. Craig put his finger under her chin and raised her face until she was looking at him.

'Why are you behaving as though you're ashamed of your verse? It was lovely. Have you written much poetry? Can you tell me some more?'

'I…' she hesitated and he saw her swallow before she spoke again.

'I used to write quite a bit of poetry and even won a competition in a ladies' magazine. I showed it to George but instead of congratulating me and saying how well I'd done, he asked me what I thought I was playing at, sending off such utter rubbish and putting my name to it. Had I not stopped to think how it would reflect on him if his peers were to find out?

'When I pointed out that my piece had won, he ripped the magazine up in front of me, told me to grow up and to stop thinking that, because I'd been able to cobble some words together, it made me an accomplished poet. He ridiculed my efforts and stamped out any belief I might have had in my ability. Looking back now, I can see he was right – it was immature scribblings.'

Craig felt a sharp pain in his hands and looked down, shocked to see them both tightly clenched into fists. He wasn't given to being violent but if George Walton had been standing in front of him right now, he'd have punched him until his supercilious fat face was nothing more than a pulp!

'Essie, you won a competition and were published in a magazine – you must have had some kind of talent. Even if your early offerings were a little rough, you'd have become better with practise. You would have grown in confidence and that gives you the courage to be more adventurous in how you express yourself. You shouldn't have stopped.'

'After the way George shredded me that day, I never wrote again. I just couldn't. His words always came back to me and I walked away from it all. To be honest, I'm surprised I remembered the lines I've just quoted.'

'Well, Essie Walton, I don't know if my belief in you holds any sway, but I think you need to try again. Don't let the Georges of this world steal your dreams. He was so wrong to act as he did and put you down like that. Your husband is supposed to support you as you support him. What made his dreams and ambitions more important than yours?'

'It's just the way it always was… always is. George does what George wants and Clarissa and I are expected to make him shine in the best way possible.'

'Given the way I've heard Clarissa talk about him these days, I think she'd be amending the 'n' in shine to a 't', personally speaking.'

It took Essie a moment to work out what he'd said but when the penny dropped, she began giggling – a sound which still sent a frisson of joy through him every time he heard it.

'I think you might be right there, Craig. I thought some distance might make her think better of him – he is her father, after all – but it seems to be the longer we're away from his controlling influence, the more she loathes him.'

'I can see how that would be – without George around to dictate what you both do, think, act, wear, etc, Clarissa is finding her own mind and, in the process, is realising her own father was stealing that from her by forcing her to bow to his will. I get the feeling she's not about to forgive him any time soon.'

'I think you're on to something there. I must say, right now, I'm struggling to find any positive feelings towards him.'

'Does this mean you're moving towards thinking about leaving him?'

'No, Craig, I'm not thinking that at all. I'm actually finding it easier not to think about him at all because I'm more at peace with myself when he's not in my head.'

'Out of sight, out of mind?'

'For now, yes. I'm beginning to feel I can breathe again and that's good enough to be getting on with for the foreseeable.'

Before he could answer, Clarissa's voice came from behind him.

'Blooming heck! That queue for the gingerbread shop was MASSIVE! Mind you, it's a tiny wee shop – I can't believe they bake all this in there. Here, you have to taste this – it's divine!'

'Since when did you start using the word "divine" as a description?'

'Since, my darling mother, I tasted this gingerbread. It's

the only word you can use.'

Craig and Essie took a bite of the proffered biscuit and both agreed it was "divine"!

That evening, after dinner at a local pub, Clarissa stayed behind to see a local band who were playing while Craig and Essie made their way back to the campsite. Craig quickly popped into Vanda and came back holding a giftbag.

'I got this for you today.'

'When? I didn't see you buy anything?' Essie tried to peek in but there was tissue paper scrunched up inside and she couldn't see past it.

'When you and Clarissa popped outside at the garden centre, I stayed behind to "go to the loo" – except I didn't, I was buying this instead. The good thing with carrying a rucksack is that you can hide things away from prying eyes.'

'What is it?'

'Open it and find out.'

Essie felt a tremor of excitement as she undid the ribbon bow holding the handles together. She couldn't recall the last time someone had bought her a gift outside of Christmas and birthdays. It was rather nice and she felt quite special.

She teased away the tissue paper, put her hand inside and pulled out two beautiful, leather-bound, notebooks. One had a little clip holding it closed, the other was tied up with a leather thong. She looked inside the bag and found a third gift – a pretty, silver, Parker pen. She looked at Craig in surprise.

'One is a journal, the other is for poetry and writing. I believe that, if you begin to keep a journal of your journey, it'll help to clear your mind and let you see how you're growing now you're out of George's shadow. The poetry is something you must try again, if only for your own well-being. Now you have those,' he nodded at the notebooks in her hand, 'you have no excuse not to.'

She felt tears begin to well up in her eyes. To have someone believe in her like this – not her abilities as a leader, or an organiser, or a baker or a cook but actually in *her*, as a person, was quite new and it left her feeling a bit shaky.

'I don't know what to say. Thank you, obviously, but…'

Craig patted the hand which was gently stroking one of the notebooks on the table.

'You don't need to say anything, Essie. Just promise me you'll use them.'

She gulped. 'I'll try but I'm not making a promise.'

'Trying is fine, I don't ask for anything more. It might be easier to start with the journal first – get used to writing again before you try your poetry. It's only a thought.'

She smiled and answered simply, 'It might.'

Later that night, when she was in her bed, she pulled the notebook with the leather thong towards her. The smell of the leather and the fresh, clean paper were quite heady. Opening it up, she picked up her new pen and, after a moment, began to write.

Hello, Journal,

My name is Essie and you and I are about to become best friends. I hope I can share my secrets with you once I feel more confident about writing them.

Today I shared a secret with Craig – who used to be known as Gerald but he doesn't like the name so he changed it – about something my husband said to me a long time ago. I'm not ready to share it again tonight but hopefully one day I can and then I can talk about how it made me feel.

For tonight though, and with this being my first entry, I'll simply say that knowing someone in the world believes in you, and thinks you can do anything, is the most wonderful feeling.

So, my first secret, just between the two of us, is that, right now, I feel amazing.

I feel cared for.

I feel loved.

E. xx

She read back what she'd written, gave a little sigh of happiness and closed the book, tying it up with the leather thong. She placed it in her bedside drawer and turning off the light, lay down, smiling into the darkness.

THIRTY-SEVEN

‘Och aye the noo!’

‘Seriously, Craig?’ Clarissa talked into the walkie-talkie handset which had crackled into life as they’d passed the “Welcome to Scotland” sign. She exchanged a smile with her mum. Since Gerald had morphed into Craig, he’d become an altogether different person. His personality had grown and so had his confidence. The diffidence which had previously been wrapped tightly around him was thrown off and a funny, witty, affable man had emerged from within.

Her mum had told her that he was now more like the boy she’d known at uni and he kept them both laughing every day. Clarissa still wondered if it had been more than just friendship between them, because they always spoke fondly of each other when they reminisced, but she didn’t want to ask in case it made things awkward.

Part of her hoped they might make it together now as a couple. She didn’t care if her parents got divorced; unlike some adult kids who went ape-shit when their parents split up, she’d be quite happy. Her father was a grade-A asshole who absolutely didn't deserve her mother. Seeing the way Craig treated them both with care and respect, and seeing how her mother was blooming as a result of this, Clarissa was realising just how much her father had domineered Essie and how he'd all but buried her alive under the weight of his expectations. Neither of them had spoken to George since they'd set off on their travels and she, for one, wasn't missing him at all.

The walkie-talkie crackled again. 'Now the fun really begins. Wild camping, here we come!'

'Wild what?' Clarissa looked at her mother who gave a small shrug.

'Wild camping! I'll explain it all when we stop at Gretna! Over and oot, ma braw wee lassies!'

'We're going to be having words, if he carries on with that!'

She grinned at her mum, letting her know she was happy to join in with Craig's silliness.

They followed the signs and soon arrived at the famous Blacksmith's shop on the edge of Gretna Green. They parked up in the car park and made their way towards the little shopping village.

'Are we going to try the Courtship Maze before we leave?' Clarissa's inner child still cried to play on swings and, in this case, get lost in a maze.

'I'm game! Essie?'

'I can't see why not, but let's find out some more about it.'

Two hours later, they were ready for the maze. The man in The Old Blacksmith's Shop had explained how it worked – there were two ways into the maze and the idea was that couples split up, taking an entrance each and then tried to meet each other on the bridge in the middle.

'Mum, why don't you and Craig go in together, I'll go in on my own and we'll meet at the bridge.'

'I don't mind going on my own if you two ladies want to be together…'

Craig bit back a grin when Clarissa pulled a face. 'Craig, I think going around a love maze with my mum is just wee bit urgh! I'm happy to go it alone, thanks.'

'Well, if you're sure…'

'I am!' Clarissa turned away but then stopped and looked back. 'Craig, you did remember your lock, didn't you?'

Craig held up his padlock and Essie waved hers too.

'See you in the middle!' he said.

They parted ways, Craig and Essie entering the maze first.

'Which way do we go?'

Essie looked around. 'I'm sure I read somewhere that you should always keep left in a maze, but that may relate to very old ones and the designers of these new ones may be a bit more savvy than that.'

'Well, shall we give it a try?'

'Might as well.'

They wandered for a bit, hitting a few dead ends and making more than one, or even two, U-turns.

'I always thought I had a reasonable sense of direction but now I'm beginning to wonder.' Essie sighed when they came up against another wall of hedging.

'I don't think a good sense of direction helps in these things.'

'I'm beginning to realise that!'

'I had an email from my solicitor today…'

Essie stopped and turned to face him. 'Saying?'

'The Decree Absolute is in. I'm officially divorced. Marjory is now completely a thing of the past.'

'And how do you feel? Any different from when you sent off the Nisi?'

'Even better, actually. I kept worrying that something could still go wrong and I'd end up being unable to get rid of her, even though I knew it was highly unlikely. But now I know it really is all over, I feel like I could float away on the breeze. I feel a bit high!'

Essie leaned in and gave him a hug. It was quite the surprise and for a brief moment, Craig didn't know what to do. It was, however, the briefest of moments and he quickly folded his arms around her back, revelling in this unexpected little luxury. The top of her head came to just under his nose and he could smell the lemony scent of her shampoo. They stood together like this for several heartbeats and then Essie released her tight grip on him – it had been a fabulous hug; good and strong, not one of those flimsy things that leave you wondering if it had been worth the effort – stepped back and looked him in the eye.

'Now's the time, Craig, for you to really begin living and, hopefully, you'll find a woman who'll appreciate how lucky she is to have you.'

He started at her words. Did she not realise? Hadn't he already made it clear that she was the only woman he wanted? He gently took her hand.

'I've already found the woman I want to spend the rest of my life with. She's the only woman I've ever loved and the only woman I will ever love. Marry me, Essie, let's have the life together that was stolen from us.'

She didn't pull her hand away and the warmth of it was coursing up his arm and into his heart. He so desperately wanted to kiss her and hold her against him forever.

'Craig,' her other hand came up and softly came to rest on his cheek. 'I'm already married.'

'Leave him. He doesn't deserve you.'

'No, he doesn't. But twenty-five years is a lot to give

up on and I really don't know if I'll be able to do it.'

'But—'

'I know,' she hushed him with a finger on his lips, 'George has made my life a misery and treated me very badly but like I said to Clarissa, I'm like the prisoner who's been locked up for many years – to suddenly gain my freedom terrifies me because I've only known the one way of life for so long. That's how I feel when I stop to consider where to go from here – terrified! Scared of the unknown and where the change of path will take me. I'm not saying I *won't* ever leave – I just can't say right now that I will. I don't want you to waste your time waiting for me, Craig, I want you to go forth and have a good life – the life you're long overdue.'

'I'll wait for you, Essie. Now I know how you felt all those years ago… I'm not giving up on you a second time. I let you go without a fight when I was young – I won't make the same mistake again.'

'I'd really rather you didn't…'

'Tough! That's how it's going to be. I'll make no demands on you, I won't force you to make any decisions and I'll be right here by your side when things are rough and you need a friend. My friendship is all yours and so is my love. I'm handing them to you on a plate and you only ever need to take what you want from it.'

'What did I ever do to make me so deserving?'

'Well, let me see…' Craig began counting on his fingers, 'You're beautiful, you're funny, you're intelligent, you're caring, you're sexy—'

'Okay, okay! Enough already!' Essie was laughing and her cheeks were flushed with embarrassment.

'I've been waiting since forever to be with you, Essie, and I'll wait till the end of forever, if that's what it takes.' He placed a small, butterfly kiss on her forehead before turning away and saying, 'Now, we'd better get a move on and find this darn bridge before Clarissa sends out a search party.'

'I wish I was there with you, Clarrie, it sounds so beautifully romantic.'

Clarissa sighed, as she looked at Ross's sweet, happy face filling her phone screen. They were FaceTiming while she waited for her mum and Craig to appear. She hadn't expected to miss him as much as she'd done since they'd parted ways in Blackpool. It didn't help when he told her how much he missed her too. He was still in Blackpool but expected his friend to be declared "back in the game" within the next couple of weeks and then he'd be heading off home to Inverness.

'It is romantic and should be shared with someone special.'

'Are you finally admitting that I'm "special" to you?'

Clarissa didn't answer right away. Ross had been open about his feelings towards her from the start. He liked her and he'd said so. Then he'd really liked her and had said so. Now he adored her, missed her like crazy, and he'd said so. She was in no doubt that he cared for her but saying the same things back was much harder. She definitely missed him, that was one thing she was sure about, but she was still working out if she missed him because she had growing, romantically-inclined, feelings for him or was it simply his easy, enjoyable, pleasing company. She'd decided to wait until they were back together again and see how she felt then.

'Well, you're definitely "special", that's for sure!'

She laughed at the mock indignation on his face.

'I'm not sure I like your insinuation, young lady! I can't see how you could make such an assertion!' He pulled a stupid face, crossing his eyes and letting his tongue hang out the side of his mouth.

She burst out laughing. 'You look like Pluto the dog from Disney! He was always my favourite!'

'It was Scooby-Doo for me, he and Shaggy always cracked me up.'

'Yeah, they were great.'

'Any sign of the olds yet?'

Clarissa looked up and after a quick glance about, spotted them approaching the steps up to the bridge where she was standing. 'They're almost here, I need to go.'

'Give them my regards.'

'Will do.'

'And to you, my little Clarrie-hen, I'm sending the biggest of cuddles and the hottest of snogs.' He puckered up and blew a big kiss to her on the screen. Clarissa felt her toes squeeze with happiness, the rest of her body joining in too.

'Hot cuddles and big snogs right back at ya!' she quipped. 'Laters!'

She hit the screen and was putting the phone back in her pocket just as her mum and Craig arrived by her side.

'Oh my, what a lovely view.' Essie lifted her camera and took several photographs. She bullied Craig and Clarissa into some of the shots before handing the camera to Craig for some mother and daughter piccies. Clarissa took the camera from Craig and insisted he stand by her mum for a couple of photos too. Looking at them together on the tiny screen, she noticed again how well they fitted together physically and how they both seemed to relax into each other. Definitely two pieces of the same coin, she thought. As she clicked away, her mind went back to her earlier thoughts of them becoming a couple and seeing them looking so right together, she wished even more for it to happen.

THIRTY-EIGHT

Their journey north carried on and Craig introduced them to "Wild Camping" which was simply being able to park up overnight in any location that took their fancy. Well, within reason of course! If they were travelling along one of the quieter B-roads, and they came across a nice little lay-by with a gorgeous view, they could park there and stay over without consequence – something that was not allowed in England. It afforded them more freedom and lifted the restraints of always having to be booked into their next campsite before leaving their current one although they still had to book into some campsites along the way in order to recharge batteries, take on fresh water and dispose of their waste.

They followed the coast road and debated on whether to grab the ferry from Stranraer to Ireland but decided not to on this occasion – maybe next year when they could do it justice and explore fully. Instead, they parked up at the popular sea-side town of Largs, took their bikes onto the little ferry over to the small island of Millport and spent a pleasing afternoon cycling around, enjoying the virtually car-free roads. They rewarded themselves for their efforts by having delicious ice-creams from the famous Nardini's café when they got back to the mainland.

They skirted around Glasgow and carried on towards Helensburgh and Loch Lomond. The weather had been holding up nicely and it was felt they'd be better off enjoying all the outdoor locations while they could. Craig was finally persuaded that his Scottish accent really wasn't the best and he reverted back to speaking normally, much to Essie and Clarissa's relief.

They bumped into Fliss and Becky – the two girls Clarissa had befriended the day she'd also met Ross – when they were waiting for the cable cars to take them up into the Nevis mountains. The girls had just come down and were extolling over the wonderful views. Their boyfriends, Tom and Mike, were hiking up Ben Nevis but Fliss and Becky were having none of that.

'Why half-kill yourself walking up the mountain when you can enjoy the thrill of a cable car ride instead? It'll be bad enough listening to them both moaning about their blisters when they get back tonight without indulging in some ourselves.'

Fliss's dry comment, sounding even more droll with her Australian accent, made them smile.

'Where are you going after this?' Essie asked them.

'We're heading over to Skye tomorrow, and after that, we'll be making our way towards Inverness. Ross is due back in town at the end of the week and he's told us we can crash at the farm for a while. I have to say, we're looking forward to having some down time and relaxing.'

Becky smiled at them as she spoke. 'Setting up in a new space every other day or so can get a bit tiring.'

'I quite agree with you on that one,' Craig replied.

'You've kept in touch with Ross, have you?' Clarissa asked.

‘We sure have, he’s a good bloke and lots of fun. Can’t wait to hang out with him again. We’ve said we’ll help out on the farm when it gets busy as a way of saying thanks for the free board.’

‘Fliss comes from farming stock so she’ll be showing me what to do. I’m a greenie townie!’ Becky laughed.

‘Then it looks like we’ll see each other again in a few weeks as we’ll also be up that way.’

‘Great stuff, Clarissa. And will you also be seeing Ross because that boy was kinda hot on you?’

‘We’ve kept in touch so most likely will.’

‘Cool! Well, this looks like your ride,’ Fliss nodded to the incoming gondola car, ‘so we’ll loves ya’s and leaves ya’s. See y’all in a few weeks.’

They said their goodbyes and the three of them piled into the cable car. While her mum and Craig ooh-ed and aah-ed over the stunning views, Clarissa wondered why Ross hadn’t mentioned to her that he’d kept in touch with Fliss et al.

‘Oh, my goodness! This is GLORIOUS! What a stunning view.’

They were standing in front of the Glenfinnan Viaduct looking out across Loch Sheil with the monument to Bonnie Prince Charlie standing proud against it. The sun was blazing out of the sky and the mountains surrounding the loch were reflected in its smooth blue waters, clearer than any mirror. Essie was clicking away with the camera, unable to believe how lucky they’d been with the weather. Scotland really did shine when the sun did.

Just then, there was a hoot in the distance and they turned to look at the viaduct. A plume of smoke rose above the trees before they were treated to the sight of an old-fashioned steam train coming around the corner and onto the old bridge.

'Wow! It's like a scene from Harry Potter and the Chamber of Secrets!' Clarissa exclaimed.

Essie changed the camera over to video mode and they watched in silence as the beautiful old engine made its way past, holding herself majestic and proud. They waved to the drivers and the passengers onboard, delighted when they waved back. The train soon disappeared into the trees at the other end of the viaduct and they stood quietly until they could hear her no longer.

'Amazing! Simply amazing!' Craig was spellbound by what he'd witnessed and it was written all over his face.

Essie took a few more still shots of the viaduct and, as she put the camera back in her bag, she turned to Clarissa.

'So, how do you know that looked like something from a Harry Potter film? Your father expressly forbade you to watch those films or read the books.'

Clarissa looked at her defiantly.

'Yes, he did, but luckily one of the girls from school took pity on me and lent me her books and DVDs when they came out. I read the books under the covers at night and watched the films on my PC. I was alienated enough thanks to all his other stupid rules. Not being able to join in with the Harry Potter chatter would have left me completely alone. At least, with Lorna's kindness, I was able to join in with something.'

'Good for you, darling.' Essie patted Clarissa on the arm.

'You're not annoyed or angry with me?'

'No, absolutely not! I wanted to take you to see the films at the cinema because I understood what a phenomenon they were, but I couldn't risk you letting something slip and your father finding out we'd gone against his wishes. Had I known you *were* so good at keeping secrets, we could've enjoyed them together.'

'I thought you agreed with him, you never spoke up against him when I asked for the books.'

'I wholly disagreed with him but all too often, it caused less trouble to keep quiet. I found out the hard way that it wasn't always worth it to disagree so I learnt to pick my battles and not allowing you to indulge in some wizarding fantasy wasn't one of them.'

'Was George physically violent towards you?'

Essie looked at Craig. 'No, he's never hit me although I'm sure he wanted to. The anger would come off him in waves and you could actually feel it wrapping around you and squeezing fear into your soul. No, his preferred method of punishment was a verbal attack. He had… has… a way of using words to cut you down and leave you feeling utterly worthless. He's very clever. Bruises on your body fade away and are eventually forgotten but the bruises of the mind stay for ever. You think they've been put to rest until something happens and all those put-downs and insults come rushing back to the fore, leaving you doubting everything about yourself and your reason for existing. Some days you cope better than others.'

'Oh, Essie…' Craig put his arm around her shoulders and pulled her tight against his side. She leant into him, taking a brief moment of comfort from his embrace before pulling away. Clarissa walked over and hugged her tightly.

'Thank you,' she whispered in her ear, 'I know you endured all this for me, to ensure I had the best opportunities in life. I wish I'd understood that at the time.'

Essie stepped back and looked into Clarissa's clear brown eyes. 'My darling daughter, I'm glad you weren't aware, you had enough to contend with, dealing with the isolation his snobbery cast upon you. You didn't need to be worrying about me too.'

She looked at the solemn faces around her.

‘Okay, enough of this serious stuff, we’re here to have fun. Let’s go and enjoy the alternate views from the monument before we head off to Mallaig. I’m looking forward to be going on the boat to Skye.’

Clarissa let out a groan. ‘Oh, Mum, PLEASE promise me you’re not going to sing when we’re on the ferry. I’m still getting over the episode in Liverpool.’

‘Girlfriend, I ain’t promising you nuttin’!’

She snapped her fingers in the air and sashayed down the path, the lyrics to “The Skye Boat Song” floating back towards Clarissa and Craig as they followed in her wake.

‘Craig, is there any chance you can change our booking to a different boat?’

‘I heard that!’ called Essie, causing them all to laugh.

THIRTY-NINE

'Okay, we're turning right just up ahead. It's almost on the bend and easy to miss so don't go too fast.'

Craig placed the walkie-talkie in the pocket on the door and tried to ignore the butterflies in his stomach. Although he spoke with his mother a few times a year, they weren't close and he hadn't been to visit since he was a boy. He'd just turned ten when he'd last been here and it had distressed him so much when the time came to go home, that his father had declared no more visits.

His mother had never been to visit them and when he'd once asked her why, she'd simply said that it would've been too painful to leave them again. He'd replied that she didn't have to leave and it had broken him to hear the sadness in her voice when she'd said her life was now in Scotland and that was where she had to stay. He'd never raised the subject again after that and the phone calls became more sporadic until they only really occurred on high days and holidays. Birthday wishes and Christmas greetings were pretty much the extent of it these days.

She still didn't know he was coming to visit – he'd kept

delaying in making that call – the fear was too great that she'd try to put him off. He was glad Essie and Clarissa were with him, there was less chance of her being rude and ungracious if they were in company. The one thing he remembered about his mother was her impeccable manners. He hoped that living in this wilderness all these years hadn't turned her into some kind of heathen.

He glanced in the rear-view mirror and saw Essie pull the motorhome onto the almost barely-there track behind him. The motorhome was taller than his little camper and he could see the branches of the trees brushing against its roof.

The track ran like this for about a mile until the trees suddenly disappeared on one side, giving a clear view over Loch Ewing and the mountains which rose steeply around it. It was early evening and the brilliant late-July sun was slowly setting on the other side of the hills, making them appear dark and fierce in its shadow. The tree break was brief and they were soon undercover in a tunnel of greenery again, following the rutted pathway until it eventually came out into a wide clearing.

Craig pulled the camper over to one side and switched off the engine. He swallowed a few times and forced some deep breaths into his lungs, trying to quell the tumbling sensation in his belly. Directly in front of his eyes stood his mother's stone cottage, built many years ago from the same local grey stone as the dry-stone wall he was parked alongside. Essie brought Marvin to a halt just behind him as he opened the door to get out. His feet had barely touched the ground when two West Highland Terriers came flying around the corner and up the sloping path, barking as they hurled themselves towards him.

'Sandy! Kirsty! Get back here now! Sit down and behave yourselves.'

The two dogs immediately plonked their bottoms on the

ground and sat, side by side, looking up at him, their mouths open with their pink tongues hanging slightly to one side, giving the appearance that they were smiling. He was about to bend down to pet them when the owner of the command came into view. The sun was behind her and he could see the tall, straight-backed figure striding his way, with her long vibrant red hair glowing like fire in the sunlight while swirling as it caught the breeze off the loch. When the woman arrived in front of him, he found himself looking into a pair of pale blue eyes. A blue so pale, it was almost silver.

'Hello, Mother,' he said, 'you haven't changed a bit!'

Essie and Clarissa waited inside Marvin, allowing Craig to have these first few moments alone with his mother.

Well, Essie assumed it was his mother although it was difficult to believe. She was stunningly beautiful and didn't look old enough to have a middle-aged son. She watched as her arms went around Craig and he was pulled into a tight embrace.

'That looks promising,' she whispered to Clarissa.

Before Clarissa could reply, the woman turned, looked straight at her through the windscreen, and beckoned them to come out.

'Here we go,' Clarissa whispered back.

They alighted from the motorhome and Essie tried to stretch discreetly. They'd been driving for almost three hours and she felt all tight and knotted.

'Welcome, welcome,' the woman said, greeting them both warmly and giving each a good strong handshake. 'I'm Flora MacDonald Wainwright and I'm delighted you've arrived here safely at last. Please come in, tea will be ready in a few minutes and the scones are fresh out of the oven.'

She turned away, leaving Essie and Clarissa feeling somewhat bemused. They fell into step beside Craig and Essie whispered quickly, 'I thought you hadn't spoken to your mum to tell her you were coming?'

'I haven't!'

'So, how come she appears to have been expecting us?'

'Buggered if I know! Maybe my dad mentioned something to her. They do still talk to each other.'

They walked down the path and around the side of the house. Both Essie and Clarissa let out a gasp when they took in the perfect location. The front of the house looked right out onto the loch and the water was lapping on the shoreline barely a hundred feet from the front door. The area along the front of the house was patioed and the sun was shining right down on to it. A table was set with four places and plates with sandwiches, savoury and sweet pastries, and a delicious looking sponge cake were already laid out on it.

Flora had entered the house but soon reappeared in the doorway.

'Please, come in. I will show you to your rooms and you can take a few minutes to refresh yourselves before we eat.'

Once again, Essie and Clarissa looked at each other before Essie replied, 'Please, Flora, we don't want to put you out. We're quite happy to sleep in our motorhome.'

'Och, you'll do no such thing. I have more than enough space for you all here. Now, follow me.'

She led them inside and Essie caught a quick glimpse of a kitchen to one side of the hallway and a lounge area on the other before she ascended the narrow staircase. At the top, Flora led them to the bedroom that was situated above the lounge, opened the door and stepped back to let them in. The room was simple but beautiful. It had two single beds, both facing the small, deep-set, window which looked out over the loch. The walls were painted white and the bedding was also white. The floorboards had been sanded and lavender-coloured rugs lay between the beds and in front of the window. They matched the curtains which were hanging from a rugged wooden pole. Essie sensed the pole had been there for a very long time. Colourful jugs around the room held bunches of lavender and the smell was glorious and calming.

'Thank you, Flora, this room is beautiful. What a fabulous view.'

'Aye, it is that. I find the sound of the water quite soothing when going off to sleep at night and the pure, clean air ensures you have a good one.'

'Is it safe to leave the windows open through the night?'

'Oh, it's perfectly safe. There's no one around these parts with a heart to burgle anyone.'

'Erm, I was actually thinking of the midges! They have quite the reputation.'

Flora let out a laugh that sounded like water running over century-smoothed stones.

'I get you! You've nothing to worry about there either, that's what the lavender is for. The wee blighters hate the smell. Keep those two jugs there on the windowsill and you'll be just fine.'

She pointed to a wardrobe in the corner.

'You'll find fresh towels in there and,' she pointed back out into the hallway, 'the bathroom is right there. That door is my room and if you need anything at all during the night, please don't hesitate to come and get me.'

'Thank you, you're very kind,' replied Essie, 'although we'll do our best not to trouble you.'

'It's a pleasure to have visitors and it'll be no trouble, I assure you. Now, I'll leave you to sort yourselves out while I take Gerald up to his old room upstairs in the attic. You know where to find me when you're ready to eat.'

She closed the door behind her, leaving Essie and Clarissa a bit shell-shocked.

'I wasn't expecting this, Mum, were you?'

'Absolutely not but if it's of any consolation, I don't think Gerald… I mean Craig, was either.'

Thirty minutes later, the four of them were sitting around the table tucking into the delectable sandwiches. Clarissa had never tasted such lovely egg mayonnaise before and said as much between mouthfuls.

'Fresh eggs laid this morning, that'll be the difference.'

'Do you have hens then?'

'I do. Technically, this is a smallholding and I'm relatively self-sufficient. Some things I trade with neighbours – such as milk and bacon for me, eggs and herbs for them.'

'You have neighbours? Where?' Clarissa looked around her and could see no other signs of life.

'They're all a few miles away but most have to pass by the track on their way to town so we have a wee deposit area where we leave the goods for each other.'

'Is that not a bit of a walk for you?'

'The road-track is a longer route than the path which cuts through the trees. It only takes about fifteen minutes each way.'

'But what about during the winter?'

'Clarissa, don't be rude by asking so many questions.' Essie placed her hand on Clarissa's arm.

'Oh, it's fine, Essie, I'm happy to answer any questions you might have. I'm aware I practically live like a hermit and it must be interesting for people who are not used to that way of life to know how it all works.' Flora looked back at Clarissa. 'In the winter, I simply put warmer clothing on. The footpath is fairly protected by the trees and gets minimal snowfall.'

'May I ask another question?'

Flora looked at her and gave her a radiant smile. 'Clarissa, you may ask as many questions as you desire.'

'I don't suppose, given your name, that you're in any way related to *the* Flora MacDonald, are you?'

The story of Bonnie Prince Charlie's escape was still fresh in Clarissa's mind and it seemed like too much of a coincidence given they weren't overly far from where her family home had been on the Isle of Skye.

'I'm not a direct bloodline descendent but I can trace my family tree back to her through cousins and the like.'

'Wow! That's awesome!'

Flora simply smiled before saying, 'Gerald, please have some more to eat. I made the fruit scones especially for you, I know how much you like them.'

Without thinking, Clarissa blurted out, 'Oh, he's not called Gerald anymore, he's—'

She stopped, suddenly aware that Flora hadn't yet been told of Craig's name change and realising he may not have told her to avoid upset. After all, no parent likes to be told the name they've given their poor child is a bit pants!

Flora looked at her son. 'So, if you're not Gerald anymore, who are you?'

'I've decided to go by my middle name, Craig. I… erm… prefer it. Sorry.'

'Och, there's no need to apologise to me, I think Gerald is a perfectly hideous name! I'm more than happy for you to be Craig.'

'But… why did you call me "Gerald" if you don't like it?'

'It wasn't my call, darling.'

Flora looked at them all.

'The tradition in my family is that the first-born

daughter is always called Flora. It goes back centuries and is almost what, I believe they say these days, non-negotiable. That's why your sister was Flora and your niece is Flora. It's something that just has to be. To ensure fairness, it fell to your father to name you and he chose Gerald after his own grandfather. I hated it but had to go with it, that was the deal. He didn't, however, bother with a middle name, so I put Craig in when I took you to be registered. I don't think your father ever noticed but I kind of hoped that giving you a decent middle name might soften the pain of "Gerald" somewhere along the line.'

'Well, it took a while to get there and I have Clarissa to thank for making the suggestion.'

'You got there in the end though, that's what matters, and you're looking incredibly well on it. Although, what's happening with Marjory? Your father told me about your wedding.'

'You knew about that? Why didn't you come? You were invited.'

'Tell me first, before I answer, is the divorce now finalised?'

'Yes.'

'Good! I didn't attend because your father informed me that she was a truly hideous piece of work and I shouldn't bother going to the effort of coming along because it would never last.'

'He said that?'

'Yes, dear. He couldn't stand the woman—'

'I know! I just didn't realise he'd passed that on to you.'

'I did have my suspicions myself, if I'm being honest.'

'How could you have possibly known? You never met her.'

'Call it a mother's intuition, we have a way of sensing these things. Wouldn't you agree, Essie?'

Clarissa looked at her mother as she thought for a

moment before answering.

'Yes, I suppose we do know, Flora. I can think of a few occasions where I've sensed when things weren't quite right with Clarissa before she's told me. Although I don't think it's as finely honed as yours seems to be. Clarissa has to at least be in my presence. I doubt I could manage it if there were hundreds of miles between us.'

'Necessity, Essie, I had to find some way of keeping the connection between me and my children.'

The wistful look she gave Craig was so full of love and tenderness, it rendered them all silent.

Clarissa took her mum's hand under the table, gave it a squeeze, and felt a warmth of love flow through her when her mum squeezed back. It brought home again how much her mum loved her and that she'd endured a miserable life with her father rather than take the risk of losing her. She knew her mum was right – George would never have let her go with her mother and he'd have destroyed Essie in every way possible to ensure she couldn't have custody of her own daughter. George never lost a fight and he wouldn't have cared about what was best for Clarissa – he'd have still gone for the win, regardless.

They all sat in silence after that, watching the sun set the loch alight with its dying rays before finally slipping down to sleep behind the mountains. With its warmth removed, the breeze off the loch turned chilly and, not long afterwards, they cleared the table and made for their beds, exhausted after their day and full from the delicious food Flora had made for them.

FORTY

Clarissa was sound asleep when Essie left the room and tiptoed down the stairs. It was early but she'd been unable to go back to sleep once she'd woken up. She'd grabbed a quick shower and was dressed with the intention of going for a walk around part of the loch. She had a yearning for some solitude and felt being surrounded by towering hills and rippling water would be the perfect balm for her ruffled little soul. She hadn't spent so much time in the company of other people since she'd been at uni. Once they were married, George would go off to work, leaving her alone every day and when Clarissa was old enough for school, she'd been alone again. She was thoroughly enjoying being with Clarissa and Craig but had occasionally missed those hours of quiet when it was just her and her thoughts.

Her hand was on the latch of the front door when a voice called out from the kitchen, 'The tea is freshly brewed if you fancy a cup.'

She turned to see Flora sitting at the kitchen table.

'I'm sorry, Flora, I hope I haven't disturbed you – I

didn't know anyone else was up.'

'Oh, you didn't disturb me, I was up and about hours ago. The best time to pick my herbs and flowers is just as dawn is breaking and the dew is still fresh upon them. That's when their powers are strongest.'

'I see.' Essie wasn't quite sure how to answer that.

'I can put the tea in a flask if you like and you can take it with you on your walk.'

'How did you know I was planning to go for a walk?'

'I can sense the disquiet in your heart, lass. A wee walk amongst all the beauty that Mother Nature has placed here will do you the power of good.'

'That's what I thought.'

Just then, the two Westies came running in. Essie put her hand down to pet Kirsty and was surprised when the dog let out a small growl. She drew her fingers away and looked towards Flora.

'Och, don't mind her, she's recently been tupped – it takes a wee while for them to settle again after that.'

'Tupped?'

'Mated. It's an expression mostly used in sheep farming but I prefer it to "mated" – it sounds nicer, I think.'

'Right. So, I'm guessing she'll be having puppies then.'

'All being well. Sometimes they don't take but it's rare. Her behaviour is suggesting she has so that's good.'

'How long will it be till the puppies are born?'

Essie looked at the little dog who was now snuffling about in the bed next to the cast-iron range, turning around several times before lying down and burying her nose under her paws as she fell asleep.

'Usually nine weeks, all being well.'

'Do you sell the puppies, are you a breeder?'

'I do sell the pups but I'm not a professional breeder. Each bitch I have only ever has two litters. My pups are in high demand and there's no many farms in a fifty-mile radius that doesn't have a Flora MacDonald Westie.'

'Were Sandy and Kirsty pups you'd bred?'

Essie put her hand down gently on Sandy's head and stroked him. Since he was pushing up against her leg, almost begging for attention, she didn't think he'd mind her touch. And she was right. As soon as her fingers began scratching, he lifted his head and forced it against her nails, trying to make her scratch harder.

'They certainly were.'

'They're gorgeous.' She smiled down at the dog by her side.

'Are you a dog lover then?'

'I don't dislike them but I've never had one.'

'That's a pity, they're great companions. Now, here's a wee bit of tuck for your walk. I baked the shortbread earlier this morning and it'll go nice with your flask of tea. Take Sandy with you, he'll enjoy the walk out and guide you back if you get a bit lost. Just say to him, "Take me home, Sandy" and he'll lead you.'

'Really?'

'Of course.'

Flora turned to the dog, gave him the same instruction and Essie watched in amazement as Sandy appeared to nod at her, as if to say he understood.

Flora caught her expression as she straightened.

'Dogs are far more intelligent than many humans give them credit for. Now, off you go and I'll see you when you get back.'

Realising she had effectively been dismissed, Essie stood up, picked up the little canvas bag Flora had placed her "tuck" in and made for the front door. She turned to call on Sandy but found him already at her heels, a look on his face which seemed to say, "Come with me, missus, I'll show you all the good spots". She looked up again at Flora only to find the woman was no longer in the room.

She let the dog lead the way out of the door, closed it behind her and, as the fresh breeze off the loch caught her hair and made it dance, she said, 'Well then, Sandy, it looks like you're in charge. Lead the way.'

The smell of frying bacon sneaked up the stairs, slipped under the bedroom door and gently pulled Clarissa away from the land of nod and into the fresh new morning. The growling sensation in her stomach gave her the final push and she opened her eyes. She saw her mum's bed was empty and the covers were neatly pulled back to allow it to air. As she stretched and yawned, her stomach rumbled again, this time more furiously. She threw her own covers back and got out of bed, unable to believe she could be so hungry after the huge tea they'd eaten last night. Pulling apart the curtains, she noticed the windows had been open all night. Ah, she thought, that'll be why – it must be all the fresh air that's giving me such an appetite. She picked up her wash bag and stepped across the hall to the bathroom. This was going to be the fastest shower ever because she was famished and that bacon smelt amazing.

Sure enough, it was barely ten minutes later when Clarissa walked in the kitchen door. It was empty apart from the small white dog asleep beside the range. On top of the range sat a huge, cast-iron frying pan and she could see the bacon rashers sizzling. She was most impressed by the lack of interest the Westie was showing in the cooking meat for she'd have expected it to be sitting to attention, trying to will the slices of meat to jump down into its waiting mouth.

Clarissa took a closer look around the kitchen – although she'd been in here last night when she'd helped to bring the tea things in from the garden, she hadn't really paid much attention. Now, however, as she was here on her own, she took the opportunity to do so.

The room was a good size, with a medium-sized bay window facing out towards the loch. Under that, was a boxed-in, window seat. Another smaller window was set in the wall directly opposite the door, the dog bed placed underneath, and to the left of that was a big, black, kitchen range. A massive free-standing Welsh dresser filled the length of the wall across from the range. The fourth wall housed an old-fashioned butler sink with a massive wooden draining board, above which a wooden shelf ran all the way along and a number of small window panes let a modicum of light into what would have otherwise been a dark, gloomy area. Clarissa surmised that, if it wasn't for the large green pine trees on the other side of the glass, there would be considerably more light penetrating the dark corners. The middle of the room was taken up by a vast, thick, wooden table. The top looked as though it had been scrubbed thoroughly on a daily basis for many, many years. She walked across and lightly ran her fingers over it. It was as smooth as the proverbial baby's bottom.

'Over two hundred years old, that is.'

She jumped at the sudden break in the silence and looked up to see Flora standing there with a small basket of eggs in her hand.

'Oh, I didn't hear you come in, Flora, you made me jump.'

'I'm sorry, lass, didn't mean to frighten you.'

'No, no, I'm fine.' Her heartbeat slowed, the initial surprise quickly receding. She reached out to feel the table again, drawn to its warm smoothness.

'Over two hundred years? Wow!'

'Yes, it belonged to a great, many times over, grandmother and has been passed down through the family over the years.'

'That's amazing. A real family heirloom.'

'It comes with the cottage. Everything in this cottage is passed on to the next in line.'

'Have your family lived here long then?'

Flora smiled. 'Over two hundred years. The grandmother – the one I mentioned earlier – helped the young wife of the local laird safely deliver a baby boy. They'd already had two failed pregnancies and when the wife fell pregnant a third time, there were fears that neither she nor the baby would survive. The laird came to see my grandmother, for she was known to have an understanding – or skill, if you like – with herbs and natural remedies, and asked for her help. She obliged, a healthy baby boy was born and the laird's wife went on to have two more children. As a means of saying thank you, he gifted this piece of land to my grandmother, along with a few more acres on either side, for her to live on and all her descendants after that. The property is entailed down through the female line of the family and so, as such, is really only ever "on loan" to the current occupant.'

Clarissa's legal training immediately jumped to the fore.

'But an act has since been passed that effectively dissolves all entails and allows the property to be sold.'

'Aye, I know, but that'll no happen here.'

'But, how do you know? You may not want to sell it but whoever inherits after you might.'

Flora turned and settled her silvery gaze upon her. Clarissa felt a strange sensation ripple through her but before she could react, it ceased as Flora moved her eyes to the frying pan and said quietly, 'I just know. It's how it's always been and how it will always be. Now, can I tempt you to some bacon and eggs, you must be starving.'

Clarissa accepted the subtle change of topic and agreed that she was rather hungry. Flora ordered her to sit, declined her offer of assistance and within a few minutes, had placed a sizable plate in front of her, brimming with bacon, eggs, baked beans and fresh toast.

'There now,' Flora said, 'eat up. The world is always a happier place when we face it with a full belly.'

As she tucked in, Clarissa couldn't help but agree.

FORTY-ONE

Craig walked into the kitchen in time to see Clarissa wiping up the last of her egg yolk with a piece of toast. He'd barely had time to utter a greeting when his mum placed a stacked plate of food on the table and told him to sit down and eat.

'Did you sleep okay?' she asked him.

'It took me a while to get off, that's why I'm late down this morning.'

'You're not late, Craig. Late is when you don't arrive somewhere by a specific time. As we hadn't stated a specific time for breakfast, you are merely following your own body clock. Dinnae fash yerself, lad.'

Craig smiled as she spoke. It had always been one of his mum's little quirks – to slip in and out of her natural Scottish tongue several times throughout a conversation. One minute she'd be speaking Oxford English, and the next, a wee Scottish word or expression would creep out to join in.

'Okay, Mum. Thank you for breakfast.'

He looked at Clarissa as he loaded up his fork. 'Is Essie

still upstairs, Clarissa?'

'No. And, actually, I don't know where she is. Flora?'

'She went out for a walk about an hour ago – needed a wee spot of time to herself. She'll be back soon.'

'But she might have gotten lost…' Craig felt a flurry of panic, placed his fork back on the plate and was halfway out of his chair when he felt his mother's hand come to rest on his shoulder, gently pushing him back onto his seat.

'She's absolutely fine. Sandy is with her, so no harm will come to her. In fact, she's on her way back now and will be here shortly. I'd best get cooking some more bacon.'

'How do you know that? And please, let me help you, Flora. We don't expect you to wait on us hand and foot.'

'I know, Clarissa, because I saw her a minute ago.' She nodded her head towards the window. 'She was sitting on the large boulder over the other side of the loch. I saw her get off and turn in this direction. Now, as much as I appreciate the offer of help, there is no need – it's nice to have people to look after. It's been a long time since I've had real company. Please, sit and take another cup of tea. Tell me what your plans are for the day.'

'I think Clarissa's hoping we'll head over to the farm of a young man she's met.'

Craig smiled as he ate, finding the blush which crept up her cheeks quite endearing.

'Oh, you've met a local lad, have you?'

'Erm, yes. His name is Ross MacKenzie.'

'Ah, one of the MacKenzie boys. Nice! They're good lads. Ross is the youngest I believe?'

'That's correct. He did say you were acquainted with the family.'

Craig poured another cup of tea for himself and Clarissa as he spoke.

'Apparently, you helped to prevent their dairy herd

becoming infected during the TB outbreak.'

'I don't know about "helped" as such. I merely provided some natural remedies which I know are supposed to increase immunity. Those, and some common sense in the way of procedures, did the trick.'

'It sounds to me, Flora, that you might share the same skills in natural remedies as your great-many-times-grandmother.'

Craig looked at Clarissa in surprise before turning to his mum.

'What's this?'

'Oh, nothing, dear. I was just sharing a little of the family history with Clarissa after she admired the kitchen table. Well, if you are heading over to the MacKenzies' today, would you mind taking some items with you? It'll save them a trip over this way and with them getting ready to bring in the harvest, I'm sure it's time that could be better spent elsewhere.'

'Of course, I can do that. We can load up whatever you need in the camper, there's plenty of space.'

'You're welcome to use my Landy while you're here – it might be less cumbersome for you, especially if you want to explore more fully, which would definitely include some rather rough tracks. I don't think your VW would survive for long, Craig, on the smaller roads around here.'

'You've got a Land Rover?'

'Yes, why so surprised?'

'It's just the way you suggested everyone came to you… I suppose I just thought you didn't go too far from home and so wouldn't have a vehicle.'

Craig felt like a child again as his mother's eye settled upon him. Did all mothers have this knack of making you feel small and stupid even when you were a grown adult? He must remember to ask Clarissa later.

'When you live somewhere as isolated as this, there are

three essential things which you need – a good generator and a good, sturdy, vehicle.'

'That's only two; what's the third?'

Flora swept her silvery-blue eyes away from Craig, towards Clarissa.

'The ability to mend them if they break!'

Her face broke into a big smile and a squeak of laughter floated out.

Just then, the cottage door opened and Essie walked in, Sandy close on her heels.

Craig felt his heart clench when he saw her loose, breeze-blown hair, the pale pink of her cheeks from the fresh air and the sparkle in her eyes. She looked relaxed, carefree and so very different from the buttoned-up woman he'd bumped into – literally – back in February.

'Grab a seat there, Essie, and help yourself to a fresh brew. The bacon is on and will be with you in a jiffy.'

Craig leant over.

'Sit! There's no need to help. Clarissa has already offered but it was refused as Mum is in her element looking after us all.'

Essie had barely parked herself upon the chair when a large, food-piled, plate was placed in front of her.

'I'll never eat all that,' she exclaimed.

'That's what you think now but once you taste those delicious fresh eggs and the newly baked, toasted bread, you'll soon finish it all.'

Craig pointed at his own cleared plate. 'If there'd been a pattern on that plate, I'd have licked it off.'

Flora placed a rack of toast on the table and was about to sit down when she glanced out of the window.

'Oh, excuse me a moment…'

She turned away and walked out of the front door, making her way towards the shore of the loch.

'What's she doing, Craig?'

He watched his mother through the glass. Flora stopped at the water's edge, appeared to sniff the air and then slowly raised her arms. She held them aloft before weaving her hands in a figure-of-eight motion above her head. She did this for about a minute before spinning around and walking back into the cottage.

Craig raised his eyebrows and was about to ask what that had all been about when Flora sat down, pulled the butter dish towards her and said, 'When you see Dougie MacKenzie later, that's Ross's father, tell him I said "seven days". He'll know what I mean.'

'What, so I've just to say "My mum, Flora, sends you a message – it's 'seven days' and you know what she means" have I?'

'Yes, dear, that would be perfect. Thank you.'

She gave him a little smile as she bit into her buttered toast and Craig realised she'd deliberately side-swiped the sarcasm in his comment. Jeez, he thought, these mothers could be right cutting creatures when the mood took them.

FORTY-TWO

'Seven days? You're *sure* that's what she said? Seven days?'

'Err, yes. Quite sure.'

Craig was not impressed at having his word doubted. It was only two words – he was more than capable of remembering them.

'Shit!' Dougie MacKenzie rubbed his face with both hands before repeating, 'Shit! Shit! Shit!'

'I don't wish to appear rude here,' Essie quietly butted in, 'but unless it's a clue for The Times cryptic crossword, would someone mind telling us the significance of this.'

Ross turned his equally worried face in their direction.

'It's how long we've got to get the harvest in before the rain comes.'

'Ah!' said Essie.

'Oh!' said Craig.

He looked at Essie as he replied, 'I'm going to guess that's not very long.'

'Not when you've got twelve big fields of crops to get in. If they get wet, they can rot, which is bad for business and bad for the bank account.'

'But the weather has been lovely up till now and there was no mention on the weather forecast of any rain coming.'

Ross put his arm around Clarissa's shoulders and hugged her close as he said, 'The Flora has never been wrong, not in all these years. She's the only weather forecast we need at this time of year.'

Dougie MacKenzie gave them all a tight smile. 'Please, excuse me. I need to try and find some spare farm hands to help or we're going to have very big problems.'

He marched off leaving Craig, Essie and Clarissa standing in the yard with Ross.

'Why do we feel that we're not the bearers of good news?' Essie asked.

'We would usually begin the harvest about two weeks from now but if there's rain on its way, the crops won't have time to dry out before cutting, or worse still, could be damaged. Dad has extra help booked for the harvest weeks but as we now have to go out early, they won't be here on time.'

'Can they not come now?'

'Sadly not, Essie, the hands work to tight schedules – they need to, to earn their money. They'll be busy elsewhere right now.'

Ross turned away from them and began to pace across the cobbles of the yard. 'I don't know what we're going to do…'

'Well, I do! We can help, can't we, Craig?'

'We can?' He looked at Essie as though she'd suddenly sprung a second head.

'Of course, we can! Ross, I concur we may not have a clue what to do but I'm sure you'll be able to guide us along. There must be something important which needs very little skill.'

'Oh, I couldn't ask that of you—'

'You didn't ask, we're offering! So, lead the way. We're only three but it's three more than nothing.'

'Actually… I've just had a thought…' Clarissa turned to look at Ross. 'Have Fliss and Becky arrived yet?'

'Yes, they got here a few days back. They're camped out over on the other side of the farm.'

'Fliss mentioned something about planning to help you with the harvest as a thank you for allowing them to pitch up here. I think her family back home are farmers and she knows what she's doing. Go and find them. That'll give you seven helpers right away.'

'I couldn't…'

'Ross, you must! This is a time when you need to accept help when it's offered. Now, tell me where we can find your father and let him know he's got seven bodies ready to help.'

Craig stood back and watched the scene playing out in front of him. He knew Essie could do organising, and Clarissa had told him a little of how she ran a tight ship down at the local WI, but this was the first time he'd seen her fully in action. It was quite awesome but also a little bit scary.

'Craig, are you coming with me to find Dougie?'

'Urm, yes, Essie, right away.' Craig jumped to attention and trotted along behind her. Yep, he thought, definitely a little bit scary.

Seven days later, they had just closed the doors on the storage barns when the rain arrived. Great big globules burst from the sky and fell with the ferocity of bullets from a machine gun. Nobody moved, however, to escape it. They simply stood still, taking in the enormity of the task they'd just, by the skin of their teeth, managed to complete.

As Clarissa had suggested, Fliss, Becky and their boyfriends had been only too happy to get on board with lending a hand. Dougie and Fraser had operated the big machinery, Ross, Fliss and eventually, after a few lessons, Clarissa, had driven the tractors to and from the barns along with Ross's grandfather, Donald, who, although retired, still mucked in during the harvest. Essie, Craig, Tom, Mike and Becky had loaded the trailers as they waited to be hitched up to the tractors. It had been hard work and the days had been long. Essie couldn't remember ever feeling so exhausted but despite the cuts and blisters on her hands and arms, the ache in her shoulders and back and the taut muscles of her thighs, she felt utterly exhilarated. From deep within her, an urge arose to let out an almighty whoop and, not caring what the others thought, she ran from the shelter of the barn into the rain-soaked yard, lifted her face skywards and hollered loudly up towards the heavy black clouds. She raised her arms and began spinning around, growing wetter by the second but she didn't care. A noise by her side had her opening her eyes and there was Craig, joining her in her madness and beside him, Fliss and Becky were also squealing and laughing as they jumped in the puddles now forming on the ground.

'You lot are pure mental,' roared Dougie, stomping about beside them, giving out bear hugs to whomever he could lay his hands upon. Essie had grown to admire him over the days they'd worked together. He was a quiet man and very patient. Whenever she'd held the pitchfork wrong, he'd calmly taken a moment to show her the correct way and how to move the crops without causing herself an injury. She saw a lot of Ross in him and it had settled her mind over how attached Clarissa was becoming to the young man. She could see the affection growing deeper between them and she couldn't help but wonder how it would all pan out.

'Seriously? Are you lot auditioning for places at the funny farm? Get yourselves inside now.'

Essie turned to see Mhairi, Ross's mother, walking towards them with some large golf umbrellas in her hand. Mhairi had been a godsend while they'd worked. She'd kept them topped-up with tea, coffee, cake, sandwiches, fruit, freshly-baked pastries and cold drinks when the sun reached its peak in the sky. They say an army marches on its stomach – well this little army had proved that point and Mhairi's delicious picnics had kept them going every day until they were finished.

Everyone ran towards the farmhouse and piled into the kitchen which was toasty from the fire burning there. Piled up in front were large towels, warming up and ready to help them all dry off. Now that the adrenaline rush was wearing off and the rain had seeped through their clothing to nestle against bare skin, there was much chattering of teeth and Essie was struggling to hold the towel she'd picked up.

'Come here, Essie.' Craig took her towel from her and proceeded to rub her hair and arms vigorously – just like her mother had done when she was a child – to get her circulation flowing again. When some feeling came back into her fingers, she returned the gesture.

They were all jostling to get in front of the warm fire when Alice, the young girl who helped out in the farm shop, came in bearing a tray full of glasses. She laid it on the table and Essie saw they all had a tot of amber in them.

'Everyone, please, take a glass,' Dougie's voice cut over the hubbub.

Once everyone had a glass in their hand, he spoke again.

'I'd like to take this opportunity to thank you all so

much for your help this last week. I can honestly say that, without you, we would not have had a full harvest and I'm sure I don't need to tell you how devastating it would have been for our little business. My thanks go especially to Essie who was adamant we could do this and who organised everyone while I sat in the office having a major meltdown. You are one awesome lady. To Essie!'

He raised his glass high.

'To Essie!'

Everyone in the room chorused as they joined in the toast.

'Oh, please, no! Stop!'

Essie felt herself growing hot with embarrassment as everyone looked her way.

'I'm simply glad we could all help and that our inexperience didn't prove to be more of a hindrance than a help.'

Dougie spoke again. 'In ten days from now, we'll be having our annual harvest dance and I hope everyone here will attend as my guests of honour.'

'Oh, will it be a ceilidh?'

Dougie laughed. 'Yes, Clarissa, it will be a ceilidh and I hope you'll honour me with at least one dance.'

'I think I can manage that.'

'One's all you're getting, old man, she's going to be dancing in my arms for the rest of the night.' Ross gave his dad a nudge in the side and got a slap on the head for his cheek.

Essie twisted to the side to put her now-empty glass on the table and caught an expression of sheer dislike on young Alice's face. She looked to see who the unlucky recipient was and felt a blow of shock to find Clarissa standing in the firing line. She immediately turned her attention back to Alice but her features now held a look of total and complete adoration as Ross moved into her sights.

Oh dear, thought Essie, that doesn't bode well. She watched Alice for a little while longer, just to see if she'd misinterpreted what she'd seen but she hadn't. The girl was moving around the kitchen picking up the empty tumblers and when she was near Clarissa, her enmity flowed from her.

Essie felt her hackles go up. She was a mother hen watching out for her young and she would not be happy if anyone thought they could behave like that towards her precious daughter. She made a mental note to have a quiet word with Mhairi later to ensure Alice knew to keep her distance from Clarissa and Ross or she'd have her to answer to.

FORTY-THREE

That same night, Clarissa lay in Ross's arms, the sound of his heart beating in one ear and the thrumming of the rain on the hut roof in the other. One of the holiday huts was currently out of commission awaiting repairs and Ross was using it while he was home. The deal was he would carry out the repairs required in between helping out on the farm. Clarissa was hoping that roof repairs were not on the DIY list.

'You okay, Clarrie?' He tightened his arm around her and pulled the blanket up over her shoulders a little more.

'Hmm, yes. Just listening to the sound of the rain – it's quite hypnotic. Very soothing.'

'Aye, I suppose it is, although, as a farmer, it's not a sound we're always that happy to hear. If it hadn't been for your mum and everyone mucking in so willingly, it would've been the cause of great despair in the farmhouse tonight.'

'Thankfully, Flora was able to prevent that. Does she often make such predictions and are they always so accurate?'

'Oh yes! Folks around here have been listening to The Flora's weather reports for years and the same with her mother before her. They've never been wrong. Those who choose to ignore them often regret it in the long run.'

'Is it only once a year for the harvest?'

'No. She lets us know when the snow is coming – which is very handy for the sheep farmers – and when it's the optimum time to sow the seeds for the crops.'

'Wow! I'm impressed. How does she do it?'

'I don't really know. Whenever anyone asks the question, the answer is always the same – she's simply in tune with the earth, the air and the sun and they reveal their secrets to her.'

'Well, I'm glad she got it right. Your family are lovely and I'd have hated for them to be struggling through the next year had she not passed on the crucial information.'

'Indeed! Now then, less of The Flora and more of us.' He nuzzled her neck in the way that made her tingle all the way to the tips of her toes. She stretched out in delight and joined him in other ways which made them more than tingle.

Afterwards, they both lay watching the dying embers in the fireplace. It had taken the damp chill off the air and the hut was delightfully cosy. Clarissa hadn't realised until today just how cold Scottish rain could be. Ross had advised it was their proximity to the North Sea that made it so icy, no matter what time of the year it was.

'Clarrie, you still awake?'

'Just about,' she murmured lazily, barely finding the energy to speak. Her eyelids had grown heavy and she wasn't too far away from slipping over to dreamland.

'I want to ask you something…'

'Hmmm…'

'You know I'm off to Japan in six weeks to begin my new job…'

‘Hmmm…’

‘Well, I’d… erm… I… would you like to come with me?’

‘What?’ Her eyelids sprung open and her journey to the land of sweet dreams ground to an abrupt halt.

‘I said—’

‘I know what you said, Ross, well… I think I know. Did you just ask me to come to Japan with you?’

‘Yes.’

She sat up and reached for her T-shirt, putting it on while her mind raced. She hadn’t expected this and needed a moment to let it sink in before she replied. When her head popped out the top, she saw Ross watching her. It was impossible to read what he was thinking in the muted, fire-lit room.

‘I don’t know what to say. This is quite a surprise.’ *And that’s quite the understatement*, a little voice whispered in her head.

‘I love you, Clarissa. And, before you reply, believe me when I say falling in love with you was never part of the plan.’

‘Plan?’

‘Yes. You know I’m going to Japan on a two-year contract to gain the additional experience I need to enable me to set up my own consultancy business when I return.’

‘I do.’ She twisted the blanket around her fingers, unsure of the emotions his words were causing within her.

‘You, however…’ he caught a hold of her fidgeting digits and held them tightly within his own. ‘You were not planned and yet I find I wouldn’t change this for anything. We work so well together. We discuss all manner of topics and we laugh at the same jokes! For goodness’ sake, you not only *get* my crazy sense of humour but you join in and make it all seem normal. It feels like we’ve both been carved from the same tree and I don’t want to lose it. I don’t want to lose you.'

'I see.'

'Is there any chance of you saying anything else?' She caught the flash of his teeth as he grinned at her.

I'm sorry, Ross, it's just... well... of all the things you could have said, this was not what I expected to hear.'

'I see.'

She couldn't help but give a little smile as he repeated her words back to her. They sat in silence as she poked about inside herself, trying to fathom what it was she feeling. In true orderly, legal, fashion, she mentally pulled a yellow legal pad in front of her and began to lay out her thoughts.

How did Ross's request make her feel? *Don't know.*

Did she feel annoyed? *No.*

Did she feel repelled? *No.*

Was she interested? *Yes.*

How did it feel when Ross said "I love you"? *Don't know.*

Did she feel annoyed? *No.*

Did she feel repelled? *No.*

Was she interested? *Yes.*

Did she feel all squishy and soppy like the heroines of almost every chick-flick she'd ever watched? *Hell, yes!*

Did she love him?

Here she paused. In her mind, she could see the list all written out. She read it over, satisfied with her responses until she came to the last question.

Did she love him?

Finally, she "wrote" out the answer, feeling a soothing sense of peace wash over her as she did so.

Yes!

She gave herself a moment to come to terms with this

inner discovery. Ross was right in everything he'd said. She couldn't disagree with a word of it.

She squeezed the fingers which had grown still by her hand as time had dragged on without her reply.

'Ross, I love you too. I'm sorry I didn't answer immediately, I… I hadn't given "us" much thought in that way, but you're absolutely right – we do seem to be the perfect fit. I certainly wasn't looking for love either, so this is as much of a surprise to me as it is to you, but it seems that love has other ideas and found us instead.'

'Does that mean you'll come with me to Japan?'

'I don't know.' She let out a little sigh. 'It's a wonderful opportunity, and it's not that I'm not interested because I am, it's just… well, Fliss and Becky have asked me if I'd like to join them when they tour around Europe next year. They're heading over to France in December and touring around until July when they'll be returning home to Australia. They've extended the invite to go back to Oz with them.'

'Oh! Right… that's also a rather attractive offer.'

'Exactly! And so is yours. Which leaves me now with the decision of which one, if either, to accept.'

'So, you hadn't made up your mind on Europe?'

'It was only mentioned a couple of days ago – I need to discuss it with my mum and I don't know how that'll go.'

'I'm sure she'll be delighted for you. I get the impression she wants you to have as many wonderful experiences as possible, maybe because she didn't get that opportunity.'

'Perhaps, but… well… I now have a lot to think about, so do you mind if I take some time before I get back to you?'

Ross lay down, gently pulled her down to his side and, as he turned to face her, he said, 'Take all the time you need, there's no pressure. You need to do what you need to do. However, in the meantime… you said you love me… how about you show me just how that goes…'

FORTY-FOUR

Essie looked around the barn and wowed inwardly at the transformation from the dusty, crop-filled building it had been when she'd stood here ten days ago. Gone were all the bales they'd worked so hard to bring in and, in their place, stood trestle tables filled with all sorts of baked goods, sandwiches, cold salads, buttered rolls and slabs of bread. A hog-roast was going in a small anti-room at the side. Another table groaned under the weight of three large barrels –a dark brewed beer, a light brewed beer, and a cider. An adjoining table was filled with various bottles of spirits and she could see additional boxes underneath, ensuring there was no chance of this bar running dry anytime soon.

Twinkling fairy lights had been strung across the rafters above her head and along the sides of the barn, giving off a lovely, gentle light and making it feel less barn-like. A small stage area had been set up and a three-piece band, in full Scottish regalia of kilts, flouncy shirts and black, buttoned jackets, were warming up with their accordion, drum kit and guitar. A DJ unit was on the other side of the room, ready to keep the evening flowing whenever the band took a break.

Essie turned when Mhairi came to stand beside her.

'Did you do all this?' she asked in wonder.

'Quite a bit of it although I did have help. Our Harvest Ceilidh is a big deal in the farming calendar so everyone pitches in.'

'Did all the farms manage to get their harvests in before the rain? I expect those four, rain-filled, days would have caused problems for those who didn't.'

'Aye, most were successful, all thanks to The Flora. We have a notification chain set up whereby we make a phone-call to the first farm on the notification list, they then phone it through to the next farm who will phone it on to the next one and so on. Within half an hour of Dougie receiving the information, everyone else would have known it.'

'That's a good setup. And it's great to know so many have benefitted.'

She looked around the room again as it began to fill up. Several of the older ladies were wearing their clan kilts although they were few compared to the younger ones who'd dressed as though they were heading off to a top London nightclub. She saw Alice come in and her outfit didn't leave much to the imagination. Essie felt it was definitely over-the-top for a barn dance. She turned to Mhairi and reminded her of the conversation they'd had a few days earlier.

'Yes, I did have a discreet word but she assured me her feelings for Ross were nothing more than those of a good friend. They've known each other all their lives, and she's always seen him as some kind of big brother, so I'd be surprised if there was anything more to it.'

'Hmm, I'm not so sure about that. I know what I saw, Mhairi.'

'I'm sure it was nothing intentional, Essie, you know

what twenty-one-year-old girls can be like. All full of angst and passion over the smallest things.'

'She's twenty-one? I thought she was much younger than that – like about sixteen, seventeen at a push.'

'That'll be the good, clean, Scottish air for you.' Mhairi grinned at her. 'Now, I need to get along, unfortunately chatting is something I don't get much time for at this event, so if I don't see you again for the rest of the night, I hope you have a great time. Go, get a drink, let your hair down and enjoy.'

She gave Essie a peck on the cheek, did the same to Craig who was walking towards her with their drinks in his hands, and then disappeared into the growing crowd.

'Everything okay?' he asked, handing over a glass of cider.

She'd chosen to eschew the wine tonight as it went to her head far too quickly, however, having just tasted the cider and been hit by its potency, she couldn't help but wonder if it had been a wise choice.

'Yes, thank you. Mhairi said she'd had a word with Alice and she denies having any kind of romantic interest in Ross. Apparently, they've known each other all their lives and she just sees him as being some kind of surrogate sibling.'

'Well, there you go then, nothing to worry about. You can just kick back tonight and have a blast.'

'Hmmm… we'll see.' Essie still wasn't convinced, however, and she'd be keeping an eye on Alice tonight – just to be sure.

'Hi, Mum, are you having fun?' Clarissa wheezed by Essie's side as she left the dance floor after a rather energetic turn of the Dashing White Sergeant.

Essie smiled at her daughter's joyful expression,

delighted to see her having such a good time. Although she'd spent the best part of the night dancing with Ross, she was also receiving numerous requests from the other young farmers in attendance. Every time Essie looked towards the dance floor, she'd seen Clarissa being swirled, burled and hurled around in one or another intricate Scottish dance. She was easy to spot in the calf-length, rich-cream, bias-cut dress she was wearing. In honour of the event, she was wearing a MacKenzie sash held together with a beautiful emerald, Celtic knot brooch that Ross had borrowed from his mother.

When she saw it, Essie wondered if the relationship between her and Ross had moved up a notch and couldn't help but worry on where it might end up – after all, it was no secret that Ross was off to Japan next month. Would Clarissa be going with him? Essie hadn't asked the question, even though she was desperate to do so, but she didn't want to look like she was interfering. This was Clarissa's life and she had to live it however she wanted.

'I'm having a rare old time, darling, although all this dancing is taking its toll. I thought I was reasonably fit but now I'm beginning to wonder.'

Clarissa laughed. 'If it's any consolation, it's just about killing me too! But so much fun – it would be a great way to go. "She died doing the Gay Gordons" – now that would be some obituary!'

They were both giggling like schoolgirls when another young man approached to ask if Clarissa would care to join him for the next dance. With a grin she accepted and gave Essie a small wave as she was led back on to the dance floor.

Essie looked about to see where Ross was. Although he'd managed several dances with Clarissa, as the son of the host and hostess, he was expected to socialise and converse with their other guests. She saw him laughing with an older couple not far from the bar area. Out of the corner of her eye, she caught a flash of bright red and when she turned her head, she saw Alice standing off to the side, her gaze flitting between Ross and the dance floor where Clarissa was whooping in time with the music. Essie's eyes narrowed when she saw the large wine glass in her hand. She'd seen Alice drinking spirits earlier and rather rapidly too. She'd hoped someone might have had a word about pacing herself but it looked like the girl was here on her own.

'Oh my, Essie, you want to try some of those whiskies they've got over there, they're fabulous. Most of them are home-brewed and are quite delicious. I think I might have slightly over-indulged.'

She smiled at Craig as he looked a little sheepish for being tiddly. She didn't mind if he was, he was as entitled to let his hair down as the rest of them. She turned her back on Alice as she said, 'Craig, you've got your contact lenses in tonight – can you see what kind of drink Alice is holding in her hand?'

'It looks…' he glanced over her shoulder and squinted, '…like a glass of red wine. One of those big glasses too.' He turned back to Essie. 'I suspect she's going to have a very bad head on her in the morning if she's been drinking those all night.'

'That's just it, Craig, she hasn't. And I don't think she's planning on drinking this one. Excuse me a minute…'

Essie began to work her way around the room towards where Alice was standing. The girl had edged closer to Ross which also meant she was nearer the dance floor and not too far from Clarissa. The same look of hostility was on her face as she watched Clarissa being the life and soul of the evening. Essie was astonished that Alice had managed to lie so well to Mhairi – it was so plain to see.

The crowd moved and her view was blocked. To make

space for the dancers, the non-dancers were gathered tightly around the walls of the barn and it was difficult to get through. She'd made some progress when she caught sight of the dance floor again. Alice was now right on the edge of the spectators and the large wine balloon was being held very loosely. A glance at the dance floor revealed the dancers were moving around the room and Clarissa was going to be close to Alice within the next few minutes – it didn't take a genius to work out what the girl had in mind. The thought spurred Essie on and, taking much less care and using her elbows much more frequently, she broke through the melee just as Clarissa's little dance group ducked under the upheld hands of their opposite number and moved alongside Alice. She saw the glass begin to tilt in a forward direction and with one last elbow in the ribcage of some poor, unsuspecting guest, managed to arrive and stand right in front of Alice.

'Oh no you don't, young lady!' Essie hissed, as she put a firm hand on the glass. She prised Alice's fingers off the stem and took it from her.

'Hey! That's my drink, give it back!'

'I'll do no such thing. You and I both know where that drink was going and it wasn't down your neck.'

'I don't know what you're talking about.'

'Like hell you don't! You've been drinking gin all night but then suddenly fancy red wine just as my daughter is nearby. I'm not a fool and don't you dare insult me by suggesting otherwise.'

The girl swayed and Essie realised she was even more drunk than she'd given her credit for. The smell of the gin she'd consumed was overpowering and was making Essie's eyes water. She put her arm around Alice's waist to hold her up, leant over and tugged Ross's shirt sleeve. When she had his attention, she said, 'Ross, I think Alice may have overdone things. Could you put this glass back on the bar and help me get her out of the barn? I think some fresh air might help.'

'I'm fine. Leave me alone.' Alice tried to push her away but Essie held on tightly.

'No! You've had quite enough for tonight. It's time you went home and when you're nursing your hangover in the morning, be sure to remember this – if I catch you *anywhere* near my daughter, a thumping headache from a hangover will be the least of your worries. I mean it! You'll keep your distance from her and from Ross and you will *not* interfere in their relationship in any way. They're together, whether you like or not, and you'd better get used to it because, if you don't, you'll have me to deal with and *that* is something you really don't want. Got it?'

Alice mumbled something and looked away. Essie grasped her chin and pulled her back to face her. She looked into the girl's eyes and repeated, 'I said "Got it"? Have you?'

Something in her tone must have gotten through because Alice gazed back at her with a look of misery on her face and then nodded.

'Yes, I hear you.'

'Good! I'm glad we've got that sorted.'

'Here, Alice, you're looking a bit rough. Tommy's waiting outside and he's going to take you home.'

Ross put his arm around the girl's waist and turned to Essie.

'Thank you for looking out for her, Essie. Tommy's one of our designated drivers this year; he'll get her home safely.'

She watched as the crowd parted to let them through. At that moment the music stopped and everyone clapped the dancers off the floor.

'Hi, Mum, you getting another drink? I think I'll join you – all this dancing is thirsty work. Have you seen

Ross?'

'Oh, he's just escorting someone outside. They've had a bit too much to drink so he's helping to get them home.'

'Okay, I'll no doubt catch up with him in a while. Now, what are you having to drink? That red wine looks tempting but much too risky when wearing a cream dress, so I think I'll give that a miss.'

Essie smiled. 'I quite agree. It could be rather messy. Perhaps a white wine would be better. Definitely not the cider though – that stuff is considerably stronger than I expected it to be. Goodness only knows what I might get up to if I stay on it! I may end up in a boxing match or something.'

Clarissa laughed. 'It would have to be strong stuff to turn my mild-mannered momma into any kind of Raging Bull.'

She turned away to tell the man behind the table what they wanted and totally missed Essie's little chuckle as she whispered aloud, 'Jake LaMotta, eat yer heart out, son!'

FORTY-FIVE

The atmosphere in the Land Rover was subdued. Craig was behind the wheel and they were following the MacKenzies' Landy to Inverness Airport. Fliss, Becky, Tom and Mike were also crammed in because they all wanted to pass on their good wishes and say their goodbyes.

Clarissa sat quietly as she looked out of the window. The sun was shining brightly and there was barely a cloud in the sky. Ross had explained that, as a rule, September was one of the best months for visiting Scotland – they normally got lovely weather at that time of the year.

She couldn't believe how quickly the last six weeks had gone by. It felt like one minute they were celebrating bringing in the harvest and now, here they were, on their way to the airport. She wondered if the time would have passed by more slowly had they not been so busy going out and about, sightseeing and being every inch the visiting tourists. Due to the harvest coming in earlier than originally planned, it had freed Ross up to spend extra time with her and, of course, her mum and Craig. It had been nice being a group of four and they'd all got on well.

There had been several day trips including a visit to Culloden Moor, where Bonnie Prince Charlie had made his last stand against the English army before fleeing back to France disguised as a maid. They'd stood in awe at the sight of the moor, taking in the vastness of the area and the rough terrain. Clarissa couldn't understand why anyone could have thought it was a good location for a battle.

'Were your family involved in the fighting, Ross?'

Ross had turned to Essie and admitted they'd not partaken in the battle. 'Clan MacKenzie was split over the Jacobite cause. One half was all for the rebellion, the other was not. My side of the family were among the rebels but on their way to join Prince Charlie's troops, they were attacked by other clans who were on the side of the British Government and that stopped us getting here.'

'You sound disappointed by that.'

'I have to confess, Craig, those clans who did line up to fight, talk about their participation with pride. Even though it near on decimated so many, there is honour among them when they look back on their history. While the MacKenzies may have gathered honours elsewhere, in the end, this is the only battle that ever really matters.'

'Right. You know your Culloden history then?'

Ross had smirked. 'It's drummed into us in school. We Scots are made to be proud of our history, whether we want to be or not!'

'But, surely you're proud of being Scottish?'

'Aye, Craig, I am. And I've got something to show you which I think you'll be proud of too.' He'd led them along one of the paths until they came to a wooden plaque raised up from the ground. It read:

Clan Donald Memorial
This headstone marks the traditional

site of a grave locally believed to be the resting place of the MacDonalds who fell in action during the battle. This stone was erected by members of the Clan Donald Society to honour all MacDonalds killed at Culloden and in battle elsewhere.

'Oh my,' Craig had whispered in wonder as he read the inscription several times over. He bent over and touched the headstone reverently, his fingers tracing the words.

'How proud do you feel now, Craig?'

When he'd raised his head to look at Ross, Clarissa had been touched to see tears glistening in his eyes.

'It's quite overwhelming, to be honest. It's something I've never given any thought to but now I'm standing here, I feel I could burst with pride and honour.'

'Aye, well, that'll be yer mother's blood rising to the fore. You may not talk like a Scotsman, Craig, but there's a Scotsman lurking no too far beneath yer skin.'

They'd walked slowly around the rest of the battle site, absorbing the haunting atmosphere and paying respect to the plaques which had been erected to commemorate where the various clans had stood as they'd headed into battle. It had been a sombre trip but they'd all agreed it was an extra special location and were glad they'd made the visit.

A few days after that, they'd upped sticks, or – in their case – lowered handbrakes, and had set off on a ten-day trek around the northern climes of the country. Ross had joined them and they'd all taken turns of driving and van sharing. It had turned out to be a lot of fun and there had been much laughter and jollity throughout.

They'd started off by heading up to the beautiful little village of Ullapool where they'd stopped for the night.

Once again, Ross had been a minefield of information, informing them how the village had been nothing more than a little sleepy hamlet until a certain Thomas Telford, the famous Scottish engineer, had come along and redesigned it in the 1700's and it became a fishing port. He also told them that it was considered to be the top geological site in Scotland and it was in this area that much information had been garnered in the Victorian era on plate tectonics.

Clarissa had been interested in the tidbits Ross was passing on but she'd been considerably more interested in the selection of pubs advertising food and live music. They'd spent the evening singing and clapping along with the locals to a resident band in a small bar near the harbour. Everyone had been extremely friendly and when they'd driven away the following day, they all felt as though they'd left a small piece of themselves behind.

It had been a quiet drive until they'd stopped for a picnic lunch – everyone was citing tiredness but Clarissa believed the imbibing of the local brew and the resultant hangovers may have been more the root of the issue. After lunch, however, they'd all perked up and the journey northwards had been livelier.

Essie exclaimed often on the ruggedness of the terrain and the stunning light of the sky.

'I now understand what artists mean when they talk about "the light" in their work. I'd always thought they painted their turbulent skies with a touch of fantasy about them but now I can see they are absolutely real and truly majestic.'

The dark clouds had rolled by above them but every now and then, they would break apart and the most glorious rays of sunshine would come spilling through and everything caught in the beam of light would sparkle with colour and come to life. Clarissa was glad she'd bought extra memory cards for the camera because her mother was snapping it every which way.

They'd continued their journey along the north coast, from the beautiful white sands of Durness all the way to John O'Groats. Along this side of the country, there were several castles – some in ruins and some intact. When asked why, Ross said he thought it possibly went back to the days of the Viking invasions, as many castles were often built upon, or extended from, old fortresses, but he didn't like to say for sure.

Essie had been over the moon and her love for castles had been well and truly fulfilled. Clarissa had enjoyed seeing them and hearing some of their gory history. Her favourite had been the 4th Earl of Caithness who'd imprisoned his son at Castle Sinclair Girnigoe, believing he was rebelling against him. After keeping him locked up for seven years, he moved his son onto a diet of salted beef, but withheld any drinking water meaning his son eventually died from insanity brought on by thirst. Hmm, she'd thought, thank goodness her father wasn't here – the last thing she needed was him getting ideas!

They had only been back at Flora's for a couple of days when Ross arrived in a state of excitement. He'd heard through the farming jungle drums that the Royal Family were due to arrive at Balmoral Castle the following day and how did everyone feel about taking a wee jaunt down towards Crathie to see if they could get a glimpse of them. Clarissa smiled to herself once again as she recalled the speed at which Essie had grabbed her things and pronounced herself ready to go. As a staunch Royalist, it was too good an opportunity to be missed. Her enthusiasm had been rewarded for they'd seen the flotilla of cars sweep by and the waves and smiles from the blue-blooded occupants had been recorded for prosperity.

Clarissa let out a small sigh and twisted slightly in her

seat. The days and nights had blended into one long, seamless movie in her head and they'd rushed her to this point. She saw a sign for Inverness airport and felt her stomach crunch up inside her.

She'd mulled long and hard over Ross's request to join him and hadn't made her decision lightly. She only hoped she'd made the right choice. She'd gone from having a life with no options only a few months before, to having so many choices she sometimes felt her head was going to explode from thinking of them all.

'Come on, Clarissa, we need to get a wriggle on. That traffic jam back there has put us on the back foot.'

She jumped out of the Land Rover and went to help her mum and Craig with the luggage piled up in the back. They each grabbed a bag and hurried towards the terminal. Her phone beeped in her pocket and, pushing the bag into her other hand, she pulled it out and saw Ross's number flashing at her.

'Where are you?' he asked. 'You're cutting it fine, you know.'

'We're just coming through the terminal doors now. There was an accident at the traffic lights just after you went through and we got stuck in it.'

'Well, you need to hurry, the luggage check-in will be closing soon.'

'I'm almost there.'

She spotted his wild red hair in the distance.

'I can see you!'

She was waving furiously as she almost jogged towards him. She glanced behind to check her mum and Craig were close by. Fortunately, they were, although Essie's face was a lovely shade of tomato red.

'Where is everyone?' The reason there had been two vehicles was because all of Ross's family, and some of the long-term farmhands, had insisted on coming along and there hadn't been enough room in one Landy for all the bodies and the luggage.

She reached Ross's side, gave him a quick kiss and then passed the bags to him. The check-in area was now quiet and they went through without a hitch.

'Right, time to find the departure gate and get through security. Come on.'

Ross put his arm around her waist and pulled her tightly to his side. His parents came running over and pointed them in the direction they needed to go.

The not-so-little group moved at a fast pace and arrived at the gate for London Heathrow within a few minutes. Everyone clamoured around them, hurling good wishes, safe journeys and lots of love into the air. Finally, they peeled away and it was only the two of them left standing alone together.

Ross looked deep into her eyes.

'Are you sure about this? It's not too late to change your mind.'

Clarissa lifted her hand and placed it against his cheek. She loved him so much. She hadn't, for a single second thought, when she'd set off on this road trip back in March, that within six months she'd have fallen head over heels with the most amazing man on the planet.

'Don't! Please! This is hard enough already…'

'I'm sorry, Clarrie. I know it wasn't easy for you.'

She gave him a watery smile as she tried to hold back the tears. The last thing she wanted was for him to go away with the vision of her ugly-crying face in his mind.

'Ross, I need to live my life before I can live yours. If what we have is worth anything, it'll survive this next year.'

She wrapped her arms around him and held him as close to her as was possible. She knew her decision was the right one – she would meet up with Fliss and Becky in

December, travel around Europe with them and when they returned home to Australia in the summer, she would go with them. From there, once she'd explored fully, she'd travel on to Japan to join Ross and stay with him until he returned home. Well, that was the plan at this time. They'd have to see if the relationship could be sustained first.

'You need to go now, Ross.'

His dad had crept over and whispered softly to them.

'I love you,' she whispered.

'I love you,' he replied. He slipped his hand in his pocket, pulled out a small box and pressed it into her hand. 'Something to help you remember me.'

He placed his hands gently on either side of her face, lifted her lips to his and dropped one last soft kiss upon them before turning on his shoeless heel, placing the hand-luggage tray onto the X-ray rack and stepping through to the other side. He waved a few more times while putting his shoes back on, then, picking up his laptop bag, he blew her one last kiss before walking around the corner and out of her sight.

Clarissa stood looking at the spot for a few more minutes where he'd been, hoping he'd pop his head around for one last smile but he didn't. He was gone and as Essie put her arm around her, the tears began to fall as she couldn't help but wonder if she'd made the right choice.

They were halfway back to Flora's when Clarissa realised she was still clutching the box Ross had given her. She opened it up and, through her tears, let out a laugh for there, nestled inside, was a silver Polo Mint. A chain was threaded through it and a small note read, *"My heart will not be 'hole' until we're together again. I love you. xx"*

FORTY-SIX

When they returned to Flora's, Clarissa made her excuses and took herself straight inside and upstairs to the bedroom. Essie said she needed to stretch her legs after the time spent cooped up in traffic jams and, passing her handbag to Craig to take indoors for her, she set off at a pace along the loch-side path. This left Craig at a bit of a loose end. He wandered through the front door and paused when he heard Flora's voice floating out from the kitchen.

'Aye, her heart'll be sore for a time but it'll soon be soothed. Good things are coming her way.'

There was a mumbled reply which he couldn't hear but Flora's response was clear enough. 'Yes, I'm hoping they'll come together too, they're perfect for each other and they make a lovely couple. There's a hurdle in the way though, which needs to be overcome. We can only try to ensure the right decisions are made.'

Craig walked into the kitchen, with the intention of saying a polite hello to his mother and her guest before going up to his own room, but when he stepped around the door, Flora was on her own, rolling out pastry on the table.

He looked around in confusion.

'Who were you talking to, Mum?'

'I'm sorry?'

'I heard voices, I heard you talking but there's no one here.'

'Oh, I was probably just thinking out loud. Don't worry about it.'

'But… I heard someone replying to you.'

Flora wiped her floury hands on a tea-towel and picked up the kettle. She walked over to the sink to fill it while saying over her shoulder, 'Ah! You've caught me out. I cannot tell a lie. You did hear voices… but they were both mine. When you live in a solitary state such as mine, you become rather adept at holding a two-way conversation with yourself. After all, apart from the dogs, there's no one here but little old me.'

Craig wasn't convinced but given the absence of another body bar his own in the kitchen with Flora, he had to accept her explanation. He sat down at the table, opposite where his mum was working and let out a large sigh.

'Did Ross get away alright?'

'Yes, he did. Although the traffic was a nightmare – he was nearly away without his luggage.'

'And how is Clarissa?'

'Probably crying her heart out wondering if she made the right decision, poor lass.'

'You're fond of the girl, aren't you?'

'I am, Mum. She's kind, intelligent, funny and caring. If I could have had a daughter, I'd have been more than proud if she'd turned out as well as Clarissa has.'

Flora took the boiling kettle and poured a splash of hot water into the teapot. She swirled it about to warm the pot, tipped it out, put in a few spoons of loose tea leaves and after filling it up, left it to brew while she finished putting together the apple and cinnamon pie she was making. In the time it took her to clean away her baking debris and wipe down the table, the tea was ready and she sat down, closer to Craig and poured out two mugs of the dark brown liquid.

She pushed one towards him while asking, 'Do you regret your life, Craig?'

He looked up in surprise. 'What do you mean?'

'Well, you gave up so much to care for your dad, putting your own life on hold until he was sorted out and then, when you were able to claim it back, everything had moved on without you. No wife, no home to call your own and, most of all, no children. I sense you'd have liked children.'

He picked up the teaspoon in the sugar bowl and dug it into the sweet, white, powder. He lifted some up and let it pour back into the bowl like a little mini-avalanche. He was silent within his thoughts for a few minutes and he appreciated that Flora let the silence flow around them, it helped him to think.

'Yes,' he finally spoke up, 'I'd have liked to have had children. I wasn't aware of how much I've missed until I came on this trip with Essie and Clarissa. I see how close they are and I would have liked that with my own son or daughter.'

'It's not too late. If you find a younger wife, you can still have it.'

He looked across at his mother and taking every effort to push down the tears which were threatening to fill his eyes, he answered, 'It's too late for that, Mum. There's only one woman I've ever loved and will ever love. If I can't have her, I would rather be on my own.'

'Essie?'

He nodded, unable to speak.

'For sure, I've never decided if this MacDonald trait is

a blessing or a curse…'

'I don't get you?'

'We mate for life, Craig. We only ever fall in love once – we're just like swans only maybe a bit less elegant.'

'How can you say that when you and dad are divorced?'

'Probably because we're not.'

'You're not?'

Flora leant across and lifted his jaw up gently with her finger.

'Keep your mouth closed, dear, it makes you look simple and you'll catch flies!'

'But… I was convinced you and dad were divorced. You haven't lived together for over thirty years.'

'That doesn't mean we don't love each other. I adored your father the first time I set eyes on him which caused a bit of a problem as I was about to be betrothed to a local boy. We weren't destined to be together but I'd been on a visit to Wales, visiting some old family kin, when I got a flat tyre on the way home. Your father drove past, saw me stranded at the roadside, and stopped to assist me. It was raining and we both ended up drenched through. Once the tyre was fixed, I asked if I could buy him a coffee to say thank you. We found a little roadside café a few miles away where we sat talking until the early hours of the morning. There's a lot to be said for these twenty-four-hour truck-stops.' She gave him a wink.

'Then what happened?'

'I asked him to come home with me, introduced him to my mum and dad as my husband-to-be and broke off my betrothal that same day. Let me tell you, that really set the cat among the pigeons.'

'Why?'

'Because MacDonald women are tied here to this land. We're the caretakers of this house and much of what goes on around us. We marry local to prevent any strife which may be caused by moving away. I'd just pledged myself to a man who was not only "not local" but was a Sassenach to boot and who lived hundreds of miles away in a place called Oxfordshire. It might as well have been the dark side of the moon as far as my parents were concerned. They didn't stand in our way though, and allowed me to marry your father and move all the way down to the Devil's own country. The only condition was that when the time came, and my mother died, I had to return to this cottage. I had a family responsibility to care for what had been left to me.'

'Do you resent that responsibility? Couldn't you have just said, "Sod it! I don't want to be here, bye-bye!"'

'No. I did want to be here. But I also wanted to be with you, Flora, and your dad. Believe me when I say that I know exactly how Clarissa is feeling right now because I was there too. Torn between following my heart, even though it was the wrong thing to do, or taking on the responsibility which had been left to me to pick up. I can tell you that, even though being away from your father is worse than every kind of hell, I don't regret the choice I made. I couldn't have lived with myself if I'd walked away from this life I'd been raised for.'

'Why didn't we all move up here with you?'

'Your father had his job – there wasn't really anything for him here. He's a proud man, he wouldn't have been happy without his work. Also, Flora hadn't long started senior school, it didn't seem fair to put her through all the upheaval of moving schools again.'

Craig thought about his sister. She'd been gone all these years and he still missed her. With their mother no longer around, she'd been the one to comfort and care for him. They'd been close and he'd felt her loss as keenly as he'd felt the separation from his mother. He looked at her more closely.

'Flora had been to visit you when she died – what

happened?'

'You know what happened, Craig. It was raining heavily when she left here. She aquaplaned just up the road on that sharp bend and the car went head first into a tree. She died of internal injuries before the ambulance could get to her.'

'But why is Matt so adamant that you can have nothing to do with your grand-daughter? I can't even mention you because he gets so riled up.'

'Flora and I exchanged heated words before she left. I think Matt blames me for her death. She hadn't been due to leave for another three days but she called Matt to say she was on her way home and she'd never return here again. I think he believes that, had she stayed the full length of her visit, she'd have arrived home safely and wouldn't have been on the road in such bad weather.'

'Young Flora is the absolute spit of her… and you.'

'Yes, I know. Your dad has sent photographs.'

'Do all the MacDonald women look alike?'

'I'm afraid we do. We have rather dominant genes.'

There was silence for a few minutes until Craig felt compelled to ask, 'What did you argue about, Mum?'

Flora looked out of the window and over the loch for a few minutes before she replied. 'Something of no importance. Certainly not something worth dying for.'

Craig felt the sorrow flowing out of her and placed his hand on her arm. 'I'm sorry, Mum, I didn't mean to drag up old memories and upset you.'

She placed her hand over his. 'Don't be silly, you had every right to ask. She was your sister and we all loved her. And I love you too, very much. Don't ever think any differently. I would have loved for you to be here with me, growing up surrounded by all this wonderful countryside, but it would've been wrong to split you and Flora up. Siblings need to stay together.'

'Do you think you and Dad will ever split up?'
His question was met with a bark of laughter.
'Craig, if we haven't divorced after all these years, I can't see it ever happening now. Like I said, I've loved your father since the day we met and I'll love him right into my grave.'
Craig suddenly had a thought. 'When Dad got ill and gave up his job, why didn't he move up here with you then?'
'The Scottish weather is not good for sore bones or joints, it's far too damp. He was better off where he was. It hurt me so much to hear the pain in his voice whenever we spoke. I did send him potions to ease his suffering but the stubborn old fool refused to take them. We exchanged a few cross words over that but he wouldn't be swayed. Anyway, young man, I didn't sit down here to talk about my sorry excuse for a life but to talk about yours. What are you going to do next? Go all out to get your girl or walk away to live a life of loneliness?'
'I think it's going to be the latter…'
For the next few hours, Craig spilled his heart out to his mum; something he'd needed to do for a very long time.

It was almost dark by the time Essie returned to the cottage. The light was shining through the kitchen window but as she walked past and looked in, she saw it was empty. She lifted the latch on the front door and was just hanging her jacket on the hook when she heard a soothing murmur in the kitchen. She stuck her head around the door and saw Flora sitting on the floor beside the range, gently stroking Kirsty and talking to her softly.
'Hey, is everything okay?' she whispered, tiptoeing in.
'Kirsty began birthing a couple of hours ago. She's

nearly done but I find it helps to be with her, giving her comfort.'

Essie crept over and looked past Flora to see three little white marshmallows wriggling around Kirsty's belly and suckling blindly, their little paws flailing in the air as they drank.

'Oh, my goodness, they're so cute!' She whispered this in Flora's ear so as not to disturb the dog who looked as though she was trying to push another pup out. 'How many more will she have?'

'This is the last one coming now…'

'Mind if I watch?'

'Of course not.'

Essie knelt beside Flora and watched her as she continued to stroke Kirsty and talk softly to her. The dog certainly seemed to be quite relaxed so she must have been garnering some comfort from Flora's presence.

After about ten minutes, Kirsty gave a little yowl, and a small watery sac was pushed out. She lay panting for a few seconds before turning around, nibbling it to free the puppy within and then licking it vigorously, stimulating it into moving. It let out a little mewl and its mother nosed it around to join its siblings at the milk bar.

'Wow! Just wow! That was so… beautiful. Thank you, Flora, for letting me stay.'

'My pleasure. It's always lovely to see a new life being born. Now, I think I've earned a cup of tea, fancy joining me?'

'I would love to, thank you.'

Essie sat watching the pups for a little while longer, totally enthralled by them. She only moved when Flora placed the teapot on the table.

'You're clearly an animal lover, Essie. Why don't you have any pets at home?'

Essie picked up her mug and took a sip.

'My father wasn't one for animals and neither is my husband.'

'I always say you shouldn't trust people who don't like animals. There's something not right in their make-up.'

Essie thought about George and his selfish ways.

'I think you could be right there, Flora.'

'Animals are good for the soul. They're simple little things really – you give them a lot of love and they'll give it right back. Much less complicated than humans.'

'My husband, George, doesn't approve of pets. We've had words about it several times – I wanted a dog for Clarissa as I think it's good for children to grow up around animals – but he was having none of it. He made it quite clear, if I brought an animal into the house, it would soon be gone... and I'd be gone with it!'

'What a lovely man he sounds...' There was no missing the sarcasm in the comment.

Essie tried to push away the feelings of turmoil she felt whenever she thought of the things George had said to her over the years. She knew she was a stronger person now but he'd battered her emotions for such a long time that occasionally it was a struggle to believe she could ever rise above him and take the plunge to leave.

Flora leant over and placed her arm around her shoulders.

'Don't let it worry you so, Essie, when the time is right, everything will fall into place. And you'll have your pup by your side. Or kitten... whatever it may be, it'll serve as a reminder of the strength you had to walk away from the one who gives you pain.'

Essie felt the tears begin to flow down her cheeks as she absorbed the comfort Flora was giving her. She knew she had to find the strength to leave George for good but it was so much easier to believe she could do it when there was a few hundred miles between them. It was another matter altogether when he was standing in front of her, face to face, and his nasty, sharp tongue was lashing her with his hurtful words and all-too-real threats.

Flora's arms tightened around her as she whispered, 'You *will* be able to sever the ties. When the time is right, you will do it. I promise you.'

Essie felt her emotions begin to soothe. Somehow, and for no reason she could explain, she knew Flora was right – she *would* be able to do it.

When the time was right.

FORTY-SEVEN

As September came to an end and they moved into October, the time came to move on. The trio felt they'd taken advantage of Flora's hospitality for long enough. The last of their luggage had been stowed back into the vans along with a year's supply – or that's how it felt – of Flora's delicious home baking.

Flora was moving between them, giving out her wonderful hugs and tears were flowing from every quarter. Eventually, they were ready to set off and with a final wave, and much blowing of kisses, the campers trundled up the rough track to the main road for the last time.

There was silence for the first few miles and then the walkie-talkie crackled. Clarissa picked it up and was treated to the disembodied sound of Craig singing, "Ye take the high road..." It was enough to send both Essie and herself into fits of laughter and the mood lightened up considerably after that.

'So, where exactly are we heading now?'

'We're going towards Aberdeen today, the Granite City – called thus because so many of its buildings are built from granite – then down towards Arbroath because Craig wants to try an Arbroath Smokie while actually in Arbroath—'

'A what?'

'An Arbroath Smokie – it's a smoked haddock! The town is famous for them.'

Clarissa gave a small shudder. 'Bleugh! I think I'll pass on that one!'

Essie grinned at her.

'Don't be such a wuss. If you're going off travelling around the world, then you need to "woman up" and open your mind to trying all sorts of new experiences – including tasting the traditional fare of the places you visit.'

'I suppose…'

'You tried haggis for the first time a few weeks back and you enjoyed that, you might be surprised and like the Smokie too.'

'It's just fish, Mum, I'm not a big fish lover, as you know.'

'I do. Well, you can taste a wee piece of mine when we get there.'

They were quiet again for a time until Clarissa voiced the question that had been sitting in her head for over a week now.

'Mum, are you sure you're okay with me going off to Europe and then around the world? Well, some of it…'

Her mum gave her a quick smile before returning her attention to the road in front of her.

'Of course, I am, darling. Why wouldn't I be?'

'You haven't said much about it and you were rather quiet the night I told you of my plans.'

'Clarissa, I'll be honest with you – it was a surprise and I've had to work at coming to terms with it. NOT because I don't want you to go – I really do – but because I'll miss you so much. It's been such a joy to spend this time with you and it's going to be a wrench letting you go, but it needs to be done. I want you to spread your wings and see life. The last thing I desire is for you to be tied down as I was. I applaud your decision to do some travelling on your own before meeting Ross in Japan – that's a brave move but it's the right one.'

'Do you think so? I'm worried we won't survive the separation.'

'I can understand why you feel that way – after all, you haven't been together for long – but I believe you're both a perfect match and you'll find a way of making it work. If you're meant to be together, then together you will be.'

'Do you feel the same about you and Craig?'

'What do you mean?'

'Well, you used to fancy him at uni, I know he used to fancy you and from what I've seen when you're together, you still have the hots for each other now.'

'Clarissa! I think I'm a bit past the age of having "the hots" for anyone.'

She noticed the blush spreading up her mum's face.

'I don't think anyone is ever too old to have that kind of feeling for someone.'

'Well, it's not anything I can think about right now. I need to sort my own life out before I can think about being a part of someone else's.'

'Are you going to divorce my father?'

Essie sighed. 'I don't know. It's not that simple—'

'Yes, it is, Mum! The bloke is an asshole! He's lied to you all these years, controlled your life, treated you like crap and behaves as though you're his little servant, there to cater to his every whim. What's he ever done for you?'

Her mum looked at her again and said quietly, 'He gave me you and I wouldn't change that for anything. I'd live every single minute again, exactly as it was, if it ensured I always had you.'

Clarissa felt a lump grow in her throat at her mum's words and her vision was blurred when she looked out of the window. What could she say to that? When her emotions had settled enough for her to talk, she placed her hand on her mum's shoulder and said, 'I love you, Mum.'

Patting her hand gently, Essie replied, 'I love you too, darling. Very much.'

The poignant moment was suddenly ended by the crackle of the walkie-talkie. Clarissa picked it up again and this time Craig's less-than-dulcet tones came over the airwaves as he sang, "Oh, Donald, where's yer troosers…"

Craig looked on as Clarissa and Essie shared a Smokie between them. Clarissa really hadn't been keen but she'd bravely taken a small piece of Essie's fish and much to her surprise, had rather liked it. With a laugh, she'd nicked another piece of the smoked delight which had caused Essie to laugh while pretending to pull the remains of her fish away. He'd offered to buy them another one but the ladies had declined saying that one between them was quite enough. Craig, on the other hand, could easily have eaten another two or three. Kippers were one of his dad's favourite meals and they'd had them often when they'd lived together, despite the stench they left behind.

He smiled at the antics of Essie and Clarissa. It was interesting watching them interact now compared to how they'd been when they'd all first set off on this journey. Back then, it had been a distinct case of mother and daughter but along the way, those lines had blurred and they'd grown closer together. They were more like best friends and Craig sensed that Essie was happy about this although they hadn't really spoken about it.

On the other hand, if Craig was being *really* honest with himself, he and Essie hadn't spoken properly about anything since his revelations in Blackpool. There had been chit-chat and laughter and they'd talked about many other things but never about their feelings or how that night had changed them – if it had; Craig just didn't know.

What he did know, even though it had never been in doubt since he'd met her again, was that he loved Essie with all his heart and soul. These months together had been the happiest of his life and he didn't want them to ever end. He refused to think about what came next even though they were working their way back south and that meant back towards home. In a few more weeks, it would be too cold to sleep in the vans and then what? The time to begin facing up to reality was creeping up on them and he had to accept that this little bubble they'd wrapped around themselves would soon be popping and real life would be waiting when it did.

He'd be going back to his empty old house – albeit freshly decorated by his niece, who had refused to send him any photographs so he had no idea what he was going home to – and Essie would be going back to… well… what? If she didn't know, how could he? As far as he was aware, she hadn't spoken to George since the day they'd left Oxfordshire. If she had, she hadn't mentioned it.

'Did you enjoy that, Craig? Did it live up to expectations?'

Craig blinked and took himself out of his head as Essie walked towards him.

'It sure did, it was delicious. My dad would have loved one of those.'

'We have a delivery service, sir, if you would like to send some to him through the post.'

Craig looked to the gentleman who'd just spoken to him. It was the guide who'd taken them around the factory, showing them how the Smokies were produced and sharing their history.

'You can do that?'

'We certainly can. All we need from you is an address and payment, and we'll do the rest.'

'Wonderful.' He looked over to Essie. 'Just give me five minutes and then we'll be on our way.'

"On their way" was taking a slow, leisurely drive towards Edinburgh. They'd booked a hotel just off the Royal Mile for a week, at the beginning of November, and were taking it easy on their way there. They passed through Dundee and over the Tay Bridge into the Kingdom of Fife, where the name of the town, Auchtermuchty, made them all smile. The main road led them to St Andrews where Essie was delighted to find another castle to add to her growing list. It may have been not much more than a ruin but the bottle dungeon more than made up for that and Essie was thrilled with it.

From Fife, they meandered back up to the city of Perth, and out to the little town of Crieff where they treated themselves to a trip around the local whisky distillery. Essie was shocked when she realised they'd been in Scotland all this time and hadn't yet visited one.

'I didn't think you'd be interested, Essie, otherwise I'd have mentioned doing this sooner.'

'I'm not a whisky drinker – it's a bit too strong for me – but I'm still interested in how they do it. This has been quite fascinating.' She picked up the small glass of whisky that was included as part of the tour and listened to the guide as she explained the correct way to drink it.

'Firstly, take a small sip, try not to take in any air as you do it, and hold the liquid under your tongue. It may feel a bit nippy at first but this goes away and you should begin to taste the flavours we discussed as we walked round. Feel free to swallow when you're ready.'

Essie followed the instructions and was surprised to find the spirit tasted quite different to when she'd tried it in the past. She said as much to Craig and they agreed to purchase a bottle of one of the malts they'd seen being bottled on their tour.

'If anyone has any questions, please feel free to ask,' the guide called out, over the voices of the tourists.

Essie put her hand up slowly. 'Are you meant to add water to whisky?'

The guide smiled. 'Adding water is a personal choice and there's no right or wrong way to do so. Some of the purists would say it's okay to add it to blended whiskies but not to malts. We say, it's all down to your own preference.'

'Thank you.' Essie followed Craig through into the shop where they debated the best year to buy. Whilst they discussed the options, Clarissa decided the whisky-flavoured marmalade sounded much more to her liking and she'd made a few purchases by the time Craig and Essie got to the tills.

The following day, they treated themselves to an overnight spa break at the Crieff Hydro and enjoyed being rubbed, buffed, smoothed and soothed at the hands of the experts on site. Craig had never indulged in such a thing but agreed that, as new experiences went, it was one of the nicer ones they'd had on this trip and he'd happily do it again.

They set off on the next leg of the journey feeling quite relaxed and their knotted muscles – all tight from sitting so often in the vans – were nice and loose meaning they were far less aggravated when their drive towards Stirling ground to a halt due to heavy traffic. They finally pulled up in the car park for the Wallace Monument and Essie looked longingly at the little minibus which was waiting to take the next batch of tourists up to the top of the crag the monument was built upon, but Clarissa and Craig had already set off on foot, determined to burn off the full Scottish breakfast they'd scoffed before they'd left that morning. Essie knew she should do the same but she was still chilled from her massage the day before and the idea of walking up the hill felt like too much of an effort. When they got to the summit, however, she was overjoyed to find she wasn't as puffed out as some of the other tourists around her who'd also opted for the less easy option. The joy, unfortunately, didn't last very long when she found they had to climb nearly two-hundred-and-fifty steps to get to the top of the monument.

'You are kidding me on!' she exclaimed when she read the sign on the door as they walked in.

'What's up, Mum, can't you hack it? Feeling your age, are you?'

'Cheeky minx! I was under the mistaken impression that today was going to be an easy day before we began pounding the streets of Edinburgh.'

'I think yesterday was the easy day, Essie. Today is payback for all the self-indulgent pampering we enjoyed.'

Craig held his hands out in front of him, his fingers pointed upwards and splayed out. 'I'll be honest, my fingernails have never looked so shiny. Maybe I should try some oyster-pearl varnish the next time, what do you think, Clarissa?'

'Oh, I'd go the whole hog, Craig, and choose the vibrant magenta – embrace your inner woman, that's what I say.'

The two of them laughed as Essie looked on in amusement. It warmed her to see Clarissa and Craig getting along and be so relaxed with each other. She understood why Clarissa was so keen for her to get together with Craig – she wanted to be sure her mum would be okay when she left to go off on her travels. Essie totally got it but she couldn't end a marriage of nearly twenty-five years just to suit her daughter's desires.

The problem was, Essie didn't *know* what to do next and she'd been putting off thinking about it. Whenever George came to mind, her stomach began to churn and it was easier to push it away with a view of dealing with it another day. Unfortunately, those "other days" were growing fewer. It was less than eight weeks until Clarissa was due to make her way to France to join Fliss and Becky, and Essie would have to go home. She couldn't stay out on the road for ever as that was just running away and not facing up to things. She'd been "running away" since March; she couldn't keep doing so for much longer.

'Hey, Mum, come on. Stop daydreaming about being back in that lovely spa and think about how many yummy square sausages you ate this morning and need to work off!'

'You, young lady, are getting far too cheeky! Any more of this, and I'll be sending you off to France much sooner than expected.'

'Oh, sure you will! You know you're gonna miss me!'

Clarissa wove her arm through Essie's and led her over to the first flight of steps leading upwards.

'Hmmm, I wouldn't be so sure about that, if you keep torturing me like this.'

Clarissa stepped back to let her go first up the stairs. 'Just in case you can't manage and need a bit of a push…'

Craig burst out laughing and Essie decided the best course of action was to just keep schtum and climb the damn steps. Fortunately, it was not one continuous climb, but three short flights thanks so the museum floors they walked around on the way up and when they did get to the top, the view was stunning, which made it all worth the effort. In the distance she could see Stirling Castle, their next destination, and she really hoped there wouldn't be as many stairs to climb there – she'd had enough exercise for one day.

FORTY-EIGHT

'Left a bit, a smidge more… Perfect! Now say prunes…'

Essie and Clarissa couldn't help laughing as Craig took the photograph. They were standing on the harbour in North Queensferry with the magnificent structure of the Forth Bridge behind them. It was the second day of their stopover in Edinburgh and they'd taken the train from Waverly to North Queensferry just so they could go over the world-famous rail bridge. They'd had a wander around the quaint little seaside village and once they'd taken the obligatory photographs, they were heading back to a cosy-looking tearoom they'd passed for some coffee, hot buttery teacakes and a chance to thaw out. The wind coming off the Forth river was cutting right through them.

Craig was staring at the photograph he'd just taken as Essie walked towards him. He had a strange expression on his face.

'Everything alright, Craig? Has the camera revealed that we really are aliens in disguise?'

'No… it's….' He took his eyes off the screen to gaze at her instead. 'I'd always believed my parents were divorced. My mum was up here in Scotland, we were down in England, they never saw each other and so I just assumed they were no longer a couple. But I was wrong. My mum told me, when we were staying with her, that they're not only still very much married but also still very much in love.'

'Wow! Even after all these years apart?'

'Yes. I was surprised when she told me but it was looking at this photograph that has suddenly made me see what I've missed all this time.'

Essie glanced at the camera as he thrust it towards her.

'I'm confused…' she said.

Craig pulled the camera back and looked at the picture once more.

'My dad has a photograph of my mother, in this exact spot, by the side of his bed. When he lived at home, it sat on the bedside table and now that I come to think of it, it holds the same position in his new home. What's more…' he glanced at Essie, 'being two blokes, the housework wasn't always as much of a priority as it should have been but…' he paused again, '…but no matter how much dust was on the furniture in Dad's room, there was never a single speck on Mum's picture. It was always pristine. I can't believe I never realised that until now.'

Essie took his arm and turned him in the direction of the tearoom. Clarissa had already gone on ahead.

'Sometimes, Craig, when we see something every day, we stop noticing it. Often, we only see it when it's gone or broken. And it's not always objects we stop noticing, it can happen with people and relationships too.'

'I suppose. I guess I'm just feeling a bit of a prat for not seeing something that was staring me in the face every single day.'

'Don't be. You had no reason to think otherwise. Now, let's get in, out of the cold, I'm perishing!'

They joined Clarissa at the table she'd commandeered next to the fireplace. The flames were giving off a delicious warmth and Essie felt her fingers and toes beginning to thaw. The weather had become more wintery over the last few days and she was beginning to feel it. The waitress came to take their order and when she left them a couple of minutes later, Clarissa leant forward. 'So, what are our plans for tomorrow? I really fancy doing a couple of ghost tours.'

'I need to run some errands in the morning, including a trip to Sight-Savers to pick up my next batch of contact lenses. The lovely Andrea in Blackpool sorted that out for me when I called her last week.'

'Ooh, Craig… do I sense a little bit of a fancy there for the "Lovely Andrea" perhaps?' Clarissa gave him a saucy wink at the same time.

'No, you do not! Behave yourself. Essie, please control your daughter, she's being cheeky again!'

Essie laughed along with Craig and Clarissa but her insides had twisted at Clarissa's words. There was no denying that Craig had definitely morphed into a good-looking man and it made perfect sense that other women would find him attractive. Who was to say that one might not come along who he found attractive too? She pushed the jealousy away. Until she sorted out her own life, she had no right to be concerned about his. She forced herself to smile.

'Sorry, Craig, but I'm afraid my daughter is out of my control these days.'

'Hmmph! Crap mother you are!'

They were still chuckling when their drinks and teacakes arrived and the chatter moved onto what tourist hotspots they still had to visit in the city.

'Ideally, I'd like a few more indoor activities, if we can manage it. That wind is bitter and it feels like it's cutting you in half.'

'Ah, we have a wee saying in these parts aboot that.'

The waitress was tidying the table next to them and turned around.

'We say, "The east wind is a lazy wind, it goes right through you!" because that's exactly what it does. You feel it right down to your bones.'

'You can say that again!' Essie discretely held her hands out towards the fire, trying to get the chill out of her fingers.

The waitress chuckled as she walked away.

Essie pulled the pocket-sized, guide book from her handbag. 'I was reading up on that Mary King's Close thing. You know, the one Billy Connolly visited when he did his World Tour of Scotland programme on the television – it looks really interesting and I'd love to go there.' She looked at Clarissa. 'Apparently, it has ghosts!'

'Oh, yes please! I like the sound of that.'

Essie turned to Craig. 'Does it float your boat? Will you be joining us?'

'Definitely. I recall seeing the same programme and would love to visit it.'

Essie returned to the guide book. 'It says booking is recommended so how about we all do our own thing in the morning – I could do with doing some boring shopping too – and we book in for the afternoon?'

Craig and Clarissa nodded their agreement as they scoffed the remains of their teacakes.

'I suppose we should, since we're kind of on the subject anyway, decide what we're doing once we leave Edinburgh. Have you set a date yet, Clarissa, for meeting Fliss and Becky in France?'

Clarissa took a sip of her hot chocolate before answering Essie's question.

'They're going over to France at the end of November

and will be pitching up at a campsite on the outskirts of Paris. They intend to stay there for about three weeks – pretty much over the Christmas and New Year period. They've been told that Paris at Christmas is rather special. I thought I'd meet up with them there as trying to catch them when they're on the road travelling would be too hit-and-miss. So, I'm currently thinking about going across around the sixteenth or seventeenth of December. I'm just trying to work out if it would be better to go on the Eurostar – which is a bit more expensive but goes right into Paris – or over on the ferry and get a train on the other side. If I do the latter, I get to see a little bit of France on my way rather than the blur of greenery which I'll get if I go on the Eurostar.'

'I suppose then, we need to consider being back home in Oxford, for early December at the latest.'

Essie felt her stomach churn at the thought. Home also meant George and finally facing up to the inevitable music that would come from her being off the radar for most of the year. She had sent a couple of short letters, via Sukie, just letting him know that she and Clarissa were doing well, but they hadn't actually spoken to each other since he'd left that morning to go to London.

'I suppose we do.' Clarissa nodded.

Craig also agreed.

Essie swapped the Edinburgh guide book for the map which also lived in her handbag. She opened it out and looked at their options for when they moved on. She placed her finger on the map and moved it along the yellow line which was the coast road down the east side of the country, and took them towards Berwick-Upon-Tweed.

'If we go this way, it will take us on to Alnwick – which has a castle I really want to visit and,' she smiled at Clarissa, 'was also in the Harry Potter movies.'

'Then I want to go there too!' came Clarissa's swift

reply.

Essie smiled. 'I thought you might. After that, we could make our way to Newcastle, down the coast to Whitby – famous for being the setting of Bram Stoker's Dracula – and then begin going inland to York and Leeds, which would take us to the end of November, more or less, and then we go home from Leeds. That'll give you some time to prepare for going to France, Clarissa.'

'I don't need to prepare, Mum, I've already got what I need. I have my passport, I can pick up a decent rucksack anywhere and I'll simply buy whatever clothing I require when I require it. To be honest, I'd be happier to go straight to France without going home first but I'll go with whatever you both decide.'

'The weather's growing too cold now, Clarissa, to be doing much more travelling in Marvin and Vanda. As much as I'd like to keep travelling for longer, I just don't fancy it in December and January.' She gave a small shiver as if to add emphasis to her words.

Craig nodded and said he agreed with Essie. The UK weather wasn't the best for road trips in the winter.

And so, it was decided, they had three weeks left.

The mood around the table turned sombre as they all came to terms with the fact their road trip was almost at an end.

FORTY-NINE

'Haggis for me too, please.'

'That'll be three Haggis with Tatties and Neeps, please.'

Craig smiled at the barman as he placed the order while Essie and Clarissa found a table. This was the second time they'd eaten in this pub and he suspected they'd be here the following night too. It was a little bit twee with its tartan carpet, wood-clad walls and Scottish "knick-knacks" on the wall but it was close to their hotel, the prices were reasonable, the staff were friendly, and the food was good and plentiful. He picked up the drinks and carried them to the table, feeling the bulge in his coat pocket bumping against his leg as he walked. Today, he'd done something totally impulsive and completely out of character, and he was about to spill the beans to the ladies. He so hoped they wouldn't be angry with him when he told them what he'd done.

He placed the drinks on the table and made himself comfortable as he listened to Clarissa tell Essie some of her plans for when she got to France. Her excitement was beginning to grow, even though there were several weeks to go before she left.

When there was finally a break in the conversation, he cleared his throat and said, 'I've done something today, which was not in our plans, and now I'm really worried you'll both be annoyed with me.'

Two pairs of eyes looked at him in surprise. It had always been a small joke between them that Craig wouldn't know impulsive if it came and bit him on the ass!

He put his hand in his coat pocket and pulled out a travel brochure, opening it at the page which he'd folded down. He laid it on the table and pushed it towards Essie. Clarissa moved in closer to her mum so she could also see.

'This is a brochure for Mexico, Craig, and this is the Moonlight Paradise resort in Cancun. I don't understand?'

He took a deep breath and said quickly, 'I've booked us on a holiday there at the end of November. All three of us!'

'You've done what?'

He looked at Clarissa, whose face mirrored the surprise also sitting on Essie's.

He took another deep breath, held it for a few seconds in an attempt to quell the lurching of his stomach, and then spoke again – this time more slowly and precisely.

'I've booked… well, provisionally booked, a two-week holiday to Mexico at the end of the month.'

He saw Essie about to speak and held his hand up to stop her.

'Please, let me finish before you say anything. Let me assure you that a trip to Mexico was *not* on the agenda when I went out this morning but I passed a travel agent and they were putting up a new window display which included beautiful photographs of golden, sandy beaches and stunning azure-blue seas with the sunlight shining upon them. I was freezing cold, the rain was lashing down and the next thing I know, I'm sitting inside with a nice hot cup of tea discussing the best resorts in the area. I made a provisional booking for two rooms because I just thought it would make a lovely ending to our trip. A chance to relax, no driving involved, it'll be warm but not too hot and we can simply take it easy before we go our separate ways in December. Please don't be mad with me, I know I've been impulsive but, to be honest, I think it'll be great.'

Essie stared at him for a few seconds before returning her attention to the brochure, reading bits out as she went through it.

'It has ten restaurants – which includes Chinese and Spanish restaurants – four swimming pools, two with swim-up bars, in-house spa facilities, a gym, several bar areas and a sports bar with televisions relaying sport from around the world. The bedrooms all have queen sized beds, that includes the twin rooms, their own optics and free bar and a double-sized jacuzzi, situated to provide a sea view while you relax.'

She stopped reading, sat back and gave him a hard stare.

'Craig, it sounds amazing, but after buying Marvin, I don't think it would be right to spend this much money on a holiday, no matter how wonderful it would be.'

'No, Essie, you misunderstand. This is *my* treat. I'm paying for it.'

'Oh, no you don't, Craig! That is above and beyond. We've played it fair and square all the way through this trip. All expenses to be split equally between us.'

'Essie, this is my "thank you" gift to you and Clarissa for letting me tag along on your road trip. You've both been so kind, you've helped me make some big decisions,' he looked at Clarissa as he said this, 'and you've shown me what it feels like to be a part of a family again. That was something which had been missing from my life for far too long. I still don't know exactly what I'll do with myself after this, but I *do* know I'll make the decision with considerably more confidence than I would have done otherwise. So, please, allow me to gift you this trip. Besides,' he gave her a sly little look, 'I happen to know you've always wanted to visit Chichén Itzá – it's one of the day-trips we can take.'

He pointed to the other side of the page where the various excursions were listed.

'How do you know that?'

'Erm, I may have let that one slip one day when Craig and I were discussing historical ruins and things around the world.'

Clarissa gave her mum a small "sorry" face.

'Look, it's not fully booked. The agents have put a twenty-four hour hold on the rooms and flights. I only need to call them in the morning to cancel or confirm, so if you really don't want to go, it's not going to cause any problems.'

Clarissa nudged Essie. 'Oh, go on, Mum, you know you want to. As Craig says, it would be a lovely, *warm,* way to end our time together. Go out in style and all that, you know...'

Craig threw her a grateful smile and she grinned back at him. It made him feel so much better to know she was on his side.

'But, what about the logistics of it? Where do we fly from? Where do we leave the vans – we can't park those in an airport car park for two weeks? What about holiday clothes? There's too much to do...'

'Well, to answer some of your questions – we fly out of Manchester, which we can easily drive to from Leeds. You can shop for any clothing you might need in either Leeds or Manchester. There's not much to do as we've managed to survive nine months on the road with little in the way of belongings and, as for parking... Well, Bobbie and Ritchie have said we can park the vans on their driveway while we're away.'

'Bobbie and Ritchie? You've spoken with them?'

Essie sounded as shocked at that as she had done when he'd presented her with the holiday brochure.

'Of course, I have. They live in Manchester… we fly from Manchester… it seemed the perfect opportunity to bring our little gang back together again. Bobbie is desperate to see you.'

'But… I don't understand… after the wedding invite debacle, I thought she'd never want to speak to me again.'

'Oh, I cleared that one up months ago. The day after you told me, actually.'

'You still keep in touch with them?'

'Damn right I do. I didn't get to see them much after Dad fell ill but we'd always have a natter every other week or so, just to keep up with everything. Then, when Facebook came along, we hooked up on there. We're still best of buddies despite the miles between us.'

'I see… I didn't realise…'

He leaned forward and picked up her hand, relief rushing through him when she didn't pull it away.

'Wouldn't you like to see Bobbie again? You must have missed her at some point over the years.'

Essie was quiet for a few minutes and he sat, holding her hand patiently, waiting for her to speak. Even Clarissa was quiet, as though she'd sensed this was something her mother needed to work out for herself. Finally, she spoke.

'Yes, I have missed Bobbie and I would dearly like to see her. I need to apologise for George's actions and hope she can forgive me.'

'Hey, she knows it wasn't your fault and she's cool with that.'

'Okay.'

'Is that "Okay, I'll see Bobbie", or "Okay, I'll see Bobbie *and* go along with your ridiculous plan to hop on a plane to Mexico"?'

Essie laughed. 'The latter. I'll see Bobbie *and* accept your very generous gift of a holiday in Mexico.'

'YAY! That's wonderful!' Clarissa let out her whoop of joy just as their food arrived.

Before they began eating, Craig lifted his glass. 'A little toast. To our last hurrah!'

The ladies chorused, 'Our last hurrah!'

They clinked their glasses together before tucking into their meal, chatting excitedly about their unexpected trip.

Craig quietly decided to himself that, if being impulsive felt this good, he might be inclined to try it more often.

FIFTY

Essie prised her hands off Marvin's steering wheel and wiped them on her thighs. The weather had finally given in to winter and the rain had been torrential for the last ten days. Driving had been a nightmare and she was glad their journey was over. Well, for now anyway. They'd just parked on Bobbie and Ritchie's driveway and the front door opened as she switched off the ignition. Although she'd done nothing wrong, she was still really nervous about seeing her old friends again. The embarrassment of George's actions made her want to curl up in shame. She still couldn't believe he'd done such a terrible thing and then lied to her about it. She looked out the window to see Craig being gathered up in one of Bobbie's famous bear hugs and they locked eyes over his shoulder. Bobbie gave her a wide, delighted smile and Essie felt her nerves drain away. She opened the door and her feet had barely grazed the gravel when she was enveloped in Bobbie's arms and the breath was being squeezed out of her.

'Oh, Essie, Essie, Essie… how wonderful to see you again. Oh, how I've missed you. Let me look at you.'

Bobbie let go and stood back, giving her the full up-and-down before pulling her back into another hug.

'You look fabulous, you disgusting woman! You've hardly changed a bit and yet, here's me, looking every day of my forty-five years!'

'Still talking nonsense, I see, Bobbie! You look amazing and you do NOT look forty-five, let me tell you!'

And she didn't. Essie was delighted to see that her friend still had the same cheeky sparkle in her eyes and the same ferocity of spirit in her face. Sure, there were a few wrinkles which hadn't been there all those years ago but none of them had gone through the years unscathed and it was the fire in her soul that would keep Bobbie young right up until she landed, singing, dancing and yelling, in her grave.

'This is my daughter, Clarissa.'

She pulled Clarissa forward and chuckled as she too disappeared into Bobbie's arms. She turned to see Ritchie coming out to greet them.

'Hey, you guys, welcome. Sorry for being slow to come out, I just had to pop the dogs in the kitchen out of the way.'

He gave Craig a manly hug and a pat on the shoulder before turning his attention upon Essie.

'Estelle Parker! Would ya look at you! All grown up and still a delight for the eyes. Come here, gorgeous, and give me a hug!'

Essie felt the joy rise up inside her that her old friends weren't holding any grudges against her. Ritchie had always had a bit of Joey from Friends about him and it made her smile. She was so happy to see that he didn't appear to have changed.

'Come on, guys, let's get inside where you can relax, unwind and have a glass – or bottle – of wine. It's far too cold to be standing out here chatting.'

Bobbie ushered them in through the front door and

Essie was thrilled when Bobbie hooked her arm through hers, just as she used to do when they were at uni, and was squeezing it tightly, almost as though she never wanted to let her go. Essie returned the pressure – a silent signal to Bobbie to let her know that, now they'd found each other, she'd never let her go again.

Clarissa looked at the food remaining on her plate while feeling stuffed to the brim. Bobbie had been cooking and the table was laden with bowls of various curries, three different kinds of rice, naan bread, poppadoms, and a plethora of side dishes and chutneys. She couldn't eat another grain and finally had to admit defeat.

'Bobbie, thank you for such a delicious meal. I am full, fit to pop.'

'It's my pleasure, Clarissa. I'm delighted you enjoyed it.'

Bobbie beamed at her and Clarissa felt a lovely warmth spread through her. Her mum had told her a little about her old friends on the drive here and the one thing she'd mentioned the most was Bobbie's warm and generous spirit. Unless she took against you that was, in which case, you were better off keeping out of her way. She had a tongue that could tear a strip off you before you were even aware she'd been offended. Clarissa said she sounded a lot like Sukie and Essie had agreed they were both formidable women.

When everyone else around the table admitted defeat too, they moved through into the lounge where Ritchie put on some soft music and Bobbie brought out another bottle of wine.

'Bobbie, we can't drink any more, we've got to be at the airport for six in the morning.' Essie placed her hand over the top of her wine glass.

Clarissa looked at the clock on the mantlepiece and was surprised to see it was only half-past five. She pointed this out to her mum who then conceded to one more glass. That was the thing with the dark nights coming down so early, it was easy to forget what time it was.

'Well then, Essie, are you looking forward to Mexico? We were there a few years ago and loved it.'

'I can't wait, Bobbie. I've wanted to go there for so long.'

'So, what stopped you?'

'Well… George isn't a good traveller and anything over four hours in a plane is a big fat no-no.'

'That's unfortunate. It must have become quite restrictive for you.'

'To be honest, Ritchie, George preferred to go on city breaks where we could take in some culture and then he could brag about it in the office later.'

'He always was a charmer.' Bobbie's comment dripped with sarcasm but it quickly turned into an apology as she realised Clarissa could have taken offence.

'Honestly, Bobbie, you've nothing to apologise for. I've finally seen the man for what he really is and you'd have to go some way for me to feel offended.'

'Now, Clarissa, it's not right to speak like that – he's still your father.'

'No, Mum, he's not my father – he's our controller! Our dominator! He cracks the whip and we're expected to jump to attention. I don't understand why you keep protecting him. Especially after all that he's done to you.'

'I'm not protecting him, sweetheart, I just don't like to talk badly of people behind their back.'

'You *are* protecting him. You still haven't agreed to get a divorce. I don't think you've got any intention of leaving him.'

'Clarissa! That's enough.'

'He's not enough though, is he? He's vindictive and cruel and every time he opens his mouth, it's with the intention of running you down. I have *never* heard him say one nice thing to you. Yet, when I ask what you plan to do, you won't give me a straight answer.'

'It's not that simple—'

'Yes, it IS that simple, Mum. I can't bear to see you unhappy with him. Just leave him and marry Craig – you're perfect for each other. He'd be a much better husband and father!'

Unable to control her emotions any more, Clarissa burst into tears. She stood up, her chair falling to the floor behind her, and ran out of the room. As she made her way back to the kitchen, she heard Bobbie say, 'Stay there, Essie. I've got this.'

Sure enough, a moment later, Bobbie walked into the kitchen, picked up the kettle and after filling it up under the tap, plugged it in and switched it on. All in complete silence. Clarissa watched as she picked up the debris on the table from when she'd been preparing their delicious meal, give it a wipe and then set down two pretty china cups, complete with saucers. A matching sugar bowl and milk jug joined them and the teapot was warmed before the teabags went in. Once the teapot was filled and had joined the rest of the crockery, Bobbie pulled out a chair, sat down and, gesturing to the chair opposite, said to Clarissa, 'Please, sit with me.'

'That's a pretty tea set,' she said, as she perched nervously on the edge of the wooden chair. She felt rather stupid now for behaving as she had done.

'Thank you. I believe that it's easier to solve problems when sipping tea from a proper china cup.'

'I'm sorry for my outburst, it was very immature. I… I don't know why I reacted so. I just wish Mum would do something for herself instead of looking out for everyone else.'

'Clarissa, you love your mum and it's heart-warming to see how deeply you care for her. I do understand how frustrating it must be for you, standing on the side-lines as she struggles to work out what to do next.'

'Why can't she see what an asshole he is? Why is she still protecting him when he's been such a bastard to her? I don't get it!'

'This is going to sound patronising but it's not meant to be – I'm simply stating a fact. When you're young, with not a care or responsibility in the world, it's easier to see everything in black and white. Sadly, as we grow older, we see things in a more gray'ish hue – and I don't mean our hair colour either. I can tell you now, the inner struggle your mum is dealing with is very much par for the course. I do voluntary work in a woman's refuge and, believe me, they all arrive there saying the exactly the same thing – they know they should have left sooner but they simply couldn't find the courage to do it. Or they kept trying for the benefit of the children. Or they couldn't deal with the guilt of being the one to break up the relationship, thinking they should have tried harder, been better wives, mothers, girlfriends... Knowing what you should do, and being able to do it, are two quite different things. The worst thing you can do is pressure your mum into making a decision before she's ready. I appreciate you think you're helping but by making her feel guilty, you reinforce the "uselessness" your father has been laying on her for years. If she feels she is useless, then she's less likely to believe she is good enough to be a person in her own right.'

Clarissa looked up at Bobbie.

'But she IS good enough, *more* than good enough. I've watched her change these last eight months and she's a much better, wholesome, person than she was when we set off. I don't want to see my father take that from her – he's stripped so much away already.'

She began tracing the wooden grain in the table with her finger.

'Then, if I may give a small piece of advice which I hope will help you both – the best thing you can do is support her. Believe that she will do the right thing when the time is right for her to do it. It might take her a month, a year, or even ten years, but never give up on her. Don't be exasperated if she says she's going to finally leave but doesn't – just keep loving her and caring for her, that's the best way to help her rebuild her faith and belief in herself. Do you think you can do that?'

'Of course. I was supposed to be travelling around Europe but I can easily cancel that to be with her—'

'No!' Bobbie placed her hand over Clarissa's. 'You mustn't do that. You must carry on as normal. How do you think Essie would feel if you gave up your dream to stay with her?'

Clarissa sighed. 'Guilty.'

'Exactly. Look, maybe if I'd met your mum again before you all set off on your road trip, I might have seen a different woman but tonight, I'm seeing a lot of the girl I went to uni with and, trust me, she's got a lot more gumption about her than you might realise. Personally, I think she'll sort this all out sooner rather than later but if she doesn't, then we'll both be by her side, holding her up until she does.'

Clarissa looked at Bobbie. 'I have to ask – didn't you think it strange that none of you were invited to her wedding, if you were all such good mates?'

'I was a hot-headed little rebel back then. I couldn't stand your father from the minute I met him and the feeling was entirely mutual. He went down the route of "divide and conquer" – he kept Essie away from us, slowly splitting us up and we saw less and less of her with each passing month. The last time we all went out together, she was wearing her engagement ring and informed us she was dropping out of her course because George wanted to get married as soon as possible. There was a promotion on the table at work and they looked more favourably on married employees. She promised us we'd be invited to the wedding but when the wedding day arrived and our invites hadn't… I assumed we'd been dropped and were no longer welcome in her new life. When Gerald… I mean, Craig, called and told us what had really happened – well, let me assure you, I was almost in the car with the intention of driving to Oxford to tell your father what I thought of him and then punching his lights out! Ritchie actually hid the car keys to ensure I didn't. I was furious. Partly at him for what he'd done but mostly at myself for the bad thoughts I'd had and for not fighting harder to remain Essie's friend.'

When Clarissa saw the sadness on Bobbie's face, she squeezed the hand that was still holding hers.

'We all make mistakes, Bobbie, but as long as you're on her side now, I think everything will work itself out.'

The vehemence in Bobbie's voice when she replied, 'If that jumped up little shit thinks he can take her away from us again, then he's got another think coming! He won't know what's hit him if he messes with me a second time!' left Clarissa in no doubt that, as a substitute cheerleader for Essie while she was away, she couldn't have found anyone better.

FIFTY-ONE

'Ladies and gentlemen, you may now remove your seat-belts. Thank you for flying Alpha Airlines and I know it's only the first of December, but the crew and I would like to wish you all a very Merry Christmas and a Happy New Year.'

Essie undid her belt and stretched her arms above her head. The ten-hour journey from Manchester hadn't been all that bad but she'd be glad to get her feet back on terra-firma again. She'd read for a bit, watched a few movies – the latest Ryan Reynold's one had been showing and he sure was a little hottie! – but sleep had eluded her and now she was shattered. Somehow, though, she had to find the energy to keep going; while it might be seven o'clock in the evening back home in the UK, it was only one in the afternoon here. They'd been up since four a.m. in order to be at the airport for six. Ritchie had refused to allow them to order a taxi and had kindly driven them there – foregoing his Sunday morning long-lie to do so.

'Here, Clarissa, put that in your bag. We can do the rest while sunning ourselves around the pool.'

Essie looked round to see Craig handing Clarissa the crossword & puzzle book they'd bought at the airport and had spent a few hours poring over as they tried to solve the puzzles together. It had been strange to see them like that – heads bent as they both chewed the ends of their pens – and Essie couldn't help but be sad that Clarissa had missed out on having a father who shared things like that with her. Although she hadn't come right out and said it, Clarissa had grown exceptionally fond of Craig and this was partly behind her outburst last night – she wanted her and Craig to get together so she could have someone who was more like a real father than the one she had.

Craig caught her eye just then and flashed her a smile. A smile that melted her to the core and which she couldn't succumb to. She knew the right thing was to leave George but she also had to give him a chance to change. It wouldn't be right to just get up and leave without talking with him to see if there was any chance of salvaging the quarter century they'd spent together. She'd finally made her decision on what to do next although she hadn't told Clarissa and Craig – she knew Clarissa wouldn't be happy about it and she didn't want to spoil the holiday. No, she was going to let her think she was still being indecisive until she left for France. It was better that way.

'Come on, Mum, time to get off this tin can and breathe in some fresh air.'

They gathered up their hand luggage and as Essie stepped out of the cabin, she was hit by the heat. The pilot had announced the temperature was twenty-eight degrees Celsius as they were coming in to land but the humidity could make it seem three or four degrees warmer. He wasn't kidding and by the time she'd walked over the tarmac and onto the bus waiting to take them to the main building, she could feel her T-shirt beginning to stick to her back. Thankfully, Bobbie had talked them out of wearing jeans on the flight and insisted they wear lightweight cut-off trousers. They'd been freezing when they'd left rain-soaked Manchester but she was grateful for them now. It was a relief to step on the bus and enjoy the air-conditioning when the doors closed and they were whisked off to go through immigration and passport control.

'Oh, my goodness! It's absolutely gorgeous!'

Essie, Clarissa and Craig walked into the lobby of the Moonlight Paradise resort and their mouths fell wide open. The brochure hadn't fully prepared them for the opulence in front of them. The floors were cool, gleaming, dark-brown marble, the walls were cream with gold gilt, stunning, crystal chandeliers hung from the ceiling, throwing their glistening rays of light all around and the piece de resistance, a fully-decorated, thirty-foot-high, Christmas tree stood right in front of them. A minstrel's gallery ran around three sides of the lobby and twinkling curtains of fairy lights flowed down around them.

'Come on, let's get checked in, dump the bags in our rooms and then explore.'

The excitement in Craig's voice helped to revive Essie's flagging energy and she felt her second wind getting up to speed. Also, there were tea and coffee facilities in the rooms – a quick shower and a strong cuppa should just about see her through until what could be considered a reasonable time to go to bed.

It didn't take long for them to register and get their keys. The receptionist took their luggage cards and assured them it would be in their rooms within fifteen minutes. She directed them to the corridor they required and advised them to follow the signs. She also handed them a couple of maps and information on opening and closing times for all the bars and restaurants along with details of the snack areas dotted throughout the hotel.

Essie was flicking through the pamphlet as she followed Clarissa and Craig.

'Oh my!' She stopped to look up at them. 'Did you know there was a second hotel on the resort? It's called "Starlight Paradise" and is approximately three-quarters of a mile away. We can either walk there or,' she looked at the blurb, 'get the bus which runs between the two buildings twenty-four hours a day.'

Clarissa smiled. 'Yes, Mum, we did know. Half of the restaurants are over there.'

'I see! I clearly missed that bit. Well, when we go over there to eat, it'll feel like we're really having a night out.'

They arrived at their rooms which were next door to each other and agreed to meet back in the lobby in forty-five minutes.

When Essie and Clarissa stepped over the threshold, they stopped dead in their tracks. The sunlight was streaming in through the double-sized patio windows which led out to a balcony adorned with two luxury wooden steamer chairs and a four-seater table. Inside, in front of the patio doors was a large, double, spa bath. Essie looked at it longingly but knew if she got in, she'd never get back out. Well, not tonight anyway.

Clarissa was filling the kettle for a quick cuppa when there was a knock at the door. As promised, it was their luggage and it had arrived within fifteen minutes. Essie was most impressed and said as much to the porter as she tipped him. She quickly pulled out a change of clothing and laid it on the bed before taking a refreshing shower. The cup of tea Clarissa had waiting for her when she got out, barely touched the sides as it went down. She looked longingly at the optics on the wall above the mini-bar – right now, it would be utter bliss to pour herself a double

G&T and just lie back on one of the steamers on the balcony. Maybe later, if she could keep her eyes open long enough. Clarissa came out of the bathroom and must have read her mind, 'Shall we be a bit decadent later, Mum, and have a sneaky drink on the balcony before bedtime?'

'That sounds like a good plan to me. Now,' she glanced at her watch, 'we'd better get a wriggle on and meet Craig.'

When they returned to the lobby, they found him in the Piano Bar perusing the cocktail menu.

'Have you seen how many cocktails are on this list? My goal is to try every single one of them before we go home!'

'Oh, great, we're going to be carrying a pisshead back to the room every night, Clarissa. I suppose we'd better find the gym – I'm going to need to get some weight-lifting in…'

'Mum, that'll be two pissheads you'll be carting back because these all sound delish and I have every intention of joining Craig in his quest.'

'Huh! Well, sod that. I'm not going to be the only sober one around here. Looks like we're all going to need liver transplants by the time we return home.'

The merry banter continued as they walked outside and got their bearings. They found the towel room where they would get their fresh beach towels each day. They checked out the pools and clocked the locations of the swim up bars. They walked a little further and came across the tennis courts and crazy golf course. Essie fancied the latter but deemed it far too warm for tennis. They stretched their legs a little further and took a stroll along the beach, the warmth of the silvery sand slipping between their toes. When they were able to see the second hotel building in the distance, they did a U-turn, agreeing to explore that side of the resort over the next few days.

'I don't know about you guys, but I'm really hungry. What time is it?'

Essie looked at her watch. 'It's nearly four-thirty. The first restaurant to open is the Italian buffet at six p.m.'

'Urgh! I don't think I can wait till then,' Clarissa groaned.

'You don't have to. According to the brochure, there's a tea and coffee area near the lobby which also has filled rolls, Danish pastries, and cookies. Let's find that, get some nibbles and then just sit down and relax.'

'Cool! Let's go!' Clarissa set off at a brisk pace, leaving Essie and Craig to bring up the rear.

'You've got to love the young,' said Craig, smiling, 'their stomachs always come first.'

Clarissa found the snack table easily enough; it was just along from the Piano Bar. The soothing notes of Beethoven's Moonlight Sonata drifted across as she reached the table and she almost physically drooled as her eyes took in the delicacies adorning it. She placed a plate on the table in front of her and began to pile on various goodies. She was just reaching for some chocolate-covered ring cookies when a soft voice murmured in her ear, 'You don't want those ones, they've got holes in them!'

Her breath caught in her throat and she spun round to find Ross standing behind her, his gorgeous smile, and cheeky tooth-gap, beaming at her. His bushy sandy hair was a touch shorter than it had been but it still stuck out at all angles.

She threw her arms around him, all the while saying over and over, 'Oh, my goodness, oh, my goodness.' She didn't know what else to say – her mind was still computing that he was here in front of her.

'Ross? Is that you?'

'Hi, Essie,' he replied over Clarissa's shoulder. 'Yup! It's me!'

'But… how?'

'Your man there, that's how!'

Clarissa and Essie both turned to look at Craig who was failing dismally at looking innocent.

'Okay,' he threw his hands up, 'I dropped Ross a text to let him know of our plans and to see if there was any way he could join us.'

Clarissa swivelled round.

'You knew about this? All those calls and FaceTime chats and you never once let on you were going to be joining us?'

'I wasn't sure at first if I could get the time off – I've only been there a few weeks – but, when I agreed to work over Christmas, which no one else wanted to do, they were quick enough to agree then.'

'So, when you said I was to text you when I landed but not to call because you had an all-day meeting…'

'I told a porky pie. I couldn't risk you calling and seeing something that might give my location away.'

'Unbelievable!' She shook her head.

'Are you annoyed with me?'

Clarissa took in the concerned look on his face and rushed to reassure him.

'Blimey! No! Of course not. It's just… I'm just… As surprises go, it's one of the best in a long time. I'd say it's right up there with the day my mum told me my father could fuck off!'

'Clarissa!'

She grinned at her mum before thanking Craig for his part in the subterfuge. 'You do know I'll never trust you again after this?'

'Yeah, yeah! Whatever…' Craig laughed with her.

She let go of Ross – albeit reluctantly – and picked up

her plate of nibbles.

'Right then, I don't know what you guys are planning, but I'm taking these,' she indicated to her plate, 'over to the Piano Bar and I will be asking the barman for the strongest cocktail on the menu because, after that surprise, I need at least one!'

FIFTY-TWO

Craig put down the Stuart James thriller he was reading and looked over at Clarissa and Ross messing about in the pool. He was glad Ross had been able to join them – his being there made the holiday feel more complete. His presence also meant he got time alone with Essie although he hadn't thought of that when he'd called him. He'd just been thinking that Clarissa would probably like having someone her own age to hang out with. Being one-to-one with Essie had been a bonus.

However, even without the extra Essie time, the holiday had been wonderful. He couldn't remember when he'd last felt this relaxed and chilled out. So far, they'd been out jet-skiing, snorkelling, and had endured the sixteen-hour round trip to Chichén Itzá. The monument had been quite something to see but Essie had been disgusted by the litter and tourist stalls which were set up around it. She said she was glad to have seen it but unlike some other places of special interest, she had no desire to return to this one. For Craig, however, the highlight of the holiday had been swimming through the river caves at Xcaret, the adventure park further down the coast. The water was so clear and, with the aid of the snorkel provided, he'd loved looking down at all the wonders beneath him. More than once he'd bumped into the walls because he'd been so enthralled and hadn't been paying attention.

Tonight, Clarissa and Ross were going into Cancun. There was a minibus taking them, and some of the other younger holidaymakers, to a few of the local bars and clubs. They'd asked him and Essie to join them but he'd declined, saying his clubbing days were long since gone. Essie had said that, as much as she would like to go out and trip the light fantastic, she would stay behind as it wasn't fair to leave the old-age pensioner on his own. Clarissa had joined in the fun by saying that since he'd disposed of the dodgy tank-tops and jumbo cord trousers, he'd been downgraded from a pensioner to a middle-aged old codger! He'd tried to tell her sternly that he wouldn't be arranging any more surprises for her if she was going to be so cheeky but had failed dismally and they'd all fallen about laughing. Essie had later confided that going clubbing now was her idea of hell and she'd much rather have a nice meal followed by a moonlit stroll along the beach. So that was what they were doing. They'd booked a table in the slightly posher, formal dress, no jeans please, Spanish restaurant. This would be his final evening alone with Essie – tomorrow was their final day and they'd all agreed to dine together for the last night. He didn't want this time to end and wasn't looking forward to going home at all.

He let out a sigh, picked his book back up and worked on immersing himself in the twisty, turning, plot. Anything to take his mind off the minutes slipping away.

Essie let out a less-than-ladylike burp which sent her and Craig into paroxysms of laughter. They'd had a few glasses of wine with dinner and had swung by the cocktail bar on their way down to the beach. They'd done a pretty good job of drinking the menu but their ambition to drink it all had fallen rather short despite their best efforts although they'd all had fun trying.

They'd picked up a couple of Pina Coladas – Essie's favourite – and brought them down to the shore to sip. As the sun-loungers had all been put away for the day, they lay on one of the double-day beds which were scattered along the beach. The sky was midnight-blue above them, the full moon a shining silver disc against it and the stars glistened like small, perfect diamonds. The waves gently kissed the sandy shore in front of them and the sound of the water was soothing and peaceful. They both lay there in silence, letting the calming effect of moon, stars and sea envelope them until Essie's windy tummy broke the mood and they began chatting.

'I can't believe how quickly the days have gone. Only one left and then it's back to reality.'

'I know. I was thinking that this afternoon.'

Essie twisted around to lie on her side and face Craig who was already lying watching her, his head propped up in his hand. The moonlight was shining onto his face and his eyes sparkled in the pale light. Once again, as it had done so many times over the last few months, her heart contracted when she looked at him. She knew she loved him and had finally accepted that she probably always would. The tiny little acorn which had been planted in her heart all those years ago at uni hadn't withered and died; it had merely slumbered until he was back in her life and with the daily watering of love he'd sprinkled on her, it had blossomed into something larger and more meaningful, just as she, herself, had blossomed under the attention he'd bestowed upon her. She'd only recently come to realise how one's self-esteem can be diminished when no one listens to you, or being told on a daily basis that your opinion has no merit or you are simply talked over. Being constantly undermined chips away at your sense of being until it becomes easier to believe you are worthless. Outside of her home, Essie had managed to don the mantle of a woman in control and Clarissa's comments on Essie's "WI face" were proof of how well she'd succeeded in hiding her insecurity.

'I'm going to miss you, Essie. You *and* Clarissa, but you quite a bit more. Do you know what you're going to do when you return home?'

This was it. Essie's heart clenched again but, this time, for an entirely different reason. This was the moment when she was going to break his heart all over again but unlike before, she knew she would be doing so.

'I do,' she answered quietly.

'And?'

'I can't throw away our years together without giving George a chance to… well, redeem himself. I'm not the same wreck of a woman who drove out of his life in March. I'm stronger now, I'm a better person than he had me believing I was and I know much of that is down to you. You've shown me how I should be treated, what respect looks like and how people who care about you behave towards you. When I get home, I'll be sitting George down and having a conversation which should have taken place many years before. He will be told, in no uncertain terms, that he needs to change his behaviour and that I will not be his doormat anymore.'

'I see. What if he doesn't change?'

'I'll cross that bridge when I come to it. For now, I have to believe that he does love me and will be prepared to work with me on this.'

Craig moved towards her, reducing the inches between them. She could smell the coconut from the cocktails on his breath when he spoke again.

'You do know that I love you, don't you?'

The lump in her throat meant it was a few seconds before she could reply.

'Yes, I do.'

'And I want you to know that I will wait till the end of forever for you.'

'You can't do that, Craig. It's not fair and I won't ask it of you. You're such a wonderful person and you must find someone who is worthy of you.'

'You're not asking, I'm telling you. And I don't want to meet someone else because it wouldn't be fair on her – she'd only be getting a tiny, little piece of my love because the rest of it belongs to you.'

The breeze blew a strand of hair over her face and he gently slipped it away, tucking it behind her ear. The soft touch of his fingers on her cheek left it tingling and their warmth flowed all the way to her toes. She couldn't tell him how she felt for she didn't want to risk giving him false hope. She knew George too well and he would toe the line because he'd loathe the idea of a divorce – that wouldn't fit into the perfect family life persona he'd spent all these years creating.

'Please, don't wait for me, Craig…' Her voice broke and tears began to slip down her cheeks. Craig wiped them away with his thumb and put his arms around her, holding her closely against him as she sobbed. When she was all cried out, she lay quietly with her head on his chest, listening to his heart beating. It was a sound she wanted to hear for the rest of her life. Knowing that she couldn't, made the tears threaten to come again. She moved away slightly so she could see his face. Without giving any thought as to the wisdom of her actions, and totally unable to stop herself, she placed her lips upon his and gave in to the kiss she'd wanted for so long. Somewhere, in the farthest corner of her mind, a tiny voice was screaming, *'NO! Don't do this, you fool...'* but she quickly quashed it. She needed this one moment to remember in the years ahead. She had to know what it felt like to kiss the man who owned her heart.

A moment passed before she forced herself to pull away. That was the moment when she realised just how much self-control she possessed because all she really wanted to do was melt further into their embrace and hold Craig in her arms until the end of eternity. It would be so easy to take his hand and lead him back to his room where they would not be disturbed but it would be unfair on him and she wouldn't be able to live with the guilt she would invariably feel. How could she save her marriage if she'd been unfaithful? Even their kiss was wrong but it was a wrong she could live with.

She looked into his eyes again. 'Goodbye, Craig,' she whispered.

She turned and swung her legs off the daybed. Without looking back, she walked away, feeling her heart shattering into a million tiny pieces with every step she took.

FIFTY-THREE

‘To Craig!’

Clarissa raised her glass as she led the toast, Ross and Essie immediately joining her.

She bent down and picked up the small gift bag she’d placed under the table before Craig had arrived. It was their last night together – tomorrow, their little group would begin to splinter. Ross would be making the long trek back to Japan and goodness only knew when she’d see him again. He’d promised to join her in Australia when she arrived there, but that was at least six months away. In three days, she would be leaving her mum and Craig to travel to London where she’d be catching the Eurostar to Paris to hook up with Fliss and Becky.

‘Craig, we got you this small gift to say “Thank you” for this wonderful holiday and giving us all a chance to really be together one last time. We hope it’ll always be filled with happy memories.’

She smiled as she handed the bag over and Craig blushed. He was an amazingly wonderful man and she really wished her mum would realise it too. She’d already vowed to keep in touch with him when she was away and was planning to send shared emails to both him and her mum in the hope it would keep them talking to each other.

They all laughed when Craig opened the smaller of the two items in the bag and revealed a keyring containing a photograph of the four of them in their snorkelling gear. It had been taken just before they'd gone into the underground caves and they were all laughing at each other in their flippers and snorkels. It was a fabulous picture and really summed up the whole mood of the holiday.

The second item was a gorgeous pewter tankard upon which the words "A Mugful of Mexican Memories. With love from Essie, Clarissa and Ross. xx" had been engraved. When he looked up from reading it, Clarissa was sure she could see tears in his eyes.

'Wow! This is—' Craig coughed and tried again. 'This is beautiful. Thank you so much. But, more importantly, thank *you*, Clarissa, for welcoming me so graciously when I joined you and your mum on your road trip. I know the purpose of your journey was to spend time with your mum and getting to know her better and I really hope you were still able to do that, even with me tagging along.' He stopped to look at Essie before turning back to her. 'Your mum is a wonderful woman with many strengths and I'm delighted to find you take after her. I know you're about to embark upon another journey which will be filled with all sorts of adventures that I can only dream of and so, with that in mind, I would like to give you this.'

He took a small box from his pocket and slid it across the table towards her.

She looked at the box. 'What is it? What's this?' She glanced up at the others but they merely smiled at her.

She picked the box up, it wasn't heavy, and lifted the lid off. Inside was a key attached to a VW leather fob. She looked up again, confusion walking all over her face.

‘I don’t understand…’

‘It’s the key to Vanda. I want you to have her when you go to Europe.’

‘But… I can’t do that… this is too much…’

‘Clarissa.’

She looked at her mum.

‘We’re concerned that you’re going to be totally reliant upon Fliss and Becky when you’re travelling. Now, they are lovely girls and I’m sure you’ll all have a wonderful time together BUT… if anything untoward were to occur, then you could be left high and dry. Also, if you fancy going somewhere which isn’t on their agenda, then you can do so and meet up with them further along the line.’

‘But… it’s Vanda! Craig, she’s your pride and joy.’

Craig smiled at her. ‘Your mum mentioned she was going to give you Marvin but I thought he might be too much, given he’s rather large, so I’ve offered Vanda in his place. She’s a left-hand drive so will be perfect for driving around Europe and I want you to have her. She needs more adventures and you’re the one best placed to share them with her. While we’ve been away, Ritchie has organised your ferry over to Calais, the insurance and international breakdown cover. You’re all set to go.’

‘But… what about when I go to Australia? She’s not going to fit on the airplane.’

Craig smiled at her. ‘You simply let me know when you’re leaving, which airport you’ll be leaving from and I’ll fly over to collect her and drive her back. It will be something for me to look forward to come June or July or whenever you go.’

Clarissa thought over what her mum had said. She saw the sense in her words and realised it had been a small niggle at the back of her own mind. Now, she could go and really enjoy herself knowing she had full independence.

She stood up, walked round to Craig, and while giving

him the tightest of hugs, kissed him on the cheek and whispered in his ear, 'Thank you. You're the best surrogate father a girl could ever have.'

She noticed the tears were back in his eyes as she pulled away. She took his hand and squeezed it and revelled in the squeeze she received back. Maybe one day, she thought, as she sat back down, he would be her father for real.

'I love you.'

'I love you more.'

'No, I love *you* more.'

'Impossible! I love *you* more.'

'When you two have quite finished! We need to go now, Clarissa.'

'Yeah, I'll be with you in a minute.'

She watched Craig and Essie gather up their belongings. Their flight had been called and they were about to board. This time, it was she who was walking away from Ross as his flight departed an hour after theirs.

'Message me when you land. I'll probably still be up in the air but it'll be waiting for me when I get off the plane.'

'I will.' She clung onto him, unable to believe how painfully her heart was breaking for a second time. She honestly felt as though a part of her was being ripped away.

'Clarissa!'

She glanced over her shoulder and saw the queue to board was rapidly dwindling. Her mum and Craig were the last in line and there were only a few passengers in front of them.

'I have to go.'

She pulled Ross's face towards her and gave him one

last kiss, pouring every ounce of love she possessed into it.

'CLARISSA!'

She opened her eyes, stepped out of his arms and, picking up her bag, turned quickly away, and ran over to the gate. Just as she was about to walk through and out of his sight, she turned back and shouted, 'ROSS MACKENZIE, I LOVE *YOU* THE MOREST!' before jogging down the stairs to catch up with her mum.

As they walked over the warm tarmac to the plane, she made the mistake of looking back at the terminus. Ross was standing at the window, watching her go. This was her undoing and the tears she'd been forcing back began to fall.

She tried to hide her face but her mum knew her too well. When they were seated, she passed her some tissues and a couple of sleeping tablets.

'As advised by Bobbie. Take these and go to sleep. Not only will they prevent jet-lag but you'll feel a bit better after some rest.'

Clarissa did as her mum advised and soon her tears dried as she nodded off.

FIFTY-FOUR

'Oh, Mum, I'm going to miss you so much.'

'No, you won't. You're going to be so busy enjoying yourself, you won't have time to miss me. Go and embrace everything Europe has to offer. Besides, I'll be coming out to see you when you get to Italy. I've always wanted to visit Florence and it would be lovely to see it together.'

'Just as long as you leave your husband behind! I don't want to see him.'

'Hush, now! He's still, and always will be, your father. You need to make things up with him at some point.'

'Hmph! We'll see. Not right now though!'

'Only when you're ready.'

Essie took her daughter in her arms for one last embrace. Inside, she was aching at seeing her go, but her head was telling her it was the right thing to do. She wanted her daughter to be independent; to know herself and grow into a strong and assertive woman. She was already on that path and her travels would only serve to develop those traits further. She was also a tiny bit jealous because it was an adventure she'd never get to experience herself. There were limits to the sacrifices she could ask George to make when she sat him down for their "talk". Travelling the world in a motorhome would be a step too far for him to take on board.

'Are you sure you have everything?'

'Yes, Mum. I think our shopping trip yesterday covered it. And, guess what, they also have shops in France, so I'm sure I'll be able to get anything I've missed.'

'Okay! Okay! Just making sure.'

Essie watched her daughter as she said her goodbyes to Craig, Ritchie and Bobbie, and chuckled as she overheard the instructions passed to her old friend that she was to keep an eye on her. Essie already knew that, now Bobbie and Ritchie were back in her life, it was going to be considerably less quiet than it had been before.

'Now, drive carefully. Call me when you get to your hotel this evening.'

Clarissa was doing the drive down to Dover over two days as Essie had been concerned that Manchester to Dover was too much driving in one day. Clarissa was booked into a hotel near Heathrow airport and would carry on to Dover the following day. Her ferry was due to depart at one-thirty in the afternoon, so she'd have plenty of time to get to the port and get on board.

The *thunk* of Vanda's door closing brought Essie back into the moment. The window was wound down as the engine started up. Clarissa popped her head out the window, smiled broadly and called out, 'Au revoir,' before moving off the driveway and disappearing around the bend in the road. A few seconds later, Vanda's throaty growl could no longer be heard.

'Right then, time for us to get a move on too, I think.'

Essie gave Craig a wane, little smile when he gently touched her arm. This was their final journey and somehow, she had to hold herself together for only a few more hours.

It didn't take long to say goodbye to Bobbie and Ritchie and promises were made several times over to stay in touch. Essie had also agreed to set up a page on Facebook when she got home so she could join their little group and always be a part of them.

'You're not getting away from me this time,' Bobbie whispered, when she hugged her once more.

'Good! I don't want to lose you again,' she whispered back.

She climbed into the driving seat, waited for Craig to join her and, emulating Clarissa, lowered her window to call out her goodbyes as she pulled onto the road and began the final drive that would take her home.

FIFTY-FIVE

Most of the journey was made in silence and in what felt like no time at all, they were pulling onto Craig's driveway. The weather forecast had predicted snow and he'd been hoping it would arrive soon and their journey prolonged but it had not and now here they were.

He jumped out before Essie had even switched off the ignition, trying to gain a few seconds to compose himself, in preparation for their next goodbye. This was probably going to be the hardest thing he'd ever put himself through in his life but he knew he had to put on his best "brave face" to make it easier for Essie. He didn't like the decision she'd made – once again, George Walton had won the fair maiden – but he respected her for it. He understood that she had to at least try and make her marriage work, but all the understanding in the world didn't lessen the pain in his heart.

He opened Marvin's side door and took out the bags of luggage stored there. As most of his belongings, bar his personal items, were going to France with Clarissa, there wasn't much to unload.

'Do you want to pop in and see what Flora has done with the place?'

Good grief, man, drag the pain out a bit more why don't you... whispered a voice in his head, and he did have to wonder what sadistic little gene inside him had thought it was a good question to ask.

'Erm… sure. That would be nice.'

Aw bugger! Now you'll always have pictures in your head of her inside your home, ya muppet! the voice whispered again.

'Oh, sod off!'

'Excuse me?'

Craig didn't realise he'd spoken aloud.

'Oh, sorry, Essie. I just realised that Flora's had a new front door put in and I don't have a key for it. I'm just hoping she had the sense to put a spare one inside the key stone.'

'Right…'

He could tell from her voice that she didn't quite believe him but he chose not to say anything further in case he ended up digging an even bigger hole for himself. He walked over to the rockery to the side of the front door and pulled out a stone near the bottom. He turned it over, opened the little compartment underneath and took out the key inside. He held his breath as he put it into the lock and exhaled with relief when the door opened.

He stepped back with a smile, gave a small, mock bow, and said, 'After you, m'lady.'

'Actually, Craig… I think it's probably better that I don't come in. I'm sure your niece has done a wonderful job but right now, I need to go home. I'm only delaying the inevitable.'

Craig felt his heart sink. He too had been putting off the inevitable.

'Okay. Another time, maybe?'

‘Sure.’ She smiled as she turned and walked back towards Marvin.

He followed behind her, admiring her hair as it swished across her shoulders and the way her hips swayed lightly as she walked. He forced the picture into his memory, squeezing it in alongside all the others he’d gathered over the months; memories he now knew would be all he’d have left once she was gone.

Essie opened the door and turned to face him.

For a long moment, they looked at each other, absorbing the essence of their closeness.

Finally, Essie said, ‘I have to go.’

He nodded, the lump in his throat rendering him unable to speak.

She climbed into her seat, closed the door and turned on the engine. She’d already reversed out onto the road when he felt his feet begin to move and he was running down the driveway after her. He banged on her window and when she lowered it, he looked up into her beautiful brown eyes and said, ‘I’ll be waiting, Essie. Till the end of forever. That’s a promise.’

She looked down at him for a few seconds and then whispered so quietly he struggled to hear before she drove off.

Craig stood rooted to the spot for several moments before falling down onto his knees, the tears pouring down his face.

He felt something wet land on the back of his neck. He brushed it away with his hand but it happened again. He looked up to see pretty, fat, flakes of snow swirling around him but the pain in his heart was so intense, he couldn’t bring himself to move and all the while, Essie’s last word continued to spin around in his head…

‘Don’t!’

FIFTY-SIX

The snow was beginning to lie as Essie turned onto her driveway. She'd put Marvin back in Sukie's garage and had picked up her own car. George would have some warning that she was back, when he arrived home later.

The sky was dark above her and just as she was opening the front door, the lamp in the hallway came on as the timer kicked in. This enabled her to see all the post lying on the floor behind it. She placed her handbag on a chair and bent down to pick it up, glancing at the dates on a few of the envelopes as she gathered them together. Some of the items were almost two weeks old. She placed them on the hallway table next to a larger pile of envelopes which, she noticed when she briefly thumbed through them, were mostly flyers and junk mail.

Her fingers brushed the table as she put the post back and left marks in the dust. Essie looked around – the house had a feeling of being abandoned and neglected. She gave a small shiver and headed for the kitchen to put on the heating. When she opened the door for the boiler, she saw the heating was on the timer and turned down low. It was just warm enough to prevent the pipes freezing. Overriding the timer, she whacked the thermostat right up – George would hate that, he deplored the house being too warm and always insisted on extra jumpers, sometimes two – but she was still adjusting from Mexico temperatures so sod it. She quickly ran up the stairs to put on a cardigan while she waited for the house to warm up and with some reluctance, took the mobile phone she'd left behind out of the drawer and plugged it in to charge while she made herself a hot drink.

The kettle was filled and switched on but when she checked the fridge for some milk, it was completely empty bar a packet of something in the last throes of decomposing. The label said tomatoes and they probably were, once upon a time, but now it was a cellophane wrapped gloopy, disgusting mess. She took them straight out to the bin and then went to retrieve the long-life milk she'd originally placed in Marvin for emergencies. She wasn't planning to clear him out completely just yet but she'd bagged up and brought some of the cupboard stock back home with her. She was now glad she had because it looked like George hadn't been living at home for some time and there wasn't much to eat.

Essie wandered through the lounge and dining room, her mug of tea in her hand, and tried to adjust to having so much space again. She picked up, and put back down, photographs of her life which were dotted around the rooms. She came to a halt in front of the old Welsh dresser where a picture of her and George on their wedding day stood.

She'd never liked this photograph, although it was George's favourite. There was something about it which disturbed her but she'd been unable to say what... until now. Now, with time away and her newly-opened eyes, she finally saw what had eluded her all these years. It was the expression of proprietorial smugness on George's face. He wasn't thinking, "I love this woman so much" as you would have expected, given the occasion. No, he was holding her close to his side in a vice-like grip and his face said, "Now she's mine!".

With a loud harrumph, the picture was slammed down and she turned swiftly towards the kitchen. Soon the radio was blaring out, the polish and duster were flying around and the vacuum was taking no prisoners. It wasn't long before the house smelt fresh, clean and like home again.

After a long hot shower to freshen up, she finally switched on the phone and waited for it to start pinging as the messages arrived. It finally went silent after a minute and a half and she looked down to see fifty-eight messages were waiting for her attention.

All of them were from George.

Her hackles went up as she read the first of his texts where he "shouted" in his block capitals that there would be trouble if she didn't sort herself out and get home immediately. This was followed by who did she think she was, showing him up like this and his final repost was that he was sick of her drama queen antics, it was time she grew up.

Essie read a few more and began laughing when she realised that he was simply repeating himself over and over with the odd variation here and there. Clearly, while he was quick enough to be vicious with his tongue to her face, he lacked the balls to put the same vitriol into writing.

With an air of boredom, she proceeded to delete the messages unread until she got to the last half-dozen. Curious to see if he'd changed his approach, or had maybe realised he now loved her and missed her, she read them.

Nope! More of the same.

She decided to delete the voicemails without listening to them.

A groan of disgust escaped her lips as she threw the phone down while a grumble in her stomach was a reminder that she hadn't eaten since breakfast.

A raid on the kitchen cupboards saw her cobbling together some tinned chilli-con-carne with boiled rice. While it was cooking, Essie went out to her car and brought in some of her luggage, including the carrier bag of re-directed post which Sukie had put in the car boot for her. She added it to the pile in the hallway and brought it all through to the dining room.

It felt strange to be sitting at her dining table again. She didn't mind eating alone – she'd done it often enough in the past – but it was different when she knew there was no chance of Clarissa bouncing through the door at any moment.

To distract her thoughts, she began going through the post while she ate. She sorted bank statements into one pile, junk mail into another and invites to several (missed) events along with miscellaneous items into a third.

The second and third piles were pushed to one side for later and she was checking through the bank statements when she noticed the payments on the rental property in the centre of Oxford appeared to have ceased. This was an old house they'd picked up cheap-ish in an auction and rented out to students at the university. Flicking back, she saw the last rent payment had come in at the beginning of May. She pushed her plate, and the half-eaten meal, to one side and looked at the miscellaneous pile. One of the opened envelopes was addressed to both George and herself and when she pulled out the contents, she saw it was a termination notice from the students who'd been renting it the previous two years, informing them that they'd completed their courses and would not be returning after the summer holidays. She turned her attention back to the statements but couldn't see any recent payments which could relate to that property. She'd need to speak to George about this. Why on earth would the premises have been left empty? Was he incapable of sorting out tenants for one of their more lucrative rentals?

Annoyed that her husband still expected her to do everything, even when she wasn't here, Essie took her plate to the kitchen, scraped the remains down the waste-disposal, washed it and put it back in the cupboard. She made another cup of tea and took it through to the snug where, switching on the television, she tried to catch up with some of the soaps she'd missed over the months.

Barely an hour had passed before she let out a large sigh and clicked the television off. Her irritated mind simply would not settle and she kept thinking about the Oxford house. A few minutes later, she was in her car and driving towards the city centre.

It was over an hour later before Essie finally parked up outside the terraced house. She hadn't stopped to consider the snow, the late-night shoppers and the seasonal revellers who'd clogged the roads all the way in. She looked at the dashboard and saw the time was just after nine o'clock. The house was in darkness and as she walked up the front steps, she saw the curtains in the front room were drawn. She knocked the door knocker and waited. When no one answered, she knocked a second time. Still no answer.

Not prepared to knock a third time, she took the spare key from her pocket and let herself in. The first thing she noticed was the carpet in the hallway. This was strange because the last time she'd been here, it had sported laminate flooring – much easier for students to keep clean. She walked into the lounge, flicking the light switch as she entered. The room was bathed in light and it was immediately obvious that the house was no longer a student rental. The bashed-up old sofa was gone and a new corner suite had replaced it. The magnolia walls were now pale blue, and heavy velvet curtains hung around the window, closed tightly to keep out the winter chill. Positioned in front of the sofa, with a bottle of wine and two glasses placed on it, was a glass and chrome coffee-table.

At that moment, she heard a creak above her head.

'Oh, shit,' she whispered.

Essie made her way to the lounge door, switched off the light and was about to step through the front door when she suddenly stopped. Her fingers sat on the door-handle for a few seconds before she turned around and returned to the room she'd just scurried out of. Five short steps brought her back to the coffee table where she picked up the wine bottle, looked at it closely, placed it back on the table and picked up one of the wine glasses. She looked at it even closer before putting it down again.

This time, when she walked out of the room, she didn't bother to switch off the light and used its beam to locate her mobile phone in her handbag. She turned on the torch app and quietly made her way up the stairs, turning it off when she reached the master bedroom. The door was slightly ajar and the sound of Elton John crooning out his love songs flowed through the gap.

Essie fiddled with her phone in the dark, taking a minute to find the setting she wanted, before holding it up and pushing the door slowly open. The plethora of candles made it easy to see the couple making love in the bed directly opposite. She waited a few seconds and then flicked on the overhead light!

'What the bloody hell—'

'Hello, George, how are you?'

Essie continued to let her phone record the interrupted action unfolding in front of her. The duvet moved and

Patricia Archer, one of the partners in George's firm, stuck her head out.

'Oh, you're back.'

'Evidently! Thank you for looking after my husband while I was away – I'm sure he's most grateful.'

While George leapt from the bed, grabbed a bathrobe from the floor and wrapped it round himself, Paddy Archer sat up and leaned back against the pillows, pulling a sheet up around her.

'While you were away? Honey, I've been "looking after him" for much longer than that. Like about twenty years longer!'

'Paddy!'

'What?' She looked at George who'd stopped moving about in a panic to shush her. 'It's time she knew. You've been promising to leave her for years, well now you can!'

Essie felt herself sway at this revelation but she wasn't going to give Paddy Archer the satisfaction of seeing her come undone.

'Twenty years?' she whispered.

'Yeah! He asked me to marry him when we were at uni. I had a big fish to fry over in the States so said no. When I returned a few years later, all set to pick up where we'd left off, I found him hitched to a mousey little nobody… you! However, since I always get what I want, I settled for the next best thing – being his mistress. I knew he'd leave you one day; I just didn't know how long it would take for the *one day* to come.'

Essie stopped the recording on her phone and put it in her pocket. George hopped over towards her.

'Estelle, I can explain…'

'Oh, I'm sure you can, George, but, for tonight, I don't want to hear it. Come to the house tomorrow morning at ten o'clock and we can talk then.'

'But… I've got a meeting tomorrow morning.'

Essie looked her husband up and down – still in the bathrobe, with one sock and shoe on and his trousers in his hand, he was a comical sight. His mussed-up hair revealed the bald patch he strived so hard to hide and despite his insistence that she and Clarissa take care of their bodies, he hadn't been living by his own code if the pot-belly peeking out from the bathrobe was anything to go by.

'George, it wasn't a request. Ten o'clock. Not a minute before and not a minute after.'

She turned to walk out the door but stopped to look back at the woman still lounging in the bed.

'Oh, by the way, Patricia, Midnight Purple lipstick is a great colour when you're a twenty-something goth, but on a woman in her late forties… not such a good look. Shouts "desperate old hag" to me. Just saying!'

And, with a big smile and a little wave, Essie floated down the stairs.

As she walked out the front door, the shock from Paddy's words dissolved and the weight of the burden she'd carried for so long, slipped off her shoulders. She became aware of suddenly feeling lighter inside. Lighter than she'd felt for a very long time.

Boy, was her journal entry tonight going to be a juicy one!

FIFTY-SEVEN

The snow was beginning to lie when Craig eventually prised himself up off the driveway. He brought his few bags into the house, locked the door behind him and staggered into the front room where he threw himself on the sofa… and hit the floor!

'What the—'

He raised his head from his prone position and saw that Flora's refurbishment of the house meant his new, modern, sofa was now hugging the wall. For as long as he could remember, the old, flowery monster with the dodgy springs had lived in the middle of the room, close to the fireplace. Being too heart-sore and body-sore to move, he dropped his head and lay where he'd landed for a time. When he did decide to shift, it was only to turn over and lie on his back, his eyes adjusting to the gloom as he began to take in the other alterations his niece had made.

The old easy chair which had resided in the bay window for so long, holding back the draught from the rickety wooden sash windows, was gone. Even when the new, custom-made double glazing went in, the chair had been put back in situ but now it was no more and in its place was an elegant, leather, Queen Anne, winged number, turned to a slight angle and with a tall, brass, angle-poise lamp beside it. Clearly, this was to be his little reading nook. To the right was a small table and when his eyes alighted upon the half-full whisky decanter and crystal tumbler sitting on it, everything else was forgotten. Despite knowing the amber nectar wouldn't ease his pain but simply prolong it, he still crawled across the freshly-sanded and varnished floorboards, hauled himself up into the chair and poured himself a hefty measure which slipped down far too easily. As did the second… and the third.

By seven o'clock, the decanter was empty and by eight o'clock, he'd finished the remainder of the bottle he'd found in the kitchen cupboard. He sat at the kitchen table and tried to decide if he felt out of kilter due to the whisky he'd drunk or because the table was no longer in the same spot where it had lived from before he was born. Deciding it was firmly the fault of the table, he stood up, muttered something incomprehensible at it and took himself upstairs to bed.

When he woke the following morning, with his tastefully decorated, pale grey and vanilla, bedroom spinning around him, the vague memory of the night before had him concurring that he'd maybe done the table a disservice and the blame for being out of sorts lay firmly on his attempt at drowning his sorrows. However, even now, he was unable to get that word out of his head.

Don't!

Round and round it went, spinning this way and that, completely out of control and careering around like a toddler on speed. Every time it hit his heart, he felt another piece splinter off and land heavily at his feet. His heart had been thoroughly broken for a second time and he realised that it was unlikely to ever mend. He'd managed to cobble it back together in his youth but now… it was shattered beyond repair and the will to fix it again was beyond him.

He dragged himself off his bed, realising belatedly that he'd fallen asleep across it, rather than in it – yet another change inflicted by Flora. He was glad to find the bathroom, at least, was still where he'd left it and spent a good fifteen minutes dowsing himself with hot and cold water, as he tried to shift the devil's own hangover from his being.

More tears fell while he was in the shower but by the time the water was turned off, and he'd dried himself fully, his pragmatic nature began to kick in. Somehow, he had to find a way to move on, despite the pain inside him, and maybe once he'd eaten a decent breakfast, he could begin putting together a business plan which, come the New Year, he could throw himself into.

He stared at his reflection in the bathroom mirror as he worked on removing the dry, nasty feel of the Sahara Desert from his mouth with his toothbrush. Dear goodness, he thought, if he was to walk into a vet's surgery looking like this, they'd be reading him the Last Rites and putting him out of his misery.

'Time to pull yourself together, man! She's gone so deal with it. Move on…' he told himself sternly, all the while knowing it was easier to verbalise it than actually do it.

He was halfway down the stairs, about to get to work on the "decent breakfast" part of his plan – although having just noticed the time, a "decent brunch" would be more appropriate – when a glance out of the long window at the turn of the stairs had his knees buckling and him grabbing the banister to prevent himself tumbling to the floor in the hallway below. He slowly sank down to sit on the step as his head reeled from the shock of seeing Essie's car driving in through the gates.

FIFTY-EIGHT

Essie was sitting at the kitchen table when she heard George's key in the door.

'Hah! Good luck with that one, sunshine,' she muttered.

Sure enough, a moment later he was banging on the door.

'Estelle! Let me in now! Estelle!'

She took a deep breath and went to open the door.

'What the hell are you playing at, getting the locks changed on my house?'

'I didn't "get them changed", George, I did them myself.'

And she had.

When she'd arrived home last night, she'd gone straight to bed, expecting to have a restless night. Instead, she'd fallen asleep as soon as her head touched the pillow and had woken this morning, just after six, feeling bright-eyed and fully refreshed.

She got up immediately and as soon as she was showered, dressed and coffee-ed, her first task had been to change the locks on the front and back doors. After all these years of renting out flats and houses, she'd picked up a few things along the way, one of which was why waste money on locksmiths every time she got new tenants when she could do the job herself.

Along with the locks, she'd also changed the combination for the garage and the remote for the front gates. They'd been open when George had arrived but they'd be closed the minute he left.

'Come through to the kitchen, George, let me make you some tea.'

She switched on the kettle and took some mugs out of the cupboard while George sat down.

'I prefer my tea in a china cup, as you well know, Estelle.'

Essie turned and placed the mugs gently on the table.

'This is my house, George, and you'll drink out of whatever vessel I give you.'

'How dare you—' He went to stand up.

'SIT DOWN!' Essie barked the words at him. 'After what I witnessed last night, George Walton, I will *dare* as much as I like. Your days of giving me orders are over!'

She glared at him until the kettle began to boil and clicked off. She walked away, sorted out the teapot and brought it back to the table. Sitting down opposite him, she began talking.

'I have one question, George, and you had better answer it truthfully. All those business trips over the years – how many of them were genuine? Especially the ones "to London" which seem to have been almost weekly over the last two years.'

'All of them.'

'Really?'

'Yes.'

'Are you sure?'

'Yes.'

'Quite sure?'

'YES, dammit! I'm quite sure.'

'Hmmm, because you see, oh-darling-husband-of-mine, I now know what a lying, manipulative, controlling, little weasel you are and, as such, I don't believe a single word that falls from your nasty, evil, viper's tongue.'

'How dare you—' he repeated, raising up from his seat again.

'Oh, George, sit down and shut the fuck up! I've had enough of your *how dare yous* – this is the twenty-first century, so get over yourself!'

Essie had to bite the inside of her cheeks really hard to prevent herself from laughing at the deep scarlet colour of his face. He looked as though he was about to explode right in front of her. She waited until he was seated again before she continued.

'Well, I think you're lying about your London trips, but the truth is, I don't really care because, I'll tell you now, I'll be seeking a divorce.'

'You will not!'

'Yes, I will, because your time for telling me what to do is over! Done! Finito! I've packed your suitcases and you can collect them on the way out. The days of lying to me – and boy, have you lied—'

'I have not!'

'— and clearly still are, have come to an end!' She ignored his interruption. 'You lied to me about the Valentine card, you didn't send it. The fact I've never received another one since should have made me realise. You also lied about my friends not wanting to come to our wedding when the truth is, you didn't send their invites and THEN, you scumbag bastard, you had the barefaced audacity to console me when I was upset and let me think they'd deliberately not attended. For that alone, never mind everything else, I am kicking your sorry ass to the kerb!

This is the last time you'll set foot in this house.'

'Ah! Good try, Estelle, but I think you'll find that it's *you* who'll be leaving. This is my house and you won't be seeing a single penny from it or from me. You'll be on your own. Don't think for one minute that you can swan off for over nine months without a peep and expect me to move out when you deign to return.'

'Judging by the dust I cleaned up last night, I'd say it was *you* who moved out – several months ago.'

Essie knew this to be true as one of her neighbours had confirmed it this morning, saying George had only been popping by every other week or so.

'Furthermore,' she continued, 'you seem to be forgetting one small, but rather important, detail…'

'Which is?'

'That you signed this house, and the Oxford house, and the three London flats, over into my name when you decided to minimise your taxable assets.'

'Why you…' He grabbed her wrist and pulled her over the table towards him.

Essie felt a pang of fear rush through her. George had never been violent in the past, his words had always been his tools of choice, but maybe she'd pushed him too far. She could feel his grip tightening when she suddenly heard a voice in her head, *The thumb is the weak spot. Push against the thumb.* In that instant, she recalled the self-defence classes they'd done in the WI. She took a breath to steady herself, looked George in the eyes, braced her hand and then pulled hard against his thumb. Sure enough, she broke his grip on her. Before he could retaliate, she grabbed both of his pinkies and pushed them back, making him cry out in pain.

'That, George Walton, is the one and only time you lay a finger on me. Now, I will say this just once, so you had better listen carefully. When you leave today, you will never return here again. Anything you need will be sent to the Oxford house, which I will sign back over to you. I will keep this house and the London flats and in return, I will not ask you for any kind of spousal maintenance.'

'And if I don't agree?'

'I have my recording from last night. Not only do I seem to recall you bragging about the new company rules you put in place five years back – you know, the ones where the senior partners are not permitted to fraternise with other employees – but I also have Paddy Archer admitting to you both having an affair for the best part of twenty years. I call that a double whammy!'

'You wouldn't dare…'

'Wouldn't I? Contest the divorce and you'll find out just how much I will dare!'

'You fucking bitch!'

Pulling his fingers from Essie's grasp, George drew his hand back and there was no mistaking his intention.

'Ah-ah-ah, I wouldn't do that if I were you, George. I've got the local police set on speed-dial and they'll be there before you can blink!'

'What the hell?'

George looked around for the disembodied voice talking to him.

'Up a bit... bit higher, left a bit, a bit more... Bingo! Hi George, long time no see.'

George looked up at the top of the fridge-freezer to see Bobbie waving down at him from the screen of Essie's mobile phone.

Essie smiled to herself. George's hens had finally come home to roost and seeing the colour drain out of his face was a pleasure to behold. She looked at her watch.

'Right, your time is up. I've said what I had to say, now you can leave.'

'I'm sorry, Estelle. Please, give me another chance.'

If he hadn't called her Estelle, she may have faltered in her decision but by doing that, he proved he had no intention of changing. She hated being called Estelle and he damn well knew it!

'Nope, sorry, George. You've had twenty-five years to be a better person. That's more than enough.'

She walked out to open the hall cupboard where she'd stashed the suitcases she'd packed that morning. She pulled them out, opened the front door and placed them on the doorstep. As George walked out, looking quite dazed, she simply said, 'Goodbye' and closed the door firmly behind him, throwing the bolts at the top and bottom as a precaution.

She watched through the window as he put the luggage in the boot of his car, got in, and after sitting staring out of the windscreen for a few minutes, started the engine and reversed out. She watched him turn in the road and drive away, letting out the breath she'd been holding as he did so.

She was about to click the remote to close the gates when a white van drove in and came to a halt by the front door. The driver jumped out and walked round to pick up a large wicker picnic hamper from the passenger seat.

Essie rushed to the door and got there just as he was figuring out how to ring the bell.

'Hi there, love, got a delivery 'ere for Essie.'

'That's me. What is it?'

He winked at her. 'I can tell you it's super fragile, so please handle with care.' He placed the hamper gently down at her feet. 'Can you just sign there, please.'

She signed the hand-held computer and took the letter he passed to her. When he'd deposited the basket ever-so-carefully inside the door, she closed it behind him and ripped open the envelope, pulling out the single page of thick, creamy, parchment inside. She unfolded the page and read the few words written within:

"Now, the time is right..."

Confused, she turned the page over but there was nothing else. That was all that was written. She placed it on the hall table and bent down to open the hamper. When she carefully pulled the lid back, she let out the loudest of gasps for there, lying sound asleep on a tartan rug, were two, small, white West Highland Terrier puppies.

FIFTY-NINE

Unable to move, Craig watched Essie open the back door on her car and lift out a wicker hamper. Even as she slammed the door closed with her heel and began walking towards the house, he still couldn't believe what his eyes were seeing.

It wasn't until he realised that she was struggling to ring the doorbell did he suddenly spring into action. He rushed down the remaining stairs and across the hallway, shouting, 'I'm coming', as he did so. A moment later, the door was wide open and there was his Essie, red-faced and slightly puffed out, standing in front of him. He stood gazing at her until she said, 'Well, are you going to leave me standing here like a plank all day?'

'Oh, sorry, sorry… come in! Here, let me help you with that.'

Craig took the basket and amidst Essie telling him to be very gentle with it, laid it on the floor.

'Essie, what are you doing here? And,' he looked down, 'what's in the basket?'

'We have a present.'

'Excuse me?'

She turned her beautiful big eyes upon him and repeated, softly, 'We have a present.'

She bent down, tugging his hand to pull him to the floor beside her and opened the basket. The puppies inside were just waking up and their snuffling little gambols, as they fell over each other to come towards them, melted him inside.

'I don't understand, Essie, why are you here with these baby Westies?'

'They're from your mum, Craig. She's sent down two of Kirsty's pups. Look, this one here,' she pointed to the one with the red ribbon, 'is the one I watched being delivered. She's always had a tiny little kink in her ear, that's how I know.'

He looked closer and saw that each had a small ribbon with a label around its neck.

"For Essie"
"For Craig"

'But I still don't understand… you said George won't let you have pets – is this why you're here, to ask me to have both of them?'

'I most certainly am not! This little lady is all mine.'

She picked the pup with her name on it out of the basket and snuggled it under her chin.

'But George—'

'Is history! Gone! Vamoosed! Disposed of!'

At these words, Craig felt his chin drop and his mouth fall open.

Essie gave him a shy smile and said, 'Why don't I tell you everything over a cup of tea, although it might be best to put some food down for the puppies first. I grabbed a click-and-collect order on the way over so while I'm sorting that out, you may want to place a few of these around.' She handed him a packet of puppy pads.

He looked at them in confusion for a moment until it dawned on him what they were. 'Ah, yes… good idea.'

It didn't take long to sort the pups out and then he was sitting across from Essie, nursing a mug of hot tea, while he listened aghast to what had occurred in the few hours since he'd seen her last.

'He's been boffing his colleague for over *twenty years*?'

'Yup!'

'And you had absolutely *no* idea?'

'Nope! He knew Paddy from when they were at uni and I never gave it a thought. I honestly believed they were just work colleagues.'

'But… all those trips to London, surely you must have suspected something?'

'Not once! He was promoted into the shoes of a senior partner who got his secretary pregnant, I didn't think George would repeat his behaviour – especially not after the way he derided the man for fraternising with the staff. But as I have learned on our road trip, the rules George expects everyone else to live by are *not* the same ones he lives by, so I shouldn't be surprised really.'

'What do you intend to do now?'

Craig found he was holding his breath as he waited for her to answer. He wasn't expecting her to throw herself into his arms and swear undying love to him, but hearing that she planned to leave her husband would be a good place to start from.

She grinned at him. 'I've told you already – he's gone! I kicked him out this morning. The locks have been changed and he is G-O-N-E! Gone!'

Essie brushed her hair back from her face and Craig froze in his seat.

'What the FUCK is that?'

'I'm sorry?'

She dropped her hand back onto the table and Craig reached over to take hold of it. With great tenderness, he pushed back her sleeve to reveal the livid, purple bruising and finger marks around her wrist.

'He's hurt you. The bastard has hurt you.' He stood up and his chair fell over with a crash behind him.

'Craig, no, it's okay, honestly. It looks worse than it is, I promise. Sit down and I'll tell you what I did to him.'

He picked up his chair and sat down heavily on it but inside he was seething. How dare that two-timing, lying, treacherous arsehole hurt this precious woman like that. His temper was churning up inside him, but as Essie explained how she'd brought tears to George's eyes and had given him a taste of his own bully-boy medicine, Craig felt himself begin to calm down. He took her hand to look at the painful marks again before walking over to rummage in one of the kitchen drawers and return with some arnica cream. He pulled his chair up alongside hers and after asking her permission to apply it, he gently and carefully lathered it all over the bruising. He then put some light gauze on top and wrapped a bandage round to protect it.

'Err, Craig, don't you think the bandage is a bit over the top?'

'It's to stop the cream rubbing off onto your sleeve. It'll absorb better like this and should, hopefully, work its magic sooner.'

When he was satisfied the dressing was secure but not too tight, Craig went to draw his hand away but Essie grabbed it.

'Craig, I… I want to say I'm sorry for the way I left you yesterday. I didn't want to hurt you, but didn't know how to leave without doing so. If it makes you feel any better, it hurt right down to the very depths of me to drive away and leave you behind.'

'No, it doesn't make me feel any better.'

Essie dropped her head and he felt a tear fall onto his hand.

'Hey,' he said, once again placing a finger under her chin and lifting her face up so he could look into her eyes. 'Knowing that you are in *any* kind of pain could never make me feel good. I only feel good when you are laughing, and smiling, and bathed in happiness. It hurts me when you are *not* any of those things.'

'I'm so sorry.'

'For what? For being brave enough to be prepared to give your marriage a second chance? For trying to salvage something from the last twenty-five years of your life? I won't lie, Essie, it broke my heart more than you'll ever know when you drove away, but I know it was for the right reasons. And nothing has changed – I will still be here, waiting for you, if, or when, you feel the time is right to move on. I won't be pushing you into a relationship or demanding more of you. Right now, this is your time for you, and I will give you all the space you need to heal from what George has done to you. I'll be your friend until you are ready for anything more.'

'Do you mean that, Craig?' she whispered, 'Will you really wait for me?'

'Yes, Essie, I'll wait.'

'Well, that's a bit pants because I was really kind of hoping you'd drag me upstairs to your new boudoir and do everything in your power to make me forget about George!'

'You what?'

Had he just heard correctly? Was Essie saying what it sounded like she was saying?

'You heard me, Craig! Take me upstairs and show me your version of heaven.'

'But—'

'No buts, Craig! I've been waiting all of my life to lose myself in someone's love. I thought I loved George once but found out the hard way that I didn't and it's been pretty damn lonely ever since. I was dying inside. When Clarissa and I started to plan our trip, I began to come alive again but it was you coming back into my life that really kick-started the process. You reminded me how it feels to be listened to… and respected… and treated like a normal human being instead of being made to feel stupid and foolish. And now I have that, I don't want to lose it.' She looked at him in earnest. 'I don't want to lose you, Craig. I did once and I nearly did a second time…'

'You've never lost me, Essie, my heart was always with you, no matter where you were. However, now that you're here, why don't I give you the grand tour of the house you declined yesterday. Shall we start upstairs?'

Craig stood, held his hand out to Essie and a bolt of happiness surged through him when she took it.

'I think that is the perfect place to start.'

Craig moved in closer, brushed a stray curl behind her ear and then buried his fingers in her hair as he tilted her head gently until their lips were almost touching.

'I love you, Essie Parker,' he said, as he brought his mouth down onto hers. He felt her lips move beneath his and he was sure he heard her mumble that she loved him. He was tempted to ask her to repeat it but that would mean breaking their kiss and he wasn't about to do that. It was too damn good. He would ask her later, because that was the one thing he was absolutely sure about…

They were going to share a lot of "laters" together.

SIXTY

Clarissa pushed open the door to the outside deck and drew in a lungful of the fresh, salty sea air. The first few miles out of Dover had been a bit squally and all passengers had been advised to remain below deck. It was only once they were clear of the port and the crappy UK weather, that they were now permitted to go onto the upper decks. The announcement was still being conveyed around the ship as she'd sprung to her feet and gathered up her coat and bag. The ferry was busy and it was claustrophobic with all those on board being confined to the indoor spaces.

She walked over to stand by the rail and watch the famous white cliffs slowly fade away. Her insides were rolling about in time with the listing of the ship but it was nothing to do with her mode of transport and everything to do with her combined nerves and excitement. Nerves because she was taking such a big step on her own and excitement for the very same reason. There had been a text from Fliss last night saying they'd hired a car and were driving up to meet her at Calais so she wouldn't have to drive back to Paris, on the wrong side of the road for the first time, on her own. This news had cheered her right up and she was looking forward to seeing her friends again.

She turned as she felt her phone vibrate in her pocket. Seeing it was a text from her mum, she went to sit on a nearby bench. The last thing she needed was her phone to land in the drink! She'd sent her mum a message just before she'd boarded the ferry and had been surprised not to receive a reply straight away. She swiped the message open and let out a squeal of surprised laughter while almost dropping her phone at the same time. She looked again closely. It was a photograph of her mum and Craig, appearing to be suspiciously under-dressed and… were they *in bed* together?

Clarissa tapped the phone. A few seconds later her mum answered and she looked decidedly mussed up.

'Hello, darling, how are you? How's the crossing? Not too rough, I hope.'

'Mum, are you in bed with Craig?' Her mum grinned back at her, moved her phone slightly and Craig came into view.

'Hi, Clarissa, everything okay?' he asked, giving her a small wave.

'I'm not sure yet! What's going on? Mum, I thought you were planning to try and resolve things with my father? Don't get me wrong, I'm delighted to see you both together, although I'd have preferred to see less of you and more of clothing…'

'Do you remember I once called your dad an asshole?'

'Yes.'

'Well, make that a two-timing asshole, darling. He's been having it off with that wrinkled old bitch, Paddy Archer, for years.'

'No way! Paddy Archer is gross!'

'Clearly your father doesn't think so. Anyway, I packed his bags this morning, had kicked him out by lunchtime, and came straight round here to begin my new life with Craig.'

'Wow! Way to go! Well done, you! That was the best decision you could have made although…where are you going to live?'

'Oh, I still have ownership of all the properties, so nothing to worry about. I won't be homeless or destitute although I'll sign the Oxford house over to your father since he and Paddy appear to have been living there the last six months. We can talk in more detail when we visit you. I just thought you'd want to know the current state of affairs.'

'I'm really happy for both of you and I wish you all the luck in the world. This is the best Christmas present I've ever had. I love you both loads. Craig, would you mind if I call you Dad?'

'Clarissa, I don't mind what you call me, as long as you're comfortable with it and if you want to call me Dad, then I'd be over the moon. What about George though? Won't it feel strange calling us both Dad?'

'Oh, I won't have two dads, just one – you. Apart from not having spoken to *George* for months now and after what Mum has just told me, I can't see me speaking to him again in the foreseeable, or even distant, future, he's never been a dad to me. I wasn't even allowed to call him "Dad" – it always had to be "Father". You've been more of a dad to me these last few months than he's been my whole life.'

She watched him as she spoke and saw his eyes fill with tears.

'Thank you, Clarissa, those are probably the nicest words anyone has ever said to me.'

'Oy! What about the words I whispered to you earlier?'

'Ouch!'

Clarissa giggled as her mum gave Craig a dig in the ribs with her elbow.

'Right, you two, I'm going to say goodbye before this whole thing becomes any freakier than it already is. I'll text you when I arrive in Paris. Love you both loads.'

She blew a few kisses and hung up, returning her gaze to the sea.

At last, her mother knew her father's secret.

Clarissa thought back to the day, all those months ago, when she'd been on her way to his office and overheard him and Paddy arguing about why he still hadn't left his wife as he'd been promising to do for years.

Her initial shock had quickly turned to anger but the one thing she'd learnt from working in a law office was to never act in haste. Elspeth's ticket dilemma couldn't have come at a more opportune moment because it gave her time away from home while she tried to decide what to do. She hadn't wanted to be the one to break the news to her mother and cause her upset and heartache. In the end, however, the problem had resolved itself and her mother would never know she'd carried her father's dirty little secret for all these months. She'd been spared the indignity of knowing her daughter had learnt of his affair before she did.

Clarissa had been happy to let her mother believe the change in her outlook had been down to Michael Duval, although his closing statement had added fuel to the fiery fury burning within her. A fury lit by her hypocritical, two-faced father.

A little credit did have to be given to the hypnotist, however – attending his show had brought about so much change – not just in her life but also for Craig and, by association, her mum. This time last year, they had each been living in their own private hell, feeling sad, lonely and downtrodden but now they'd come together and become a family.

Furthermore, had they not chosen to go travelling, she wouldn't have met Fliss and Becky. She'd still be all wrapped up tight in the little box her father had forced her into. Instead, she'd broken out and was about to discover all the wonderful things the world had to show her.

And, lastly, but by far the most important, was Ross. He was showing her what real love is. Real love is supportive, it's caring, it builds you up and it carries you when times are bad. It allows you to be free and to be yourself. It doesn't hurt you, or fence you in or make you feel small and insignificant. True love makes you feel magnificent and that you can do whatever you set out to do.

A small rumpus from the other side of the deck broke into her thoughts and when she looked up, she could see France beginning to appear over the horizon. She made her way across to the opposite end of the deck, her tummy buzzing as her next adventure drew close. She watched the land on the horizon grow bigger before turning around to take a selfie of the skyline behind her and sending it to Ross.

She was sitting in Vanda with the engine running, preparing to move off the ferry, when her phone pinged. She quickly read the text:

"A beautiful picture. Now go and enjoy the beginning of the rest of your life. I love you! xx"

Clarissa quickly replied.

"I love you too! xx"

"The beginning of the rest of her life..." She liked that sentiment. It felt like she'd been waiting since forever for her life to start and now that it was finally here, she was ready to grab it with both hands. Her waiting was over.

ACKNOWLEDGMENTS

They say no man is an island and 'they' are absolutely right. It's impossible to do this job without the help and support of so many people. The longer you do it, the longer the list becomes of all those who cheer you on and hold you up. If I was to try and thank everyone who stands by me, we would need a second book to ensure no one was missed off. So that end, I'm going to keep this short.

My Main Man:
Mr Mogs, for always listening when the ideas begin to flow.

My A-Team:
The Wee Mammy, my sister, my dad and my mother-in-law – thank you for always being at my side.

My Bestest Bestie in the Whole World:
Kym, your never-ending belief gets me through the self-doubt.

My BFF:
Stuart James Dunne, the phoenix who came back stronger and showed me that for every down there is a better up.

My Cheerleaders:
Sue Baker, Michaela Balfour, Megan Gibbons, Kathleen Becker, Karen Harrison, Samantha Curtis, Mark Fearn.
Thank you for shouting my name whenever and wherever possible.

My Editor:
John Hudspith who always manages to make every manuscript better than I thought possible.

My Cover Designer:
Berni Stevens for such a fabulous creation. Looking forward to seeing what else is to come.

My Facebook Groups whose members are the best:
Kiltie Jackson's Speakeasy, Fiction Café Book Club, Chick Lit & Prosecco and TBC – The Book Club.

My Readers:
Thank you SO much to everyone who reads my books, leaves reviews, recommends them to friends, and gets in touch to let me know how much
you enjoyed them.
You guys are the reason I'm still doing this and while you are out there reading,
I will continue to be here writing.

xxx

ABOUT THE AUTHOR

Kiltie Jackson spent her childhood years growing up in Scotland. Most of these early years were spent in and around Glasgow although for a short period of time, she wreaked havoc at a boarding school in the Highlands.

By the age of seventeen, she had her own flat which she shared with a couple of cats for a few years while working as a waitress in a cocktail bar (she's sure there's a song in there somewhere!) and serving customers in a fashionable clothing outlet before moving down to London to chalk up a plethora of experience which is now finding its way into her writing.

Once she'd wrung the last bit of fun out of the smokey capital, she moved up to the Midlands and now lives in Staffordshire with one grumpy husband and six feisty felines.

Her little home is known as Moggy Towers even though, despite having plenty of moggies, there are no towers!

Since the age of three, Kiltie has been an avid reader although it was many years later before she decided to put pen to paper – or fingers to keyboard. Her debut novel was released in September 2017 and her fourth book was a US Amazon bestseller in Time Travel Romance.

Kiltie loves to write fiery and feisty female characters and puts the blame for this firmly on the doorsteps of Anne Shirley from Anne of Green Gables and George Kirrin from The Famous Five.

If you would like to read more about Kiltie, you can find her on the following:

Website: www.kiltiejackson.com

Facebook: www.facebook.com/kiltiejackson

Twitter: www.twitter.com/KiltieJackson

Instagram: www.instagram.com/kiltiejackson

ALSO BY KILTIE JACKSON

A Rock ‘n’ Roll Lovestyle

An Artisan Lovestyle

An Incidental Lovestyle

A Timeless Lovestyle

Printed in Great Britain
by Amazon